# THE
# QUEEN'S
# DAUGHTER

Ocean

Bergen

NORWAY

SWEDEN

North Sea

DENMARK

Baltic Sea

SCOTLAND

The Scottish Marches

IRELAND

WALES

ENGLAND

FRIESLAND

SAXONY

POMERANIA

SLAVINIA

POLAND

PRUSSIA

SILESIA

Oder R.

Sarum Winchester London

Canterbury

Southampton

FLANDERS

BRABANT

LOWER LORRAINE

Rhine R.

Mainz

THURINGIA

Dresden

BOHEMIA

MORAVIA

Atlantic

NORMANDY

Gisors

Paris

BRITTANY MAINE

CHAMPAGNE

FRANCONIA

HOLY ROMAN EMPIRE

UPPER LORRAINE

Danube R.

SWABIA BAVARIA

STYRIA

Loire R.

POITOU

Poitiers

BURGUNDY

CARINTHIA

La Rochelle

Saintes

Limoges

AQUITAINE

Auvergne

Rhone R.

ARELATE

LOMBARDY

Venice

HUNGARY

LEON

Pamplona

NAVARRE

GASCONY

TOULOUSE

Genoa

Ravenna

CASTILE

ARAGON

Saràgosa

Pisa

Corsica

PAPAL STATES

Toledo

Barcelona

Monte sant Angelo

Rome

Taranto

Sardinia

Naples

KINGDOM

Mediterranean

Granada

DOMINIONS OF THE ALMOHADES

Monreale Palermo Cefalù

SICILY

Messina

Reggio

Strait of Messina

OF

N W E S

EUROPE c. 1200
Scale of Miles
0   50  100      200       300        400

The Zisa Palace, Palermo

ESTONIA

LITHUANIA

Novgorod

TERRITORY OF NOVGOROD

BULGARIA (KAMA)

Elm tree at Gisors

ENGLAND

English Channel

Barfleur

Gisors

FLANDERS

Meuse

Rouen

Normandy

Paris

Champagne

HOLY ROMAN EMPIRE

Brittany

Maine

Anjou

Loire

Touraine

Berry

Burgundy

Bourges

Caspian Sea

Atlantic Ocean

F R A N C E

Poitou

La Marche

Bourbon

Saintes

Angoulême

Auvergne

Aquitaine

Dordogne

QUERCY

Bordeaux

Alans

Black Sea

GEORGIA

Possessions of Henry II about 1180

French Crown land about 1180

Gascony

Toulouse

St. Gilles

Arles

prov.

Mediterranean Sea

Boundary of France in the 12th century

0    50    100   150

miles

RUM

KHELAT

KURDISTAN

BYZANTINE

Constantinople

BULGARIA

EMPIRE

Thessalonica

Durazzo

EPIRUS

Athens

ACHAIA

EMPIRE OF NICAEA

RHODES

Crete

LESSER ARMENIA

KINGDOM

of

Kyrenia

Famagusta

CYPRUS

Limassol

Antioch

ORTUQIDS

Mosul

ZANGIDS

Euphrates R.

Tigris

Tripoli

Damascus

Acre

Horns of Hattin

Arsuf

Jaffa

Jerusalem

Ascalon

Gaza

ARABIA

a n     S e a

Illustrated map by Laura Hartman Maestro

Alexandria

EGYPT

Cairo

# THE QUEEN'S DAUGHTER

SUSAN COVENTRY

HENRY HOLT AND COMPANY

NEW YORK

Henry Holt and Company, LLC
*Publishers since 1866*
175 Fifth Avenue
New York, New York 10010
www.HenryHoltKids.com

Library of Congress Cataloging-in-Publication Data
Coventry, Susan.
The queen's daughter / Susan Coventry.—1st ed.
p.     cm.
Summary: A fictionalized biography of Joan of England, the youngest
child of King Henry II of England and his queen consort, Eleanor of
Aquitaine, chronicling her complicated relationships with her warring
parents and many siblings, particularly with her favorite brother
Richard the Lionheart, her years as Queen consort of Sicily, and
her second marriage to Raymond VI, Count of Toulouse.
ISBN 978-0-8050-8992-9
1. Joan, of England, 1165–1199—Juvenile fiction. [1. Joan, of England,
1165–1199—Fiction. 2. Princesses—Fiction. 3. Kings, queens, rulers, etc.—
Fiction. 4. Great Britian—History—Angevin period, 1154–1216—Fiction.
5. Sicily (Italy)—History—1016–1194—Fiction.] 1. Title.
PZ7.C83395Qu 2010    [Fic]—dc22    2009024154

First Edition—2010
Map by Laura Hartman Maestro
Printed in the United States of America

1  3  5  7  9  10  8  6  4  2

*for*
**BRAD**

# THE
# QUEEN'S
# DAUGHTER

PROLOGUE

THEY SAID HER FAMILY DESCENDED FROM THE DEVIL. BY the age of seven, Princess Joan knew the oft-sung tale by heart. She loved to roll the heroine's wondrous name around on her tongue—*Melusine*.

One of the earliest counts of Anjou, Fulks the Black, had returned from an unexplained journey with a mysterious bride, a woman of unearthly beauty—Melusine. The countess bore four sons in quick succession. For their sakes, Count Fulks suffered his wife's hot temper and strange ways.

Her most provoking habit was to leave mass before the consecration of the Host. When Fulks could no longer tolerate the resulting scandal, he commanded three of his knights to prevent her next departure from church. The following Sunday, when Melusine rose during mass, two men seated behind her stood to block her exit. The third knight barred the door.

The priest marched down the aisle, determined to see her take Communion. But as he brought the body of Christ to her lips, Melusine turned away, eyes flashing fire. At once her skin sloughed, revealing scales. Serpents writhed in her hair, and a twisted tail emerged from beneath the hem of her skirt. Recognizing a daughter of Satan, the knights fell back in horror. Melusine gathered her howling sons in her claws and flew out the window but, in her haste, dropped the youngest.

The later counts of Anjou descended from that boy.

Joan's father, King Henry II of England, was born count of Anjou. He took fierce pride in the tale, blaming his own hot temper on Melusine's blood. Joan's mother, Eleanor of Aquitaine, often added that the king had no lack of sins to excuse. Sometimes, when her brothers ran wild, courtiers crossed themselves, whispering, "From the devil they've come, to the devil they'll return." Joan hid her own temper as best she could. Even so, once, in a fury, she bit her nurse, and the woman called her "Devil's child."

Her mother found her weeping. She smoothed Joan's hair and petted her. She said, "Remember, a good girl says her prayers and listens to her mother."

Eleanor said the devil could not claim a girl who was good.

# PART ONE

# PRINCESS JOAN

ONE

*Poitiers, Poitou County, France, February 1173*

WE'RE GOING ON A JOURNEY, TESSIE," JOAN SANG TO HER
poppet. The words were drowned by grousing men dragging wooden trunks along the floor. Lifting the rag doll to eye
level, she waggled the limp head back and forth so Tessie could
acknowledge her delight.

Her father had been in London and came to Poitiers on his
way south to the city of Limoges, another of his French fief-
doms. He was going to bring them along—Joan, all four of her
brothers, and Mama. Did it mean he was no longer angry? She
squeezed Tessie tighter. It must; she couldn't bear it when Papa
was angry.

"Hurry. The king is waiting," her nurse said, coming up
behind. "Must you bring that dirty toy?"

Joan tucked the doll under her arm. The trick was to ignore
Agnes, not argue.

"Oh, no!" Agnes said, her eyes drawn to two men lifting a
heavy cedar trunk. "Not that one, the smaller. And be quick."

Joan pressed her lips tight to keep from laughing. Her father
had arrived in Poitiers two days ago. He had said they wouldn't
depart until Friday, three days hence; but this morning at dawn
he altered his plans. The servants were just as flustered as Agnes,
who swore the king enjoyed turning the household upside down.

"I'm ready," she said. "I'll wait out—"

"Child, if you step outside that door . . ." Instead of finishing the threat, Agnes took one last squint-eyed look around. The beds were stripped bare. The traveling trunks, packed to their limit, made a labyrinth across the floor. "Lord help us if we've forgotten anything."

Joan snatched the nurse's bony hand and pulled toward the door. "I want to get to the wain before John."

She always fought with her younger brother over the best spot. Straw mattresses would pad the cloth-canopied wains carrying the queen's retinue, but the mattresses never reached into the far recesses. Those unlucky enough to be seated near corners would spend half the ride trying to keep their bottoms from slipping onto the wood.

Agnes followed her downstairs, but without enthusiasm. When they emerged from the stairwell, the gallery stretched before them, lit along both sides by tapers, black smoke painting the gray stone walls. At its end, an arc of pale winter sunlight marked the doorway to the courtyard. Joan slipped her hand from her nurse's, her body tensed to run.

Agnes sighed. "Don't act like a wild sprite of the woods, child. Look. There's your mother."

Queen Eleanor had stepped from an adjoining gallery, the sunlight framing—so troubadours attested—the most beautiful woman in the world. Listening to those singers had taught Joan how men measured beauty: white hands, red lips, a crown of dark hair, eyes full of light. Though she was fifty years old, Eleanor of Aquitaine continued to inspire poetry, every word of which rang true to Joan.

"Mama!"

"Good morning, sweetling," Eleanor called, then turned back and beckoned. "Hurry, John. Your father is waiting."

Still clutching Tessie, Joan ran to where two streams of people and baggage converged at the intersection of the passages. She saw John trailing behind his nurse, clinging to her skirts.

"Come, John, I'll race you," Joan called, knowing the challenge was unfair. Six years old—a year her junior—he was also small for his age and timid. John's face was taut, but he nodded. Agnes caught up in time to overhear.

"Joan, don't—"

"Let them go," Queen Eleanor said. "They may as well run now. They'll be cooped up in the wain until daybreak tomorrow."

That was all Joan needed to bolt, John at her heels. She decided to let him win. He passed her on the steps to the courtyard, where they crashed into the wain almost simultaneously. The groom tending the horses glowered. Her father's journeys put everyone in a bad mood.

"Help me up, John," she said, smashing Tessie as she grabbed the iron handles jutting up from the side of the wain.

"No, I want to go first."

A deep voice scolded, "Where are your manners, boy?"

She smiled. It was Richard—her champion. Though all of fifteen, her second-eldest brother never treated her like a baby the way Henry and Geoffrey did. Henry, eighteen this month and puffed with pride, condescended to her and thought himself generous. Fourteen-year-old Geoffrey fixed his efforts on impressing his brothers; when he paid her any attention at all, it was to tease.

Richard said she *should* love him best because she took after him. They both had red-gold hair, wide foreheads, and blue eyes.

Mama once jested they both also had Angevin dispositions—like Melusine. When their father said that was a good trait, Mama had laughed.

The memory stole away her smile. Her parents hadn't laughed together in so long. Papa used to summon them to his other castles all the time, but now, he rarely bothered. And when he came to see them in Poitiers, he generally stormed off in a temper after only a few days. It seemed whenever Mama and Papa were together, they argued.

Richard scooped Joan up like a kitten and tossed her through the curtain. She landed on the scratchy mattress.

"Tessie!" she yelled, poking her head out.

Richard picked up the doll and handed it to her. He turned to their brother. "What about you, Johnny-boy? Will you ride to your lady on horseback or be delivered in a wain?"

John looked up at his brother. His mouth hung open, and his dark eyes were blank.

"What lady?" Joan asked Richard. They ignored John as he struggled to grasp handles too high for him, hopping and bumping against the wain.

Richard smirked. "Never mind. It wasn't meant for your ears."

She hated when her brothers kept secrets. Her mother said a queen's daughter had to be aware of everything happening around her. If men wouldn't tell her, it was her duty to find out.

"I'll ask Mama."

He mimicked the high pitch of her voice. "Ask Mama." Then: "Or be patient for once. You'll find out."

Knees scraping against the wood, John hauled himself over the edge of the wain and landed in a heap. He popped up triumphantly. "I did it!"

The queen's retinue approached. Richard backed away to let a groom set a stool behind the wain. Their mother stepped onto it.

"Richard says we're going to see John's lady," Joan said.

Eleanor glanced over her shoulder at Richard and scowled.

"I didn't know it was a secret," he said, sulking. Joan was glad he didn't look at her. She hadn't meant to tattle, not really.

"It isn't." Eleanor faced the wain to address Joan. "We are going to Limoges to meet the count of Maurienne. Your father thinks his daughter will be a good match for John."

Joan frowned—he was no prize for any man's daughter. He was "John Lackland" unless one of their older brothers died. The king of France had assigned the mocking epithet, pointing out that Papa had more sons than lands to bequeath.

"Why would the count give his daughter to John?" Joan asked.

"He won't. Unless your father promises Chinon, Mirabeau, and Loudun."

"But those castles are supposed to be Henry's."

"Your father expects Henry to yield them to John."

Joan's joy dripped away like water through her fingers. Henry and Papa did not need another reason to fight. Richard said nothing, but his face was sullen.

"What does Henry think about that?" she pressed.

Her mother looked away. "Richard, find your horse. Your father is ready to start."

QUEEN ELEANOR SAID ONLY FOOLISH RULERS WERE UNFAMILIAR with their own domains, so Joan peered through the gap in the russet curtains and studied Limousin's countryside until it grew dark. They passed through fields brown with last year's grain, edged with clusters of neat cottages. Here and there, villagers emerged to watch them pass. Some waved their hats—they looked like flailing spiders. She didn't mind when Agnes pulled her from the curtain and told her to sleep.

When day broke, they were near enough to the city that she could recognize the terrain. Limoges was built largely of stone and sat on the bank of the river. Joan watched the walls grow larger until they filled her sight. The aged brown castle had a few narrow windows set high in the towers, and forbidding ramparts overhung with wooden hoardings.

The portcullis stood open in welcome. Though King Henry was not due for another three days, the lord of Limoges knew her father. The court had probably been prepared for a week.

Amid the disorder of unloading, Joan tied Tessie to her skirt, beckoned John, and slipped away from their guardians. There were children in the castle; there must be something to do. She led John into the courtyard, crowded with men and horses. A ramshackle cart partially blocked her path; it held barrels of ale, some of which had been cracked open. She hurried past the sour smell of rot and drink.

Across the yard, by the far wall, Richard stood surrounded by what her mother would call a gaggle of brigands. Joan waved but he didn't see. She didn't recognize most of the swaggering youths flaunting their swords and talking loudly. Closer, a group of boys about her age crouched in a circle fraught with motion. What were they doing?

"Come, John."

She crept up and squeezed between two of the boys. Field mice, prodded with sticks, skittered down lanes drawn in the dirt. Disgusted, she stepped backward, crunching the toes of boys who closed in around her. One wrested her arms behind her back and yelled, "She wants to see!"

Another plucked up a brown mouse by its tail. He thrust it, arch-backed, limbs splayed, into her face.

"John!" she shrieked, turning her head and shutting her eyes. She heard scuffling. Tiny feet scrabbled in her hair. Squeaking near her ear—

"Richard! Riii-chaaard!"

A smack sounded, and her tormentors scattered. Strong hands caught her under the arms. She looked up, expecting her brother. Instead, she saw a stranger.

"Are you hurt?" He looked Richard's age and was similarly lean and compactly muscled. But his eyes were nothing like Richard's. They were gray as mail, soft as petals. Strands of tangled brown hair curled across a beardless chin. His mouth was set in a thin, hard line.

"No." She felt queasy.

"Just frightened." The hardness disappeared from his lips; he sounded amused.

She pulled from his hands. "I'm not frightened."

"Then I must compliment your convincing imitation."

Why come to her aid just to mock her? She tried to answer as her mother might. "Your imitation of courtesy, to the contrary, leaves much to be desired."

"Oh-ho! Fine thanks, lady!" he said, laying folded hands across his heart. His voice held the accent of the south—Occitan, her mother's native language. "After I rescued you—"

"From a mouse, not a dragon. How much gratitude—"

Interrupting with laughter, Richard came at last. "So, you've met my sister."

"Your sister?" Her defender's mouth dropped open.

"Couldn't you guess? My mother's image."

The knight looked at her. She flushed. She stood before him, a ragamuffin in her traveling dress and a layer of dirt, plaits mussed by a frantic rodent, all too aware she would never match her mother. Staring back with offended dignity, she resisted the urge to smooth her dress or rub the dust from her face.

Richard said, "My mother's tongue, I meant. The poor girl *looks* like me!" Laughing again, he clapped the knight's arm and turned him back toward the far wall where the others waited. He called back over his shoulder, "Joan, does Agnes know you're scuffling in the courtyard with stableboys?"

Angry with him, she didn't answer. She looked at John, whose hunched shoulders and long face told her how frightened he'd been.

"I tried to kick them," he mumbled, rubbing his arm.

"If you hadn't slowed them, they'd have put the mouse down my dress. You are my champion, John."

He straightened his shoulders and beamed.

"OUCH!"

"Sit still and it won't hurt." Agnes raked the comb against Joan's head. She gritted her teeth. Agnes was not allowed to beat her, so when she misbehaved, her nurse combed her hair.

Agnes cared little for all she had suffered. As if the mouse and the fair knight's insults were not enough, now she couldn't find Tessie. Charisse, the kindest of her mother's attendants, had helped look through the baggage, although Joan knew the hunt would be fruitless. Tessie must have fallen loose in the courtyard, and Agnes would not let her return to search.

Joan sat on a stool in her mother's antechamber, where several of Eleanor's ladies were primping. The room was awash in fluffing dresses and the wafted scent of flower petals and sweet herbs the ladies tied in packets to their underskirts. Chattering blended to a low-level hum.

She tried to hear everything. Her father and mother had been in council all afternoon. Clenching her hands in her lap, she prayed her father hadn't given any of Henry's castles to John. This journey was turning out to be unpleasant enough.

Charisse, in a brown robe and blue girdle that flattered her blond hair and slender figure, threaded through the ladies. "I'll do the plaits, Agnes."

Charisse was famous for her plaiting—long, even, intricate braids that lay perfectly flat. The queen let no one else touch her own smooth black hair.

Agnes sniffed and stood aside. Joan sighed with relief when the comb changed hands.

She heard one of the maids giggle. "No, he's a brute. But did you see the fair son of Toulouse?"

She perked up. Toulouse?

"Wet behind the ears. Let him grow a few inches first." The scornful voice belonged to Amaria, Mama's pretty, green-eyed favorite.

To Joan's dismay, the rest was lost in the prattle. She thought of what she had been taught about Toulouse. By right, the county belonged to Mama. Lying just south of Aquitaine, the Toulousain had been part of the duchy held by Mama's grandfather, until it was stolen from him. Years ago, Papa had tried to win it back, but France supported the current count because he was married to the French king's sister. Why would a vassal of France be here?

Mama said men needed swords to fight but women had better weapons. A queen—or a princess—needed to know everything about her enemies. Maybe Mama didn't know the count was here. She could be the one to tell her!

Charisse patted the braids against her head. "You look very pretty. That blue gown makes you seem ten, at least."

Joan smiled her pleasure, though she knew Charisse's kindness had motive. A grown girl would not mourn the loss of a doll.

Amaria stepped into view, holding out her hand. "Come, child, I'm supposed to bring you to the Green Hall. The barons will be paying respects to the king and queen before supper."

That meant she would have to stand still for another endless ceremony, a smile pasted on.

The Green Hall took its name from the marbling of its stonework, intricate and pretty. She stood in the receiving line beside her mother and in front of Amaria, who would prick her if she slouched. To ignore the torment of hunger pains, Joan tried tracing the green veins of the marble with her eyes. She started at the ceiling, then followed the squiggles down the wall like lines on a map until her gaze bounced off the head of a vassal and went climbing back up.

On the fifth descent, she saw the young knight who had rescued her. His soft light-brown curls brushed the top of his shoulders. Garbed in scarlet, with a jeweled clasp at the shoulder, he looked handsomer than he had in the courtyard. At least now he was combed and washed. And so was she, if he cared to look. He stood with an older man whose blue tunic was too tight. Gems splashed across his breast and weighed down his hands. He had dark hair and small eyes—an untrustworthy face. If this was her knight's father, she decided she would not like either one.

Between her mother and father stretched a twenty-foot line of courtiers. On her mother's right, the countess chattered, a nervous laugh following each sentence. Joan glanced at her mother to gauge her level of impatience then followed the direction of her gaze to the scarlet knight and his ill-favored father. She tugged Eleanor's sleeve.

"Who is that man?" she mouthed.

The queen peered down her nose. "The count of Toulouse."

That was the count? "Why is he here?"

Her mother leaned over to answer. "To pay homage. He put his wife aside. She fled home to France." Then she straightened, leaving Joan to draw the conclusion. If Toulouse lost the friendship of France, the count would need to make peace with Papa. Would Papa let him make peace? Mama would not like it if he did.

Being a princess made her head hurt. What did Mama need Toulouse for, anyway? If Papa seized it, where would that leave the young scarlet knight?

The count was greeting her father. She watched carefully as he stretched out his hands to clasp Papa's, then leaned forward to speak into his ear. Papa jerked back, scowling.

Joan rose up on the balls of her feet, her mouth falling open. She snapped it shut. What had the count said? Maybe the son had heard—the knight's fine features were distorted with anger. No, not anger—disgust. She recognized a son's disgust with his father.

Her brother Henry wore the same expression often enough. But what did it mean?

The count backed away, the young knight with him. Papa's face was cold as he greeted the next man in line.

What did Mama think?

Joan's curiosity turned to shock. Her mother had paled; her mouth was drawn into a tight circle. Could Mama be frightened? The green marbling blurred before Joan's eyes. She stood confused and miserable until the crowd began to disperse. Her mother stepped back against the wall, dragging Amaria.

"Find out what he said," the queen commanded.

"How, my lady?" Amaria asked.

"The boy heard. Quickly, get him away from the count."

Amaria sped away.

Papa was angry at her champion's father? And for some reason that worried Mama. Swallowing hard, Joan asked, "Mama, what—"

Her mother shook her head. "Never mind. This does not concern you."

But everything was supposed to concern the queen's daughter. Joan's lower lip quivered, and she bit it before her mother noticed. How might Amaria coax words from her knight? Despite the necessity, she didn't want him to yield.

"What if he won't tell Amaria?"

Her mother looked at her sharply. "Tell her what?"

"What the count said that made Papa so angry."

"God's teeth! Your nose is longer than your ears are big. Don't worry about what the count said." She drew a breath. "We must go in to supper. Keep a smile on your face and your eyes on your bread. Don't make your father any angrier."

Joan crossed her arms to contain her frustration. Papa wasn't angry with *her*.

A steward directed the diners to their seats. Long tables draped in finely woven sky-hued linen formed three sides of a rectangle. King Henry sat in the center of the head table between the count of Maurienne and the lady of Limoges.

Joan's place was on her mother's right, at the end of the head table. Diagonally, at one of the long side tables, sat the count of Toulouse with his son. Her own father preferred to sit apart from his children—it took several minutes before Joan located her older brothers, each surrounded by a group of friends. John didn't behave well in company; he was already abed.

A swarm of servants burdened with clanking platters entered, bringing the scent of roast pork and apples. The hall grew louder with appreciative and impatient murmurings. Joan caught sight of Amaria weaving back.

The noise formed a barrier around the queen. Amaria bent between Joan and her mother. "I'm sorry, my lady. I couldn't get near. The boy never left the count's side. I— Oh, no, lady! He's looking over here."

"Don't look at him!" Eleanor snapped. "The king is watching."

Joan felt cold seep under her skin. Her mother's knuckles were white. Something was very wrong. The count must have said something about Mama. But he hated Mama. Why would Papa listen to him? Would Mama's concern make her look guilty?

She silently prayed, Please, God, please. Don't let them fight again. But she knew they would. Mama had no reason to send Amaria to the count unless she feared his words.

But Joan had a reason.

"Go back." Her high-pitched voice sounded loud. "Go back to the count. Ask if you may speak to his son about Tessie."

Amaria turned, face stupid with incomprehension.

"What are you talking about, child?" Her mother's voice was heavy.

"My doll. I lost her earlier in the courtyard."

"I can't think about a doll now."

"He was there. The count's son was there. Amaria, go ask him if he's seen it."

Her mother searched her face. "Joan, this isn't a game."

"I'm not playing a game. I want Tessie." Steadily, she said, "Papa won't be angry if she's just helping me."

Her mother's hands clenched and unclenched. "It's all I have. Amaria, go ask Lord Raymond if he's seen Joan's doll." Staring after the departing maid, she added, "If your father hangs me, child, it will be on your head."

Blood roared in her ears. Would Papa be fooled? When Amaria returned without Tessie, she could shriek. She could bawl and roll about on the floor. Papa would be so angry with her he'd forget about whatever the count had said.

Heart thudding in her chest, Joan watched as Amaria simpered before the old count. He laughed. The maid said something to the scarlet knight, who swept his gaze across the room, found Joan, and smiled. Never had anything warmed her like that smile. He answered Amaria. She nodded and hurried back through the crowd.

Charisse stepped aside so Amaria could again lean between Joan and her mother.

Amaria's eyes were wide. "Lady, he has it."

Joan felt woozy but managed to clap with exaggerated

delight in case her father was watching. Her mother drew a deep breath.

Amaria continued, "He says if the princess is distraught, he will produce it immediately. It is in his chamber."

"Ha!" Now Mama smiled, though the curled lips appeared more smug than pleased. "He wants you to go to his chamber? While everyone else is at supper?"

"Not me, lady. Princess Joan."

The smile disappeared. Joan had never seen her mother look nonplussed before.

"God in Heaven! What is he doing?"

"Mama, he's returning my doll. Let me go."

Her mother's eyes turned toward the ceiling, as if seeking guidance, but she blinked so rapidly perhaps she meant to stem a flow of tears. Then, lowering her head, she said, "Amaria, go with her. Don't let Raymond touch her. Don't let her out of your sight."

Joan felt important. Her mother was worried about letting her go to a man's chamber! And she was helping the queen. She stood. Her knees were only a little wobbly. She took Amaria's hand and crossed the floor.

Her knight rose as she approached, then bowed. "I'm sorry. I should have sent it back to you right away."

She nodded, not trusting her voice.

"By your leave, Father?" Lord Raymond asked.

"Hurry back," the count answered, without bothering to acknowledge her.

As they walked the narrow gallery to the chamber, he said, "You are fully recovered, I see. I doubt as much can be said for the mouse."

She wanted to giggle, but her throat was too tight. He was so calm. Could it be he had heard nothing untoward about her mother? But, no. She remembered the disgust on his face.

"I found the doll after you'd gone. I asked Richard, but he didn't know if it was yours."

"He didn't know Tessie?" Joan halted. She felt betrayed.

His step slowed, and he smiled at her. "Men don't spend a lot of time studying poppets." They walked on. "At any rate," he continued, "I hesitated to entrust it to him. I meant to inquire—"

"God's teeth!" She hoped to sound flippant. "I didn't accuse you of stealing my doll."

He laughed out loud, and she flushed with pleasure at her success.

They stopped in front of a dark oak door that had massive handles.

"Will you come in?" he asked, pushing open the door. The gray stone walls, unadorned, were lined with trunks draped in scarlet cloths bearing the twelve-pointed golden cross of Toulouse. There were five beds in the room, one neat and four rumpled. Several woolen blankets lay on the floor.

Raymond waded across the blankets to the neat bed. From under it, he took a large leather sack. He plunged in his hand, rifled for a moment, and pulled out Tessie. Joan rushed to him and took the doll. Tears flooded her eyes. She felt like an idiot, but she was not crying for Tessie. She didn't know why she wanted to cry.

He touched her shoulder. Amaria came a step closer.

"I—" Joan stopped. She didn't want to do this. "I have to ask you something. You don't have to answer."

He sighed. "I was afraid you would." He withdrew his hand.

"You don't have to answer. I don't want to cause trouble for you. With your father."

He chuckled without humor. "That is strangely generous coming from one in your family. Strangely generous and unbearably sad."

Joan bristled. "What did your father say to mine?"

His eyes flickered to Amaria then back to Joan.

"I don't want you to betray your father's trust," she said again, almost hoping the subject would close.

"My father's only intent was to stir up discord in your family. He won't care if I dip my finger into the pot and stir it some more."

The bitterness in his voice fed her fear. Her words came out as a whisper, "I don't understand what you're saying."

He touched her shoulder again, but this time his grip was firm. She looked up into his face as if he had commanded it. He studied her a long moment from behind darkened gray eyes; then his lids lowered, and he said softly, "I'm sorry. I should not have made you the go-between. They're going to ruin your innocence. God as my witness, I do not willingly help them." He stood back, his hand dropping to his side. "Tell your mother to be careful. My father said, 'There is treachery afoot. Beware your wife and your sons.'"

She stared at him. Treachery? Her brothers and Mama?

"Do you understand now?" he asked.

"No."

"I'm glad of it. Tell your mother what he said. Maybe it will come to nothing."

Joan's feet were rooted to the floor.

"Take her back to the queen," the knight ordered. As Amaria

bundled her out the door, she heard him say, "God go with you, child."

Mama looked up expectantly and smiled to see Tessie, but Joan found she could not repeat Lord Raymond's words. When Amaria did, Mama's face didn't change. She said, "That is all? Hmph. The count's impudence must have angered him."

Supper progressed as if the air held no hint of trouble. Joan watched her father eat, laugh, rise from his chair to pace and talk to other men, all as in a typical meal. Lord Raymond did not return to the dining hall. Joan was glad. She didn't want to face him.

When her father and the count of Maurienne announced John's betrothal, Joan spied on her brothers. Henry was scowling. His friends beside him scowled, too. Richard's face was impassive. Geoffrey frowned.

"Mama? Did Papa agree to give John the castles?"

"Yes, child."

Twisting her hands in her lap, she asked, "Henry knows?"

"Yes, he does."

After supper, they were obliged to pass right by her father. He laid a stern hand on her shoulder and demanded, "Joan, where did you disappear to with that ruffian?"

She looked up. "I lost my doll. But he found it." She lifted the doll to show him.

He scooped her up into the crook of his arm. "You lost Tessie!"

Tessie! Papa remembered Tessie. Her heart crumpled before it could swell. She nodded.

"Well, well. We must make him a present. What should we give him?"

She tried to think of something outlandish. "A horse?"

"A horse for a doll?" He laughed loudly, turning her back and forth. The men beside him laughed, too. "A horse it is, then." He set her down and turned to his wife. "You shouldn't let her wander off with young men. Especially men with reputations."

Eleanor raised an eyebrow. "I doubt the young lord misuses children."

"Mother your daughter, Eleanor. I'll see to our sons."

## TWO

IN THE MORNING, THE MEN GATHERED IN THE COURTYARD
for a hunt. Standing with Agnes in the arched gateway, Joan
peered into the horde, hoping to find her brothers and wish
them good fortune. Men called to each other and whistled for
their dogs. Horses trotted about, splattering mud. She knew the
disorder was less than it seemed, but she found it frightening
nevertheless.

There was Papa. Astride the large brown mare he favored for
the chase, he rose half a head taller than the lords flanking him.
When he saw her he smiled, but after last night, she did not trust
his good humor.

Across the yard, the men of Toulouse waited in a tight cluster. Her knight was seated upon a fine strong destrier, black as
soot. She recognized the horse, a brute that had once kicked in
the head of a groom. Her father never let his own sons near it.
Was this how the king rewarded kindness?

She heard the blast from the herald's horn and watched the
hunters depart through the main gate. The flash of scarlet
mounted on black receded from her vision. Lord Raymond rode
with confidence, showing off his skill. Mama would say he
should show better sense. What if he were hurt? She gnawed on
her thumbnail until Agnes brushed her hand from her mouth.

"I must take you inside, child."

"Can I see my mother?"

"No. She is busy with the countess. I'll take you to the nursery where the other children are playing."

"I don't want to play. I am not feeling well. Can I go to our chamber?"

Agnes looked at her with pity. "Yes, Joan."

The large room comprising the second story of the guest tower was, thankfully, unoccupied. Agnes sat in a chair near the window and took up her mending; Joan sprawled on the bed they shared and played listlessly with Tessie. If Papa was angry again, it was Henry's fault—Henry, the "young king." Ever since his coronation nearly three years ago, all he and Papa ever did was fight. The coronation had only been performed because Papa had taken ill and wanted to ensure the succession. He recovered, yet the way Henry had been acting recently, so impatient, you'd think he wished Papa *had* died.

Joan crossed herself quickly; she hadn't meant that. To chase away wicked thoughts, she tried humming a hymn she'd learned long ago in Fontevrault Abbey. Very few such memories of her early life remained, only songs, snatches of prayer, the wrinkled, kind faces of nuns whose names she no longer recalled.

When she turned five, Mama had claimed her from Fontevrault and brought her to Poitiers. There Eleanor ruled in her own right as duchess, although Richard, as heir to Poitou and Aquitaine, had already taken charge of the soldiers. Mama was so proud of him.

Agnes said, "Would you sing something else, Joan?"

She hushed, feeling guilty. Agnes had been with her at the abbey. Quiet, pious, and not very pretty, perhaps she would have preferred to stay there.

"Will you play merels with me?" Joan asked.

Agnes laid down her mending. "If you like. I thought you felt ill and didn't want to play."

"I don't want to play with people."

The nurse produced the board and pegs from one of the trunks. Richard had taught Joan the game, where players took turns placing pegs in holes in the board. Three pegs in a row meant she could capture his peg. She must also remember to block his rows, so he could not take hers. Richard always won, but still it was more fun playing with him. Agnes didn't like merels.

They played until the nurse tired and gave Joan a piece of cloth to embroider. Time passed so slowly, she started to doze in her chair, but Agnes woke her, saying she should not sleep now or she would lie awake at night. So she sat and gazed out the window.

"Child, come away from there. You look like you're in a trance."

Joan slid from her stool and paced about the room. There was no point watching for the return of the hunters. The window faced the wrong direction.

"Joan, you are wearing a rut in the floor. What is bothering you today?"

She thought of everything that bothered her: the horse her father had chosen for her champion, Henry's peevishness whenever Papa was around, Richard's indifference, the count's warning, her mother's fear. And last night she had taken the queen's side against the king. She had only meant to help Mama, not hurt Papa.

The door to the chamber burst open to admit Charisse and a bevy of maids.

Charisse said, "The hunters are back. The king is going to Chinon. We must pack."

Joan shuddered with misgivings. It was only mid-afternoon. Hunts usually lasted till dusk.

"He's in a foul mood," Charisse continued. "He dismissed six of the young king's companions."

Joan sat hard on the bed and groped for Tessie. Why would Papa send Henry's friends away? Charisse began throwing clothes into a trunk, taking no care to sort or fold them.

Agnes asked, "Was there any—?"

"Nothing. There was nothing. No one knows what happened. The king was seized with a violent fit of temper and ended the hunt."

"Where is the queen?" Agnes asked.

"She's already in the wain, waiting."

"And the princes?"

Charisse stopped and looked at the nurse. All around them, maids gathered up ribbons and clothes, pillows and combs, tossing them into trunks and banging the lids shut.

"Still on their horses, but the king has men all around them."

Joan's heart pounded so hard she thought she would faint. "Like prisoners?"

Charisse turned to her. "Oh! Oh, darling sweet, no. Not like prisoners. Like naughty boys. He just wants them back in Chinon so he can scold them in private."

"Scold them for what?"

"I don't know, sweet. Just hurry. Let Agnes run you down to the wain. The servants will be here for the trunks any minute."

Amaria appeared at the door. She clutched the jamb and

leaned forward, pressing her hand to her bosom as she struggled to catch her breath. "Joan!"

Joan jumped up. "Yes?"

"Come now! The king is accusing the queen of hiding you away. He wants to leave!"

"But I've been here all day."

Amaria beckoned her forward. "Come. I'll take you."

Together they ran to the stairs. At the top of the stairwell, Amaria paused to gasp for air. "I had to search all over for you," she said.

"Amaria? No one is hurt?"

"No."

"What is going to happen?"

"Sweet Mother Mary, Joan. How should I know?"

Amaria hurried her down the steps, then through the semi-enclosed walkway connecting the guest tower and great hall. The hall was filled with courtiers and ladies who smirked behind their hands as Joan passed. Papa stood at the door, arguing with the red-faced lord of Limoges.

The lady of Limoges spotted them, and relief broke across her face. "Here she is, sire."

Her father whirled about and glared at Joan. "Where were you hiding?"

"I . . . I . . ." She started to cry. Why was he so angry?

"Put her in the cart."

A man lifted her and carried her away. He didn't take her to her own wain, but to an open two-wheeled cart that held a few kitchen girls and boxes of larder supplies. Too frightened to complain, she wondered if her father would fault the man or if he'd done it on the king's instruction. But why punish her? What had she done?

DUSK FELL, BUT THE CORTEGE DID NOT HALT FOR SUPPER. THE kitchen girls shared their meager scraps of bread and cheese with Joan. If they hadn't, she supposed her father would have let her starve. It drizzled, and she thought he might rescue her from her misery. Instead, she huddled for a long time under a fusty, wet blanket with the other girls.

It was night when the rain stopped. Clouds dispersed, revealing a full moon bright enough to light the way. The cortege changed horses at a village Joan did not know, then pressed on. The rain had converted the dirt road to mud. Drivers led their horses in a snaking pattern to avoid the quagmire. Joan's cart swayed side to side as if rocked by waves. One by one, her companions drifted off to sleep, but she sat upright. She didn't like traveling at night, especially without Agnes, and since the way was unfamiliar, she couldn't guess how long it would take. Limoges was in the Limousin, south of Poitou, while Chinon lay to the north in Anjou. Mama liked to claim southerners had better manners, that northern Frenchmen were almost as barbaric as the English and the Irish. But Joan had not been impressed by any courtesy in Limoges.

Night gave way to the chirruping arrival of dawn, and Joan became conscious of awakening maids and stamping horses. She must have slept after all.

Her tongue felt thick, and her throat, parched. When one of the girls produced a skin of water, she had no choice but to drink from it. The water tasted of dirt. She wondered what the servants were thinking. Her father was famous for impetuous

changes in his itinerary—maybe it was nothing more. Even as
the hopeful thought formed, she recognized it as vain.

Fog settled upon them during the morning hours, and when
it lifted, spitting rain began. They stopped only for fresh horses.
Joan thought her father must care more for his beasts than for
his children. At last, after a long day's rolling passage northwest
through dormant vineyards and fields sharply scented with rot-
ting chaff, the road began its descent to rejoin the Vienne River.
Ahead, she could see the many pale gray towers of Chinon
Castle. The sprawling fortress sat atop a spur of rock, its lower
walls nearly hidden by trees.

When they drew near, the castle gates opened. The castellan
met them, and servants flocked to unload the carts. The weary
kitchen girls followed a steward sent to fetch them. A groom led
away the horse and cart. Joan stood alone at the castle door while
people swarmed about with purpose. She knew Chinon. It was
her father's most important fortress in Anjou. She could make
her way to the right chamber. But she was afraid to leave on her
own. What if Papa were to look for her again?

Agnes found her. "Oh, Joan! You are as wet as a fish."

"It rained." Her eyes welled with tears.

"Come. We'll find some dry clothes."

"Where is Mama?"

"With the king."

"And my brothers?"

Agnes looked away. "With the king, too."

"Can I go to them?"

"No, child. He didn't send for you."

Her shoes left damp marks on the stone floor as she followed
Agnes to their chamber. Inside, maids arranged the bedding and

aired dresses as though it were just another day, but Joan could not shake away her fear. Agnes helped her out of her wet gown and chemise and into dry ones. Then she combed Joan's hair as gently as Charisse would have.

The other maids left when they completed their tasks. Only Agnes remained.

"Can I go to find John?" Joan asked. He wouldn't be with Papa. Her older brothers excluded him from their schemes. Still, he might have heard what happened on the hunt.

"I think you should stay here."

Agnes found her some sewing. Joan was tired after the night's poor sleep followed by a tedious day of travel. Her stitches zigzagged and her thread tangled. When she nodded off, Agnes didn't wake her.

She woke when Amaria brought stewed pears and boiled eggs, and she ate until her stomach felt bloated. "Amaria, what is happening? Did Mama and Papa argue?"

"Probably." She shrugged. "I don't know."

"Where is Henry?"

"Joan, don't badger me."

Joan frowned. Her mother said a princess had to be aware of all the undercurrents at court. She would be angry that everyone was keeping her daughter in the dark.

"I want to talk to my mother."

Agnes chided, "Be patient, Joan. They've fought before. You know that."

She knew. But it hurt every time.

In the evening, bells called them to supper. With relief, Joan noted her mother and father together at the head of the table, though her father looked sullen and her mother defiant. Her brothers sat apart—Richard and Geoffrey in their usual company. Since that was their preference, it wouldn't have worried her, except the young voices were unnaturally muted. Henry sat among a group of older knights. Throughout the meal, she watched him cast furtive glances around the hall—he looked as though he were measuring the distance to the doors.

Agnes bent over her shoulder. "You are not eating, child. Are you unwell?"

She nodded without thinking.

"Come, I'll take you back to the chamber. You're better off in bed."

She rose and followed Agnes; no one stopped them. She thought it likely no one cared that they'd gone.

LONG AFTER SUPPER MUST HAVE ENDED, CHARISSE CAME TO the chamber. "Are you awake, sweet? The queen asks if you are ill."

"May I go to her?"

Charisse pulled at her fingers, then nodded. "But if she says you must leave, don't argue. Don't give her any more trouble."

"Is my father angry about what the count of Toulouse said?"

"He's always angry about something. Don't fret so much."

The passage that led to her mother's quarters stank of burning oil, and the lamps cast overlapping shadows to menace them as they walked. Charisse brought Joan to the antechamber, where six maids already lay two to a bed. She knocked on the door to the queen's bower.

Amaria opened it a crack. "Lady, it is Princess Joan."

"Let her enter," her mother said. She sat in bed, her legs under a gray linen sheet. Heavy blankets were kicked to the footboard. Her unbound hair fell past her shoulders, and her eyes were swollen—she looked tired. "Joan, what is wrong?"

"I don't know, Mama. I'm frightened."

Her mother sighed. "Come here."

Joan climbed into the bed and felt comforted by its softness and the lily scent of her mother's hair.

"Why are you frightened?" Eleanor asked.

"Because no one will tell me what is wrong."

She thought her mother smiled for a moment. But then the regal face grew stern. "Why don't you tell *me*? What do you think?"

"Papa is angry. He's angry at Henry. And . . ." Joan's breath rushed out. "Count Raymond spoke to Papa." Her mother nodded. "And . . . and I spoke to Count Raymond's son."

"Are you afraid your father is angry with you?"

"No." She was, but it was the least of her fears. "He doesn't care what I do, Mama."

Her mother hugged her. "Sweetling, I told him Amaria talked to young Raymond. You just wanted your poppet."

Joan's heart lightened. She hadn't hurt Papa. He didn't know.

"He's not suspicious of you. He won't let me speak to your brothers, but I doubt he'll keep you from them—he knows how you worship Richard. Tomorrow morning you must try to see Richard. You must find out what your father said to him."

"But—"

"Shush now." She laid her hands over Joan's. "A princess must be brave. And she must know whom to trust. You trust Richard, don't you?"

She nodded. She trusted Richard. She wanted to trust her mother, too.

"You're a smart girl. Someday, we'll make you a queen, won't we? Where would you like to be queen? France?"

Joan wrinkled her nose. She didn't feel like playing her mother's favorite game.

"Shall we marry you to young Philip?" Mama pressed.

Joan shook her head. Her family did not like France, even if Henry was married to Margaret, the elder of Prince Philip's sisters, and Richard was supposed to marry Alice, the younger.

Mama laughed, a little trill. "Lie down, darling."

She laid her head in her mother's lap.

"What about Jerusalem?" she said, smoothing Joan's hair. "Or Sicily? Or maybe you could be an empress."

"Mama," she groaned, "I don't want to marry a king. I want to stay with you."

"Sweet Jeanne." The Occitan pronunciation caressed like an endearment. Her mother pulled the sheet up and lay beside her. Snuggled in her mother's arms, Joan fell asleep.

GASPS AND THE SCREECHING OF WOMEN IN THE ANTECHAMBER woke her. Joan sat up and clutched her mother. Pale dawn light filtered through the shutters, enough to see armed men storm through the door. The knights drew up short before the half-dressed queen.

Her father led them. "Where is he?"

"Who?" her mother asked.

"Your unholy whelp."

"Unholy? That would be yours, then. Melusine's blood."

"Better sons of the devil than sons of yours. Where is Henry?"

"Henry?" Joan thought her mother sounded surprised, but

the surprise was lost in laughter. "Sire, he was in your care, not mine."

Her father drew close, his face choleric. Joan ducked as his hands flew out from his sides. He dragged the queen from bed, one hand on her arm, the other in her hair.

"Where is he?"

Eleanor steadied herself and pushed away the king's hands. "He was imprisoned in *your* antechamber last night. How could you have lost him? Where are his guards?"

"One is dead. The other, missing."

"Who killed the dead one? You or Henry?" She laughed again. "You fool. Henry must be halfway to France by now."

"France?" His jaw slackened. "Not France, Eleanor. Henry is too soft for treason." His voice was so even, so cold, Joan couldn't tell if it held hatred or hurt.

"If you believe that, then seek him where you will."

Her father ground his teeth, thinking, then he turned to the knight at his right. "There are five or six castles where he could be heading. Send out search parties . . . and one also to the French border. The young king must be apprehended." He looked back at Queen Eleanor. "If I do find him in France, he will find himself in hell."

She smirked. "You won't find him anywhere if you and your brigands keep loitering here. Look at Sir Rufus gawking at Joan."

Joan gasped. The young knight's eyes widened, and his face flushed red. She pulled the linen up to her chin. Her father glared at him, then at her mother.

"I'm bringing Henry back, Eleanor. And when I am through

with him, he will curse the womb that bore him." His voice was thick with anger.

"Your children hate you." Hers was ice-water thin. "You cannot blame me for that."

CHINON CASTLE WAS HER FATHER'S FORTRESS. THOUGH ITS exterior was starkly beautiful, the interior was merely stark. In older parts of the castle, condensation dripped from the walls so regularly that green moss grew on them in sheets. In Poitiers, niches held cushioned benches or flowers; here, they held spiderwebs or nests of mice.

Joan made her way through the east gallery. It was now late afternoon. The tapers on the wall were spaced too far apart—even when all were lit, the gallery was dark. The gloom suited her purpose. She was hiding.

After everything that had happened that morning, she would rather disappear altogether.

Her father had given orders for Sir Rufus to be blinded by hot irons. The punishment took place in the tilting yard just before morning prayers. Unwilling to watch, Joan stood behind the door to the yard, but she heard Rufus scream.

The grumbling knights nearby did not fault the king. Everyone knew Mama had accused Rufus falsely to hasten the men out of her chamber. But didn't Papa know that, too?

She wondered who would have borne the blame if the gift horse had thrown the young lord of Toulouse.

She turned a corner, reaching her destination in ten more paces. The secluded alcove had been a chapel under one of Chinon's previous lords. It had fallen into disuse, its furnishings scavenged for other chambers, but a pretty stained-glass window remained, allowing a thin patch of brightly colored light to dance across the floor. She liked to pretend that it was her own chapel, or a nursery for Princess Tessie.

Joan slipped through the arched entrance and sidled along the wall to sit where no one walking past could see her. She had overheard many things from this vantage point, since the gallery was often used by servants, but she didn't expect any answers to fall upon her ears. Did Henry run away because of what the count of Toulouse said? Could he really have gone to France? Mama always said to answer a question, start from what you know.

Mama taught that a princess must not only understand the policies of the realm, but she must also understand its enemies. Joan understood why the king of France was their enemy. King Louis of France put his first wife aside because, though she'd given him two daughters, she'd failed to produce a male heir in fifteen years of marriage. His first wife was Mama, Duchess Eleanor of Aquitaine.

What happened next was one of Joan's favorite stories. The French king had treated Mama cruelly, leaving her alone and disgraced, prey to any lowly lord who thought to enhance his lands by seizing hers. To whom could she turn? Who could be so bold as to offer her succor, when to do so meant angering the powerful king of France?

One of the king's own vassals did—Prince Henry of England, duke of Normandy, count of Anjou. Papa! A scant eight weeks after the annulment, Papa stunned Christendom by marrying Mama. Within a year, she gave birth to a son.

King Louis's humiliation was not yet complete. The next

year, Papa became king of England when Stephen—the usurper—died. Papa was now wealthier and more powerful than his overlord. And Mama was a queen again.

Joan especially liked the way Papa told the story. He ended it there. Mama emphasized the consequences.

As duke of Normandy and count of Anjou, Papa was still King Louis's vassal. Mama was too, since Aquitaine was still a French duchy. They could not refuse to pay homage. What kind of example would that set for their own vassals? But Papa did not believe a king should bow to a king. While Joan had been in Fontevrault, Papa and King Louis had almost come to war more than once. Not even the dual marriage alliance, Henry wed to Margaret and Richard betrothed to Alice, could secure peace between two such bitter rivals.

So four years ago, Papa had settled the contentious issue of homage by yielding the French fiefs to his sons. Henry became count of Anjou and duke of Normandy. Richard became duke of Aquitaine and count of Poitou. The county of Brittany went to Geoffrey. The boys paid homage to King Louis; since then, there had been an uneasy truce.

Joan scratched lines in the dust on the floor. Henry was not just a sworn vassal of France, he was also King Louis's son-in-law. Just how friendly were Henry and the French king? If Henry asked for France's support, would there be war? Suddenly, horrible questions stretched out before her, leading where she did not want to follow. If Henry fought Papa, whose part would Richard take? And then Mama—

*Beware your wife and your sons.*

Joan whispered, "No." She clasped her trembling hands and forced her mind to reason. Richard was content ruling Aquitaine.

And Geoffrey was just fourteen—he would not commit treason on Henry's behalf.

The count of Toulouse wanted only to sow discord in her family. His words had no meaning.

Yet, where was Henry?

Slumping against the wall, Joan fought to hold back her tears. Could she ask Richard? Did he know Henry's plans?

Bells chimed and echoed through the corridors, calling the household to supper. Joan jumped up and rubbed her cheeks with her sleeve. She didn't dare be late.

She ran through the empty gallery, slowing when she reached the door to the great hall. There, Agnes stood beside Charisse, wringing her hands.

"I'm here. Agnes, I'm here."

Agnes saw her. "Oh, child," she said, reaching out an arm to envelop her. "Please tell me where you are going before you disappear."

"I'm sorry."

"Your face is filthy." She dabbed at it with a handkerchief. "Let me see your hands." Joan turned up her palms, and Agnes sighed. "Come along. It's too late to wash you."

She followed Agnes to a low table, relieved she would not be on display while she dined. Looking across the room, she saw her mother at the head table, sitting between two of Papa's Normans— men she knew Mama did not like. Charisse slipped into place behind the queen.

At the opposite end of the table, her father sat beside the French princess. Alice was fourteen, sweet-faced, and starting to blossom. Papa had taken her as his ward years ago when her betrothal to Richard was first arranged. Alice lived in Poitiers, but

Papa often summoned her to Chinon. She became haughtier with each passing year, and Joan was glad Richard snubbed her. She wished Papa would snub her, too; but he still took her onto his lap as if she were a child.

The line of courtiers entering the hall began to taper off. Joan squinted, confused. Too many chairs remained empty. Too many chairs—

She whipped her head around to look at her father; her chest ached as she drew in a breath. He rose but leaned one palm on the table. His eyes bulged with the tension in his clenched jaw. Joan followed the direction of his gaze back to the gaping vacancies at the table.

Richard and Geoffrey were not there.

The room buzzed with confusion. Joan felt danger closing in.

The queen stood also, and her voice cut through the whispers like the sharp edge of broken glass. "Richard and Geoffrey will not make war on their brother. Nor will they break their oath to their sworn lord, the king of France."

All eyes focused on the king and queen. Her mother's back was as rigid as the wall behind her. Her powdered white face glowed beneath her dark veil. The wide, deep-blue sleeves of her robe fell like folded wings over her clasped hands. If not for her mother's perfect calm, Joan would not have been surprised to see her fly to the ceiling like Melusine.

"They have returned to Poitiers," Eleanor said.

Relief washed King Henry's face clean of fury, as though he had wiped it with a wet cloth. Joan stifled her cry. Richard and Geoffrey had not gone to France, but her father's relief meant he believed they might have.

He stood straighter and said in a deep, measured voice, "I

would not ask my sons to kill each other. Did I build this king-dom so they might tear it apart?" His harsh laughter flooded the room. "Join your frightened children in Poitiers. I have no need of you here."

Joan's eyes burned. John sobbed loudly, but she was too old to cry in an assembly.

The queen nodded. "As you will, sire."

The corners of her mouth turned up and her lids lowered as she took her seat at the table. The king let out so long a breath he seemed to deflate. He sat down with force, scowling.

Joan wondered which of her parents had won.

# THREE

K ING HENRY II OF ENGLAND WAS KNOWN THROUGHOUT
Christendom for his energy and the speed of his military
campaigns. Men who had fought against him told cautionary
tales of his armies appearing from nowhere, in far-flung loca-
tions, after traveling distances that should have been impossible.
One duke's sarcastic complaint—"his steeds have wings"—had
been repeated until it gained a strange credibility.

But Joan knew her father's horses possessed no wings.

The previous dawn, four days after Richard and Geoffrey's
flight, she had climbed into a small wain with Agnes and four
lady's maids from Chinon. All day and all night they swayed and
lurched, suffering the grinding screech of the axles and bumping over rocks in the road. They ate soldiers' rations tossed into
the cart by an unseen cook. If her father covered ground quickly,
it was because he never stopped moving.

Sleep eluded her throughout the long night, though she tried
every trick, even piling blankets beneath her head until she
nearly sat up straight, which didn't prevent her teeth from clack-
ing together every time a wheel met a hole. The wain was loud
with the creaking of the wheels, the rustling of the canvas roof,
and the moaning of unfamiliar maids.

She was exhausted and stiff. Worse, she felt abandoned. Her
elder brothers had left her behind, and her father had packed the
still-weeping John off to Fontevrault as soon as the queen's

cortege rattled out of Chinon's gate. Joan didn't know why he had not sent her to Fontevrault also, or to Poitiers with Mama. And she was too frightened to ask.

They were on their way northeast to the castle of Verneuil in Normandy—four days' journey from Chinon and less than a day from the French border. Bishop Gilbert of London and Bishop Jocelyn of Sarum had gone ahead to Paris to ask King Louis to return the wayward son to his father. There was half a hope the pious French king would be sympathetic. Even so, her father intended to reinforce his petition by positioning an army in Verneuil.

There was no longer any doubt that the young king had gone to the French court. Two days ago, Henry's chancellor and chamberlain had returned to Chinon. They said they had deserted him at the bank of the Loire when they saw he would not be dissuaded from his treasonous course.

Joan rolled onto her back and watched the black of the waxed russet roof lighten to gray. She heard the cooing and whooping of birds. Then hoofbeats alerted her to movement outside the wain. The wheels ceased rolling. The curtains parted, allowing a sliver of pale light to cut across the floor of the cart.

"Joan, girl?" Her father's voice was husky with his attempted whisper. He thrust his hand through the folds of cloth. "You're awake? Come to the curtain."

Joan scrambled across protesting soft bodies. Her knees slipped from blankets and flesh to the hard wooden floor. She pushed her head outside and drew in a breath of fresh air. The trees were budding, but the dawn air was cold and frost glistened on the ground.

Her father held out his hand. When she had twisted halfway

through the tangled cloth, he wrapped his arm around her waist and hauled her onto his saddle. Her skirts bunched beneath her thighs; she squirmed to smooth the wrinkles. He loosened his grip and wrapped his cloak around her, enveloping her in warmth.

"Did you sleep?" he asked. She shook her head. "No? Neither did I." His deep chuckle bounced her against his stomach. "In a few hours, we'll rest the horses and eat. Do you want to ride with me until then?"

"Oh! Yes, Papa!"

He spurred forward to rejoin his knights. Joan peered from the cloak. She recognized several of the faces. Sir Rufus's brother was there; she shrank behind the cloth. No one smiled a greeting. They looked tired and serious.

Her father needed less sleep than most men. His voice held no trace of fatigue. He pointed out landmarks and remarked on the hunting. Then he dropped to a confidential tone, a teaching tone, to make sure she took note of her surroundings. See the way the breeze stirred the trees. Smell the faint acrid hint of smoke. A soldier should take note of odors that did not belong to the locale. If there wasn't a village nearby, an enemy camp might be hidden in the woods.

She nestled against him, knowing he talked to hear his own words of wisdom. He taught his sons the same way, but his sons were not there.

He pointed out an eagle's nest. She leaned back to look and almost fell from the saddle. He gripped her arm.

"Remember to keep your weight centered. You know better."

"Yes, Papa." Her face felt hot. His lessons ceased. When he did not deign to talk to her for the next few miles, she regretted the silence.

"Joan, girl? You haven't lost Tessie again, have you?"

Her heart thumped. Now she wished the silence had not ended. "No, Papa. She's in the wain."

"Tell me, how did the young lord of Toulouse happen to gain possession of your doll?"

"I dropped her in the courtyard. Some boys were teasing me, and Lord Raymond chased them. I . . . he said he found Tessie after I left."

Her father coughed then cleared his throat.

"You were with Amaria when she talked to the boy, weren't you." It didn't sound like a question, but he waited for her answer.

"Amaria didn't talk to him. I did." She felt his arms about her stiffen.

"I wondered. Will you tell me what you two discussed?"

"I asked him what the count said to you. You looked so angry, I was afraid."

"What did he say?"

"He told me what he heard. His father said you should beware of Mama and Henry."

*"Henry?"*

She could envision the crooking of his eyebrow, like a drawn bow, and was glad she did not have to look him in the face.

"He said 'your son.'"

The crunch of the horse's hooves on the hard dirt sounded loud. Her father's heart sounded loud, too, or maybe it was her own. She should have told the whole truth.

"So, you reported this to your mother."

"Amaria did. But I would have. I was frightened. I didn't know what he meant, and I wanted to know."

"Did your mother explain?"

"No." Again, silence fell. It lasted so long, Joan decided she preferred the sound of talk, after all. "I suppose I know now."

"Do you?"

"Henry has gone to France. If he doesn't come home, you will fight him."

"Mmm," he said. Then, "Hmph," as if considering something. With one hand, he tucked the cloak tighter. "Is there anything else you would like to confess to me?"

"No, Papa. Mama doesn't tell *me* anything, either." She said this so woefully, it sounded ridiculous. But it had a surprising effect. Her father laughed.

"Your mother likes to play with secrets, doesn't she? But you and I don't like secrets. Perhaps it is because we have nothing to conceal. Honest people don't need to keep secrets. Remember that, Joan, my girl."

"Yes, Papa." She wondered what else he wanted her to say.

"Shall we make a pact? An honest one? I won't conceal things from you, if you don't keep anything from me."

"I wouldn't," she protested. He must know *she* would never plot—

"You would if you thought I might hurt Henry."

Joan frowned, confused.

Over her head, he continued. "I don't blame you. My girl, I swear to you, none of your brothers has anything to fear from me. I would let them strike me down dead before I would harm one hair of their precious hides. Henry will come home. I will forgive him. But I will kill anyone who stands in the way of our reconciliation. You can understand that, can't you?"

She did understand. Moreover, she believed him. Papa wanted what was best for them. So did Mama. Only . . . she didn't think they agreed what was best.

THREE BURGHS BOUND TOGETHER BY COMMON OUTER WALLS made up the city of Verneuil. Each was enclosed by a separate inner wall and a deep dry trench. Craftsmen and tradesmen lived in the East Burgh. The Lesser Burgh housed wealthier townsmen and clerics. King Henry's men would be in the Great Burgh, which was dominated by the castle keep and its outbuildings. The Great Burgh had the highest walls and backed against the River Avre.

From her perch in her father's saddle, Joan listened to his talk of the city as they approached. He called the castle impregnable, then laughed and excepted the time he'd besieged it.

Once inside, Joan immediately decided that she had never seen an uglier castle. Small windows were set so deep in the thick gray walls of the keep she felt entombed. Adjacent to the keep, joined to it by a covered walkway, was a three-story tower. The upper two floors were subdivided by wattle-and-daub partitions into tiny chambers all packed with men waiting to make war on her brother. She waited, too, wondering if her father would be true to his word.

After a fortnight, the bishops returned from France. Her father allowed her to sit in the back of the council chamber while they made their report.

"Sire, there is no good news," the portly Bishop Gilbert stated. "When we presented King Louis with your message, he said, 'Who is it that makes this request?' We repeated, 'the king of England.' "

Bishop Jocelyn took up the tale, frowning so worriedly a ladder of creases ascended his forehead and disappeared under his miter. "He said, 'That cannot be, for the king of England is here with me. But if his father, who was once king of England, still claims the title, let him be made aware the whole world knows he resigned his kingdom to his son.' And then he dismissed us, sire. We had no opportunity to speak to the young king."

Joan bit her lip. It was King Louis's fault! Surely, if Henry had been allowed to hear the bishops, he would have repented.

Her father ground his teeth. "The king of France fancies himself a wit."

Bishop Jocelyn's wrinkled face shook with earnestness. "Sire, I urge you to look to the security of your castles and people. Your son has drawn you into conflict with France."

Her father nodded. "We are prepared. My son will learn a lesson about war."

JOAN, TOO, LEARNED ABOUT WAR. THE FIRST LESSON WAS THAT a man renowned for quickness must also know when to be patient. Her father hired several hundred mercenaries and told them to wait. For three weeks, he met with messenger after messenger, men eager to curry favor by bringing bad news. Vassals all over Anjou, Limousin, and Angoulême rose up to lay waste to his strongholds, but he scoffed at suggestions that he subdue them.

"Richard can deal with the local barons. Should I scatter my army throughout the realm seeking troublemakers while King Louis invades Normandy?" He would deal with traitors after he had brought Henry to heel.

The second lesson was a bitter one: Trust no one. A lesson doubly learned.

Shortly after Easter, Joan found out Richard and Geoffrey had joined Henry in France. Not only that, but Richard had been knighted at King Louis's hand. The French king's vassals vowed to assist the young king in expelling his father. And the three princes swore they would make no peace with their father without France's consent.

It put her father in a terrible temper. Joan felt it best to stay out of his way. But one night as she was readying for bed, a knock on the door interrupted her prayers—a summons from the king. Joan recognized her escort—Sir Robert of Chenowith, one of Papa's closest advisers. He appeared uncomfortable and did not speak as they walked. He opened the door to the king's chamber but did not go inside.

Her father sat on the edge of his bed, his head in his hands. He raised it at her approach. The skin beneath his eyes sagged. The chancellor Geoffrey Ridel was present also. Joan didn't like him. His eyes and lips were yellow-hued, and he always smelled like horse urine. She made a point of wrinkling her nose as she walked past him to the bedside.

Papa said, "She was raising all of Poitou and Aquitaine in Richard's name and her own, Joan." Joan stared. Did he mean Mama? His voice turned harsh and he spoke past her. "The devil take her, I'd gladly hand her over myself."

"Sire," interrupted Chancellor Ridel, "it is treason, plain and simple. Treason is punishable—"

"I know how to punish treason." He pounded his hand against his thigh, sounding angry and weary all at once. "That is not the issue."

She'd arrived in the middle of their conference. The king and chancellor were not yet finished arguing. But her father *had* sent for her.

"Papa, what happened?"

"Your mother was taken by agents of mine."

"Taken? Why?" Joan stomped her foot, though she would rather have thrown herself on the floor and wailed. Mama's vassals in Aquitaine and Poitou had old quarrels against her father. If they chose to rebel now, it showed only that they knew how to seize opportunity.

"She was riding with a light guard." He spoke with a brittle patience that made her think he'd planned exactly what to say. "They caught her halfway to the French border, disguised in men's clothes. If you have a more benign interpretation of these facts, you're welcome to put it forth for my consideration."

She turned her head. Her father's face was a blur. The young lord of Toulouse had said they would rob her of her innocence. He'd said it as if innocence were a good thing. What a fool.

"What will you do to her?"

"She's been imprisoned."

"Where?"

"That is a secret."

"A secret?" She blinked, but the tears rolled down her cheeks. "A secret, Papa?"

"Your brothers mustn't know where she is."

"Do you think I would tell them?"

"Ah, Joan, girl." He caressed her chin with one finger. "Of course you would. This way, you will not have to tell." He stood, putting his hand on her back and pointing her to the door.

She walked away, her legs stiff as pikes. Sir Robert pushed

the heavy door open when she pulled on the handle. As she passed through, she heard the chancellor's voice.

"I told you it was a mistake, sire. She's proven useless as a hostage. Why would holding her curb the queen's treachery? You've been more conscientious of her care than her mother would have been. And you can't believe her brothers care a whit—"

Sir Robert yanked the door shut.

QUEEN ELEANOR HAD SAID MEN NEEDED SWORDS TO FIGHT, but women had better weapons. What would she say now? Know your enemies? Joan didn't even know whose side she was supposed to be on.

In May 1173, the count of Flanders invaded the Norman–French border at Pacy. Joan did not need her father to keep her informed—with all the excitement in Verneuil even the lowliest stableboy knew the young king and Duke Richard were with the count.

With Geoffrey under his wing, King Louis brought the French army to the Norman Vexin. A buffer between France and Normandy, the Vexin had been Princess Margaret's dowry. Joan knew some might say Louis was within his rights to claim it for his son-in-law, but they wouldn't say it in front of King Henry. The French took the first castle late in June.

Papa yelled at everyone. She expected him to leave—half hoped he would—but instead he dispatched his mercenaries against the count of Flanders's men.

When the mercenaries drove the Flemish from Pacy, the count moved to the Vexin to join King Louis. The combined armies headed west to Driencourt where they succeeded in capturing another of Papa's castles. But during the short siege, the count's brother was killed by a crossbow bolt. The count returned home to settle his brother's affairs. Papa laughed at his haste to abandon the French cause, then announced it was time to take his own knights to the field.

A celebration was held on the eve of the army's departure. The great hall was so crowded Joan feared she'd be trampled. The king appeared at the start of the feast. His eyes shone with enthusiasm—as if war were no different than a hunt.

The celebrants quieted to hear the chaplain's brief blessing. When he finished, shouting erupted once more. Apparently the promise of bloodshed sent spirits soaring—her father's included. Boasting of old battles and basking in compliments, he hadn't sounded so jovial for a long while.

The table grew slippery with spilled wine. Papa ate three puddings, but Joan felt ill and barely touched the food. How could he be so excited when they were fighting her brothers and only one side could win?

AS SOON AS KING HENRY TOOK HIS ARMY TO RELIEVE Driencourt, King Louis descended upon Verneuil. Within four days, the French army had pitched camp outside the Great Burgh, decorating the rolling green hills with colorful tents and banners, patchworked with clearings for horses. Carts formed a semicircular wall to the rear. In a fanciful mood, Joan might have pretended a fair had come to Verneuil, but this was no time for fancy.

From the ramparts, she watched a crowd of soldiers struggle to push a war engine into position—a trebuchet, she guessed—an ugly thing of beams and ropes and chains. She tamped down her dread. Hugh, lord of Verneuil, promised the wall would hold a long while. Young Henry's banner fluttered amidst those of King Louis's other vassals. The hot July wind carried the scent of pitch and French smoke.

Sir Robert found her. She watched him approach; he grimaced all the while.

"Princess, don't come up here alone."

"Where is Richard? I don't see Aquitaine's standard."

"We think he has gone to rally the Poitevin rebels."

"Will my father go to Poitou after Driencourt?"

"I expect he will come here first."

"Why?" She lifted her chin defiantly. "We are well fortified. Lord Hugh says we can defend Verneuil until winter."

His expression softened. "Listen to you, Stout-Heart. Who is 'we'?"

She sniffed, annoyed by his condescension.

"If King Louis attacks," he continued more seriously, "we can defend ourselves. But he doesn't have to fight, he just has to wait. We depleted the town's food stores, sojourning here so long." He hesitated before adding, "The garrison is strong, but I have doubts about the burghers. If they decide to open the gates—"

"Open the gates? My father will boil them alive."

"If they are starving, they might be willing to risk boiling."

Surely they would not surrender while sheltering King Henry's daughter. Scowling to hide her anxiety, she demanded, "Did my father instruct you to frighten me?"

"He instructed me to see to your safety. If it comes to it, we'll sue for your safe passage to Fontevrault. You'll be safe with the nuns." The knight bit off a piece of his thumbnail, his face doubtful.

"What else is wrong? You may as well tell me. You know I'll find out."

"Nothing." He sighed. "Only the enemy is not supposed to know you are here. Your father was worried they might try to take you hos . . . hostage." He blushed faintly.

The word made her cold; his reluctant acknowledgment of what they'd overheard embarrassed them both.

"They'd have to take Verneuil first."

In a rush, Sir Robert said, "Lady, I know the young king. He would clear a path in his own ranks with his sword to let you walk through."

"That is kind of you to say." She turned away and stared at Henry's banner so Robert would not see her eyes tear. "They still have to take Verneuil first."

ON AUGUST 6, ONE MONTH INTO THE SIEGE, THE HUNGRY burghers begged the French for permission to send to King Henry for food. If he refused, they promised to surrender the city. King Louis agreed on the condition they surrender in three days' time if relief had not arrived. Sir Robert was forced to negotiate Joan's safe passage to the nunnery, although Joan begged for, and received, the same three days' grace.

On August 9, the king of England appeared on a hilltop overlooking Verneuil. Joan heard that the army he'd managed to march was half the size of the French force, but King Louis did not make time for a head count. As they fled, his men set fire to the Lesser Burgh and grabbed what prisoners they could.

Joan watched from the ramparts again. Sir Robert had led the garrison from the castle to join King Henry; they chased the

French back toward the border. She could see small pillars of smoke far in the distance. For a while, she thought she heard shouting, but then she didn't hear anything. After a time, she descended the stairs and went back inside to wait for her father.

The next morning, she found him. She walked alongside, half running, as he headed for the dining hall.

"Did you see Henry?"

He spat on the floor. "Fine company he keeps. Men with fast horses."

"Did you see him?"

"No."

"He wasn't hurt?"

"Henry is a fast rider himself." He stopped and put his hands on her shoulders. "But look at you, standing your ground. Should I hang Sir Robert or put him in prison and forget to feed him?"

She shrugged off his hands, furious he would tease when she had been so worried, hurt he had not come to talk to her.

"Are you angry with him for letting Henry know I was here? Or for not letting Henry know sooner?"

He grunted and started walking again. "For letting your whining supersede my orders."

Joan dug in her heels. "Next time you should make your orders clearer."

"God's feet!" He whirled about so abruptly, she flinched. "Your mother must be mute since you've stolen her tongue. There won't be a next time. Tomorrow you go to Fontevrault."

"Papa! But . . . but . . . that isn't fair!"

He rolled his eyes—to Joan, a worse chastisement than a cuffing. Yet instead of scolding her, he muttered, "This is the damnedest war I've ever fought. It is hard enough to do battle without injuring my adversaries, and now I have to keep one eye on them and the other on you. Do you want me to lose?"

She waited a moment before answering sulkily, "No, Papa."

"Then help me, Joan, girl." He stepped closer. With one finger he lifted her chin. "Go to Fontevrault with a smile."

JOAN WENT TO THE ABBEY FEIGNING A SMILE, BUT HER FATHER asked too much if he expected her to continue pretending contentment. Summer passed and autumn came and still the king fought his sons. Joan grew weary waiting for letters that never arrived.

When the abbess sent for her, Joan tiptoed into the parlor, expecting only another reprimand for fidgeting during mass. Sir Robert stood by the window.

"Princess." He made a small bow. There was more gray in his hair, and his face was brown with sun. She looked at his fine-fingered hands. The nails were well kempt. He smiled at her. She breathed—the news was good.

"Sir Robert, I'm glad to see you."

"You've grown an inch, Princess Joan. You'll be as tall as Richard."

She frowned. Agnes had just finished letting out her hems. The nurse told her no man wanted a wife taller than he was, as if she could control her own growth.

"How is my father?"

"Hearty. He sends his love."

"And my brothers?"

"No doubt repentant. Alive, despite their best efforts to get themselves killed."

"And my mother?"

The smile left his face. "That, I don't know."

"She is alive?" Blood pounded in her ears. If he said he didn't know, she would faint.

"Yes, of course she's alive. The witch will outlive us all."

"Thank you, Lord God," she whispered. She would stop fidgeting in church. "How goes the war?"

"You can't imagine how those words sound coming from your little mouth. You are how old, Princess, seven?"

"I'll be eight next month. The twelfth of October."

"Ah, yes. That's right. I knew I was here for a reason. Your father has a present for you."

"Where?" Her eyes darted to the shadows behind him. She heard him laugh.

"Not here. In Gisors."

The kings of England and France traditionally made their peace treaties in Gisors, under a tall, spreading elm tree.

"Under the elm tree," Sir Robert said, echoing her thoughts.

"Oh, Robert! My father has won!"

"He is *winning*. He asked your brothers to meet him, and they have agreed. Will you come?"

In answer to his question, she threw her arms around his waist and embraced him.

ON SEPTEMBER 25, 1173, AN UNSEASONABLY CHILL WIND BLEW in Gisors. Joan sat atop a hill on a high, cushioned chair, with a pelt across her lap for warmth. Agnes had opted to stay in their tent at the foot of the hill. Four knights attended Joan—one was a handsome young man named Sir Walter. She knew him because of his father, also Sir Walter, who was often called to the king's council. Papa spoke of the elder Sir Walter as one of the few sensible men in England. He was the lord of Sarum, a far-away place on the chalk downs of Wiltshire. Joan had once asked Mama what a chalk down was, and Mama pursed her lips and answered there was no reason to know.

From her perch, Joan could see the elm tree. If it had not been so windy, words might have reached her; today she could only sit and watch.

Her brothers rode to the parley three abreast, Richard tall and fair and straight-backed. She thought he might be taller than their father if they stood side by side. Henry dismounted and stood with his arms crossed. She could not see his face. Geoffrey stepped to Richard's side, bumping him and not moving away—he must be terrified of Papa. King Louis's vassals crowded beside them; Louis kept back a pace.

Her father's company looked finer. They flew England's banner high, as well as those of Anjou, Poitiers, Normandy, and Aquitaine.

She wished she could hear something, or at least see the men's expressions. Everyone stood so still it was impossible to tell if anything was being said. Joan shivered under her wraps and wished her brothers would hurry and concede.

She saw a great shifting of men. The treacherous earl of Leicester, who had allied with King Louis early in the war, now broke from the French ranks. He was waving his arms in the air, and she could hear a faint voice. He must be shouting.

"Oh!" Joan jumped up. Had the earl drawn his sword? She could see nothing in the confusion. Guards encircled her.

"Come back to the tents," young Walter said and grabbed her arm.

"I want to see my father."

"I said come!" Walter slung her over his shoulder. She beat on his back while he hauled her down the hill to the camp. In front of the tent, red-faced from the effort and breathing hard, he dropped her to her feet.

"What happened? Tell me!" She wondered if he was making her a prisoner. But that was silly—she was Papa's prisoner already.

"Be quiet, girl. Go inside." He shoved her.

She stumbled inside, and Agnes rushed toward her. "Joan! What is it?"

She wrapped her arms around Agnes's waist and sobbed. Over the shouting of men and the whinnying of horses, she could hear young Walter yelling to someone that she was safe.

Sir Robert came to the tent. Agnes brushed the stray wet hair from Joan's eyes.

"What happened?" Joan asked.

He started to stretch a hand to her and then pulled back as though remembering his place. Hollow-voiced, he said, "King Louis won't let your brothers make peace."

## FOUR

KING HENRY VISITED FONTEVRAULT JUST ONCE DURING the winter. Joan waited impatiently while he spent two days with John before coming to see her.

She thought Gisors had aged him. He was growing stout. He rambled over dinner, seeming not to notice the meager plate the nuns had provided, their usual meatless fare. Fighting had resumed immediately after the conference; this time, England was not spared. The earl of Leicester invaded from the south, and King William of Scotland attacked from the north, but her father's English subjects remained steadfast. He had been able to divide his time between Normandy and Poitou and let England see to itself. He told her Richard had tried to take the port town of La Rochelle. When that failed, he took the riverside city of Saintes.

"It was a good plan, taking Saintes." He scratched his beard and looked over her head. "If I were a little older, and he were a little older . . ." He bent his gaze back to hers. "If it was five years hence, Joan, girl, I'd tell you to put your eggs in Richard's basket."

He would say no more about the war, except that they'd agreed to a truce until spring. He was spending the winter in Poitiers. Joan asked after her mother, but he took a large bite of bread and chewed a long time. When he spoke again, it was of something else.

Before leaving, he kissed her head and told her to be good. As if she had any choice in Fontevrault.

He returned in mid-May.

The fighting had been heavy early in the spring, but now the rebels were cooling their heels. She thought her father was pre-occupied. He talked little but paced quite a bit.

"I've decided to go back to Verneuil. Will you come, or are the memories too frightening?"

"I wasn't frightened in Verneuil, Papa."

"That's right. You hadn't the sense."

She frowned at him. "Why are you moving?"

"I don't like Poitiers. It smells of your mother."

"Why did you spend all winter there?"

He looked at her sharply. "It was close to the battlefront. I wanted to be sure no one disturbed the truce."

"Oh." It didn't make sense. Wouldn't Poitiers have been a better choice?

Her father must have noticed her puzzlement because he laughed. "It's a castle filled with baby princesses. It was a horrible winter. There were five of them, with one brain among them."

Joan counted. Henry's wife, Margaret, must be there. And Margaret's sister Alice, if she was still intended for Richard. And of course John's betrothed, the little heiress of Maurienne. Anyone else?

"Was Constance there?" The young countess of Brittany, Geoffrey's fiancée, had come into her father's wardship.

"Yes, and little Emma of Anjou." He laughed again but did not sound happy. "Not so little. I'm going to give her to Prince David ap Owen of Gwynedd. I can use a bit of Welsh support. If the Scottish king breaks the truce, I'll be hard-pressed to beat him back again and still fight the French and your brothers." He ground his teeth and looked at something on the wall.

Joan felt unsettled. Did he fear the Scottish king so much? "Who is Prince David?"

"A Welshman. He has a rival claim to the throne. Like a hundred other Welshmen." He shook his head. "What do you think, Joan, girl? Will you come to Verneuil and keep the womenfolk from driving your poor father to lunacy?"

She rolled her eyes, said, "Who will keep me from lunacy?" and smiled when he laughed.

Joan badgered Agnes to have her baggage prepared by the following day. Agnes showed so little enthusiasm for traveling, however, that Joan asked her father if they might leave her behind. She told him she was too old for a nurse, but the truth was Agnes's ill spirits weighed down her own. The king said he supposed there would be women enough.

She thought she would enjoy being with females who were not oblates, nurses, or nuns but soon discovered otherwise. The princesses in Poitiers bickered and gossiped among themselves, then quieted whenever she drew near. Worst was Alice's haughtiness. She was not even married to Richard, yet she acted as though she were queen over everyone. When Joan complained, her father told her to leave Alice alone.

She grew impatient to leave Poitiers behind. Thankfully, her father could dismiss courtiers and servants as quickly as he marched an army. Within a week, they left for Verneuil.

ONE EVENING LATE IN JUNE, A LARGE COMPANY OF KNIGHTS arrived. The hungry men descended upon the torch-lit dining hall in a clamor that brought all the women of the castle running. Hurrying to join her father, Joan bumped into a man she recognized as old Sir Walter, the lord of Sarum.

"Pardon me, sir," she said, blushing at her clumsiness.

"Princess!" He smiled a greeting, surprising her. Of course she expected him to know her, but it always surprised her when men behaved kindly.

Young Sir Walter came up beside her. "Father, there is a place—oh, excuse me, Princess." He made a deep bow. His hair was combed smooth and severely parted. His eyes were bluer than her father's. He was handsomer than ever and obviously knew it. She remembered the rude way he had treated her in Gisors.

"Sir Waldo," she said with the slightest of nods. It was gratifying to see the smile freeze on his face and confusion cloud his eyes. She turned back to the father. "I have other people to greet, if you will excuse me."

As she walked away she heard the son ask, "What did she call me?"

Old Sir Walter answered, laughing, "I believe she called you a fool."

The glow from her small triumph quickly faded. Something important was happening. Otherwise, these men wouldn't be here. She wove through the crowd until she reached Sir Robert. "We meet again, sir."

He rubbed his hand across his forehead. "Lady, I don't know anything."

She laughed. "Yes, you do. You might as well tell me. You know I'll find out." She didn't really expect him to tell her anything before telling the king. It didn't matter that the other knights close by were watching—she was pleased just to see him. Sir Robert was the exception to the rule; she had come to expect kindness from him.

Bells sounded, and servants began bringing platters heaped with slabs of venison and warm puddings of bread and goose liver. They were supposed to be tomorrow's supper. She wondered what the steward would find to serve instead.

The knights jostled each other to find a place on the benches alongside the tables. Joan looked for her father; he was sitting beside Alice.

While they ate, Sir Robert went to the king's side and spoke in his ear. Henry's face darkened. Before the feast ended, he rose and left the table with Robert—Joan noticed several other knights leave their places to follow. Swallowing her pride, because she couldn't swallow her impatience, she slipped up to the head table and sat in her father's seat.

"What did Sir Robert say?" she asked Alice. Joan was irritated when the girl merely shrugged. "Didn't you listen?"

"He was talking to the king, not to me." Alice popped a piece of bread between her wine-stained lips.

"You were right there!" Joan bit her tongue. Scolding would not accomplish anything. Yet how could Alice have lived alongside Mama for so long and learned nothing?

"I don't know. Something about Wales. Or Scotland."

"About Prince David ap Owen? Or King William?"

Alice's forehead wrinkled. "Which one did the king have a truce with?"

"King William."

"It was him. He broke the truce."

THE RENEWED SCOTTISH OFFENSIVE SO WORRIED THE KING that he no longer dared leave England to its own defense. Taking an advance force north to Barfleur to arrange passage across the channel, he charged Sir Robert to follow with the women. Princess Alice complained from the moment her plump bottom touched the cushion of the wain. Three hours into the ride, Margaret slapped her—Joan decided Henry was blessed in his wife.

When they arrived at last in Barfleur, Alice shoved Joan aside to be first from the wain, then flung herself into the king's arms. Joan blinked in surprise to see her clasp her arms around his neck and kiss him. Her father put his hands on Alice's arms, but not to dislodge her. For a moment, he gazed intently into her eyes. Finally, he pushed her away and turned.

"Joan, girl, the boat is waiting. We sail tonight after the baggage is loaded. I'll allow—"

"Jeanne."

Joan whirled at the sound of the voice. Her mother stood several paces behind, surrounded by guards.

"Mama!"

A knight put his hand on her shoulder.

"No," the king said, "let her go."

She ran to her mother's embrace, breathing in lilies and herbs. "Mama, where were you?"

"Oh, sweetling. A few places I couldn't be found. Where did he keep you?"

Joan's throat tightened. Her mother believed she'd been no more than a prisoner. "Fontevrault."

"Have you had a chance to talk with your brothers?"

"No. I saw them, though, at Gisors, before—"

"That's enough." Her father came up behind. "Ask me, Eleanor. Don't use the girl."

Her mother didn't answer. She tilted her head slightly and

looked down her nose. Joan tried to memorize the way she did it. The queen spoke—malice made her voice thin.

"War agrees with you, Henry. You look quite virile for an old man."

"Confinement agrees with you. You look very docile."

"The way you like your girls," she answered mockingly. Her gaze passed over his shoulder to where the other princesses still stood.

The king winced. "Don't be petty. You used to be so much cleverer. We're going to England. I know how well the weather suits you."

"Where in England? The weather varies."

"Tut-tut. Joan is listening."

He gestured with his head, and Eleanor's guards closed around her. Her mother walked away, her back straight as a mast. How could they do this to each other?

That evening, forty ships set sail, heavily loaded and riding low in the water. Joan didn't even know which one her mother was on. The princesses sailed with the king. He had them locked in the hold, safe from the ogling of sailors. Except for Alice. The king kept her somewhere else.

JOAN WANTED TO HATE HER FATHER, BUT HER RESOLVE WEAKened when they disembarked in Southampton. As the other princesses were placed into a wain bound for the English stronghold of Devizes, he came like a penitent and asked her to accompany him to Canterbury. She knew he didn't have to ask.

When she answered, "Yes, Papa," though she meant to sound indifferent, he smiled and hugged her hard, saying, "My loyal girl."

Still, he did not explain the choice of Canterbury over the Scottish Marches. That task fell to Sir Robert, who said the count of Flanders and her brother Henry also were coming to England. Because the king feared the latest setbacks were evidence of God's displeasure, he was going to Canterbury to perform penance for Archbishop Becket's death, penance he had promised the Church years ago.

Joan knew Thomas Becket's story. As chancellor, he had been her father's closest adviser and friend. Yet when Papa managed to arrange for his appointment as archbishop of Canterbury, head of the Church in England, Becket repaid the honor by opposing every royal command. Four years ago, renegade knights murdered him in Canterbury Cathedral. Her father was blamed, though it had not been his fault.

They traveled to Canterbury with minimal escort, sending the bulk of the army to await them in London. Just outside the city, they stopped so the king could be stripped of his finery. Donning a hair shirt, he walked barefoot through streets thronged with burghers and beggars, who watched with such solemn quiet Joan's skin crawled. Did they think him guilty or was the silence evidence of their awe?

She rode with Sir Robert until they drew close to the cathedral, where the whole party dismounted. The sun on the white facade made her eyes ache.

From the arched doorway, golden cherubs smiled down upon them, but to Joan, the angels seemed to laugh at the king as he passed. He proceeded through the nave to lie prostrate before Becket's tomb. The bishop made a long-winded speech absolving him of guilt, then every one of the monks gathered to lash him. Joan wept until her cheeks were raw.

Sir Robert led her away from the cathedral at sunset, leaving her father to spend the night at the foot of the tomb. No one bound his wounds. She was afraid he would die.

"He won't die," Sir Robert said. His voice was hoarse. She leaned against him, and when he took her arm, she noticed his hand. Crusted blood darkened two of the nail beds.

"I can tell the state of the kingdom by your fingernails."

He looked startled, then put his hand before his face. "They'll grow again."

In the morning, they returned for the bishop's mass. Her father still lay on the marble floor before the tomb. Joan had not slept and now fought nodding off by staring at him, willing him to move so she would know he lived. Afterward, the bishop raised him up and gave him a drink of blessed water as well as a phial of the martyr's blood to keep for a relic. Joan was so relieved she almost ran to him, but Robert whispered she must wait.

Outside the cathedral, a crowd had assembled again. Sir Robert brought the king's horse. Joan watched her father struggle to mount. His guard gathered, shielding him from the eyes of his subjects until he was seated. They rode away amidst an explosion of cheers. Whatever they had thought yesterday, now the people adored their king.

A few miles from town, the cortege stopped. Henry entered a wain and did not come out until they reached London's White Tower two days later. Sir Robert and a physician attended him. Joan paced before his bedchamber, awaiting his summons. When her legs could no longer bear weight, she sat on the cold floor.

Sir Robert came out just as Joan heard far-off church bells ringing compline.

"How is he?" she demanded, jumping to her feet.

"The physician is letting his blood."

They waited in silence until the physician emerged.

"Princess Joan? He asked for you."

Joan pushed past Robert, through the door. The smells of a sickroom assaulted her: old bloody bandages, a chamber pot, the vinegary smell of medicinal wine. A lamp burned near the darkened window, but the wick had not been trimmed, and it gave off more smoke than light.

"Joan, girl? Come here." His voice sounded thready.

She hesitated a moment before stepping forward. He sat sideways on his bed in the dim light, leaning back on his hands with elbows locked. His face was frighteningly pale and deeply lined. The physician's young apprentice sat at the bedside rubbing unguent onto his cracked, purple feet. Joan stared at the bruises, unable to look upon the welts on his back.

"Papa, why did you do that?"

He kicked the apprentice on the shoulder, nearly rattling him off his seat. "That's enough, ham-hand. Get out."

Knocking over the stool as he jumped, the young man fled the room.

The display of temper gave her courage; he wasn't dying. She asked again, "Papa, why?"

"It's too hard to explain," he grumbled, settling back gingerly on the pillow propped high against the headboard.

"But—"

"Do you love me?" he demanded.

She nodded, eyes brimful of tears. He could ask such a thing?

"If I ever lost *your* love, I'd suffer worse to regain you."

Was it God's love he felt he'd been lacking? Did he fear his sins had turned his sons against him? "Papa—"

"Shut up, girl. Just sit there until I fall asleep."

It was her presence he wanted, not her questions. She lay on the floor. London was hot in July, and flies swarmed in through the unshuttered windows. She envisioned them settling on her father's wounds and felt sick.

She tossed and turned and had started to doze a little when a shout sounded at the door.

"What is it?" her father asked, sitting up with a grimace.

"Sire!" Robert's voice filtered through the heavy door.

"Robert? God's feet. What is it, Robert?"

Robert came inside, carrying a taper. In the flickering light, his eyes were wild. His hair stood on end. In a high, unnatural voice, he said, "Sire, King William of Scotland is captured."

"When?"

"The day after your scourging, sire." He sounded as if he couldn't quite believe the miracle he reported. Joan hugged her knees, dazed with disbelief and joy.

The king rose from his bed and whispered, awed, "God be thanked, and Saint Thomas Becket the Martyr." Then he shouted. "Have London's bells rung until dawn!"

Robert left the chamber. Her father turned to her. "Find my shirt."

She helped him slide the shirt over the crisscrossed wounds on his back and shoulders. How had he known what had to be done? Because he knew everything. Who could defeat God and her father?

"God does love you, Papa."

He wrapped an arm around her waist and smiled. "He might, but I was talking about Becket." He lifted his eyes heavenward and shouted, "You knew I meant you no ill. You've won,

Thomas!" He turned back to her and rasped, "Now, Joan, girl, now, I will win."

WHILE JOAN'S MOTHER WAS STILL QUEEN OF FRANCE, KING Louis answered the pope's call for crusaders. Mama scandalized the world by taking the cross and traveling to the Holy Land alongside him. It was a fiasco—even Mama admitted so—and the pope banned women from crusading ever again.

Abandoned in London Tower, Joan now understood why she had done it. There was nothing worse than being left at home to wait. At least she had Sir Robert's missives to keep her informed.

The count of Flanders and the young king retreated from England to join the French siege of the Norman castle of Rouen. When her father broke the siege and chased them all out of Normandy, King Louis suggested another parley at Gisors. Negotiations failed because Duke Richard did not attend.

Sobbing, Joan tore Sir Robert's letter into tatters.

A few weeks later, she heard her father had been persuaded to meet with Henry and Geoffrey. He offered generous terms provided they deny their brother support for the duration of the war. Then he took an army to Poitou to deal with Richard.

For a month, Joan waited, on tenterhooks, until Sir Robert returned.

"Your father has been chasing your brother all over the dukedom."

She looked at his hands, but they were curled into fists. "Did he catch him?"

"They met at Montlouis."

"Did they fight?"

Robert shook his head. "Duke Richard fell weeping at the king's feet."

The image brought tears to her own eyes. "What did my father do?"

"He drew Richard up and gave him the kiss of peace. It is over."

Joan let out a breath she felt she'd been holding since Chinon. It was over. Her father forgave them everything, just as he had said he would. He had kept his word.

Now he must forgive Mama, too.

THE KING CELEBRATED AT ROUEN WITH A FEAST BEFITTING the return of three prodigal sons. The tables and walls were draped with bright cloths, the lamps burned high with scented oils, musicians played harps to accompany the meal of eels, whitefish, and boar. Jugs of wine were set at every third place so merrymakers could refill their own cups. The king's laughter sounded above the din as he roamed about the hall.

Joan sat beside Richard. She could not take her eyes off him. He looked as Papa must have when he was younger—strong and handsome. His haphazard dress did not disguise the confident man he had become. His bow-shaped lips, eager to laugh, poked out of a tangled red-gold mustache and beard.

"Joan, I heard you held Verneuil against Henry," he said. Henry shot him a dark look. Richard said, "Next time, I want *you* at my back instead."

He laughed as she choked. When she recovered, Joan pushed aside her bowl. Her brothers were horrible.

"Where is Mother?" Richard asked, pinching her arm.

"Everyone says you sat in Father's lap the whole war and listened to his poison."

"I was in Fontevrault." She wanted to rub her arm but wouldn't give him the satisfaction. "He sent Mama to England but wouldn't tell me where."

"Why not?"

"Because he knew I'd tell you."

Richard's lips bunched beneath his mustache. "So then, sister mine. We must convince him you won't."

JOAN SAT BY A NARROW WINDOW IN THE GREAT HALL, STABBING a needle into cloth. Around her sat three lady's maids of Rouen, taking advantage of the waning afternoon light. Richard entered the crowded room, and Joan tried to make herself small. All week he had been saying cruel things.

Instead of joining the men gambling near the hearth, he came closer. Squatting beside her, he murmured, "Did you know Sir Rufus died? The poor blinded knight?"

"Richard, stop," she said through closed teeth.

"By his own hand. Just after you left Chinon."

The needle pricked her finger, and blood beaded at the tip. She stuck it into her mouth.

Richard rose. "Be more careful, Joan."

She watched him move to the soot-blackened hearth; the firelight made his hair shine red. The knights edged aside to make room. He knelt for the dice and started winning at once.

Yesterday, he had told her Mama tried to escape Poitiers only because Papa had threatened to kill her. The day before that, he had crept up behind her while she prayed in the chapel and whispered women's names in her ear. "These are some of the king's lovers. The ones Mama knew about. He liked to torment her."

Joan fled the chapel. But she couldn't flee every time Richard entered a room. She couldn't even tell herself not to listen to her brother's lies. She wondered if he knew about Alice.

At the hearth, Richard laughed loudly and rose from his knees. Men beside him groaned, slapping at his legs while he stuffed coins into his purse. She looked away, but too late. He caught her watching and came back to the window.

"Toulouse is a beautiful place. Warm and golden pink with sunshine all year round. They speak our language there." He slipped from Norman French to the tongue of the south, Occitan. She heard her mother's voice in Richard's and loved him even as she cursed his trick. No one else in the room would understand. "The troubadours are gayer. The wine is round and sweet in your mouth, like a kiss. Jeanne, Toulouse belongs to our mother. It's part of Aquitaine." He put his foot on the low rung of her stool. "Count Raymond came with Toulouse in his hands and put it into our father's. He paid homage to Father and then Henry. Last of all, he paid homage to me. *I* am duke of Aquitaine."

"You are too prideful. I'm sure Papa didn't mean to slight you."

His scornful gaze raked her. "You are a cow, sister mine. He slighted our mother. And if you think it was not intentional, you're a worse fool than I thought."

"I'm not a fool!" Both her parents had said she was smart.

"Prove it. Find out where Father is hiding her. Before something happens to her."

Yet it was impossible for Joan to even talk to her father, much less learn secrets. When her ninth birthday passed unnoticed, she realized the king had no interest in his daughter now that he had his sons back.

The knights hunted, hawked, and gambled. No one but Richard paid her any heed at all.

Within a few weeks, her father grew restless. He announced that they would soon return to England, to Devizes, so Henry could be reunited with Margaret, but he had other plans for Richard. In southern Aquitaine, many of the lords had taken part in the rebellion. Now Richard must punish them by razing their castles and demanding tribute in the name of the king.

During Richard's departure, she hid in her room, playing merels alone on the floor. As soon as Richard was gone, her father came to her. He squatted to talk at her level.

"Joan, girl, you must forgive your brother."

"Forgive him?"

"He was heartsick you didn't turn out to kiss him good-bye."

"Richard was?" She tasted gall. The filthy, lying—

"He said not to blame you. He said you had to hate someone for what happened. Joan—"

"The devil!" She understood what her brother was doing. If she hated Richard, she wouldn't carry tales to him. At least, that's what Papa would think.

"He's no greater devil than the rest of us. Please. For your old father's sake?"

Joan almost burst, trying to contain her frustration. The more she protested, the less her father would believe her. No doubt he'd been watching the way she ran from Richard.

"He *is* a worse devil, Papa! I don't hate him." Even her own ears recognized how false the contradiction sounded.

He patted her braids. "You should have kissed him. Hatred will ruin you."

It was too late. She'd already been ruined by the people she loved.

OLD DEVIZES CASTLE WAS MASSIVE, BUT IN A STATE OF DISRE-pair. The king's cortege arrived at the western entrance and passed through battered wooden gates. The west wall had been patched with stone that did not match the original. The knights' tower, obviously the newest addition, stood apart from the keep as though disdainful of the company. Joan tucked her chin to her chest and sighed, letting the curtains of the wain fall shut. She would not like Devizes.

The court gathered to greet the party. Margaret met her husband with a restrained smile, though Henry gathered her up and called her his pretty queen. Alice stood back, darting impatient black looks at the king. When he finally noticed, she folded her arms across her chest and narrowed her eyes. Joan thought her indignation was ridiculous. Surely Papa would find her ridiculous, too.

It pleased her to think he would despise Alice. Maybe he would even send her back to France. Richard wouldn't mind—he had never liked his fiancée.

After greeting the king's cortege, the crowd began to disperse. Lady Anne, the mistress of Devizes Castle, accompanied Joan to a bedchamber, fussing all the way about its comforts. The fire was warm, the chamber aired each day. After the lengthy journey, Joan didn't care so long as the bed did not move.

"Queen Margaret will join the young king." The lady pushed

open the door. "So you and Princess Alice will have this to your-selves."

In the middle of a tiny, round gray stone room sat a single bed lumped with blankets.

Scowling, Joan said, "I'd rather share a pen with a sow."

Lady Anne sniffed and looked over her head. The hostess might prefer to put them all in with the swine.

"Never mind." Joan sat on the bed. "This will do."

The lady nodded. "My maids are here to serve."

Joan let a girl undress her and slipped between the crisp linen sheets. She said her prayers quickly and buried her head in the pillow, determined to fall sleep before Alice came to the room. In the morning, she was still alone. She twisted the sheet in her hand. Alice must have been with Papa. But she was Richard's betrothed! What was Papa doing? Why would he want Alice?

Joan remembered Mama's advice: To solve a puzzle, start from what you know. Alice was a daughter of France. She was countess of the vast estates of Berry. But what if King Louis found out what Papa was doing? Bad enough if Richard were to lose the dowry, but . . .

Joan clapped a hand to her mouth. What if Papa planned to marry Alice himself? Then, not only would he keep Berry, but King Louis would think twice about making war again.

A hundred objections crowded her mind, but none calmed her. If it were true, it meant Richard was right—their mother was in danger. Papa couldn't marry Alice unless Mama . . .

If men would not tell her things, it was her duty to find out. She had to find out where her father was keeping her mother. Richard needed her help.

*  *  *

JOAN HAD FREE RUN OF DEVIZES CASTLE AND SOON DISCOV-
ered niches near the meeting halls where she could conceal herself. But six weeks passed, and she grew discouraged. No one
ever spoke of anything important in those halls. Her father held
confidential discussions in the anteroom to his chamber, on the
second floor of the knights' tower. Except for the rare instances
of the king's invitation, Joan had no business there.

Then, one afternoon after she'd nearly given up hope, a score
of her father's adherents arrived to great welcome. Among them
were the old and young Sir Walters. In the crowded great hall,
Joan found the elder. Remembering his earlier kindness, she
decided to approach him.

"Sir, I'm glad you're here. It has been so boring."

"Don't tell me you prefer warfare."

"Oh, no. We must not mention the war." She gave him her
sweetest smile. "Where have you been? Not with Richard?"

"No, lady. I've been home in Sarum."

"What brings you here?"

His face clouded, then cleared. "Waldo has come for the
hunting."

She laughed and pulled on his hand. "Will you sit with me
at supper? I'm tired of all these women."

Just then, she caught sight of the younger Walter drawing near.
He wore a blue silk tunic, an extravagance he must have thought
made him look grand. He bowed low, then lifted his eyes to hers.

"Princess." He reached out his hand as if he would take her
fingers. He was treating her with a deference her years did not
warrant. "I hope you have forgiven me," he said.

"For what, sir?"

"For Gisors. It was my first assignment after my dubbing. I was green wood and frightened for your safety." His blue eyes shone.

She caught her breath. She didn't know how to answer.

He said, "No? Then it will be my quest to prove myself to you."

She nodded, embarrassed to feel her face flush.

"Excuse me," she said, moving away to lose herself in the crowd.

The meal was typically boisterous. Hunting was fine near Devizes, and several meats, hot from the spit, sizzled on platters. Hounds crawled back and forth under the tables looking for tidbits. A servant heaped Joan's trencher full of eggs pickled in brine. She ignored the other men, chins well-greased, faces ugly with shouting, and watched only her father. Several times he rose and went to talk to old Sir Walter. The final time, he laid his hand on the knight's shoulder for a moment before returning to his seat.

She had to find out why they had come.

Chewing slowly, barely tasting the food, she considered talking to young Walter but immediately discarded the plan. She would have to eavesdrop on old Sir Walter and Papa.

She yawned and asked a maid to take her to her room. After undressing her, the girl turned down the bed. Joan dismissed her. She waited a few minutes to find courage. Then she pulled on her gown without bothering with underskirts and laced it as best she could. She slipped from her room, down the darkened hall, and out onto the rain-softened ground of the courtyard. She ran across the mud to the knights' tower. With a heave, she opened the creaky wooden door. Inside was dark. She stood, shivering, breathing hard.

She knew the second-floor hallway curved behind her father's chamber, so the room could be accessed either through the anteroom or through a back door. She could hide in the chamber and sneak out through the back as soon as she heard the conference ending.

She took a deep breath and started up the spiral stairs to the hallway. In the dark, she felt along the passage, testing each step. Just then the tower door below creaked. Flickering torchlight scuttled up the walls.

"Father, it is a mark of his favor. Think what it means!"

She was sure the voice belonged to young Walter. In the stairwell, there was nowhere to hide. Terrified, she bolted up the last of the stairs. Her footfall was quiet. She whirled around the corner and flattened herself into a recess in the wall. Her chest ached from holding her breath.

Old Sir Walter said, "You put too much stock in the king's favor."

"He trusts you."

"I have no wish to be a jailer. It's not as if he'll ransom her."

"It won't be forever. And if we make ourselves useful in this—"

"You aim too high."

"Father, you sell our worth too cheap. I can make the girl—"

Joan strained to hear more, but the voices died away down the hall. She stood, mulling the words. Her heart beat faster. She knew where her mother's next prison would be.

Before she could step from her hiding place, she heard the door open once again. This time, a crowd of drunken men climbed the stairs, laughing and arguing. They passed by without noticing her. Supper had ended; more would be returning.

Her mouth was dry as sand. There was no choice but to run. She flew down the stairs, one hand on the newel. At the bottom, expecting another step, she jarred her ankle and fell against the door. She felt a sharp pain and heard cloth tear as the door bounced ajar, then bumped back against her. A protruding nail had rent the skirt of her gown.

Shaking, Joan pushed the door open. The courtyard was empty. Exhilarated, she sprinted across the yard. Now it was but a short bolt to her chamber.

A glimmer of light underlined her door. Hadn't she blown out the candle? She slid inside.

Alice sat up in bed. "Where were you, Joan?"

Joan stammered, "I—I forgot something in the dining hall. I couldn't find the maid so—"

"You lie." Alice climbed from the bed, smirking with satisfaction. She pulled on a cloak and grabbed Joan by the arm. "We're going to the king."

Joan could not bring herself to beg Alice for favor. Instead, she pulled her arm from the other girl's grip. She curled her lip and said, "It will be your word against mine."

"Look at your dress. You were crawling about in the mud."

Fear slashed through Joan like a dagger. If she fought the bigger girl, she would lose. She must be calm. What if she confessed? She could say she did not have a chance to hear anything. Her father might even laugh.

She let Alice drag her to the king's chamber. He was deep in conversation with Henry. Alice interrupted, talking fast and pointing out Joan's torn skirt and dirty hems.

Her father raised his hand, his face purple, his eyes slits. Joan stood stock-still with fear. He slapped her so hard she could not hear his words over the ringing of her ears.

Henry stepped between them.

"Father! She's a child. Think what you're saying."

"She's your mother's child—I'd put nothing past her. Girl, who were you with? I'll have him broken."

Papa had hit her! Her cheek felt numb, and blood filled her mouth.

Her brother protested, "Who would dare touch her?"

"Damn you, girl. Speak to me."

She mumbled, "I was trying to come here. Everyone came back too soon."

His eyes narrowed. "Why?" Then he said at once, "Never mind."

"Father, what harm can she do? She's a child."

"Henry, get out. Take Alice. I need to speak to Joan."

Joan watched them leave. Her legs shook—she was afraid he meant to hit her again. When the door closed, he looked at her a long time.

"Do you want to know where your mother is?" he asked.

Her head spun. She nodded.

"Very well. I'll send you to her."

## FIVE

TRAITOROUS SONS COULD BE FORGIVEN, BUT WHAT OF A faithless daughter? Joan didn't know. Would she be imprisoned for the rest of her life?

Two unfamiliar knights bore her away from Devizes. She rode with the elder one, wrapped in fur against the cold. In the early hours of the morning, they stopped in a small village where she was entrusted to the wife of a tavern keeper. They waited for three days before moving on, but no one told her why. She wondered what her brother Henry had thought when she disappeared. Would he guess Mama's destination as she had? Would he send word to Richard?

Sometime during the fourth night, old Sir Walter joined them. In the morning, the two knights turned back the way they had come. Sir Walter looked unhappy.

"Are we almost to Sarum?" Joan asked.

"We'll be there today. Your mother is there." Perhaps they had been traveling slowly so he might fetch her first.

"Yes, I know."

He didn't seem surprised. He loaded her bundle onto his packhorse then lifted her into his saddle. "Lady, I don't want you to think of yourself as my prisoner. You are my guest."

"Can I leave Sarum if I want to?"

He didn't answer.

"Can I send a message to Richard?"

He mounted behind her. "My son is eager for your arrival."

"I don't like Walter."

"No? Well, he can be difficult to like." He dug his heels into the horse's side and urged it forward, leading the packhorse.

They were not so far from Sarum. They crossed the Avon on a creaking wooden bridge and left the river's edge while the weak sun was still high. After traversing scrubby fields, a shallow stream crusted thinly with ice, and then more scrub, she could see a forbidding castle rising in the distance above a high ring of earthworks. The gray stone was almost invisible against the gray sky. Sir Walter let the horses break into a trot as they drew closer.

They circled around to approach the east gate. The horses' hooves clattered against the plank bridge spanning the dry ditch. The gatehouse lay before them with the castle keep rising behind on the high point of the hill.

Joan noticed movement on the stone walls, then the gates opened and a cluster of people spilled out. Three ladies stood with her mother, and six knights, including young Sir Walter.

"Joan!" Queen Eleanor strode forward without a glance at her captors. No one stayed her. Imprisonment had done nothing to diminish her; Joan could almost believe she ruled here.

Old Sir Walter handed Joan into his son's arms. The young man's nose wrinkled, and he set her down quickly, as though she had been bedding with rats.

Her mother swung her up into an embrace. In Occitan, she murmured, "Jeanne, Jeanne. What have you done?" She kissed her cheek several times as she stooped to set her back down.

Joan closed her eyes to breathe in the familiar lily scent of her mother. It would be all right. Mama was pleased.

"Papa caught me spying."

"Sweetling, I taught you better." She laughed, sounding delighted. Changing to Norman French, she said, "Come inside. Charisse will faint when she sees your hair."

"Charisse is here?"

"And Amaria." Eleanor frowned. "He only allowed me two of my own maids."

A petite, brown-haired woman close behind them said, "My lady, anything you need—"

"Yes, yes." The queen waved off her words. "Joan, this is Lady Penelope. She and Sir Walter have been very kind."

Lady Penelope stopped to curtsy, then hurried to catch up. Joan nodded over her shoulder, feeling uncomfortable. How did one behave toward one's jailer? She would have to mimic Mama.

After passing through the arched gate, a short walk across the inner bailey brought them to the keep. They had to climb a series of steep, winding steps to reach the door. A narrow passage opened into a second story hall. Joan wished young Walter would move away from her—he stood so close she was afraid she would trip.

Lady Penelope said, "Princess, we are very pleased to have you here. You may sleep in your mother's antechamber with her maids."

"I'll take her," the Queen said. "You can send her things later, although it hardly seems worth the effort. Henry clearly has no idea. . . ." She turned a critical eye on her daughter. "And send a maid with warm water. Joan, have you washed at all these past two years?"

"Mama." She squirmed.

"Come, Charisse will be glad to see you."

Joan followed her mother out of the hall unguarded. Perhaps

Sir Walter really would treat them as guests. But as they walked to their chamber, she noted the dark, damp walls, felt a chill wind course through the gallery, and knew she was in prison. There was no need for Sir Walter to guard them as long as they were here.

YOUNG WALTER LEFT AFTER A FORTNIGHT. JOAN ASSUMED HE was reporting to the king, but who could blame him for finding any excuse to escape? She had never seen a place as gray as this castle. At night, she dreamed wistfully of the crisp air and bright sunshine of Poitiers and understood Papa's cruelty in exiling Mama to Sarum. Each morning, they woke in darkness, dressed, and stumbled across the bailey to the chapel to pray by candlelight. They ate a gray meal of bread and tepid gruel, then hurried to fit a day's tasks into the few hours before the dreary sun abandoned Sarum once again to the dark and the cold.

The household supped early and passed the long evenings in the great hall, listening to the mournful howling of the wind. The women crowded beside the hearth to spin or embroider while they gossiped. The men sat against the single wall lit by a lamp, drinking wine and talking about hunting and tournaments. Joan listened, eyes on her sewing, mimicking her mother. She couldn't imagine what Mama thought of such petty talk. How could Eleanor, who believed a queen should influence kingdoms and empires, bear being trapped here at the end of the world?

WALTER WAS COMING HOME FOR CHRISTMAS; THEY WATCHED from the walls as his party approached. Joan stared at a knight in gray at the fringe of the company. She thought . . . and then she was sure. She ran down the stairs two at a time.

"Sir Robert!" She caught his leg before he had a chance to dismount.

"Princess." He smiled. "Let me get down before my horse squashes you."

As soon as his feet touched the earth, she flung herself into his arms. "I'm so happy to see you."

"I'm glad to see you, too. Your father sends his love."

Her smile hurt her cheeks. As she took his hand to lead him inside the gate, she heard, "Princess Joan?"

It was Walter. He bowed, and she nodded. He looked miffed, so she dropped Robert's hand and walked closer. When she held out her hand, he squeezed her fingers.

"It is good to see you, lady. You're lovely in that gown."

"Thank you." She blushed. Charisse had cut down one of the queen's old dresses to make her a new one for her tenth birthday. "Excuse me, please."

"Yes, of course." He bowed again.

She caught the wary look on Robert's face, but it was fleeting, and he smiled when she came back to him. She led him up the steps, babbling about Sarum, warning him to be careful of the ice or he might slip. Inside the door, the queen waited.

"Robert? This is a surprise." Her voice was tense. Joan looked up sharply. Her mother's face was pale.

"Lady." Sir Robert bowed. He straightened and said, "They are well. They are all well."

"God is merciful," she said, pressing her lips into a thin line. "So why are you here? To free us?"

Joan didn't like when her mother used that mocking tone.

Robert shook his head. "I have another matter to discuss." He paused and scratched his nose. "We needn't speak of it now."

The rest of the travelers had come into the hall. Lady Penelope dispensed orders to servants and directions to the knights while holding on to young Walter's arm.

"Speak of what?" Eleanor asked. "Why did Henry send you?"

Joan watched Robert glance toward Walter before speaking. Walter was dragging his mother closer. Then Robert looked at the queen. "He wants your advice, lady."

"*My* advice? Henry, Henry." She laughed, a rolling trill deep in her throat. "Tell me, Robert, how can I advise my lord king?"

Robert coughed into his hand. "He has had an offer for Joan."

The queen stopped laughing. Behind her, young Walter halted abruptly.

"One worth considering?"

"He believes so. He puts it to you. King William of Sicily."

Joan caught her breath. The queen folded her arms across her chest and smiled.

SIX

A
T LAST, ELEANOR HAD SOMETHING TO DISCUSS AROUND
the evening fire.

King William II of Sicily had made generous concessions. He agreed to marry Joan at once, not keep her as ward until she came of age. Her coronation would immediately follow the wedding. And she would be given a wealthy fief—the county of Monte Sant'Angelo—which would remain hers even if he died. In return, he insisted she arrive in Sicily before the end of the new year.

Sir Robert claimed King Henry's counselors had protested Sicily's haste. Benumbed with shock, Joan could only think they had not protested very hard. Surely Mama would find some fault with Papa's arrangements.

However, after the first night, talk of the terms ceased and was replaced by talk of the kingdom. After all, a wise ruler must know the domain. Joan listened, trying to absorb it all while praying her mother would yet change her mind.

Before the Normans conquered Sicily, chaos had reigned. Eleanor said King William's great-grandfather and grandfather had forged a united kingdom—more or less. Without a strong leader, it would crumble back to what it had been.

Joan wanted to ask, What sort of man is the king? She only dared ask, "Is King William strong?"

"He is young. But he has been king for almost ten years, and the kingdom has not crumbled. Sweetling, you will help him be strong."

Two weeks after Christmas, Sir Robert took his leave. Old Sir Walter and a few knights attended his party as far as the earthworks. The ladies waved from the walls. Shivering despite her wraps, Joan watched until the last banner faded into the mists. Her mother stood beside her; Eleanor neither waved nor shivered. She was as unmoving as the icicles hanging from the balustrade, and the satisfaction in her unblinking eyes was every bit as cold. The queen would not change her mind.

Early the following morning, Walter cornered Joan on the stairs on her way to breakfast.

"Come here," he said. "I have a secret."

"Come where?" If he meant to go behind the stairs, he could go by himself.

He grabbed her wrist. "I want to tell you something."

When she tried to wrench away, he pulled her close and put a hand over her mouth. He dragged her behind the stairwell and pressed his forearm across her chest. She swung her arms, but her blows just made him scowl.

"Be quiet. I don't want to hurt you." He pushed so hard the back of her head ground against the stone wall. "Will you listen?"

She thought: *Idiot*. How did he expect her to answer? It was hard even to breathe. She opened her eyes as wide as they would go.

"You don't want to go to Sicily. You'll never see anyone you love again. And King William is . . . he's practically a Saracen. He has infidels in his court."

As he eased the pressure against her mouth, she twisted her head sideways. "Let me breathe or I will faint."

He moved his hand cautiously from her mouth to her shoulder. Despite her resentment, she didn't renew her struggle; she was curious to hear what he might have to say.

"Mama says the king is a Norman."

"He has Norman blood. That doesn't make him a Norman. His mother is Navarrese. He keeps a harem of Saracen slaves. Do you know what that is?"

She shook her head.

Walter's eyes narrowed. "Slave women. He will add you to his harem like a slave."

"Liar."

"You don't have to go. Just do what I say. I won't hurt you any more than I have to." He kissed her ear. His lips felt cold and wet.

"No!" She twisted back and forth frantically. If he didn't let go, she would scream.

"Hold still, girl." He grabbed a handful of her skirts. "Do this and no one else will have you. Your father will have to give you to me. You want to marry me, don't you?"

"*Marry you?*" Her mouth was too dry to spit. "Why would I want you?"

His hands fell to his sides, and his eyes widened in disbelief.

Had he actually imagined she wanted to be his wife? She rubbed the back of her hand roughly across her ear where his lips had touched her.

Hoping to shame him, she said, "What kind of man kisses children?"

Instead of showing remorse, he sneered. "Ask Princess Alice. Or ask William of Sicily why he would marry you so quickly. Some men prefer little girls."

ELEANOR OF AQUITAINE HAD BEEN THIRTY WHEN THE POPE annulled her first marriage. Her new husband, Henry the duke of Normandy, count of Anjou, heir to the English throne, was nineteen. Joan had always known that, but she had never given it much thought before.

Did Papa stop loving Mama because she was too old?

She was passing time in her mother's chamber before supper. The back of her embroidery was one large knot, which she had been trying to disentangle before Mama inspected the work. She couldn't stop thinking about what Walter had said that morning. Why *did* King William want to marry her so soon?

"Mama?"

"Don't sit with your knees in the air like that. Put your feet on the floor."

Joan thumped her feet down. "How old is King William?"

"A good age. He is twenty-two."

"Why is that a good age?"

"He's not an untried boy but not a doddering old fool, either. And a girl should marry a man at least ten years older. Men prefer young wives."

Then it was true. Would he tire of her when she was no longer youthful? With grave voice, she asked, "How young?"

Her mother peered at her over her own sewing. "Child, you worry too much. There is nothing to be afraid of. King William will not want to lie with you before your courses start. That will be another three or four years. You will feel ready by then."

Lie with? *Some men prefer little girls.* Was that what Walter had meant? Her palms began to sweat.

"But, Mama, what if—?"

"If he takes you before that, it is no sin. You will be his wife. Remember, Joan, a queen's first duty is to give her husband an heir. If he comes to your bed, you must make him welcome. Then he'll be patient if an heir is slow to come." Eleanor looked back at her needlework.

Conflicting fears jumbled together in Joan's brain. She took a breath and blurted out, "Mama, what is a harem?"

Now her mother gave her a long, hard stare. "A harem? Why do you ask?"

"I heard King William has one."

"Who in the world would tell you a thing like that?"

"I don't know who said it. I was listening behind a wall."

Her mother laid down her cloth and frowned. "There is a rumor that William's father kept a harem. He adopted many Saracen practices, so it might be true. But, Joan, it is also rumored the old king stood seven feet tall, had a knotty black beard that grew to his knees, and could lift his horse. I taught you to listen when people talk. I did not teach you to believe everything you hear."

Joan heard irritation in her mother's voice, but her question hadn't been answered. "So, King William doesn't have a harem?"

"Are you asking if the king takes slaves to his bed? He's a man. If you want to keep other women from your husband's bed, be in it."

Joan hadn't meant to anger her mother, but now she was more confused than ever. How was she supposed to make her husband welcome? What did the old king do with all those women in his bed?

Amaria said, "Princess, you are tiring your mother. Come. I'll help you dress for supper."

Joan followed her, surprised by the maid's solicitousness. Amaria filled a washbasin and helped her clean her hands and face. She smoothed Joan's gown, brushed her hair, and tied a ribbon in it, deftly, without Charisse's stray caresses, then said, "Has anyone ever told you anything about what men do?"

"What they do?" she repeated.

She knew men and women must lie together when they were married, and it was a sin if they lay together without being wed. *Like Papa and Alice.* She had ciphered that lying together made babies come. And illegitimate children were God's punishment for such sins.

Yet as far as what men actually did . . .

"I suppose not."

Amaria sighed. Very quietly she said, "Would you like me to tell you?" Joan nodded. She needed to know.

When Amaria explained, Joan could scarcely credit it. She remembered Walter grabbing her in the stairwell and felt ill. Too embarrassed to ask questions, she merely nodded her understanding, then followed the maid to the dining hall.

Joan was glad Amaria knew so much about men, but she had said nothing about William. Joan knew she'd have to try asking her mother again.

At last, one night while speaking of Sicily, Eleanor wondered aloud if Joan ought not to learn Greek. Although the Sicilian kings were Normans—just as Joan's ancestor William the Conqueror had been—and Norman French was the official language of both courts, the Sicilian kings were said to speak all the languages of their realm. William was known to be fluent in Greek, Arabic, and Latin as well as French.

Joan lifted her head. "What else do people say about King William?"

One of Lady Penelope's maids answered, "He is supposed to be the handsomest man in all of Christendom."

The queen's lips pursed. Joan pouted. They were patronizing her.

"I don't want made-up stories."

Her mother sighed. "It isn't a story. King William's comeliness is well known. He was crowned three days after his father's death because the kingdom was not stable enough to tolerate any delay. He was just twelve, and there was general fear his father's enemies would kill him or undermine his rule. His advisers even suppressed word of the old king's death until his coronation was under way. But the chroniclers said the new king emerged from the ceremony shining fair as the sun, and even the most hard-hearted opposition melted before him."

Joan stared, mouth agape. Then she snapped her jaw shut. "Hmph. He didn't do anything to win over his enemies except look handsome?" She heard some of the maids titter. She thought of Walter. "It wouldn't win me. I don't like handsome men."

Her mother laughed out loud. "What sort of men do you like?"

Joan folded her arms across her chest. "An intelligent king is better than a handsome one."

"True. King William is supposed to be intelligent."

Her mother's mood was expansive today. What else could she learn? Quickly, she added, "I like kind men."

It was the wrong thing to say. Her mother frowned. "A kind man makes a weak ruler. Kindness is a luxury only serfs can afford."

Tears stung Joan's eyes as she recognized the truth of her mother's words. No one would ever call her father kind. Or Richard. Henry was said to be the kindest of her brothers, and Papa had once called him soft. There was Sir Robert, but he was only as kind as Papa allowed him to be.

"Then I shan't love him."

In Poitiers, she had heard enough troubadour poetry to know the queen put great stock in love. Perhaps she would not have to marry King William if she didn't like him.

"God's teeth, child, don't be stupid. There is no greater fool than a woman who loves her husband. Unless it is a woman who believes her husband when he says he loves her. Don't believe otherwise or you'll be hurt."

The room fell silent. To Joan's surprise, it was quiet Lady Penelope who finally spoke.

"Not all men are so cruel, Princess. I would not gainsay your mother, but perhaps you will find something to love in King William. Even if he is not kind, he has no reason to treat you ill."

Joan nodded to acknowledge Lady Penelope's thoughtfulness but could not find voice to thank her. It occurred to her that old Sir Walter was kind, but he was lord of nothing but Sarum. She was going to marry a king.

MORE RAIN FELL IN A SARUM SPRING MONTH THAN FELL IN A year in Poitiers. In the midst of a May thunder shower, unexpected messengers from the king appeared. They were sodden to the bone; Lady Penelope insisted they wring themselves out by the hearth fire in the great hall before they announced their purpose. When she was assured they were fit to address the queen, they were at last given audience. They had come to fetch the prisoners and take them to Winchester.

"King William's ambassadors will be there," said the bishop of Norwich.

"So soon?" Eleanor asked. "My, my, the king of Sicily is impatient."

"No, lady. It isn't that. It seems . . ." The bishop coughed. He glanced at Joan then back at the queen. "It seems there is a consideration the previous ambassadors neglected."

Eleanor frowned. "He wants to change the terms?"

"No, no. It is just King William was disappointed his ambassadors did not have a chance to see the princess." He lowered his voice. "To be sure her countenance is pleasing."

"Pleasing!" She laughed, laying a hand on her middle. "Oh, Joan. Your husband-to-be is a vain man. What fun you will have."

Joan's stomach turned over. What if she wasn't pretty enough for the king? She was too tall, she knew, and still growing. She looked too much like Richard, not enough like Mama.

The bishop's nose wrinkled. "I daresay this is too much trouble for you and my lord king to find so amusing. We are to bring you and the princess to Winchester. The king regrets he cannot attend you there, but he said"—he took a deep breath and rolled his eyes upward, saying words he clearly had been instructed to say—" 'Tell Joan to smile. Her scowl would scorch a dragon's eyeballs.' "

Eleanor laughed again. "How soon do we go? I'm not overly fond of Winchester, but anything is better than Sarum."

Joan cast a glance at Lady Penelope. Her eyes were down, her cheeks pink. She wished she could tell Lady Penelope that *she* would miss Sarum.

IN WINCHESTER, JOAN MET THE AMBASSADORS FROM SICILY, led by the bishop of Troia. He was a short, funny man with an even funnier name, which she could not pronounce. He made a great fuss over her, touching her hair and calling her lovely.

The queen stayed a long time in conference, and when she finally rejoined Joan in the small bedchamber, she stood a moment in the doorway, brows knit. Joan's smile faded.

"Do you understand what that was, Joan?"

She did. It meant she had to go to Sicily. She tried to remember the words the bishop of Norwich had used. "It means there is no . . . no impediment to the marriage."

Her mother walked over to where she sat and looked down at her. "There never was. You're a pretty girl—I don't mean to say you are not—but they would have praised you even if you had been a toad. They had no wish to insult your father."

The room seemed to shrink even smaller. "Then I don't understand."

"This farce was King William's way of showing strength. By imposing a last-minute condition on the marriage, he meant to downplay the importance of the alliance. By agreeing to it, your father showed the match is more important to us than it is to William."

"Why did Papa agree to it?"

"Your father is a practical man. He wanted the alliance."

Joan took a deep breath. "Why do I have to marry King William, Mama?"

Her mother looked away. "Charisse, bring me a chair." When she was settled beside Joan, she took her hand. "Sweetling, the right alliances are good, but wrong alliances are disastrous.

Emperor Barbarossa has offered his daughter to William. If the Holy Roman Empire allied itself with the Sicilian kingdom, Rome's independence would vanish. The city would be swallowed whole."

Joan considered this. She knew all the Germanic kingdoms were loosely united under one great ruler, the emperor. They called their confederation the Holy Roman Empire, claiming it was the true heir to the Roman Empire; Mama had once told her that Barbarossa imagined he would conquer all of Italy one day also.

"Joan? The empire would be far too strong for anyone to oppose. By marrying William, you make many very powerful men happy: your father, the king of France, and the lord pope."

"What about King William? Did he want to marry the emperor's daughter?"

"I doubt it. Sicily would become part of the empire. He has fought against Barbarossa already to prevent that. On the other hand, it could mean William's son would eventually become emperor. I don't know where William's ambitions lie. But his counselors prefer you."

"I feel like a chess piece."

"That is what princesses are. But come now. You do have some choices. They will allow you to bring a maid and six knights as guards. William will likely snatch away the knights for his own use, but I thought . . . we could send for Agnes, if you like, but she doesn't travel well. Would you prefer Charisse?"

"Oh, Mama!" The gift delighted her, but seeing Charisse's lowered eyes, Joan sobered. "Charisse should have a choice, too."

"Charisse's alternatives are Sicily or continued imprisonment with me."

"I'll go to Sicily, lady," Charisse said.

The queen didn't bother to look at her. "Yes, I thought you might."

THEY SPENT A MONTH IN WINCHESTER WHILE JOAN'S trousseau was prepared.

In early August, Henry came to say good-bye to his daughter. Guards escorted Joan to a dark round room high in the west tower, and she understood Papa would enter through the west gate so there would be no possibility of a chance meeting between the king and the queen.

She'd been sitting on a thin cushion on a stone bench for what seemed an hour before he entered. A servant hurried in behind him and set down two large bright candles, then scuttled out. Papa gazed upon her a long while. His cheeks were hidden by his beard, now streaked with gray. His lids drooped until he cocked his brow and smiled. "Joan, girl. You've grown."

"Did you expect otherwise? Did our jailers do wrong to feed us?"

The smile faded. He turned from her, but not before she saw him rub his eyes.

Joan felt a burning in her throat and fought the desire to run and press her cheek against his chest. She might never see him again.

"William is a fine man," he said. "I wouldn't have agreed to this if he wasn't."

"Mama says it is a good match."

"Aye, then. Listen to your mother." He sounded tired. His gaze wandered about the room. "Are you pleased with your trousseau?"

"Mama says it is adequate. I am to thank you for your generosity."

"God's eyes, girl. You're my daughter. I'd not send you off a pauper." He hooked his thumbs into the girdle at his waist. "What will it take for you to give me a smile?"

Joan sat very still. If she asked him to release Mama, they would fight. She murmured, "You haven't given Mama any money for clothes."

"She lacks clothes?"

Joan scowled.

"Fine. I'll tell the exchequer to give her an allowance. I'm not mean. I didn't think of it."

"Will you let her see Richard?"

"No."

"John?"

"No. It's taken me this long to purge them of her poison. Come, Joan, I don't want to argue." When she said nothing, he sighed. Then he spread wide his arms. "Come and embrace me. I know you are not truly angry at me for sending you to your mother. And Lord Walter said you were lively enough."

"You asked of me?"

"Of course." His jaw slackened—his injured look.

Slowly, she rose from her bench and let him wrap his arms around her.

"Be good, Joan, girl. Make me proud." Then he kissed her cheek, but she would not kiss him in return.

Later, when she saw her mother again, she was glad she had not kissed him. The king sent word he would release Eleanor from prison provided she took the veil. She could be abbess at Fontevrault.

"He could have our marriage annulled, but then your brothers might be declared illegitimate. And Aquitaine and Poitiers would revert to my control. Henry cannot repudiate me. He'd have to set me free." Eleanor laughed. "I might remarry poor Louis."

"Oh, Mama, don't go to Fontevrault!"

"Of course I won't, Joan. I am not a nun. Good Lord. What is your father thinking? Could he have gotten a child on Alice? He probably thinks he'll marry the tart."

Mama knew about Alice? Joan swallowed and held her tongue. Of course. A queen had to be aware of all the undercurrents at court. A queen had to know everything about the realm's enemies. A queen must be familiar with the resources and workings of her domain. A queen must make her husband welcome in her bed, give him heirs, but not be fool enough to love him.

The only thing Mama had failed to explain was why any woman would want to be queen.

## SEVEN

IT WAS A GENTLE MID-AUGUST CHANNEL CROSSING, BLESSED with sunshine and favorable winds. Joan pushed away a tide of memories of other crossings, other journeys, pleasant and unpleasant, as they sailed from Southampton to Barfleur.

She ate little on board so, in Barfleur, she was hungry enough to eat a piece of fish that did not smell right. Then, for the first time in her life, she felt sick enough to die.

Her escorts bore her to the infirmary of a Cistercian abbey outside the city. The bishop of Troia prayed over her so vehemently it frightened her. The bishop of Norwich ordered her knights to take the rich trousseau to Chinon for safeguarding, and that frightened her more. At last, her stomach calmed, and she was able to keep food down, but barely. Ten days behind schedule, they put her into a wain and moved slowly southward.

Five days later, in Normandy near the city of Mortain, Sir Robert joined their party, though when she first heard his voice she could not believe it was him. He swore at everyone, even the bishops, as she had never heard him swear. The cortege halted.

"Princess?" he called at the curtain.

Charisse laid her hand on Joan's brow, but she pushed it away.

"Sir Robert?"

The curtain parted. She saw him and forced a smile.

"Princess, you are as green as a toad. Come here."

She crawled out to him over Charisse's protests. He lifted her onto his horse and mounted behind her.

"You've grown again."

"I'm not doing it on purpose."

He laughed. "No, but you are making a liar of your father. He said you travel as well as he does, and now we hear you've been vomiting a path from Winchester to Sicily."

"I feel better now."

Joan breathed deeply and rested against him. Though the air was oppressively humid, the familiar scent of horse and leather comforted her. Robert's low, steady voice made her feel safe. He said he would accompany her to St. Gilles, where she would depart for Messina with Sicilian attendants. But first he was taking her to Poitiers to see Richard.

"Richard? But . . . doesn't Papa think I will tell him we were in Sarum?"

"It doesn't matter. The queen is not in Sarum anymore."

The cortege plodded along a crest that bisected vast fields pungent with rye. In the distance, a cluster of bare-chested serfs bent and straightened, swinging large scythes. Two men pushed at an ox as if they expected something from the animal. Heat rose in waves from the earth, and the bright sun made Joan's head hurt.

Robert spoke of her brothers. Henry was still discontent— the king had not yet given him any authority or any armies to command. He spent all his time in tournaments, running up outrageous debts. Richard had made great gains in Aquitaine. The local nobility feared him, and most paid him homage as their duke.

"Is Richard content?"

"It's hard to know. He tells the king repeatedly that the nobles of Aquitaine will not cease agitating for the release of their duchess. As long as the queen is imprisoned, Duke Richard will not have peace in Aquitaine. Of course, he wants her freed as much as his vassals do."

So, Richard was still battling with Papa. "What of Geoffrey and John?"

"Count Geoffrey divides his time between serving in Duke Richard's wars and playing in tournaments with the young king. It is as if he cannot decide what kind of man he will be. He's very clever. A little unnerving. He watches everyone but doesn't say much. And John is with your father again. Your father spoils him."

Of course he did. John was the only one who had never betrayed him. The news did not make her happy or sad, only hollow inside. After so much had happened, nothing had changed.

JOAN STAYED TWO WEEKS IN POITIERS. SHE HAD MISSED HER mother's home—the capital city of the county of Poitou and seat of the duchy of Aquitaine. The court had revived under the auspices of its duke, who filled it with handsome knights, beautiful ladies, musicians, and troubadours, just as Eleanor had done. In the baileys, the dazzling blue of the heavens and green of the grass seemed unreal after the dull sameness of Sarum's gray sky and chalky earth. Inside, bright reds and golds decorated the walls and furnishings; the noise swirling the air was music and laughter, not Sarum's incessant wind.

The night before she was to leave, Richard threw a feast for her. He teased her into drinking unwatered wine. When she was nearly asleep at the table, he put his hand on her hair.

"Henry told me what happened. You'll be a fine queen, sister mine, a courageous one. I never meant for you to be a prisoner, too."

"I was in Sarum," she said, lifting her head. He had never asked.

"There was nothing I could do. Not yet. I'm sorry, Jeanne."

"Don't be sorry for my sake. I was with Mama. But Robert says she isn't in Sarum now."

"Don't worry. If Father doesn't free her soon, I will."

"Please don't fight again, Richard," she said. His lips tightened. "Richard?"

"If he frees our mother, I won't. I have no other quarrel with Father. I certainly won't be stupid enough to take Henry's part again."

"Henry's part? What do you mean?"

He ruffled her hair. "Nothing, Jeanne. Nothing. Old quarrels. Go to Sicily and forget about us. Go make William happy. The world could use more happy men."

THE EASTWARD JOURNEY THROUGH AQUITAINE AND PROVENCE to St. Gilles was over before Joan wished it to be. Southern France was as beautiful as her mother had said. Lavender painted the hills purple and blue, the sweet fragrance mingling with that of grapes. In each castle where they rested, they were welcomed by lyrical Occitan voices. But when they arrived in St. Gilles, Joan was disappointed. The buildings were squat and unadorned. Sailors infested the narrow streets, and even with the escort of knights from the castle, they made slow progress. Worse, she could not escape the fishy sea odor that still made her queasy.

St. Gilles belonged to the count of Toulouse, but in his

absence, the castle was maintained by a local nobleman. Joan was surprised to find a pretty castle in such an ugly place. It was small, but with uncommonly large windows and square-hewn stone walls. Inside, the woodwork was ornamented and polished. Embroidered panels depicting bright, happy tournaments and hunts decorated the walls.

The castellan's wife was pretty too, and they had a daughter who looked to be twelve or thirteen. She smiled with teeth so crooked Joan wondered that she had not learned to smile with her mouth closed. Her name was Ermengarde, which suited her. She was friendly, with such a lively laugh that Joan forgot about her teeth.

Ermengarde said she would move to her mother's chamber so Joan could have her bed.

"Oh, no," Joan said, in a burst of goodwill. "Please stay with me. I haven't had a girl to talk to in . . . well . . ." In truth, she could not name a friend.

"I'll stay tonight if you like. But they tell me I talk in my sleep. You may be glad to be rid of me tomorrow." Then she proceeded to talk so much Joan wondered how she could have anything left to say when she slept.

The castle was crowded because of its distinguished visitor—everyone in Provence had come to pay respects. That afternoon, Joan spent two solid hours being bowed to and fussed over. She nodded so many times she thought she'd shake her head loose. Her stomach began growling loudly. Then, just when the end of the receiving line was in sight, a commotion sounded at the door, and the line grew again.

Ermengarde's eyes lit. "They are back from the hunt. My brother Aimery and his friend Lord Raymond."

"Lord Raymond?" Her pulse bounded. There were a hundred young Raymonds in southern France, and the only one she knew would be in Toulouse. Still, her eyes darted over the newly swelled crowd until she saw him, impossible to overlook in brilliant scarlet and blue. His hair was wind-tousled and longer than the fashion. Several young knights formed a circle around him, as if each wanted to be as close as he could, but they parted to let him take a place in line. He looked at her, squinting in question. Did he imagine she would not recognize him?

Joan forced her attention to the lady curtsying before her. She repeated the woman's name and thanked her for her kind wishes. The next knight, a minor southern baron, kissed her fingers. He told her how much he loved Papa and Richard. She barely listened. They all said the same things, to no purpose. She would not even remember their names.

Finally, Lord Raymond stood before her. With exquisite poise, he slipped to one knee. When he rose, she held out her hand. He took her fingertips, but she twisted her hand and let him kiss her palm as if he were her equal in rank or had the privilege of her particular friendship. His eyes bound her more firmly than his hand.

He said, "I had not hoped you would remember me."

"My memory is poor, but not so poor as that. You saved me—"

"From a mouse," he interrupted, a slow grin spreading across his face. "Not a dragon."

She smiled, flustered by a memory that was not exactly flattering, yet flattered he remembered all the same.

"How is Tessie?" he asked, letting go of her hand.

Growing so warm she thought she would melt to the floor,

she murmured, "Your memory is astounding. I cannot remember bishops. You remember poppets."

He shrugged. "I have a facility with names. I would prefer a more useful skill, but sometimes it serves."

She wanted him to stay, to say more, but there were other courtiers to greet before supper and it was already late. Worse, she felt tongue-tied. How could it be that Eleanor's daughter had not learned to banter with men?

Lord Raymond glanced over his shoulder at those still waiting to pay their respects and grimaced. Then he bowed. "Lady. It's a great pleasure to see you again and to see you so well." He abandoned her to the rest of the court.

Ermengarde jiggled her arm. "You know Lord Raymond?" she whispered, eyes wide.

"We've met before."

The next baron stepped before her. Joan drew a deep breath, nodded, and smiled.

Not until supper did she have a chance to talk to Ermengarde. In a warm hall of yellowed gray stone, they ate a rich feast of mutton and gravy over bread. The dark red wine of the Rhône Valley was prized throughout southern France, and the steward did not stint in the serving. Joan sat at the table of honor, but since the room was crowded with important people talking to anyone who would listen, she and Ermengarde could whisper back and forth without fear of chastisement.

"Why is the lord of Toulouse here?" she asked. He had not come all the way for her sake.

"Oh, Princess! Then you don't know him well?"

"No. We only met once."

Ermengarde lowered her voice. "I'll tell you the story, but you mustn't tell anyone who told you. It isn't fit for your ears." She giggled. "Or for mine. He got a babe on a girl in his father's court."

Joan's face fell. She was disappointed in the story. And in him.

"Princess, that isn't all. She's a lady, not a servant, but her father hasn't anything, and Lord Raymond insisted he would marry her."

"Marry her?" He couldn't be more than twenty. He was heir to Toulouse. Yet he imagined he could marry for love?

"They say it was a terrible scene. The count flew into a rage and called the girl any number of things." Ermengarde's voice rose with excitement, but she lowered it again. "They say Lord Raymond struck his father. And his father threw him out."

"Oh!" Joan tried to think of an appropriate response. "Did the count disown him?"

"No. But Lord Raymond had to come here. As soon as he left Toulouse, the count bought off the girl's father and married her to a lowly knight at court. Lord Raymond was furious when he found out. He rode back into Toulouse with several of his fellows and stole away the baby."

"He did? What could he do with a baby?"

"It is here. A little boy, they call him Bertrand. Lord Raymond has a nurse for it. And he says he won't go back to Toulouse until his father allows him to bring the boy to court."

"That is . . ." Joan screwed her face into a knot. Stupid, she thought. Such a fuss over nothing. "Tenderhearted. Is he . . . is Lord Raymond despondent?"

"Over the lady?" Ermengarde laughed edgily. "If the cure for heartbreak is more of the same."

Joan glanced over at Lord Raymond's table. He was talking to Aimery, his face animated, gesturing with his hands as though estimating the size of some hapless prey. With a broad smile and a red face showing his amusement, Aimery slapped down Raymond's hand. The young lord laughed, ducking his head to the table.

"They're like two brothers," Ermengarde said, nudging her. "Don't you think?"

"Very," she agreed, to please her new friend. But she wondered if this was how other peoples' brothers behaved.

LORD RAYMOND DID NOT SPEND TIME IN THE GARDENS, SO Joan saw little of him. He was at supper, of course, but though his father was overlord of St. Gilles, young Raymond sat with his knights far from the head table. She dared not look for him for fear Charisse or Ermengarde would notice.

She had been in St. Gilles nearly three weeks when her escorts finally arrived, just in time for her eleventh birthday. She stood in the courtyard with Charisse and watched twelve carts loaded high with her dower gifts and trousseau rumble through the gates. The coverings had been peeled back to display the king's bounty. Three entire wagons held gowns of wool and linen, shoes, hose, and undergarments. The others held silver plate, ornate golden cups and altar pieces, finely embroidered linens and curtains for the marriage bed, livery for her guard, and gifts for King William, including two gold-leaf books from her father's own collection.

Several groups of mounted knights crowded the courtyard. Joan saw Lord Raymond nearby with a small knot of men. She wanted them to take notice of her dowry. Instead, they noticed her guard. One of the men was unusually short and clubfooted.

"Would you look at that? The king sent five knights and a dwarf."

Joan whirled to see the speaker, one of Lord Raymond's knights. She heard the others laughing. Raymond did not even smile.

"He must be tied to the saddle. Come." The grinning knight beckoned to his fellows. "We'll have a tournament."

Joan wanted to shout, to warn the men, but they would never hear her.

Lord Raymond nudged his mount into the man's path. "It will be no credit to you if you unhorse him. And certainly no credit if you try and do not succeed."

The knight's face flushed. "My lord—"

"You heard me."

The knight nodded. Looking more angry than abashed, he backed his horse behind his lord's. The other knights exchanged glances, but Raymond seemed unperturbed. He dismounted and tossed his reins to a squire standing with his party, then stepped toward Joan.

His bow was perfunctory. "Lady, I had hoped to see more of you, but it looks like you'll be leaving us soon."

"Yes. Thank you," she managed to say.

Raymond's jaw hardened. He looked at his feet and then back at her. "Princess, I apologize for the poor breeding of my fellows."

"They will improve with you for example."

He barely smiled. "No, I doubt it. Though it is pleasant to think so." His voice changed. "I'm glad to know you'll have champions accompanying you."

It struck her as an odd thing to say. "Will I need champions in Sicily?"

Now he did smile. "Everyone needs friends."

They stood together a moment. Joan had a sudden wish for Ermengarde's tongue. She was so afraid of saying the wrong thing, of sounding childish, she could not speak at all.

Raymond said, "I've never been to Sicily, only to the Holy See, and I was too young to remember. But I've heard the island is awe-inspiring in its beauty, rivaling even Toulouse."

"My mother says nothing compares with Toulouse." She bit her lip. She shouldn't have mentioned her mother's claim. And he couldn't return to Toulouse, could he? Her face felt hot.

He leaned closer. "Here is your chance to tell me I will always be welcome in Sicily."

Charisse said, "Lady, Sir Robert will be waiting. I'm sorry, but we must go. Please excuse us, sir." She hardly curtsied before steering Joan away.

Joan didn't know what to think. Charisse's behavior bordered on rude, and while trying to make conversation had been uncomfortable, nevertheless, she had wanted to try.

"Princess, stay away from Lord Raymond. He is not suitable company for decent ladies."

Joan stopped short. "But, Charisse, he—"

"I heard. His fellows are little better than brigands. He can barely control them. Lord Raymond is not fit company for you."

IN LATE OCTOBER 1176, TWENTY-FIVE SHIPS FROM THE SICILIAN fleet massed in St. Gilles harbor. Joan was surprised to discover she knew the counselor who greeted her in King William's name. That is, she knew of him. Richard Palmer was a Norman, a friend of the late Archbishop Becket. He had gone to Sicily when Papa and Becket parted ways, and there he was made bishop of Syracuse. Mama called him sensible and had said to look for him in Sicily.

Now here he was—a short man with piercing hazel eyes, light brown hair fading to gray, and frown lines that seemed ingrained. He might well frown, considering the news he bore.

Winter gales had begun, and sailing was treacherous. Two hulks carrying gifts for King Henry had been lost at sea. They dared not take the direct route to Palermo but, rather, would sail close to the coast of Italy, cross the straits to Messina, then travel overland to Palermo. If they hurried, they could still reach Sicily in time for Christmas court.

Her own counselors voiced no objections. At daybreak, Charisse roused her from bed to dress and board the ship. Joan was obliged to take leave of her counselors and hosts with little ceremony. Sir Robert's face was taut. Ermengarde wept so hard she could not speak.

The young lord of Toulouse came to the hall to pay his respects. Charisse had been relentless in her chaperonage—Joan had exchanged no more than greetings with Lord Raymond. Even now, Charisse stood close by her side.

As Raymond bowed, Joan stretched out her hand. He kissed the fingertips, but before releasing her, he squeezed her fingers.

"God go with you, Princess."

She took a breath. "You are always welcome in Sicily," she said before Charisse could prevent it. She was rewarded with his smile.

"And you are always welcome in Toulouse." Then he rubbed his chin. "*You* are. I'd prefer you not to bring Richard with an army at his side."

He seemed to be joking, so she laughed.

Charisse said, "Lady—"

Raymond bowed. "I will not keep you. Safe journey, Princess Jeanne."

Jeanne. Only Mama and Richard called her Jeanne. Even in the south, the Occitanian speakers pronounced her name with the Norman accent. She would never hear it again.

Joan said, "Good-bye, Lord Raymond. Thank you for your kindness."

He was not smiling now. Walking away, she thought she felt his eyes on her back.


THE KNIGHTS SAILED ON A SEPARATE SHIP, SO JOAN HAD ONLY Charisse and the churchmen for company and sailors to avoid. She kept to her small, airless room in the forecastle. The bed was narrow and the mattress uneven. Fine linen sheets had been placed in the room, but mice nibbled holes in them. Droppings littered the floor, though Charisse swept it clean twice a day. The cook served fish more nights than not. Joan gave up trying to eat anything but bread and dried fruit.

As they crept along the Mediterranean coast, trying to dodge the worst storms, Joan fell ill again. They were forced to put in to harbor first at Genoa and again at Pisa, where she had to be carried ashore.

She understood they could not stay long in Pisa. The Pisan lord would not turn away the sick daughter of King Henry of England but found the presence of so many Sicilian ships in his harbor unsettling. The admiral of her small fleet insisted they sail down the coast until they reached Sicilian territory. They would have to stay in Naples until the weather improved.

Richard Palmer greeted each setback with foul temper. Joan

thought he blamed her for her illness *and* the weather. She wished for the strength to match his foul temper with her own.

En route to Naples, Joan lay abed, wondering if she would ever feel well again. Closing her eyes made her dizzy, but when she opened them, the pounding in her head grew worse. Charisse had gone out to the deck for air and stayed longer than usual. Her absence was irritating.

The door opened. Charisse flew to the bedside. "Joan! Princess Joan, I heard . . . did your mother know? She couldn't have, kept so isolated in Sarum. Oh, but Joan!"

Joan sat up. "Charisse, what on earth—"

"The bishop of Troia and Bishop Palmer were on the deck arguing. I didn't mean to listen, but then I heard Bishop Palmer shout that he would bring you to Sicily on time if it meant delivering a corpse. I hid behind a barrel and heard every word. King William has been betrothed before. To the daughter of the Greek emperor. The Sicilians prepared for the ceremony, and the king went to meet his bride, but she never appeared! Can you imagine?"

"But what has that to do with me?" Her father was a practical man. King Henry wanted the alliance, even if the Greek emperor did not.

"Only that it explains why Bishop Palmer is so determined to see you reach Sicily. They don't want their people reminded of the king's humiliation. Or thinking it is happening again. Thank God, the bishop of Troia's counsel prevailed. He insisted it is enough for you to reach Naples."

Joan was in no mood to be appreciative. King William had wanted to marry someone else. She lay down and turned her back. "The bishop vouched for my appearance, didn't he? He must not want to deliver me looking like this."

JOAN DID NOT REMEMBER HER ARRIVAL IN NAPLES. WHEN SHE woke in a high, soft-mattressed bed surrounded by a double wall of curtains, Charisse said she had been asleep for two days. She tried to climb from the bed, but the ground swayed beneath her, forcing her to lie back down.

She was hungry, though. The lady of the castle sent a plate heaped with bread and mild cheese, and Joan finished every bite. When the food stayed down, Charisse's brow relaxed.

"This is Naples?" Joan asked.

Charisse nodded. "We could have been here faster if we'd traveled overland."

"Surely not." Joan shifted uncomfortably. Naples had not been on the itinerary. The sea route to Messina should have been faster, even allowing for storms. If her frequent requirement for unscheduled stops had delayed them that much, no wonder Bishop Palmer was angry.

"Well, merchants have. There is word of your family. Would you like to hear it?"

The news could not be so bad, or she would not share it readily. Joan nodded.

"The little countess of Maurienne died. Prince John is betrothed again. To your cousin Hawise."

The countess was dead—John would not get Henry's castles, after all. Joan shook the futile thoughts from her head.

Charisse looked away, eyes narrowing. "There is also news from Toulouse. Lord Raymond has married."

"Married! But . . . but . . . to whom?" The mother of his babe had wed someone else, according to Ermengarde.

"The heiress of Melgueil."

Joan thought hard. Melgueil lay between St. Gilles and Montpelier. Money was coined in the city, so it was very wealthy. She could remember hearing nothing of its daughter. "When?"

"Just after we left. The count allowed Lord Raymond to return to Toulouse provided he wed immediately."

So, likely his father chose the bride. "What do they say of the heiress?"

"Princess—"

"I am curious, Charisse. He was kind to me. I wish his happiness."

After a pause, the maid said, "She is older than he is. They say she is plain but presentable. Wealthy enough to make up for any faults he might find."

"I hope they are suited."

"Suited?" Charisse snorted. "What woman could be suited to a man like Lord Raymond? Put him out of your head now, Princess Joan."

WHEN JOAN WAS WELL ENOUGH TO VENTURE FROM HER CHAMber, she found the lord of Naples eager to show her the city. Charisse agreed she might visit the cathedral. Its strange splendor eclipsed anything she had seen in her father's lands. The lord said the strangeness was due to Greek influence. Joan stared a long time at a mosaic of the Virgin. Arched wings partially obscured the halo above her head; the long, straight black hair and dark robe accentuated the whiteness of her skin. It made Joan think of Melusine.

In contrast to the cathedral, the castle was small, oval, and plain, the result of the city being razed time and again by too many conquerors. They had given up lavishing money on a castle that was sure to be burned. Laughing, the lord claimed Naples had a penchant for supporting weak rulers. Then he hastily amended, "Until King William, of course."

Whether the climate in Naples or Charisse's ministrations were responsible, Joan's health continued to improve. Each time she caught her reflection in glass or polished metal, she saw her cheeks becoming rounder, the dark purple hollows fading from under her eyes.

At last, she felt well enough to attend supper in the great hall; even Richard Palmer smiled as she took her place. The men spoke eagerly of reaching the island of Sicily. After keeping Christmas, they would travel down the mainland shoreline to Reggio, then sail across the narrow Strait of Messina. The road along the rocky hills of the island's northeast coast had been recently widened and smoothed to ease the overland journey. Their eagerness infected Joan. After all, she was going to be queen of a kingdom wealthier than England, and as warm and beautiful as Aquitaine. Armed with all Mama's teachings, she'd make William a good queen.

After supper she retired to her chamber, but she did not feel sleepy. She lay in bed fidgeting awhile. Then she sat up and plucked Tessie from the pillow. "We're going on a journey, Tessie," she sang.

# PART TWO

# QUEEN JOANNA

# EIGHT

*Palermo, Sicily, October 1179*

Q UEEN JOANNA!" THE TUTOR RAPPED ON THE TABLE BESIDE
   her. Joan jumped: The harsh Sicilian pronunciation of her
name grated on her nerves. "You are not paying attention."

"I beg your pardon." She tore her gaze from the mosaics of
smiling maidens and fantastic beasts decorating one wall of the
chamber. Although this palace had been her home for almost
three years, she'd never noticed before that the lions eyed the
maidens as if they would devour them.

Beneath the tight dark curls plastered against his forehead,
Master Eugenius's eyes narrowed in accusation. "You have not
been concentrating the entire morning."

He bent his paunch over the table and slammed her book shut.
His breath smelled of olives. Or perhaps the odor emanated from
his hair.

"You are wasting my time. You used to be such a diligent
pupil. These past few months . . . well." His voice lowered as he
straightened and turned away, muttering loud enough for her to
hear. "It's to be expected. The female mind is not capable. . . ."

Joan bit her tongue, knowing he wanted her to argue so he
could turn her words against her. She had learned that her only
hope of victory was in silence.

He gathered his things and set his hat upon his head.

"Tomorrow then. But if you're still gathering wool, I'll speak to the queen mother again."

Rising from her thick-cushioned chair, she silently cursed the luxury that threatened to swallow her whole. She would never feel at home here. Palermo was as foreign to her now as when she had first come. And this morning the memories of her arrival were as vivid as if it had been days ago, not years.

*Joanna. Poor thing. You're just a child.* William's aunt, the Princess Constance, had greeted her with those words.

Just a child—Joan had imagined it would be different when she finally met William. She'd spent two weeks at the Favara, a Saracen-style palace outside the city, while preparations were made for her triumphal entrance to Sicily's capital.

At last, Bishop Palmer and the Queen's Guard conveyed her to the city gate, where King William waited with his entourage. He shone as fair as the sun, just as her mother had said. He wore a wide scarlet mantle of silk twill, embroidered with lions attacking camels, that engulfed his torso and legs, covering so much of his horse he resembled a centaur. Little use to remind herself she did not like handsome men, or that women who loved their husbands were fools. She wanted to love him. Yet he did not even deign to smile at her, his eleven-year-old fiancée, as he murmured words of welcome she could not hear.

A thousand torches lit the crowded streets. Wide-eyed, she tried to see everything, but everything blurred. The illuminated procession ended at the Convent Saint Maria. William abandoned her at the portcullis, looking through her as he bid her good night. They were apart until their wedding eleven days later. Throughout the ceremony, he focused all his attention on the archbishop of Palermo, so she did also. When the archbishop placed their hands together, William's was cold. As soon as they were united, she was whisked from the cathedral to the Royal Palace. In the Palatine Chapel, even more magnificent than the church, William laid a crown upon her head and spoke over her in Latin. At the wedding feast, she sat between the queen mother Marguerite and Princess Constance.

It must have been midnight—she had been wide awake but dreaming—when they put her in a litter bound for this palace, her new home. Not even the Favara's splendor had prepared her for the Zisa. Modeled after the palaces of Turkish caliphs, the Zisa took its name from an Arabic word meaning "magnificent." Pale gray stones reflected the moonlight. The rectangular palace rose three stories tall, its angles softened by the arched windows. A wide gallery welcomed her, vibrant with colorful mosaics, noisily alive with water flowing from a fountain into a pool.

So long ago. She *had* been a child. Instead of taking her place beside her husband, she had been consigned to this nursery, shelved in a jeweled box like a relic.

But Queen Joanna was a child no longer.

Summoning her mother's tone of voice, she said, "Good day, Master Eugenius."

With an unwilling bow and a sniff of disapproval, he took his leave.

When the door shut, she slumped back into her seat and listened to the footsteps fading, until all she could hear was the gurgling coming from the fountain next door. He was right, of course. She was distracted.

A soft rap on the door alerted her to Charisse's return. Three taps and a pause, then three more before she had a chance to respond. None of the other maids knocked in quite the same way, polite but insistent.

"Lady?" Charisse opened the door and stepped inside, frowning. "Master Eugenius is gone? You didn't call me."

"No. I wanted a few minutes' peace."

Shaking her head, Charisse came closer. Pursed lips accentuated the fine lines around her mouth. "You shouldn't dismiss him early. You know it irritates him."

"I don't care."

"You know that's not true."

Joan dropped her head to her hands. Charisse was right. Master Eugenius was not so bad. After all, he kept her sane.

The first year in Palermo had been unbearable. Boredom had deadened her mind to every thought save longing for home. At last, Marguerite had noticed her listlessness and suggested the tutor. Joan didn't mind Master Eugenius's irascible condescension most days. He was the first person in Sicily who seemed to behave naturally. Her studies, more interesting than anything she had been taught in Fontevrault, provided a reason to wake in the morning. And as she began to learn Greek and Arabic, she could understand a little of what the servants whispered among themselves. Yet Master Eugenius's lessons could not cure homesickness.

"Lady?" Charisse said, laying a hand upon Joan's hair. "Do you feel well? I know it is strange, but if you feel sick or have pain—"

"I don't feel anything. That is what I find strange. I had thought to feel different." She sighed. "You . . . you haven't told anyone?"

"Who would I tell? Master Eugenius?" Charisse laughed, a short chirrup that sounded sad. Joan knew she missed Eleanor's entourage. If it had been Marguerite's intention to isolate her daughter-in-law from court gossip, she could not have found a better arrangement. "But you know you cannot keep this a secret. You're nearly fourteen. The queen mother—"

"I know she's anxious, but I feel so ashamed."

"There is no shame in becoming a woman. Come. It's a beautiful day. Have your supper in the garden."

Nodding acquiescence, Joan walked alongside her through the Fountain Room. The marble floors shone in the sunlight streaming through the windows. The fountain sprayed thousands of ephemeral rainbows into the air. They bypassed the broad staircase that led to her apartments, going instead to the small arched doorway to the garden, Joan's favorite part of the Zisa. Lengthy pathways wound through flowerbeds and patches of crisp-scented herbs, past clusters of tangy orange and sweet fig trees. Scattered alcoves contained half-hidden benches; waterways fed by fountains crisscrossed the paths. In her secret thoughts, Joan referred to it as the Garden of Eden. The only thing missing was temptation.

The vast perimeter of the garden was enclosed with a high wall she suspected the eunuch guards patrolled. If there was a gate, she had never stumbled across it. But the grounds were extensive enough that she need not see the wall if she didn't care to be reminded she was in a prison.

"I'll go ask Sati to bring you something to eat," Charisse said, after settling Joan on a stone bench close to the rosebushes.

A few shriveled blossoms clung to the stems. Warm breezes stirred the mulch, lifting a mixed scent of damp bark and old blossoms to her nose. Autumn in Palermo was nothing like Sarum. Here the seasons scarcely seemed to change.

Her stomach rumbled. What was taking Sati so long? William's mother had given her the woman as a wedding present. This particular handmaiden—she didn't like to think of them as slaves—had been set over the others because, in addition to her own native Arabic, she spoke the universal Norman French of the court, as well as enough Greek to communicate with the cook and kitchen maids. Joan relied upon her heavily, yet had not been able to forge a bond as her mother had done with her favorites. Whether Sati maintained her distance because she had been born an infidel or because she was a slave, Joan couldn't guess, but it was another thing to dislike about Sicily. She could count only Charisse and Princess Constance as friends.

At last, Charisse returned, leading the handmaiden. Sati's slippered feet glided along the stone path. As always, she looked beautiful, with her flawless olive skin and brown eyes that seemed at once scornful and sad. Balancing a silver tray on one arm, she avoided a mud puddle and reached Joan's side.

"My lady," she murmured, setting the tray on the bench.

Joan wrinkled her nose. The dish was swimming in sauce; she couldn't recognize the meat. "What is it?"

"I did not inquire."

Joan tore a piece of bread and dipped it into the sauce. It tasted of wine and salt. Perhaps it was fish.

"Why aren't you eating?" Charisse asked, nudging the tray closer.

Joan made a face. "They cook all the flavor away and then add sauce so it tastes of something else. I want my meat to taste like meat and my fish to taste like fish." Knowing she sounded petulant, she dipped her bread in the bowl for another bite. She sighed and looked at the ground. The padding between her legs was becoming sticky. She had no appetite, even though her stomach felt hollow. After a moment's silence, she got to her feet.

"Pardon me for being out of sorts today. I suppose I simply fear change."

JOAN SAT ON A GILDED BENCH, WATCHING WATER DROPLETS form patterns in the air before cascading into the collecting basin. How many hours of her life had been given over to this, the endless false rain of the Fountain Room? Unwilling to be idle, Charisse sat nearby hemming a gown. Two other handmaidens stood in a corner, their handiwork discarded on a chair. They had been discussing something very seriously for quite a while; perhaps they were arguing. Charisse sent them occasional disapproving glances, which they ignored.

Joan stifled a sigh. Would anyone notice if she transformed into a marble statue? She imagined Master Eugenius haranguing a statue and giggled in spite of her mood.

Sati poked her head through the arched doorway. "My lady, Queen Marguerite is here."

Joan jumped to her feet. "Bring her in."

*How did Marguerite know?*

She turned to glare at Charisse, but the maid's eyes were wide with surprise. Hastening to the door, Joan curtsied en route as the gray-haired dowager entered with a loud rustling of silk and the scent of wood anemone.

"Lady mother. How good of you to come."

"Joanna." William's mother enveloped her in a stiff-armed embrace. "I've heard glad tidings. William will be so pleased."

Joan stole a glance at Sati, whose shadowed face gave nothing away. Though she had at times felt intimidated by the maid's sulky efficiency, she had never imagined her disloyal before.

"You won't tell him yet?" she ventured, blushing.

The queen mother patted her shoulder almost fondly. "It's high time you took your place at court, or Constance will grow old pretending she is queen of Sicily." A brittle smile appeared, then disappeared.

Queen Marguerite did not like the princess. Constance had a mercurial temper, but Joan made excuses for her for the sake of the times she was kind. At twenty-five, she was still unmarried and likely to remain so until Joan either bore a son or proved barren. As the last living child of William's grandfather, King Roger the Great, Constance stood next in line for the throne. They could hardly choose a husband for her until her true worth was known. If Joan did not provide Sicily's next king, Constance would be its next queen. They did not want to accidentally seat the wrong man on the throne simply because he was Constance's husband.

"Come, dear. I've brought my seamstress to see to your dresses. You're a wisp. I think a few layers of lace underneath will help." Smiling, the queen mother took Joan's thin arm in her plump one and steered her toward the door. "We'll make you ready to join Christmas court."

JOAN HAD EXPECTED MORE FANFARE. THE KING WAS NOT EVEN present when she arrived at court in mid-November, four weeks after her fourteenth birthday. The queen mother, hovering about to boss the servants, told her he was in Monreale, conferring with the architects of his new cathedral. He was often in Monreale, she explained; the project consumed his attention.

Joan found the apology effusive. Apparently, Marguerite also believed William should have been at home to greet his wife.

The Royal Palace was an immense structure of pale stone tinged with pink, with high, arched windows set in blocked towers. Surrounded by greenery and waterways, it did not resemble a Norman castle any more than the Zisa did. Queen Marguerite showed Joan to her new apartments, an interior suite of four rooms located on the second floor toward the rear of the compound. The chambers were larger than those at the Zisa but similarly arranged, with a bedchamber for Joan, one for the maids, a room for dressing and bathing, and an anteroom to serve as day chamber.

Joan noticed a door leading directly from her bedchamber to a balcony. Curious, she stepped outside and breathed in the rich scent of flowering carob. Stairs led from the balcony down to a pretty garden court. But her appreciation was marred by the sight of the surrounding high stone walls.

"Lovely," she assured Marguerite, returning quickly inside.

"In the spring, there will be gorse and bird's-foot, brought especially from England. William had his best gardener design it for you."

Joan forced a smile. Somehow, she doubted William's involvement.

Most of her belongings had preceded her, and two more cartloads would follow. While she settled in—handmaidens finding their places, arranging furniture in the day chamber, a familiar eunuch slapping Charisse's low bed beside her own— Joan wondered if she'd merely exchanged jails. After all, she had only moved inside the city walls. Ensconced in a curtained litter between Charisse and Sati, she had not even been allowed to peer out at the scenery during the short journey. Another of

Sicily's absurd prohibitions—someone might catch an unauthorized glimpse of the queen.

*The queen.* She felt her heart flutter. At court, she would not be a prisoner. She would be William's consort, his helpmeet, as Mama had been before—

The queen mother sighed loudly. "Joanna, dear, you look tired. Rest awhile. We've decided, for the time being, you will take supper here in your room."

SINCE THE DAYS OF KING ARTHUR, CHRISTMAS COURTS HAD held a glamour of high expectations. Joan's father had always filled his halls with vassals at Christmastime, using the occasion to fulfill old promises and make new ones, to promulgate laws he knew would be popular, to pay and extract payment of old debts. Sometimes there would be weddings before the feast days began, and celebrations would be doubly joyous. Joan had always loved Christmas court.

Palermo's court, too, burgeoned in December, but she knew this only because she was permitted to attend morning prayers in the Palatine Chapel. There she sometimes caught sight of William, unless business had taken him from the Royal Palace early or kept him away overnight. Memory had not exaggerated his beauty. He wore floor-length, richly colored tunics and elaborately draped girdles that made him appear more a Greek emperor than a Norman king. But Joan had no opportunity to speak with her husband. He sat at one end of the balcony, surrounded by guards and pages, while her seat was at the opposite end between Constance and Marguerite.

From the balcony, she observed the worshippers gathered in the nave or gazed on mosaics that preached the Old Testament with a splendor the poor priest could never hope to match. Each day the chapel was crowded with new faces.

"Who is that, there—beneath Noah's feet?" she whispered.

A squat man with a long pointed nose and a shiny bald head had carved out a space for his entourage on a bench close to the altar. The crest of William's house, two lions eating camels, was emblazoned on a banner held by his page.

"Tancred of Lecce." Constance sniffed. "My nephew."

Joan almost giggled. The nephew was twice Constance's age.

"The mother claimed Duke Roger fathered him," Queen Marguerite explained, her lips tight. "Roger hadn't the sense to deny it."

Duke Roger would have been William's eldest uncle, but he had died young—too young to ever claim the throne. And Tancred was his illegitimate son.

"What has he done?" Joan asked, impressed that the two women should both dislike him. Agreement between them was so rare.

"Rebelled against my husband any number of times. He spent as much time in prison as out when William was a boy," the queen mother said in hushed tones. "But when William became king, he granted a general amnesty."

The priest began speaking, and Joan could ask no more questions. She watched Tancred throughout the service, pleased by the design of the balcony that allowed her such a view while ensuring a measure of privacy for the royal party. Those gathered below could only spy on her by twisting their heads away from the altar and craning their necks.

Tancred was a fidgety man, crossing and uncrossing his legs, scratching his pate, rolling his shoulders as if he had a pain.

The woman beside him, her face hidden under a veil, sat still as a stone. Joan wondered if William had noticed this new arrival. What did he think of his cousin?

Carefully, trying not to draw attention to herself, she shifted sideways to glance at William. Her eyes met his. She started and blushed, then turned her face quickly forward. He'd been watching her. Her palms dampened, and she wiped them against her skirt. She passed the remainder of the service in agony, moving her lips but neglecting her prayers. Was he still watching? She held her shoulders straight and tried to make her neck long.

At last, as the priest recited the closing prayer, the temptation to peek again grew too strong to ignore. She looked back, expecting to catch his eye. William had already gone.

EACH DAY AT DUSK, WHILE THE REST OF THE COURT SUPPED IN the dining hall, Sati and two eunuchs escorted Joan from her apartments to the library to meet with Master Eugenius. By order of the king, no one else was allowed to be present during the hours she spent there. She loved the untidy room with its wall of shelves reaching from ceiling to floor, holding nests of old papyrus scrolls alongside stacks of parchment and rows of codices. It had a faintly musty smell and numerous dusty niches. Scattered around sturdy tables were mismatched chairs and worn benches.

"Tell me about Tancred of Lecce," Joan demanded that evening, pushing aside *Stephanites and Ichnelates*, a Greek translation of fables from the East.

"Tancred?" wheezed Master Eugenius, perched atop a ladder to reshelve scrolls left on the table by some careless scholar. He often raged against King William's policy of allowing open access to his library. At Christmas season, it was worse. "Why?"

She heard distaste in his voice, but it meant nothing. The tutor disapproved of everyone.

"Queen Marguerite says he was a rebel."

"And you have a natural interest in such men."

Joan frowned, considering the comment a veiled criticism of her brothers. "I am curious about Sicily. I want to know about the old king's reign."

Master Eugenius lumbered down the ladder. Dust and flakes of parchment stuck to the oil in his hair. He came closer, squinting. "That is a time everyone else would prefer to forget. Besides, Tancred has made his peace with King William."

"But not with the queen mother or Princess Constance."

"Queen Joanna, the grudges people nurse are their own business, not yours."

"My mother says a queen must be aware of all the undercurrents at court."

The tutor's eyes opened wide, but he quickly huffed and squinted again. "Why would you think Tancred capable of stirring any currents in Sicily, let alone 'undercurrents'?"

He sounded vaguely amused, which angered her.

"I suppose, here in Sicily, women are not allowed to think?"

"Women should never think. It causes any number of problems."

Now she was sure he was mocking her. She glared at him, looking for a weakness, and realized by the fine lines around his mouth and eyes that the blackness of his hair must be due to walnut husk dye. He was Tancred's age, if not older.

"Whom did you support, the old king or the rebels?"

To her surprise, Master Eugenius laughed, his large belly shaking. "Had I supported one or the other, I'd be long dead."

Her nose wrinkled at the odor of cowardice. "But in your heart, surely—"

"In my heart? I despised them both."

Joan rolled her eyes. "Is there anyone you don't despise?"

"Currently?" His smile was thin, but appeared near conspiratorial rather than sneering.

"Don't trouble yourself to answer. I suppose if our lord king were deposed tomorrow, you'd be at liberty to despise even him."

"Of course not," he protested without fervor.

Joan sat quiet a moment, thinking through what he had said and did not say. She tapped her fingers idly against the worn table, knowing the sound irritated him. There were factions at every court. Here, with the conflicting interests of the Greeks, the Muslims, and the Latins—Norman French and Lombard Italian—division must be rife.

Her mother said a queen must know everything about her realm. Would Eugenius teach her? He had gone back to the shelves but did not scold her for the noise she made. It occurred to Joan suddenly and with some surprise that Eugenius did not despise her.

NINE

HER MOTHER ALWAYS SAID A WOMAN'S HANDS SHOULD never be idle, much less the hands of a queen.

Yet surely Mama had not intended that a queen be required to sew silk. The cloth puckered under the slightest tension, but if she left the threads too loose, they matted and frayed. Her rosebud looked like a splatter of blood.

"It's not as if I'll wear it," Joan grumbled, laying the veil on the arm of her chair.

In Palermo, noblewomen followed the ridiculous Saracen practice of covering their faces when they went out in public. But aside from the chapel and library, she despaired of ever being allowed even to venture outside her apartments.

Charisse held a torn sleeve up for scrutiny, silk cascading over her legs and onto the floor. Without looking at Joan, she chastened her: "The queen mother will expect to see *some* progress."

Sighing, Joan picked up the fancywork. William's mother had given her the veil, along with silk floss and a few threads of spun gold. Yet seeing the disastrous consequence, Marguerite probably regretted the gift.

Still, it was not the embroidery causing her ill humor. Joan was angry, to no purpose, with William, who had been absent from morning prayers the past three days. According to Marguerite, he had taken a group of noblemen from the mainland to see his cathedral. Joan was angry he had never taken her to Monreale, angry he misled her by staring at her earlier, angry that he apparently had no interest in her at all.

Sati entered the anteroom with a tray of oranges and cheese.

"Finally," Joan sighed, rising and leaving the veil on her seat cushion. She plucked a slice of fruit from the tray.

"Your pardon, Queen Joanna. The queen mother delayed me with a message for you."

Joan raised an eyebrow, sucking the sour juice from her orange.

"Queen Marguerite asks you, in King William's name, to attend supper tonight. An embassy has come from the king of England."

Joan gasped, almost coughing. She had not dined with Sicily's nobles since her wedding feast. "Who? Who has come?" The news must be good. She refused to let fear intrude on this moment of liberation.

Sati shrugged. "Englishmen."

"You must send word to Master Eugenius if you will not be at lessons," Charisse said.

Sati said, "The queen mother has spoken with your tutor."

"Of course she has," Joan said, a little wildly. Surely, William would no longer ignore her after seeing how her countrymen regarded her, how Papa's vassals treated the beloved daughter of the king of England. And the Englishmen would carry tales back home. Papa would hear of the splendor of Palermo's court, the health and happiness of his daughter. Joan trembled with excitement. What did she want Papa, perhaps even Mama, to know?

"Charisse," she murmured, "do I want to impress my husband or my father's embassy?"

"My lady?" Charisse frowned.

Sati asked quietly, "What impression do you wish to make?"

"I want them to know I am queen." Her words hung in the air. She wanted William to remember she was *his* queen. She wanted her father to be proud.

Pinching her lower lip, Sati answered, "They will know," then regarded Joan appraisingly.

Joan delivered herself into the hands of the Saracen. First, she was bathed. The tub was large enough to submerge her whole body at once. As soon as the water began to cool, Sati commanded two handmaidens to lift her out and dry her with rough linen towels. Then they soothed her chafed skin by rubbing scented oil on her arms and chest. She smelled roses, the sweetness cut by a hint of saffron.

Sati chose the gown—a deep blue silk covered with Greek patterning in silver and yellow embroidery. The bodice was padded in the bosom and tight through the waist. After Charisse pinned her hair under a veil, Sati teased out a few strands to lie at the nape of her neck. Then she applied ash-based color to her eyebrows and lashes and painted her lips the dark color of wine, an unnatural shade for a mouth. Joan resisted the urge to lick the stinging paint from her lips, certain the bitter taste would linger on her tongue.

"There," Sati said, pushing her before a long, narrow mirror. The woman staring back was unfamiliar: Queen Joanna, not Princess Joan.

Already it was dusk; the eunuchs of the Queen's Guard escorted her. She expected to stand in a receiving line and greet her husband's courtiers as she'd seen her mother do so many times. Instead, she was directed to wait in a small room off the dining hall until someone came to claim her. Finally, a young page fetched her to join her husband outside the door to the hall.

"My lord." She curtsied deeply, praying the trembling of her legs would not be noticeable.

William acknowledged her with a half smile, looking over her head. He crooked his arm for her to hold.

"Lady Joanna," he said, his voice surprisingly gruff. So ordinary a voice should not emerge from so exquisite a face. She understood how his father's enemies forgot their grievances at the mere sight of him. Curious and eager, she laid her hand on his arm and let him lead her into the room.

The courtiers were already seated around the massive tables, too numerous to count at a glance. The entire roomful rose, then bent their knees and bowed their heads. So, she and William were not expected to greet the guests before supper? How strange Sicily was. How inaccessible its king, like an emperor or god.

William's place was obvious, a wide chair at the center of the head table. The empty seat beside him must be hers. She stole a quick look around the table. It accommodated twenty or so: Bishop Palmer and Archbishop Walter of Palermo representing the Church; the queen mother and Constance; the duke of Apulia and Tancred of Lecce. With a start, she recognized Lord Anfusus of Devizes in the seat to the right of William. Devizes—the ancient castle where she had betrayed her father's trust so long ago.

She sat beside her husband, thrilled with the way the courtiers followed in little rippling waves. At the other tables, men and women sat intermingled. Only at the head table did the men sit to the right and women to the left. She was tucked in between William and Constance, but William immediately focused on the lord of Devizes. Disappointed, Joan turned to Constance.

"Who painted your face, child?" Constance said. "And that gown! You're trussed up like an odalisque."

Joan's hand flew to her mouth to hide the lips she knew were too bold. It hardly mattered that Constance was equally painted. On the Sicilian princess, Sicilian fashion did not appear out of place.

"Oh!" Constance said hurriedly, patting her shoulder. "I'm sorry, dear. You look beautiful. Truly, you do."

Joan blinked back tears, too embarrassed to be grateful for Constance's attempt to be kind. Had William also found her paint and dress garish?

The woman beside Constance, Tancred's pinch-faced wife, added, "Queen Joanna, you are a great beauty. A jewel in our lord king's crown."

Humiliated by their condescension, Joan tried to blame Sati. But why would Sati want to make her look foolish?

Servants began serving food: thinly shaved roasted duck drizzled with sweet, tangy sauce accompanied by slices of melon. Joan pretended fascination with her plate to avoid talking with Constance. She wished she could sink into the floor.

"Joanna." Her name sounded voluptuous when William mispronounced it. She turned, her cheeks hot and stomach fluttering. "Lord Anfusus says you and his wife are acquainted."

"Yes, my lord," she murmured. The lady of Devizes would not remember her fondly. Her spirits spiraled downward. She hated Sicily.

"Princess Constance will bring her to see you. Tomorrow, if you like?" He wore a smile as benevolent as an elderly priest's.

Miserable, Joan asked, "Where is she?" Why wasn't she at the table?

Lord Anfusus said, "Traveling tired her. We deeply regret she could not attend supper."

William leaned his head closer to hers. "The lady is with child."

Joan nearly choked. The lady of Devizes was fully forty, perhaps older. Before Joan could speak, Lord Anfusus laughed. William looked from one to the other.

"She doesn't know I've remarried," Anfusus said. "I'd forgotten how long the queen has been away from England."

"Three years," Joan said. Not so long for a man to lose a wife, remarry, and laugh about it. She decided she did not like this English lord.

"You remember Ermengarde? Of St. Gilles?" Anfusus asked.

"Ermengarde! Ermengarde is here?" The old lecher nodded. In a moment, her world had changed. Ermengarde would tell her everything and more.

Constance touched her arm. "Who is here, my lady?"

"A friend of mine from France."

William was smiling. The beauty of his mouth entranced her. He said, "Constance, tomorrow you must bring the lady to visit Joanna."

Joan beamed as she turned to the princess.

"Of course, my lord king," Constance said. "I live to serve."

Something flashed in the princess's eyes before she blinked and looked away. Joan jerked to see if William noticed. His eyes had dulled. He looked hurt, like a scolded boy.

Confused, Joan waited for someone to speak, but the next moment, a servant reached between her and William to ladle stewed meat into their bowls. William shifted to lean toward Anfusus, almost putting his back to her—she could barely hear what they said. William promised to take the visitors to Monreale. Lord Anfusus said something about the Pantocrator, a mosaic of Jesus on his heavenly throne, at the cathedral in Cefalù.

"You must see the foundation of Palermo's new cathedral," Archbishop Walter bellowed.

The men directed their discussion farther down the table to include the archbishop. It hurt her head to try to listen. Why was the archbishop building a new cathedral? She'd been married in the old one, and it had seemed splendid enough. Were there not enough churches in Sicily?

Three more courses followed, accompanied by drink; it grew terribly loud in the hall. Joan picked at her food and tried to think of visiting with Ermengarde. Then she would have conversation enough to last a year of suppers. But that didn't allay her current anxiety or loneliness. Why was Constance angry that she would see an old friend? It made no sense.

Unless . . . a dark thought snaked into her consciousness. The princess's anger might have a different basis. Who usually sat in the queen's chair? William had not seemed shocked or displeased when he greeted his elaborately decorated wife. So why had Constance accused her of dressing like an . . . an odalisque?

A horn blew, and the doors opened at the far end of the chamber. Servants swept in to clear away the last course, and more followed with trays of sweets and heavy wine. A space opened up in the middle of the hall as diners at the lower tables moved toward the walls. Joan roused from her torpor to watch the entertainments.

Half a dozen musicians entered the hall, blowing horns and banging drums with tinkling bells, accompanied by dancing girls. Twelve Saracen slave girls skittered across the floor barefoot, wearing strange robes of gauzy white cloth. The music was unfamiliar and eerie. At first, Joan could but stare, fascinated. As the girls twirled and writhed, the fabric shifted, lifting and falling with the breezes created by the movement. It embarrassed her to watch.

The other women at her table returned to their conversations after the merest glance at the entertainers. William, too, continued his discussion with Bishop Palmer over the heads of the Norman embassy, who were rapt. The dancers undulated closer. When they stood directly in front of the table, the Normans leaned forward in their chairs.

William turned from the bishop to attend to the dance. He wore the same detached half smile Joan was learning to recognize. Yet his eyes glittered with amusement as he leaned toward Lord Anfusus. He murmured something. Anfusus's head bobbed up and down, but his stare didn't falter. William's smile broadened for just a moment.

At the conclusion of the dance, William signaled to a servant behind him, who pulled back his chair. When the king stood, the entire assemblage followed. He waited for their obeisance, then held out his bent arm for Joan. He escorted her from the hall, her ladies falling in step behind, accompanying her as far as the stairway that led to her apartments. His own private chambers were near the front of the Royal Palace, up a different set of stairs.

"Did you enjoy supper?" he asked when she released his arm.

"I did." Taking a chance, she said, "I'd like to attend more often."

"You would?" Wrinkles appeared on his forehead.

Joan nodded, wondering how such a simple request had flummoxed him.

"We can arrange that." He sounded unconvinced. Joan wanted to ask who "we" was. Was he not king? Was she not queen? He opened his mouth, shut it, then opened it again. "I . . . I thought I would come to your apartments later. If you would have your maids make you ready."

*Now?* Feeling cold and hot at once, she managed to murmur, "Of . . . of course."

"Good." He let out his breath, sounding relieved. Joan dared not look at the faces of his guards or her own maids as the two entourages separated to ascend different flights of stairs.

Her handmaidens crowded after her into the bedchamber, murmuring irritatingly in Arabic as they scurried to obey Sati's harsh-voiced commands.

This was her chance. She must please William. This was her chance. The words rolled around and around in her head.

As Charisse unlaced Joan's gown and helped her wiggle from it, another handmaiden brought forth a pale yellow dress, little more than a shift, to cover her chemise. Joan stood still while she tied the single row of laces loosely up the back. Glancing down at the bodice's simple needlework, Joan realized there was no padding in the bosom. She shivered. How could she please him? She wasn't ready, not really a woman at all.

"You needn't worry," Sati said, approaching with paint to refresh Joan's face. "They say the king is a gentle lover."

Joan froze. "*They* say?"

Poised with a red-pigment stylus before Joan's mouth, Sati's hand wobbled. She drew back. Slowly, her taut frown relaxed, and she continued with a subtle shrug, "Rumor, my lady."

"Has he a mistress?" It was a foolish question. He was a powerful man with a child for a wife. Of course he had not been chaste.

"He keeps slaves," Sati said. "At the Cuba. They are of no consequence."

"Enough consequence to cause gossip," Joan protested.

"Of course." Now Sati sounded impatient. "Do you imagine women would not whisper about such a king? You are very much envied, my lady. Even his slave women are envied."

Before Joan could ask anything else, Sati brought the stylus to her mouth and began darkening her lips. The slave dancers had all been painted. Were the harem girls? Was this what William liked?

A knock on the door to the anteroom announced the king's arrival before they had time to unbind her hair. Sati herded the handmaidens from the bedchamber. Joan stared at Charisse.

"What do I do?" she whispered.

"Oh, Joan. Whatever he wishes. It will be all right." Looking as if she might cry, Charisse ran her hand down Joan's arm. It did nothing to alleviate her panic.

William entered; the distressed maid flushed, curtsied, and fled. Joan wished she could flee also.

"Joanna?" he asked, blinking. He seemed befuddled, as though unsure he had come to the right place.

"My lord," she said. Her voice was so low and deep it sounded as if she had a catarrh.

Red came to his cheeks. "You needn't be frightened." He slid past her, unwinding his girdle, then tossed it onto a high-backed chair near the balcony door.

Joan's face had never felt so heated. Her arms and legs would not move. Mute, she watched him sit and raise his tunic to his knees to unlace his boots.

She had to say something. The first thing she could think of popped from her mouth. "Do you always wear such tunics?"

William looked up at her quizzically.

"How do you ride?" Her father had shunned long tunics except on the highest of state occasions, claiming a man could not sit a horse dressed like a priest.

He stood and pulled out the sides of the tunic. "The cut is fuller than it appears." For a moment, he stared at the rich bro-cade, as if reassuring himself the answer was correct. He let go and faced her. "Will you need assistance?"

"W-with my laces." She turned around, trembling as his fin-gers touched her back. He pulled the gown open and helped peel it from her shoulders. It slid to the floor. She couldn't turn around; he would see how thin she was.

Behind her, she heard the rustling of clothing. The long tunic sailed by and landed on the chair with his girdle. "You needn't remove your chemise," he said. "Come. Lie down."

She shuffled past, trying to conceal herself, and climbed quickly onto the bed. He sat beside her, wearing a silken under-shirt that reached his thighs. He smelled of soap. His legs were the color of cream, sparsely covered with light hair, and spindly. No wonder he hid them.

"Lie down," he said again. He lay on top and began sliding against her. She thought his mouth brushed her hair, but then, with a click of his tongue that sounded irritated, he raised his hips and began pulling at her chemise. "Pull this up or you will have to remove it."

After she complied, William fell heavily against her and she cried out.

"Don't," he said. Joan bit her lip and willed herself not to sob as he made her his wife. His whole body tensed and then slackened. He sat up. Paint from her face had smeared across his undershirt. Without looking at her, he rose to find his tunic. She watched him pull it on, then sit to put on his stockings and boots. Still silent, he stood again and picked up his girdle, but laid it over his shoulder. She suspected he could not drape it properly alone.

"I won't trouble you any more than necessary, Joanna," he said, his voice high, almost whining. "But you understand, we must make an heir."

There was no answer she could make, except to nod and watch from the bed as he walked to the door in the dark. He fumbled with the handle. Relief that it was over mingled with the cold realization that she had somehow failed. They had exchanged no more than a dozen words.

"My lord?" she said, her heart beating fast, amazed at her own boldness. He turned. She could barely discern his face. Was he frowning? "Will you be going to Monreale again soon?"

"Monreale?" He said it as though he did not recognize the word. She felt an urge to slap him.

"Will you?"

"Yes. Yes, of course, I will. Barisanus has just completed his brass door. They'll be installing it. . . ." His voice trailed off. She wished it hadn't. For the briefest moment, he'd sounded impassioned.

"Would you take me to see it?"

"The cathedral?"

She could almost envision the wrinkling of his forehead, his confusion. She wondered if it was her accent that made him seem lost when she spoke.

"No, the mosque," she said sarcastically, in the careful Arabic Eugenius had taught her.

William laughed, but it was forced. He said, "I didn't think it would interest you. Of course, you must see it." She heard his hesitation and half expected him to say, "We can arrange that."

"Soon?" she pressed.

"Yes, soon. Good night, Joanna."

Pale light flooded the room for a moment and then the door shut.

EARLY THE NEXT MORNING, WILLIAM'S MOTHER AND AUNT brought the lady of Devizes to the queen's apartments. Ermengarde sprang forward to wrap Joan in a warm embrace.

"Princess! It is so wonderful to see you again." Joan felt the small swell of her friend's belly pressing against her own body. Over Ermengarde's head, Joan saw Constance smirk; Queen Marguerite's eyes widened with horror. Joan stiffened. Her friend's careless tongue had just disadvantaged them both before William's mother and aunt.

Ermengarde drew back. "I beg your pardon. I meant, my lady queen."

"You gave no offense. I'm delighted you're here. Please, sit." She gestured to the benches against the wall, plumped with pillows. A fire in the hearth staved off the light chill from the windows—the shutters had been left open to allow in the sun.

The women sat, Joan beside Ermengarde. She beckoned one of her handmaidens to bring a tray of sweets and an infusion flavored with carob.

Blanching, Ermengarde said, "No, thank you. My stomach is too easily turned these days. All these delicacies—I will forever regret that I did not sample any while I had the chance."

"Come to Sicily often," Joan said, "and you will have no cause for regret."

Ermengarde rubbed her middle. "Anfusus wanted to leave me in Devizes. If I were not carrying his child, he might have annulled the marriage for the ruckus I raised." The smile on her face showed she did not mean it. She actually seemed happy. Perhaps it was the baby. Joan's hand went to her own belly. Last night would be worth it, if William's seed took root.

"Why is your husband here? Did my father send him?"

"His chancellor did. Trade issues, my lady. Wheat and wine. Anfusus tried to explain but I . . ." Ermengarde shut her eyes and let her head loll sideways, then giggled.

"How did you come to be the lady of Devizes?" Joan asked, knowing once started, Ermengarde would need little coaxing to talk—little coaxing but abundant guidance. Ermengarde could not distinguish what was important from what was not.

"Just after Lady Anne passed, Anfusus's son died in a tournament. He is not fond of his daughter's husband, so he needed a wife." Blushing, she looked at her hands. "Someone young. He didn't care whether she had property or not. Your father spoke to Count Raymond. The count spoke to my father. They thought it a good match."

"So, my father and the count of Toulouse are on better terms?"

Ermengarde laughed. "My lord and I are not so important as that. Count Raymond saw no better use for me."

Joan detected a note of sadness in her laughter. "Is Lord Anfusus good to you?"

"He's very good," she said, raising her head and voice to include the other ladies. She would not say otherwise in front of strangers. Ermengarde, too, had matured.

"How is your brother?"

"Wonderful. Count Raymond knighted him. He's very proud. He is going to be married to a cousin of the duchess of Narbonne. She's sweet. She has hair the color of—"

"And what of his friend? Count Raymond's son?"

Charisse coughed. Joan ignored her.

"Lord Raymond?" Ermengarde's smile faltered, then reappeared even more bright. "He is well. But I think not so happy. He remarried, you know."

"Remarried? But what about the heiress of Melgueil?"

"They were married only ten months when his father declared her barren and arranged an annulment."

"After ten months?"

Her expression grew thoughtful. "He never wanted to wed her in the first place. Yet everyone said he was kind to her."

"Not kind enough. Why did the count want the marriage ended?"

"Oh, Count Raymond and the viscount of Carcassonne had been warring over some border territory. Someone suggested Lord Raymond marry the viscount's daughter to seal a truce. He could hardly be married to both of them."

"What happened to the girl?"

"She went to Fontevrault. What else could she do?"

Joan noticed Ermengarde rubbing the swell of her belly and made a quick prayer: God grant them a son.

"So, why isn't he happy with the daughter of Carcassonne?"

Charisse's embroidery scissors clattered to the floor and all heads turned.

"I beg your pardon," she murmured, retrieving them. Joan did not misunderstand the interruption. Charisse thought her too interested in the heir of Toulouse.

"Tell me about my brothers," Joan said as they all settled again. "I confess I am frightened to ask."

"They are well. Queen Margaret gave birth to a boy—did you hear? But it died in three days."

Joan crossed herself. "When?"

"Two years ago. No, almost three. They say your father took the news harder than the young king."

"I pray they will have another. What about Richard?"

"Duke Richard is quite the warrior. In Toulouse, we try not to mention his name." Ermengarde blinked as she smiled. It was a jest, yet not a jest. "Oh, but your older brothers were all together at the coronation of the new king of France."

"King Louis is dead?" Her thoughts churned. What did she know of the heir, Prince Philip, except that her mother once considered him a potential husband for her? Papa called the French king's son a monkey-faced boy with brains to match. And Richard had said he was an untrustworthy friend but a worse enemy.

She should have been told. Mama would be so disappointed in her. Monarchs died, heirs died, and she did not even know.

"No, no," Ermengarde said. "But he will be soon. Prince Philip was crowned king in November, just before my husband and I set sail to come here. The young king is seneschal, of course, so he had to attend. And Duke Richard and Count Geoffrey went to pay homage."

"Did my father attend?"

"No. Nor Prince John. Your father plans to make John king of Ireland. If the Irish allow it." She added hastily, "Of course, they will do as the king wishes."

Joan laughed to set Ermengarde at ease. "Who can say what the Irish will do?" Still, the room grew silent, and Ermengarde fidgeted. "I'm glad my brothers are not still bickering," she mused aloud. "But I do wish they would find common cause with my father, instead of standing beside the king of France."

"He is their overlord," Constance reminded her, her lips curling.

Joan was not in the mood for Constance's ill temper and answered with equal petulance. "Yes. But the king of England is their father."

"My dears," the queen mother said, getting to her feet, "we cannot let morning prayers begin without us. Joanna, we'll see you in the chapel."

Reluctantly, Joan rose. "Please come again, Ermengarde. I'll show you my garden."

"*Oc*, Queen Jeanne," Ermengarde said, using her native Occitan. Joan thought she put stress on the pronunciation of her name and wanted to embrace her again.

"We'll bring her," Queen Marguerite promised. She patted Joan's hair. "I know our Joanna misses England still. But when she becomes a mother, she will feel more at home."

Joan blushed. Everyone must know her marriage had finally

been consummated—there was no such thing as privacy at court. Her eyes flitted to Constance, who still glowered. No matter. Constance could be as ill-tempered as she pleased. William had promised to take her on a journey. An old friend had come to tell her all the news of home, and perhaps by the time Ermengarde left they would both be with child.

## TEN

WITH THE ENGLISH DELEGATION IN PALERMO, JOAN HAD expected her routine to change. She was disappointed. When William took Anfusus to Monreale, Ermengarde felt poorly and did not accompany her husband. No one thought to invite Joan.

She did not attend supper with the court again until Christmas Day. Though the meal was sumptuously presented, the mood in the hall was subdued. Constance whispered that the guests needed time to recover from the previous night's feast. Joan wondered if Constance had presided in the queen's place on Christmas Eve.

Ermengarde visited frequently, escorted each time by both Constance and Marguerite. It was as if they trusted neither Joan's visitor nor each other. Ermengarde had not lost her talent for filling a room with chatter, but Joan learned no more about her family except that Eleanor was still her husband's prisoner. Ermengarde provided that information with obvious discomfort, and the other women tactfully stared at their handiwork while Joan wiped her eyes.

February arrived and, with it, favorable tides for setting sail from the island. Ermengarde came to say good-bye, accompanied by Queen Marguerite.

"Where is Constance?" Joan asked, surprised.

"She sends her regrets," the queen mother said. "William

asked her to accompany Lord Anfusus while he visits the silk workshop."

"I'm afraid I can't stay long," Ermengarde said, sallow from fatigue, her eyes red-rimmed. "There is much to do before we board. I feel so queasy, and Anfusus says it's my own fault for insisting on coming." She forced a smile. "I'd do it again though, lady."

Joan took her hand and squeezed it. She knew how awful sea travel could be when one felt ill. "Come into the garden. Have one last walk about in peace, on solid ground." She glanced at Queen Marguerite, who appeared tired also. "Charisse," she said, gesturing toward the queen, "lend your arm to my lady mother so we might all enjoy the garden."

"Thank you, but I'll await you here." Queen Marguerite moved to one of Joan's cushioned benches. "My legs have swelled again. I can barely walk."

Joan quickly pulled a stool over to prop her mother-in-law's feet, noting the grayness of her skin. "Are you feeling well, lady? If you like, we'll stay inside."

"I'm fine. Go, walk." She smiled weakly.

Joan regarded her doubtfully. Was the queen more ill than she appeared? It was unlike Marguerite to yield to infirmity. Or was she wrong to believe Marguerite determined to listen to her every exchange with Ermengarde?

"We will not be gone long. If you need anything—" Joan started to indicate Sati, but Marguerite interrupted.

"Sati will attend you." Marguerite spoke with the firmness of a command.

Joan watched the girl lower her eyes and nod. Marguerite leaned back in her chair, a satisfied curve to her lips. It occurred to Joan that Sati was privy to everything that happened in her innermost chamber. And that the queen mother was uncannily well informed.

Sati turned to follow her mistress but did not lift her chin or meet Joan's gaze. It was impossible to read her expression.

With a tilt of her head toward the doorway, Joan returned her attention to the open, uncomplicated Ermengarde. "Shall we?"

Ermengarde smiled her assent. They descended the stairs, the maid in tow.

"It's so good to have a word alone with you," Ermengarde murmured.

Joan put her arm around Ermengarde's waist, drawing her closer. She led her friend toward the fountain. It was plain, compared to others she'd seen in Sicily, but the water fed into a pool containing fish of all different colors. She liked to pretend the fish had been William's idea.

"Shall we sit?" she asked, pointing to the bench beside the fountain.

"No. I want to walk. It's only that I have an ache in my side. Queen Marguerite assures me it is nothing, just the baby growing." She continued pacing.

"What did you wish to talk about?" Joan asked. If this was nothing more than Ermengarde's usual chatter, the queen mother would find no reason to criticize. Still, there might be something important in it. Had one of her brothers sent a message?

Ermengarde's face crumpled. "Perhaps I shouldn't say anything. I wouldn't dare, except I've lived with the shame for so long. I thought I could tell you, because you knew him. You'd understand. Besides, I can confess to you and not have to see it in your eyes every day."

Joan stared. What had she done? "Good heavens. Whatever it is, it can't possibly be as terrible as you think."

"You . . . you asked about Lord Raymond."

Joan nodded.

"I . . . I kissed him."

"You *kissed* him?"

"He kissed me. Oh, Joan, it happened two years ago. Lord Raymond was in St. Gilles, and I . . . I cornered him in the garden. My father was giving me to a man I had never even seen. And I knew Raymond's father would force him to marry another woman against his wishes." Her voice softened. "Raymond looked so surprised and concerned to see me there without my maids. I don't know how I ever found the courage to do it."

"No," Joan breathed. "Nor do I." She felt a knot in her stomach, admiration mixed with disapproval. And something else she couldn't name.

"I told him I didn't want to marry Anfusus. And that if *he* took me—"

"Ermengarde!" Her knees almost buckled. She remembered young Walter grabbing her in the stairwell with a similar plan. "Ermengarde, you didn't!"

"As soon as I said it, I wanted to die. All my life I've loved him. I never dared hope he might love me."

Joan didn't know what to say. She turned her head, unable to look at her friend.

"That's when he kissed me. I'll never forget it. I would have done anything . . . but he moved away. He looked anguished, or—oh, I don't know. He said my brother is one of his closest friends. And we were betrothed to other people. He said he was sorry, but we shouldn't be in the garden alone. He does love me; I am sure of it. But I'll never see him again."

"It is better that you don't," Joan said, nauseated with confusion.

"I know. His father would never let us marry. I'm fortunate to have Anfusus. And with this baby . . . oh, but, Joan. I'll never forget how he kissed me. The look on his face. It's so unfair."

"Life isn't fair," Joan mumbled, echoing her mother. It was the wrong thing to say. She hadn't intended to sound so insensitive, but she felt angry with Ermengarde. She had a husband who doted on her, a station above what she might have expected. She had a baby in her womb. And she had been kissed with passion by a man who loved her. By Lord Raymond. Life wasn't fair.

Ermengarde wiped the tears from her face with the back of her hand but made no answer. *Ermengarde* was speechless.

Joan tried again. "I'm sorry. It must cause you great sorrow. I don't know Lord Raymond well, but he seemed very kind. At least you can draw comfort from the fact that he loves you—too much to dishonor you."

"Anfusus must never know. They say he was always faithful to his previous wife, even after she fell so ill." Ermengarde sighed raggedly. "And I think it would be hard to be wed to Lord Raymond. I doubt he could be faithful, even to a woman he loved."

"Is he truly so . . . wicked?"

In a low voice, Ermengarde said, "He fathered two daughters after he remarried, with different women, neither his wife."

It was true what Mama said about men. And true that women were fools to love them.

"You'll be more content with Lord Anfusus."

"I'm glad I told you. It has weighed so heavily on my heart, but I could not confess to the priest."

"You were young and confused. It was a mistake, not a sin." Joan doubted the words were convincing, though Ermengarde nodded and tried to smile. "Come, we should go back."

Arm in arm, they returned to Joan's chamber and embraced one final time, bringing tears to Joan's eyes. Ermengarde left with the queen mother.

Sati's deep voice sliced through the quiet. "You were kind to her, my lady."

Joan felt a slash of fear. Sati had heard her excuse Ermengarde for trying to give herself to a man she could never marry.

Defensively, she snapped, "I don't suppose the queen mother would approve."

Picking up a cup Marguerite had left beside her chair, Sati said, "It is your good fortune she does not know."

FIVE DAYS AFTER ERMENGARDE'S DEPARTURE, JOAN'S FLOW came a third time. So many weeks had passed she thought she might be with child, but Charisse said it was always so the first year. Until a girl's body adjusted to womanhood, the intervals would be erratic.

This time she ached deep in her belly and experienced a headache so severe she was forced to take to her bed for the better part of two days. Finally, she recovered, but did not return to lessons with Master Eugenius until her flux had ceased. As soon as she arrived, he began grumbling and set her to reading geography, knowing she hated it.

When she left the library, Sati, waiting by the door with two eunuchs, greeted her with a smile. "A message for you. The king will come to your apartments after supper. We must hurry to prepare."

Already disgruntled by the tutor's treatment, she found Sati's news further cause for frustration. William ignored her except to come to her bed.

Sati and another slave, Fatima, drew her bath while Charisse aired the bed linens and swept the chamber. Sati rubbed her skin with a saffron-tinged oil, leaving it tingling with a faint yellow glow. Charisse brought an armload of blue pimpernel from the garden to decorate the washstand and left the balcony door open for air. The breeze felt deliciously cool after the heat of the bath. Sati provided a light cotton chemise, dyed pale green and embroidered around the neck and hem with primroses. Cotton was even softer than Sicilian silk, and Joan giggled as the cloth brushed her skin.

"There are some things I do like about Sicily," she murmured.

A tray had come from the kitchen, so she ate her supper quickly then rinsed her mouth with rosewater. She walked around her bedchamber, enjoying the cool air rustling against her chemise. She felt a ridiculous urge to run down into the garden and dip her feet in the fountain. Instead, she merely walked to the door and stared over the balcony.

A quarter-moon shone thinly through the clouds. Had it been day or night when Ermengarde found Lord Raymond alone? She imagined meeting Raymond in her moonlit garden.

"Lady? The king is here," Charisse said.

Joan hurried to her bed and climbed under the sheet. "Let him enter."

William walked into the room.

"It's chilly in here," he said, frowning. He noticed the balcony door and started to close it, but instead he paused and gazed into the darkness. He stood quietly for what seemed a long time.

At last, he shut the door and turned. "Did you enjoy your friend's visit?" he asked. "The one with child?" he added as if she had so many visiting friends he needed to make himself clear.

"Yes," she said. She shouldn't be annoyed by his fatuous attempt at conversation—at least he was making an effort. Then she guessed—of course, that was why he had come. Someone had informed him she had not conceived; he must try again.

He paced across her floor twice before stopping beside a chair. He sat and pulled off his shoes, then stood to lift the hem of his tunic and peel off his stockings. He dropped the hem and faced her. With the Greek-style tunic covering him from shoulders to floor, he might as well have been fully dressed.

He sat on the edge of her bed. She thought he looked distracted.

"Would you like . . . some wine?" he asked.

She shook her head, then added quickly, "Would you, my lord?"

He nodded but made no move to summon a servant. Seeing no other option, Joan left her bed. She crossed the room, feeling naked in her chemise, and pushed the door open a crack.

"Charisse. Bring some wine, please. And two cups." Her voice shook. Perhaps wine might help, after all.

She walked back, aware of William watching her. He pushed the sheet to the foot of the bed and gestured for her to sit. When she reached for the sheet to cover herself, he said, "Don't," the word rattling in his throat.

She remembered snippets of troubadours' lays—of men's covetous glances and lovers' scorching stares. She forced herself to meet his gaze and found it not appraising, but troubled. He blinked and turned his head.

Charisse knocked, then brought in the wine. Averting her eyes, she set the jar and two cups on the table by the bedside and hurried out. William poured and handed Joan a cup. She sipped slowly, watching him drink. When he set his cup aside, she took another large gulp and handed hers to him to place on the table. He lay back on the bed beside her, and she wondered if she was expected to touch him.

William sat up abruptly. He drank more wine. Then he stood, unwrapped his girdle, and pulled his tunic over his head. His chest was thin beneath the white shirt, his hips narrow, his arms soft. Had he ever lifted a sword, she wondered?

He flopped back onto the bed. "Oblige me," he said brusquely.

"What do you want me to do?"

With a grimace of what seemed to be irritation, he sat upright, shook his head, and stared past her. She couldn't bear to look at him either.

"Joanna?" he said suddenly.

"Yes?"

He made a noise, as if he meant to say something, then thought better of it. For a long moment, he sat without speaking on the edge of her bed. "How old are you, Joanna?"

"Fourteen."

"How old is your friend?"

Her gut knotted. "Ermengarde? Sixteen, perhaps."

She heard his breath come out through his teeth. He muttered something she could not catch. He thought she was too young. Two years was too long to wait. The count of Toulouse had waited but ten months.

"My lord?" she said, panicked.

"Hmm?"

What could she say? She said nothing, just picked at the sheet until he looked at her. His eyes were round and sorrowful, edged by dark crescents.

He had been strange tonight, gazing outside, approaching her with reluctance. It would be difficult for him to lie with her, she realized, when he had experienced no such difficulty the first time.

"Are you well?" she asked bluntly.

His eyes widened in surprise, then he shifted away from her. "Do I seem ill?"

"You look tired." She thought she should not comment on the other.

"Tired? I suppose I am." He drew in a long breath and let it out slowly.

She wanted to ask what he did that made him so tired. The palace was full of secretaries, notaries, and clerks, but she had no idea what any of them did. She wanted to understand how William governed.

"Is there anything I can do?" she asked.

He stared at her with the wrinkled forehead that annoyed her so much. "No. No, there is nothing. I'm tired because I haven't been sleeping."

"Why not?"

"Why?" He smiled his disinterested half smile and answered not to her but to a space above her head. "I haven't been sleeping because I am agitated with the archbishop."

"Archbishop Walter?"

"He was my tutor once, did you know? He taught me how to appreciate architecture, how to search for meaning in Greek philosophies, how . . ." William sighed. "But now, he searches for obstacles to throw in my path. He spends enormous sums on his cathedral, in hope of convincing the pope we don't need another archbishopric in Sicily."

"But we do?"

"Yes."

Clambering to sit up on her heels rather than reclining, she begged, "Explain to me why."

"To thwart the archbishop."

Joan laughed. "That is circular logic."

This time he looked straight at her, the absent look gone. "The kings of Sicily have been granted authority over the Sicilian Church equal to that of a papal representative. This privilege was bestowed upon my grandfather in gratitude for services rendered to the Holy Father, passed down to my father, then me, and confirmed by each successive pope. The archbishop claims the rights should now revert back to the Church."

Joan understood all too well the politics of king against archbishop, the tenuous balance of power between church and state. "That's why you're building the cathedral in Monreale?"

"A cathedral and an abbey. The abbey will be of the Benedictine order; its abbot will automatically be accorded archiepiscopal status. Palermo's archbishop will have no authority over Monreale."

"And will Archbishop Walter find his diocese reduced?"

"Several parishes have already been transferred to the control of Monreale."

Joan smiled at his cleverness. William had substantially diminished Archbishop Walter's power—and enhanced his own.

"How did you get the pope to agree to such a scheme?"

William did not return the smile. Had she offended him?

He cleared his throat. "You wanted to see the construction? We'll go tomorrow, after morning prayers."

"Thank you." She untucked her legs and sat back on the bed. William waited a moment longer, then stood and gathered his things. He was leaving. He might be too tired to lie with her, but was he coming to like her better?

"Sleep well, my lord."

He had already turned away. "Perhaps I will."

SATI AND CHARISSE SKIPPED MORNING PRAYERS TO PACK THE queen's trunk, in case they were delayed in Monreale overnight; Sati ordered Fatima to accompany Joan to the chapel. As they entered the balcony, Princess Constance whirled around and slapped the slave for stepping on her hem. Joan slid between them at once. The dress was not torn, not even soiled.

"I will discipline my own maids," she said stonily. Constance glared.

Joan walked past the princess, allowing Fatima to scuttle into place. Constance's face was a thundercloud, while the queen mother smiled and smiled. One was never happy unless the other was sullen. Joan shook her head. A careless maid was not the source of Constance's irritation, yet whatever the issue this morning, she didn't care. She wanted no part of their rivalry. God forbid they would expect her one day to take sides.

She peeked once or twice at William, but he was fervent in his prayers. She prayed earnestly also—that she would soon carry William's heir, that he would enjoy her company.

Charisse and Sati met her outside the chapel, where a litter waited. For the brief walk from the front gate, all three wore heavy veils as protection from sharp-eyed would-be gawkers. Joan couldn't imagine anything more absurd. Except, perhaps, being required to travel in a litter as if she did not know how to sit on a horse. It would slow the entire cortege. She hoped William would not resent the pace.

It was well after midday when the quiet of the countryside gave way to the noise of the city. At last the litter halted, shifted, and she heard William's voice.

"You may come out."

They veiled their faces and Charisse pushed apart the curtains. William offered his hand to help Joan disembark. She took his arm as they mounted the steps to the north porch of the cathedral.

"God's teeth," she swore, tripping. She could scarcely see through the opaque veil. Her legs were clumsy and tingling from the long, cramped ride. "I might as well be blind in this fool hawk's hood."

She thought she heard a gruff chuckle. William pushed back her veil.

"I won't tell my mother if you don't," he murmured in her ear. She smiled at him, but he was already looking elsewhere, sweeping his hand out across the view. "It will be grander than the cathedral in Cefalù." He sounded awed, as well he should. The gleaming, white stone building, even incomplete, was massive. "There is a cloister behind. You should see it now—you won't be allowed once the monks move in."

He walked quickly up the stairs, with no trace of the previous night's lassitude. She had to skip to keep up. He paused before the entrance, a large brass door intricately engraved with Greek archers, saints, and a frightening depiction of Christ's descent into hell.

Joan caught her breath. It was sublime.

"Barisanus's work?" she asked, glad to remember the name of the artisan.

He smiled. "Yes. See?" He gave it a light push and the door swung open. Perfectly set on its hinges, it did not even squeak.

"Marvelous," she said, following him inside.

Sunlight filtered through the casements and unfinished roof. It was the largest cathedral she'd ever seen and the only time she'd ever seen one being erected. Workmen crawled about the scaffolding, seemingly oblivious to the presence of the king. The sound of hammer on stone rang from all corners in a discordant chorus, while dust burst forth at intervals and rained down from above.

"How splendid," she murmured.

"Yes. Well, it will be. The walls will be covered from one end to the other in mosaics."

"So many?"

"Ah, Joanna, yes."

"The greater glory to God." A man's deep voice boomed.

Joan jumped. "Bishop Palmer!"

"Sire. My lady queen." The bishop bowed to William first, then Joan. "Impressive, is it not?"

William slipped his arm from her hand. "Richard, the queen must be returned by sundown, but that should give you an hour or two."

"More than adequate, my lord."

"Be sure she sees the cloister."

The bishop nodded. "Yes, sire."

"My lord, where will you be?" Joan demanded.

William's head jerked back as if the sound of her voice startled him.

"The king has a conference with the chief engineers," the bishop answered smoothly.

Joan fixed her eyes on William, hoping her disappointment was not evident. With feigned indifference, she asked, "You'll return tomorrow?"

"No." He wrinkled his brow. "Afterward, I'll be hunting."

"At the Cuba?" He kept his harem there. If he had had trouble lying with her, it was not because there was something wrong with *him*.

He nodded, then his gaze faltered. "In the deer park," he amended.

Joan heard a shattering of glass somewhere off in the distance. William heard it, too, because he cringed. She hoped it was something large and beautiful and expensive.

## ELEVEN

MASTER EUGENIUS SNATCHED A YELLOWING SCROLL FROM her hands. "Queen Joanna, I must insist you confine your studies to what I've assigned."

"I thought King William did not believe in censorship."

"For *scholars*, lady." Eugenius sniffed. "Some things are inappropriate for a wife."

"Pah." The scroll had been loose on the library table, in plain view, and the artful Arabic lettering caught her eye. It was a love poem—she'd deciphered that much before Eugenius's confiscation. "My Arabic would improve more quickly if you gave me something interesting to read."

"Not this interesting," he grumbled. He rolled the scroll tightly and stuck it in a basket on the floor.

The suffocating humidity of too many long August days had made her testy. Being trapped in the library—stale-aired and close, even at dusk—did not improve her mood.

"Has the king read it?" she demanded.

"I wouldn't know."

"I thought you said he's read everything in here."

"Everything of worth," he said, reaching for his copybook and quill pen. "You left off—"

"But you have read it."

Eugenius's quill paused above the vellum. He began again. "You left off at the eighteenth line of book six."

"Why did my husband bother to acquire a work without worth?"

"It was a gift."

"A gift?" *Love poetry?* She narrowed her eyes. "From whom?"

"My lady, I don't—"

"From whom?"

"The Greek Emperor Manuel Comnenus." She must have appeared dumbfounded because one side of the tutor's mouth twitched in amusement. "Did you expect a lovely Almohad princess?"

"No. Although that would be a more interesting tale." Joan did not wait for him to accuse her of frivolousness. "So, when did the emperor send my husband this gift? When William was supposed to marry his daughter?"

He nodded, apparently unsurprised that Joan knew of her husband's previous betrothal.

"Was the king disappointed the girl did not arrive?"

"He was insulted," Eugenius said. Then he cocked his head and bit the end of his quill. "Rather the *realm* was insulted. The king mourned," he mumbled around the pen.

"Oh."

The quill fell to the table. "Lady, he did not mourn the loss of Princess Maria. His younger brother accompanied him to Taranto to meet her. On the return to Palermo, the prince was struck with a lethal fever."

"How terrible for William," Joan murmured. Losing a brother was one tribulation she had been spared.

"More cause for him to hate the Comneni."

Joan eyed him sidelong. Here was an interesting avenue to

explore. "Master Eugenius, I am shocked. Does my husband truly hate the Greek emperor?"

"That question would be better directed to him."

His response dug a hollow in the pit of her stomach. She had not spoken alone with William in six months, not since he had abandoned her in Monreale. Turning her palms up and forcing a smile, she said, "You know the king speaks ill of no man."

Eugenius snorted. "Which will serve him better in heaven's kingdom than here."

"Was his father any different?"

"The old king mistrusted everyone. With good reason. It's hard to believe he lived long enough to die a natural death."

She paused, knowing if she interrogated him he might clamp his mouth shut; yet curiosity drove her on. "Are any of the old king's enemies still living?"

"Huh. You know of Tancred."

"Only that he exists. Are there others?"

Eugenius shuffled away, slippered feet scuffing loudly, to feign concentration on a row of codices on one of the shelves. Joan rose and followed until she stood at his side.

He said, "Perhaps the king does not want you concerning yourself with—"

"He abhors ignorance, even in a wife. That is why I have a tutor."

Eugenius licked his lips and would not look at her. "It is not what I am supposed to teach."

"Who decides what I am allowed to learn?"

He turned his back to her again.

"Who tells you what is acceptable? Queen Marguerite?"

He didn't answer.

She ran her finger along the shelf, making a trail in the thin layer of dust. "Are you a teacher or aren't you?"

Finally, slowly, he turned around. "What do you want to know?"

"Tell me about Sicily's past. How it shaped King William."

He sighed. "You are very intelligent, milady. I will give you your history lessons. But don't blame me if you discover things you'd have rather not learned."

SICILIANS DID NOT WILT IN THE SUMMER. CONSTANCE, IN PARticular, seemed to have blossomed with the scarlet poppies that year, growing more pleasant and smiling more the hotter the weather.

"Heat has not always made you so sullen. Did the summers feel milder at the Zisa?" she said, gently teasing. "Or perhaps you found them less stifling because you had greater freedom there?"

It was true, though Joan had not appreciated it at the time—she'd been permitted free run of the Zisa and its gardens. Here she could not leave her apartments without her eunuch guards. Before she could consider how to respond, Constance continued, "Have a cool drink," raising a hand to summon Sati. But when the maid brought the water pitcher forward, the princess shook her head. "No. That has been sitting out in this heat. Bring a new one."

Sati turned to Joan, one eyebrow arched in question. Water from the kitchens would be no cooler. Joan held back a huff of irritation. Constance often made unreasonable demands of the slaves. Yet the maid could not be permitted to give offense.

"Go, Sati," Joan said with a nod.

The girl bowed, then bore the pitcher from the room.

Constance smiled and took a bite of the honey cake Joan had offered. "This is delicious. Why aren't you eating?"

"It's too hot for such heavy food." It was too hot even to walk in the garden. They sat in the day chamber, curtains drawn against the sunlight. Fatima lazily swished a fan to stir the air.

"Normans," Constance laughed, with a toss of her head. "Are you still homesick?"

"Sometimes." And yet, where was home? Poitiers? Fontevrault Abbey? Sarum? She had been in Sicily for three and a half years. She had never lived in one place for so long before. Shouldn't Sicily be home?

"But . . ." Constance's gaze shifted slightly. "You are not unhappy?"

"Certainly not. What reason could I have to be unhappy?"

In the nave of the Monreale cathedral Joan had almost been hurt by her husband; she had vowed it would not happen again.

"You don't find the king . . . neglectful?"

"He's busy, as a king should be."

"Yes, he is." Constance smoothed her palms over her skirt. "Still, Queen Marguerite thinks he should make more time for you."

Marguerite had been hinting that Joan should make a greater effort to draw William's attention. It had never occurred to her the woman might be putting similar pressure on her son. But she was not so naive as to discuss the queen mother's maneuvering with the princess. One would have to be a fool to become entangled in their rivalry.

"Although," Constance continued, "if he neglected his other duties, she'd scold him for that too." She settled back into her chair. "And you? Have you wearied yet of all Marguerite's . . . advice?"

Joan forced a smile. "I am always grateful for it."

Snickering, Constance said, "As am I." Her brow puckered, and she leaned forward. "Dear, just remember that Marguerite has had a difficult life, and sometimes her own wishes are contradictory. If you try too hard to please her, you may find you've alienated her instead."

"I don't know what you mean."

"A maiden shouldn't speak of such things, but I worry . . ." Constance paused, stealing a glance over her shoulder, though they were alone but for Charisse and Fatima. "Joanna, who knows what Marguerite's imagination might conjure? Especially if William *were* to begin spending more time with you. What if Marguerite were to think him too preoccupied with his pretty young wife?"

"Hmph. That is hardly reason for concern."

Constance's eyes narrowed. "Marguerite is jealous of her son's time and attention. And please do not be offended, but . . . she is suspicious of your mother's reputation."

"My mother—" Joan started to protest.

"Bewitches men. Oh, I know it is all gossip and troubadours' exaggeration, but Marguerite . . . well. Some days she complains you are too childish for William, but more often she moans that it was a mistake to marry her son to Eleanor's daughter."

Joan fought to understand. A mistake to marry William to her because of Mama's reputation? She knew her father had been unfaithful, but Mama?

"Joanna." Constance's voice was gentle. "Don't be frightened. You must simply demonstrate your youth and innocence when you are with William. Then he will have no cause to complain of you."

How much more innocent could he expect her to be? She knew she had not pleased him sufficiently. Was Constance saying that was a good thing? Clearly, Mama had not taught her enough about the politics of the bedchamber.

"I . . . I don't understand."

"It would set Marguerite's mind at ease if you were more . . . reticent when William—"

Sati walked into the room, her face smooth as a mask. Constance turned red, and her hands fluttered up from her lap. "No, of course you don't understand. I'm speaking nonsense. And here is our water. It is cooler, I hope?"

"Yes, lady," Sati said huskily.

Joan glanced from one to the other. Constance looked as though she'd been caught cheating at merels. What else had she intended to say before Sati returned? What would Sati report to Marguerite?

JOAN ASKED HERSELF, HAD SHE EVER LOVED CHRISTMAS COURT?

This year, fewer of the king's subjects made the journey to Palermo, and William appeared even less interested in the festivities than usual. The court was distracted by a more momentous occasion than the anniversary of the Savior's birth. William had decided—or had been informed by his *familiares*, the three head counselors of the realm (Bishop Palmer, Matthew of Ajello, the chief notary, and Caid Richard, the chamberlain)—that it was time he toured his domains. The king would leave following the feast of Epiphany, visiting Messina first and then the mainland. He was expected to be absent from Palermo for more than eight months.

For Joan, remembering the constant movement of her father's court, it didn't seem strange William should make such a journey. Rather, it seemed strange that his leaving Palermo was deemed such an event.

To her dismay, she learned she would not be permitted to accompany him but would instead be sent back to the Zisa for her own "restful retreat." Marguerite said Sicilian women preferred the comforts of the palace to the rigors of travel. Politely, she had reminded Marguerite that she was quite accustomed to traveling and would not be discomforted. She wanted to see more of Sicily. Marguerite said she would be a distraction, and said it so coldly Joan saw she should have listened to Constance. Now the queen mother would be watching her even more suspiciously.

How did they expect her to give him an heir?

Once again, William caught her off guard. Four nights before his departure, he appeared at the door to her apartments. She had already changed from her gown into a nightdress, a shift of plain blue cotton.

"My lord!" Joan gasped.

Behind her, the women shuffled out of the way, tidying pillows and picking up strewn garments.

"May I come in?" he asked, flushing slightly. "I should have sent word."

She stepped back to allow him entrance. Did a man need to send word to his wife? She couldn't imagine her father sending a courier around to her mother when he wanted to lie with her. She must be one of the duties he needed to attend to before his tour began. Irritation put sap in her veins.

"Come in, sire." She turned on her heel and led him into her bedchamber, past the bowing handmaidens.

When they stepped into her chamber, she took a deep breath and considered. She must make him desire her without appearing wanton. If only she had known he was coming. She hadn't bathed or painted her face. She probably looked like an English shepherdess. Now what should she do? What did his slaves at the Cuba do to tempt him?

"Shall I help you with your tunic, sire?"

"Pardon?"

"Your . . ." she gestured to his clothes. She'd have to unwind his girdle first, she supposed.

"Oh. No." He began undressing. She pictured herself sitting at his feet and yanking off his boots—the thought was so ridiculous she almost snorted. She had to look away.

But what would he think? She forced herself to look at him again. He was staring at the wall, absently untying the laces of his leggings. Whatever he was thinking about, it wasn't her embarrassment. His mind was not even in the room.

"My lord? Shall I close the shutters? Are you chilled?"

"Pardon?" He seemed almost to startle at the sound of her voice.

"The shutters? Shall I close them?"

"Are you cold?"

"I asked if you were."

"No. No." He pulled off his hose. "Lie down, Joanna. The bed will be warmer."

Again he wore his long undershirt and allowed her to keep her nightdress on. But when he lay down beside her and lifted their clothes, his skin felt clammy.

He hadn't asked for wine, but she smelled it on his breath; he was breathing through his mouth as if ill with catarrh. Then he grunted hard through his nose, and an efflux of blood spilled onto her shoulder and pillow.

"Oh!" Joan grabbed the girdle draped across her footboard and pressed it to his face, pinching the bridge of his nose as the nurse used to do when John suffered nosebleeds. William's face was pale, with purplish crescents beneath his closed eyes. For a moment, with his head pressed against her breast, she felt a wave of tenderness.

At last the hemorrhage ceased. Color came back to his face. William rose from the bed, arms and legs graceless. He wadded up the bloodied cloth and stuffed it into the hearth fire, sending a sickeningly sweet cloud of smoke into the air.

"I'm sorry," he said. His gruff voice now sounded far away. "I frightened you."

"No. I wasn't . . ." She should have admitted to fright. What else was there? Disgust? Pity?

They looked away from each other, half dressed, their business unfinished and neither about to suggest they start again.

William cleared his throat. "I will be leaving soon. For Messina."

"Yes." She wondered if she dare ask him for permission to accompany the tour.

"When I return you will be . . . a little older."

Joan flushed. God help them. She was no temptress. And he could not exert himself without bleeding from the nose. She could imagine Mama *and* Papa throwing up their hands in disgust. She no longer wanted to go with him. She wanted him gone.

## TWELVE

JOAN SIGHED AND FLIPPED THE CLOTH SHE WAS EMBROIDERING to check the tension of the thread. Constance had spent many lengthy hours providing companionship. The princess's deft fingers could create peacocks and lions, but Joan contented herself with simple repetitive patterns.

She was having a hard time concentrating. For two lonely years she had been living at the Zisa as though in exile. Thoughts of William filled her head. He had eventually returned to the capital after his eight-month tour, but no one ever bothered to recall her to the palace. Nor had her husband seen fit to visit her. Banished from his company, how was she supposed to fulfill the duty of a queen?

She drew a breath, feeling her face grow warm. For the past few months she had been dreaming of her husband. But sometimes it was not William. She did not know what rumors were whispered about her mother, yet it shamed her to think wantonness might truly run in her blood.

She glanced at Charisse, hoping she had not attracted scrutiny with her sighing and blushing, but the maid's nose was buried in her own needlework. They were otherwise alone, seated in the main hall on the second floor with its large windows where they might enjoy the view back toward the city. Luxury no longer overwhelmed her, and this was the best of the palace's rooms.

Fatima entered, smiling. "My lady," she said in labored French, "Master Eugenius has come."

"God be praised!" Joan exclaimed, springing from her chair. Her tutor had been ill for a month—or claimed to be. More likely he had been ill-tempered.

She hurried down the stairs and passed through the damp Fountain Room to the small antechamber Eugenius still preferred. Whatever brought him back, he was welcome.

He rose as she entered.

"My lady." He bowed. His hair was thinning, yet as artificially black, sleek, and olive-scented as ever.

"Master, I see you are better. I'm glad."

"Huh. You see what you wish to see. One does not recover from old age."

She smiled, knowing enough to flatter his vanity. "You're not old. What have you brought?" She gestured at a leather satchel on the table. He stepped forward, blocking her from reaching it.

"The archbishop received a letter from England. He allowed me to copy a portion."

"Oh! Oh, Eugenius!" Joan could hardly catch her breath. News of home! She rubbed her itchy palms against her skirt, then tried to step around him. He held up his hand.

"In a moment, lady. That news is old; it will keep. I have other that is bitter."

"Bitter?" Not trusting her legs, she turned and sat in the closest chair.

"Concerning Constantinople."

"Ah." Only more about the Greek Empire. "Tell me."

"The young emperor and his mother have been overthrown. By a cousin of the late Emperor Manuel Comnenus, a man named Andronicus Comnenus. He killed them all—Emperor Alexius, his mother, even Princess Maria and her husband."

*William might have been Maria's husband.*

She murmured, "So, this Andronicus is now emperor? What does it mean?"

"It means a cruel, craven man is in control. His first action was to incite the Greeks to massacre the Latins in the city. A shortsighted prejudice, and unfortunate for the empire. It has earned him the enmity of all of the West, especially the French king."

"Philip?" She searched her memory for anything she'd heard about Philip's involvement with the East. Eugenius always told her she should be more conversant with the politics of the Eastern Empire, but he was a Greek. In truth, she cared less about Constantinople than Poitou.

"His sister Agnes had been betrothed to Alexius."

Her stomach sank. "Did Andronicus kill her, too?"

"Worse. He wedded her. She is only twelve years old and he more than sixty, but they say he made the marriage true."

Joan hid her face in her hands, sick with pity. "What will King Philip do?"

"Do? Nothing. He is too busy with your father and your brothers. Read the letter. I will leave it with you." Eugenius reached for his cloak, hung over one of the chairs.

"You won't stay?" she asked, rising to her feet. She would have welcomed more conversation.

"I cannot, lady. The night air chills my chest. I had hoped to come earlier, but the roads were still muddy from last night's rain, and it smells of more to come."

He draped himself in the heavy cloak. His face was craggier

than she remembered, and his chest had grown thin. Rain never used to keep him from the Zisa.

As he bowed to take his leave, Joan reached for his arm. "Thank you, Master. I appreciate you remembering me."

"Huh," he said, hunching his shoulders. "You're not forgotten here, though you like to complain it is so."

She withdrew her hand and pouted. Only Eugenius would scold her for trying to be kind—Eugenius and Mama. Kindness was weakness.

As soon as the door closed, she snatched the letter from the bag. He had copied the portion he thought would be most interesting to her, but out of context it took a few starts before she got her bearings.

Richard's unruly vassals had taken up arms again. Two of the most quarrelsome, the Angoulême brothers, found a new grievance and rebelled, allying with Aimar of Limoges.

Limoges. For a moment, memory transported her back to the Limousin castle where John's betrothal had been announced. She had once harbored such childish hopes—her parents' reconciliation, her brothers' more honorable behavior—all dashed by young Lord Raymond's revelation. The same Lord Raymond who wanted Ermengarde but could not have her, the same lord who sometimes visited her dreams.

Joan forced her concentration to the page.

Richard drove the disloyal brothers from the Angoulême; but they had powerful friends in the region, all of whom disliked him. The Angoulême brothers, seeing they could not defeat Richard, fell back on a more devious plan. They appealed to King Philip, calling him the rightful overlord of the French lands. And Philip, the snake, accepted their homage.

Joan drew her arms tight across her chest and read on, knowing what was to come. Papa would not accept France's interference. Sure enough, in May, the king brought his own forces to join Richard's and ordered Henry to help his brother as well.

Joan skimmed the rest to be sure those she loved had not been hurt. Richard and Papa would win, but it left her uneasy. Henry had been friendly with King Philip and many of the disloyal barons. How did he feel about being ordered to fight against his overlord and allies? She knew him. He would be disgruntled. And how would it affect Richard to discover how much he still relied upon his father's strength? She knew this answer, also.

Papa would lord it over him, and Richard would not be grateful. He would be enraged.

DURING WHAT JOAN HAD COME TO CONSIDER HER EXILE, Constance was a regular companion, but the queen mother had visited infrequently. When she did, Joan noticed how little she could walk without resting, how short of breath she became when she talked. Marguerite had not been to the Zisa at all for the last several months.

Constance assured Joan the illness was not serious but admitted that, in the summer past, William had summoned a consultant from Salerno, where the best physicians learned their skills.

Throughout autumn, Constance said little about Marguerite. Joan grew even more anxious. Then, on the first of December, the queen mother arrived in a litter, followed by two empty wains.

Joan waited in the Fountain Room while a man dressed in black with a long white beard escorted Marguerite inside. Joan embraced her. She was not as plump, but her flesh felt doughy. Still, she could walk and her skin was pink.

"Lady mother, I am so pleased to see you. You look well."

"I feel better." She waved her arm to indicate the man she'd brought, who stood a few feet behind her. "This is Genuold, my physician. He agreed to talk with you."

"With me?"

Queen Marguerite nodded and gestured for him to step forward.

Genuold approached Joan and stretched out his hand. When she extended her own, instead of bowing and kissing her fingertips, he took it, spread her fingers, examined her nails, and, to Joan's horror, sniffed her palm.

She pulled away. "What in God's name . . . ?"

Genuold smiled, crinkling his eyes at her, before whirling to face Marguerite. "She looks sound. Thin, yes, but I believe that is constitutional. Her flesh is not wasted."

"And the other?"

"The other?" Joan interrupted. Her face flushed with embarrassment, but anger lurked just behind. They had been discussing *her* health?

The physician continued to talk as though she were not there. "Most likely she was merely too young."

"Perhaps," Marguerite conceded, turning toward her, chin up and eyes slanted down. "William wants you back at the palace. You are no longer a child. You have responsibilities and cannot continue to hide."

"*Hide?*" Eleanor of Aquitaine's daughter did not shirk her duty. Joan drew herself up tall. "I did not ask to be sent here."

Marguerite's chest heaved. When she spoke, her voice bit like a dagger. "William said he felt like a monster when he tried to take you to bed. Constance says you complained of being a prisoner at the palace. You refused to eat—"

"That is absurd!" She wanted to refute the charges but managed only to insist, "I never refused to eat."

Genuold chuckled, risking their wrath.

"If she was a child," he said gently, "it is clear that she is no longer. Look at her, a rose in bloom. I suggest simply putting the two of them together. Your concerns will soon disappear."

As the anger on Marguerite's face slowly subsided, Joan noticed the wrinkling of the skin beneath the paint, the filminess of the queen mother's eyes. She was old.

Mama would be growing old also.

"You must come back to the Royal Palace," Marguerite said, the haughtiness gone. She sounded resigned, which was worse.


JOAN WAS SEVENTEEN NOW. BY TACIT AGREEMENT, NO ONE would treat her as a child, and she would not use youth as an excuse.

Throughout the winter, William came to her bedchamber every two weeks, except on feast days or during her flux. She learned that he would talk if she asked about the cathedral. With the structure finally complete, Pope Lucius signed a charter granting Monreale archiepiscopal status. Archbishop Walter could do nothing but admit defeat. William began commissioning the mosaics he had so long desired.

Speaking of the cathedral animated his face in a way that made him doubly handsome, but after a few minutes he would always stop abruptly, as if remembering his purpose. He would glance absently around the room, then offer her wine and drink a cup whether she accepted or not. Wordlessly, he would undress. He never kissed her and never spent the night in her chamber. After the first reunion, her wicked dreams ceased altogether. At least she now knew wantonness was not one of her faults.

She did her best to please him, but as soon as the winter rains ceased and spring's sun dried the grounds, he began hunting again and all but abandoned her bed.

EVERY MORNING AFTER PRAYERS, CONSTANCE AND MARGUERITE came to her apartments to stitch and talk—endless inconsequential prattle. In Marguerite's company, Constance had become sour-tempered again. They were barely capable of civility to one another, disagreeing about everything from yesterday's supper to which bird produced the song coming from the garden. Joan could not understand why they picked at each other over issues so petty, especially as it became clear that Marguerite's health was failing again. Couldn't Constance be more accommodating, for charity's sake?

The beginning of June's new moon coincided with the arrival of visitors to Palermo from Ravenna, one of William's fiefs on the mainland. Dancers performed at supper. From the corner of her eye, Joan watched the way they rolled their hips in front of William. He didn't come to her chamber that night, but did the next.

"How are the mosaics progressing?" she asked.

"Well," he said, unwrapping his girdle.

"Have they finished the apse as you'd hoped?"

"Not yet." He sat heavily on the bed beside her. His face was drawn. "I know this is unpleasant for you, but we must—"

Joan's mouth dried, and her eyes moistened. Had he been staying away for her sake? "I know. I don't mind, truly."

He grunted, flushing. Turning from her, he stood and pulled off his tunic.

She reclined and waited for him to lie on top of her. He squeezed her breast, stopped, started again, and stopped. He rolled away from her and sat up. Elbows on his thighs, he pressed his head into his hands.

She understood: He *could not* lie with her. The thought both offended and terrified her.

"William?" she whispered.

He looked at her, face empty of expression. "What is it?"

"I want to please you, but I don't know how."

He groaned. She had said the wrong thing.

"You please me well enough." He heaved to his feet. As he pulled his tunic back over his undergarment, he said, "I shouldn't have come tonight. I have too much on my mind."

"Will you talk to me?"

After a moment's hesitation, he sat back down. She leaned forward, watching his face.

"What is troubling you?"

"Do you know anything of Constantinople?"

Aware she was being patronized, she said, "Andronicus Comnenus seized the throne. He slaughtered the ruling family and married the young French princess."

His eyebrows rose. "How was he able to succeed?"

"The Greeks were tired of being ruled by emperors with Western sentiments. They saw Andronicus as one of their own."

"Yes," William said, scratching his leg. "Yes. Who discusses these things with you? Not Constance?"

"Constance?" She tried not to snicker. "No. My tutor, Master Eugenius."

"Ah, Eugenius." A smile flitted across William's face. "A clever Greek. Supercilious, though."

"Yes." She smiled back. "Why are your thoughts turned to Constantinople this evening?"

"A nephew of the late Emperor Manuel Comnenus has come to Sicily, named Alexius, like the murdered son. He's in Naples now, trying to raise support for his bid for the throne. He will likely come to Palermo next."

During her history lessons, Eugenius had once said William regretted his father's military losses in Tunis and hoped one day to return Sicily to the glory of his grandfather's days. Had William even greater ambitions in the Mediterranean? Did William see a role for Sicily as far as Constantinople? Joan examined her husband, trying to see him differently.

"Will you help him?"

"I don't know."

"What do your advisers say?"

Eugenius had explained how William governed with a heavy reliance on many advisers. The most important were his three *familiares*. Bishop Palmer spoke for the Church, but unlike Archbishop Walter, Richard Palmer understood that the interests of the Sicilian Church were best served by preserving a strong Sicilian kingdom. Matthew of Ajello was the chief notary and had been since the reign of William's father. Eugenius grudgingly admitted that Matthew was a brilliant man. During a time of great unrest in the previous reign, all the land registers had been maliciously destroyed. It should have meant chaos, since all grants, charters, and taxes were officially recorded in the registers.

But Matthew reconstructed them all from memory. Caid Richard, the chamberlain, was the final member of the trio. He was a baptized Saracen. Although Eugenius did not hold him in high regard, Joan suspected this was because the previous chamberlain had absconded with part of the treasury, renounced his baptism, and gone to join an infidel army. Eugenius did not trust any baptized infidels.

William shrugged off her question. "Different things. They know a hundred different ways to avoid saying yes or no."

He didn't ask her opinion, but she gave it anyway. "The empire is divided. Alexius is asking out of weakness. You would be aiding him from strength. Who will have the power when Alexius sits the throne?"

A shadow passed between them as his expression grew thoughtful. "But if we lose?"

"Alexius loses. Not Sicily."

"Hmmm." William rubbed the same spot on his leg. "That is an interesting way to look at it." He stood and tossed his girdle over his shoulder.

"Well?" she asked as he walked to the door, "Are you going to aid Alexius?"

"I don't know." He opened it. "Good night, Joanna."

*Faintheart*, she thought. He would not take Constantinople.

If God did grant her a son, she would not bring him up in Palermo among eunuchs, churchmen, and clerks, but send him to Richard to learn to be a true Norman king. She rolled over and buried her face in her pillow. If she had a son.

AT MIDSUMMER, SATI'S REPORT OF THE UNEXPECTED ARRIVAL of an English embassy filled Joan with misgivings. When she heard the name of the ambassador, Sir Robert of Chenowith, she fainted dead away from fear.

It was a miserable experience, fainting, like being swallowed whole by a beast, too exhausted to fight. She woke with both elbows bruised and a knot on the back of her head. Charisse dabbed her face with a wet cloth. When Joan tried to push it away, her hand fell back on the pillow.

"Steady, lady," Charisse warned.

"Someone is dead."

"Queen Joanna," Sati said, resonating calm, "the king has summoned you. You must be strong."

Charisse and Sati escorted Joan to her husband. She had never been in the throne room before. Standing around the perimeter were a few noblemen she did not recognize, two scribes wearing ink pots in slings, several eunuch guards with sheathed swords, and Caid Richard. Mosaics covered the vault and upper walls, depicting gardens and orchards, exotic predators and prey, creatures of myth. The same skill that had gone into the Palatine Chapel had been applied here, but with its secular theme, the results were startlingly different. In her fear, she felt she'd stepped into a peculiarly beautiful nightmare.

William took her by the arm and led her to side-by-side golden chairs. Despite its burnished glow, the seat felt hard and cold.

He sat in the larger chair. To Joan's surprise, he laid his hand over hers. "Bring in the messengers."

Sir Robert walked slowly into the room with two other men, who held back while Robert approached and bowed low. Joan stared at his clenched hands.

"Sire, Queen Joan, I deeply regret bearing this news."

William nodded and said gruffly, "Say what needs to be said."

"Lady, the young king is dead."

"Henry?" Her eyes welled with tears. Her throat tightened. Yet she thought, *Thank God. Not Richard. Not Mama or Papa.* "How?"

"A fever."

"Oh." It was not so terrible. Innocent death was God's will.

"There is more. He had been at war with your father. The whole realm was at war. The young king threw in his lot with King Philip and the southern French rebels. They have devastated Aquitaine, desecrated churches. A great many good men perished." He halted. "It was as if the devil possessed him."

"Where . . . where was Richard?"

"With your father."

Her chest cramped. Even drawing breath hurt, yet she had known. "He was a fool to fight them together."

"He almost won," Robert said bitterly. "It was a hard-fought war. The young king's adherents nearly killed the king twice, once in ambush and once while peace negotiations were in progress. Your father was more aggrieved by their dishonor than—" Robert bit his thumbnail. "When Henry fell ill, the king could not believe but that it was another trick. Only too late did he realize . . ."

Joan could not think of her father's grief and be strong. "Tell me they reconciled," she begged, tears spilling over.

"The king sent his ring as token. Your brother knew what he had done. At the last, he tried to atone, dying in a hair shirt, curled on the floor. He gave his possessions to the priest who shrove him." Robert's voice broke. "Except your father's ring." *I know the young king. He would carve a path through his own ranks to let you pass through.* Poor Henry. People said he had the most

· 192 ·

generous spirit of all her brothers. Papa called him the weak one. "He died clutching it to his heart."

"Papa," she moaned. Above all, he had loved his sons. He loved her, too, yet she had not kissed him when they parted. For Mama's sake. "Did someone tell my mother?"

"The king sent word."

Of course. As he had sent Robert to her.

Her terrible brothers. Why couldn't she hate them? Papa said hatred would ruin her, but love was no better.

William dismissed him. "Thank you. I'll speak with you again." He stood and put his arm around Joan, drawing her to her feet. "Come, Joanna. We'll bring your grief before God."

He took her to the Palatine Chapel, where they were met by the queen mother, Constance, and Bishop Palmer. The bishop took her hand and drew her to an altar bright with candlelight and sharply scented with burning wax. She had never thought him a godly man until that moment, when he knelt with her to pray. He asked the Lord's forgiveness upon Henry, and asked Him to heal her father's grieving heart. He prayed for her comfort, and peace for England and Aquitaine. When he finished, his cheeks were damp.

"Thank you," she murmured.

"War is a terrible thing. So much misery for so little purpose. Sicily is blessed with King William."

"Yes," she said, nodding toward her husband, who seemed rattled by the mention of his name.

"More blessed still when the succession is secure," Marguerite said.

Richard Palmer turned and said balefully, "In God's time, lady. Not yours."

Joan felt glad to see Marguerite flinch at the rebuke and

pitied William, whose eyes were cast down. He said, "Joanna, I'm sorry. I . . . I lost my brother also."

"Thank you." It was awkward comfort, yet comfort nevertheless. She was not alone in Sicily. Though they did not brandish love as a sword, as her family did, perhaps it was better to love coldly rather than to burn so hot.

"I'll see you to your chamber, if you wish," he offered hesitantly.

Before she could accept, Constance said, "I'll take her, poor child. My lord, you've got more important business to attend."

AS MUCH AS SHE WANTED TO SEE SIR ROBERT, JOAN COULD NOT go to supper. At daybreak, her grief was still too raw, and she remained in her room. But word came from William—he was going to Monreale. If mourning permitted, would she like to accompany him?

During the journey, Charisse wept with her while Sati handed them handkerchiefs and poured sips of wine. By the time they reached Monreale, Joan felt calmer.

William helped her climb from the litter. "I want you to see the mosaics in the apse. A wall of saints. The first panel is nearly complete." He marched up the stairs of the north porch. She developed a stitch in her side keeping up with him and wished she had drunk a little less.

It was darker in the cathedral than she remembered, but of course, the roof was now complete above their heads. William looked back at her and smiled, beckoning for her to hurry.

She crossed the floor, crunching discarded bits of colored glass beneath her feet. Masons' dust stung her nostrils. Approaching the apse, she slowed. Figures of saints in various stages of completion dappled the walls. William gazed upon one in particular: a likeness of Archbishop Becket. Half smiling, William turned.

"What does this mean?" she demanded.

"It is Saint Thomas," he said. His forehead crinkled.

"I have eyes. I can see who it is." She had watched her father flogged because of Becket's treachery. If the physical resemblance were not insult enough, his name was emblazoned above the image. Her breath came fast. Too fast. And then she could not breathe at all.

Charisse caught her as her knees buckled, and cupped her hands over Joan's nose and mouth. Lights flashed and receded into darkness. But as she inhaled her own warm exhalations, her head slowly cleared. She glared up at William. "Why did you do this?"

"I . . . I thought . . . Constance said—" He stopped. His skin looked gray. "Joanna, I must have misunderstood."

"What is there to misunderstand? He betrayed my father! He was a liar, a hypocrite—"

"Joan!" Charisse put a hand on her shoulder. "Lady, shush. You are distraught."

William bent over her. "He has been canonized. You mustn't profane his memory in my cathedral."

"You shouldn't have put a devil in your cathedral. It will be cursed. I curse your damn cathedral!"

William slapped her cheek, so gently she doubted he'd left a mark. Joan tucked her feet beneath her and stood. She couldn't bear him another minute.

"I'm going back to the palace."

"I think you should wait—"

"You are the stupidest man who ever drew breath! Why should I care what you think?"

She hated his wrinkled brow, the confusion in his eyes. The blackguard had hit her! And she hated him because even his blows were weak.

WORD OF THEIR QUARREL SPREAD QUICKLY. OF COURSE, SHE was faulted. Sympathy for her grief was short-lived; Sicilian sentiment held that the English princes were the devil's own sons and whatever ends they achieved they no doubt deserved.

Although not strictly confined to her apartments, there was little cause for her to go elsewhere. William spoke no more than a formal greeting at supper. The ladies of the court, even Constance, treated her frostily. Queen Marguerite, who might have mediated, could not. Almost at once, she had taken ill and was bedridden.

In late September, when Joan thought things could get no worse, a messenger appeared at her door.

"You must come at once. The queen mother is dying."

She took in Marguerite's chamber at a glance, its walls and furnishings gray in the semidarkness. Dust swirled in the faint shaft of light seeping through a gap in the curtains. The air stank of illness. In a vase next to the door, flowers crumbled.

Marguerite lay in bed. Her face was bloated, her hair dull, her eyes closed. William, pale and red-eyed, sat in a chair by her bedside, holding her hand. Constance stood near the window, clutching a handkerchief.

"Joanna," William said. "Mother, Joanna is here."

Marguerite's eyelids opened. "Good," she whispered. "Good."

Joan drew closer. Marguerite pulled her hand from that of her son.

"Remember your promise."

He swallowed convulsively. "Yes, Mother."

"I'll speak with Joanna."

"Yes, but I'll come back."

He beckoned to Constance, who followed him slowly. Joan knelt beside Marguerite.

"Lady?"

"End your quarrel."

"The quarrel is over, if William will pardon me."

"You are good."

Joan's lashes fluttered down. No, she was not. She'd been filled with resentment and plots of revenge.

"Constance said . . . Becket . . . you admired—"

"Oh, Lady Mother, it doesn't matter. Truly it doesn't."

"It does." Her eyes opened wide. She wheezed, "I should . . . before . . . but he promised."

"What promise?"

"She must marry . . . far away . . ." Marguerite shut her eyes. Her chest rose and fell.

Joan's heart ached. How terrible it was to be a royal woman. No doubt Constance would rather have been wed long ago than be kept in reserve as insurance against the young queen's failure. And poor Marguerite. She had likely married the monstrous old king against her will.

She pressed her cheek to Marguerite's cold hand; the queen mother's chest had stopped moving. Joan knew she should summon William but could not. As her tears wet Marguerite's sleeve, she thought: *Who will hold Mama's hand?*

Who would hold her own, when her time came?

## THIRTEEN

KING WILLIAM WITHDREW TO HIS APARTMENTS, SEEING NO one but the *familiares* and then only to discuss funeral preparations. Constance was no better, escaping to the Zisa with her maids.

It was left to Joan to preside over the mourners who came to pay their respects, a more difficult task than she had imagined. As Eugenius cynically commented, if they must make the trip, they would bring their grievances along. Despite his prejudices, Joan relied heavily on her tutor for insight into the requests of the petitioners as well to what motivated the *familiares'* responses.

Then Tancred of Lecce asked for an audience. The bald, overdressed man kissed her fingertips with clammy lips and held on longer than he should. He said the count of Acerra had asked him to intercede in gaining Princess Constance's hand in marriage for his heir, a boy of eighteen. Making eyes at her, he said he was sure the king would look favorably upon the request.

Joan intended to refuse; but to her surprise, all three *familiares* and Eugenius also ardently opposed the match. Perversely, perhaps because it was the first time all four had taken an identical stand, she wavered. The loyalty of Acerra was questionable, but wasn't that why such matches were made? The only thing that mattered to Joan was that Acerra was in Sicily. They wouldn't have to send Constance away. Couldn't the others consider Constance's best interests?

She decided to take the question to William herself and discover exactly what his promise to Marguerite had been.

He agreed to see her—his mother must have also told him to mend their rift. A page opened the door, leaving as soon as she entered. The curtains were drawn, and it was hard to see by the light of the single oil lamp.

William rose from his chair to greet her but did not seem to be standing fully upright. His tunic was a dull brown and rumpled as if he had been wearing it a long time.

"Joanna, thank you for coming."

Thank you? This was not a comfort call. Had he expected her sooner?

"My lord, how are you faring?"

William sighed, turning up his palms. "I owed her everything. I didn't do nearly enough."

"I suspect every son would say the same. That is the nature of mothers and sons."

"Perhaps. But I always fell short of her expectations."

Shaking her head, she said, "I doubt that, William."

"It would have been nice," he said wistfully, "if she had seen a grandchild born."

"Oh!" Joan fell back a step, as if he had stabbed her.

"No, Joanna, no. I didn't mean . . ." He lifted a hand toward her, then dropped it, the helpless gesture magnified in the elongated shadow on the wall. "I never say the right thing to you."

She let her breath out slowly. No, he never did, but her words had been equally thoughtless at times. "I . . . I'm sorry for what I said . . . in the cathedral."

"The error was mine." He sighed so heavily he seemed to be taking blame for more than the inappropriate mosaic.

Joan walked closer. Thomas Becket was revered throughout Christendom. How could William have known she yet bore a grudge when even her father had forgiven his foe? "We should put it behind us. Your mother would want—"

He made a noise deep in his throat. "What did she say?"

"She hadn't time to say much except that we should end our quarrel. And that you promised to see Constance married."

"I will."

"But must you banish her?"

His mouth fell open.

Joan continued in a rush. "Couldn't she marry a Sicilian baron? Forgive me, but your mother was too influenced by the past. Surely you see no threat from Constance."

"No," he murmured, shaking his head, looking at the floor.

"The count of Acerra has asked for her for his son."

"Acerra? No. That won't do."

"Acerra seems far enough away to me."

He raised his head. "Would you have me break an oath sworn to my mother on her deathbed?"

The lamp flickered, and they both glanced toward it.

Letting out a long breath, she answered, "Of course not."

The curtains shifted with a breeze that became trapped in the folds. For the first time since she had entered his chamber, William straightened.

"I promised my mother I would send Constance from Sicily."

He would not accept Acerra. But perhaps she could still keep Constance close awhile longer.

"You will not exile her immediately, will you?"

Averting his eyes once more, he said, "There is no hurry. But she must be wed."

TWICE, JOAN WENT TO THE ZISA AND WAS TURNED AWAY by Constance's maids. The third time, she demanded they admit her. Constance was sullen at first, but Joan talked gently of nothing until, worn down, the princess dissolved into tears.

"Joanna, forgive me. I thought you . . . she said *you* wanted to be rid of me. I should have known." She wept harder, while Joan stared in disbelief. "I'm sorry. I haven't been able to think. William does not respond to my messages. All I know is you will banish me."

"It is not my will." Joan thought she would break apart with pity. When Constance's tears subsided, she said, "Come. Let's take a walk in the garden."

They exited through the side door into the vast pleasure garden. They walked along winding paths and passed several tucked-away benches but did not stop to sit. Perhaps the garden was not such a good idea. It was November, and most of the plants were dormant, with leaves spotted or brown.

Joan broached the topic with caution. "Have you never thought of marriage?"

"Of course I've thought of it."

"Is there no one who interests you?" She felt certain William would take Constance's wishes into account.

Turning half toward her, Constance said, "The duke of Aquitaine."

"Richard?" Her voice was a high, wavering thread. "He is already betrothed."

"I'm joking. He sounds barbaric. Yet I can see you're none too anxious to share him."

It was not a question of sharing Richard—he would always love his sister best. Lifting her chin, Joan said, "He is the most courteous man alive."

"I didn't mean to offend. I'm merely demonstrating that my wishes count for nothing."

Whose did? After discussing several possibilities with William and his advisers, Joan had decided the fault did not lie with the suitors. Richard Palmer seemed to block his ears whenever any of the others spoke. Matthew of Ajello and Archbishop Walter disagreed about everything on principle. Caid Richard thought the princess should return to the convent, a position he reiterated each time anyone suggested a match. She'd even solicited Eugenius's opinion, but he'd stared at her with the flat, uninterested eyes of a fish and said he wasn't a matchmaker.

Constance's husband would never be chosen by committee. The only way to see her married would be for William to make a decision and stand firm.

"Constance, you needn't be so glum," she said, with too much irritation to be comforting. "You won't be banished anytime soon."

OVER TIME, THE KING PUT ASIDE HIS GRIEF, RETURNING TO THE chapel, the counsel chamber, hunting, and finally, the conjugal bed. He spoke to Joan more often now, a consequence, she supposed, of the death of his mother and absence of the princess. Whether he listened to her, she couldn't say.

"William?" She had come up with the perfect solution to Constance's quandary and was impatient to discuss it.

Two weeks ago, in early March, the long-awaited Alexius Comnenus had arrived at court. A handsome man a few years younger than William, he had fierce eyes and a curled mustache that Joan thought made him look wicked. Yet his voice had been soft, even tremulous, as he presented his case before the throne: Andronicus did not deserve to be emperor. He tortured opponents before killing them. Until marrying the child princess, he had lived in open sin with his own niece.

Alexius reminded them sternly that King Baldwin IV of Jerusalem was a boy and a leper, and that in the Christian states that had been established in the Holy Land internal dissension was rife despite the constant threat of infidel aggression. It was rumored that Andronicus had made overtures to the Saracen war chief, Saladin, and it was feared he might betray his Christian neighbors.

"What if Constance married Alexius?"

William rose to dress without replying, his face peevish. Perhaps she should have given him a moment, but if she waited too long he would be hurrying to leave, and she would lose her chance to make him talk.

"Think of it, William!" Alexius had no army of his own. If Sicily's army conquered Andronicus, William might name his choice of emperor. Sicily's king would be the true power behind Alexius and Constance. Moreover, William, a Roman Christian, would unify the peoples in the neighboring crusader states in a way the Greek Andronicus could not. "Sicily would not only gain control over the Greek empire, but prominence over all of Jerusalem and the Holy Land." She had been thinking of it for a fortnight. It was a plan worthy of Queen Eleanor.

Pulling his silk tunic over his undershirt, William said, "I am considering aiding Alexius. How could I not give it every consideration? But he is not the right man for Constance."

"Then no one is right," she grumbled, slapping her hands against the sheet. "What is wrong with Alexius? She will be an empress!"

"No."

"Why don't you at least ask Constance? Bring her here to see him."

"Joanna! I have said no."

The vehemence of his voice startled her into silence. He sat to pull on his stockings, avoiding her stare.

"But you haven't said why."

He sighed, one hand on his thigh, then stood. The tunic brushed his stockinged feet as he cast about for his slippers.

"There," Joan said, pointing beside her bed table. "William, I'm willing to accept your judgment. I simply wish you would explain to me why."

He plucked up his slippers and faced her. "Alexius has nothing but promise."

"But if Sicily commits to aiding—"

"It will come to naught if we lose."

Joan fumed. "Had your grandfather prefaced his engagements with 'but if we lose,' Sicily would still be in the hands of the Saracens. My father never began a war in his life, trembling to think 'if we lose . . .'"

William's face slackened. Joan could not tell if he was wounded, considering her words, or merely wondering where his girdle had fallen. It was exasperating being married to a man who would not fight.

"Make the betrothal conditional." This seemed an even better plan. "If we win—"

"Don't be a fool," he said, shaking his head. "The *familiares* will never consent to Alexius."

"Why?" The question died in her throat. Her blood turned to ice. *Because the queen is barren.* Sicily must not be given to the Eastern Empire.

"What are they saying?" she demanded. Infuriated by his startled expression, she grabbed the cup at her bedside and threw it. Wine splotched his tunic; he stared at the stain, crestfallen. "Have they told you to put me aside?"

He clutched his slippers close to his chest, eyes rolling upward with resignation. "They cannot even find a husband for Constance. Do you think they could agree upon a new wife for me?"

"Send me home to my father. They'll find you a new wife quick enough. That's what you want, isn't it?"

"Of course not."

"Why?" She felt perched on the edge of a precipice, as though her very life hinged upon his response.

He answered without irony. "A different marriage could be worse."

If he had spoken maliciously she might have borne it, but William was not a man who ever teased, for cruelty or for fun. Tilting her head back to look down her nose at him, Joan spoke with cold anger laced with her mother's mordacity. "I suppose it might, though I can't see how."

His vacant expression would remain forever etched in her memory. If only she had thrown the lamp rather than the cup. Then she might have set him afire.

*　　*　　*

THOUGH IT WAS THE CAPITAL OF A MEDITERRANEAN KINGDOM, Palermo could not lay claim to being Sicily's busiest port. Messina boasted a harbor protected from the sea's tempests by a long curved spit and waters so deep even the largest merchant ships sailed right up to the docks to unload their wares. Seven years earlier, Joan's first sight of the island had been Messina. She remembered gaping at vessels lined up like horses in a stable, while salt breezes and tar cleansed the air of the rotten sourness of fishing boats. Though she had begged a few moments simply to watch the ships bob up and down, the bishop of Troia hurried her along, promising that Palermo's harbor outshone Messina's for beauty.

Yet in all this time, she had never visited Palermo's port. Sicilian kings did not greet disembarking dignitaries. No matter how important the embassy or highborn the guest, it was as if travelers did not deserve notice until they reached the Royal Palace.

Not even ambassadors from the Holy Roman emperor.

Joan had been nursing her newest grudge against William for two days when word flashed through the palace: A ship had put into harbor carrying messengers from the Holy Roman emperor Barbarossa. She and William received a fat bishop with white hair, yellow fingernails, and the smoothest tongue she'd ever heard, who dared pretend that the man once known as "the scourge of Italy" was now Sicily's dearest friend. At last he came to the point: Barbarossa's eldest son and heir, Prince Henry, needed a wife. Advisers had suggested the Sicilian princess. How soon could negotiations begin?

Words poured from his mouth like water from a fountain, and Joan nearly laughed at the corked expressions of the *familiares*, who could not object until the king spoke. But William would not interrupt. By his glazed eyes, she knew he had stopped listening.

When the bishop finally gave up speaking, William seemed to startle awake at the silence. He said a mere "thank you" before the whole room began speaking at once.

Raising his hand for quiet, he announced in a mild tone, "As you can see, you've given us much to discuss."

With a benign smile, he dismissed the bishop and his men.

The bishop refused to be disappointed; he just smiled falsely and said he would talk with the emperor and return. Before going, Barbarossa's ambassadors met with Alexius. He openly admitted their purpose had been to suggest that a combined effort against Constantinople would more likely succeed. Alexius now pressed for a Sicilian alliance with the Holy Roman Empire.

After the bustle subsided, William could no longer find excuse to absent himself from Joan's chamber. His voice, when he spoke, was even gruffer than usual. Coming from deep in his chest, it sounded as if he could not breathe through his nose. "What did you think of Barbarossa's ambassadors?"

She raised her eyebrows at him. "The bishop was as oily as tunny fish."

"Heh?" he said, squinting. "Oh, how he talked."

Joan huffed. It was like speaking to a wall.

He said, "If the Holy Roman emperor's forces join us in Constantinople, we will defeat Andronicus."

"And Barbarossa will be lord over all."

William's forehead creased.

Joan scoffed, "Do you think the Scourge will sit Alexius on the throne and return home?"

"He is an old man. And his son is weak. More likely Barbarossa will die and his son will find his resources overextended. The Greeks will overthrow young Henry's rule."

Grudgingly, Joan finished the thought. "It will cost Sicily less and gain us more in the end."

"But Barbarossa wants the alliance sealed with a marriage contract."

"You can't . . ." Her mouth felt tacky. The Holy Roman Empire was no less a threat to an heirless Sicily than the Eastern Empire. "Constance cannot marry the future Holy Roman emperor."

"I know." William sighed. "But perhaps, by the time the bishop comes back . . ." He rubbed his nose roughly. "Genuold thinks . . . thinks I should lie with you more often."

"You've discussed me with your physician?"

"Joanna, please," he said irritably. "I should not have to beg permission."

"God's feet, William. You're bleeding again."

He saw the streak of blood on his hand and paled. "It is nothing."

She fished a piece of linen from the drawer in her bedside table and dabbed above his lips. "No, there isn't much. I think it has stopped." She gave him the cloth. Reluctantly, she said, "If Genuold believes it will help, come as often as you wish."

He rose and put on his clothes. "I'll come again in . . . in three days?"

"I'll be here."

He smiled weakly and put his hand to the door. After he left, she realized she had misspoken. He did not come because he wished to, but because he had been told he must.

The next morning, William failed to appear in the chapel. She whispered an inquiry after his health only to learn he had gone hunting. Black thoughts filled her head, blotting out the words of the priest. When prayers ended, she decided to leave the city also, to visit Constance. By hinting at their proposal, she might learn how the princess felt. Moreover, she could talk about Richard and Papa and perhaps be comforted.

Guards at the front gate admitted her, rousing the servant who should have been minding the door.

"There is no need to announce me. I'll find the princess." Joan headed for the stairs.

"She is in the garden, my lady," said the flustered doorkeeper. "She wanted time alone."

"In a temper?" Joan asked, hiding her smile.

The doorkeeper nodded, then shook her head and reddened.

"Charisse, wait for me. If she doesn't want company, we'll leave."

She slipped out the side door, glad for a few moments alone in the sun-warmed garden. She strolled past a red carpet of poppies, inhaling sweetness until she thought her lungs would burst.

Constance was not on the bench near the rosebushes where Joan expected to find her. She walked on. Near the cerise and purple sweet pea, she slowed, imagining she heard Constance's voice. But the maid had said she was alone.

Joan began watching where she set her feet, creeping along the path. A bench hidden in a bushy alcove was also empty, but the alcove was definitely the source of the voice. Constance sounded weepy.

There was a low rumbling answer. Joan halted. Could Constance have a lover? Little bumps of excitement rose on her flesh. She walked faster toward the sound, and now she could see a place where the bushes had been flattened. They were hiding!

The man's voice rumbled again, sounding almost like William. Nearly close enough, Joan knelt on the crumbly earth and tried to see through branches and twigs.

Constance sat on the ground, feet tucked beneath her robe, hair disheveled. Her face was streaked with tears.

"You lie!" That, Joan heard well enough. "You want to be rid of me."

A man leaned over, elbow into the mud. He had hair the color of William's. She heard the gruff voice say, "You know that's not true."

Twigs scratched her face, but Joan could not move. Not even to swallow the viscous saliva that suddenly filled her mouth.

"You think you can gain my silence with a crown?"

"Darling, I gain nothing." *Darling!* "But this is wrong. You know it is wrong."

"You said . . . you promised . . ." Constance sobbed so hard she could not continue. Joan clutched her abdomen.

"Constance, we must do what is right. For your sake—"

"You don't care about me. The harlot's daughter has won! You deny me everything and give her all. You cover her with kisses that should be mine. You dream by her side."

"I *never* kiss her! I barely speak to her. I swear, I do only what you know I must. I've kept my promises—"

"No! You promised you would never abandon me. Yet now you say I should be an empress." With a gasping breath, she cried, "I never wanted a throne."

William put his hand on her shoulder, but Constance pushed it away. Still as death, Joan could not tear her eyes from the scene. Then he moved, throwing one leg over Constance's lap, pushing her to the dirt. Joan saw his face in profile, taut with anguish. Constance's arms encircled his neck. He kissed her with a passion Joan had not believed him capable of.

She doubled over and retched. The horror of their sin filled her, and she could not be emptied of it. She vomited loudly, crashing against bushes too weak to bear her weight. Vaguely, she was aware her noises had startled them. Then awareness dissolved into nothing but dark.

She woke in her old bedchamber. Her forehead ached, and when she put a hand to her hair, she found it matted with blood.

"My lady!" Charisse cried, coming to kneel beside her bed. "She wakes!"

In a moment, Genuold was leaning over her, his beard falling onto her face. "Can you hear me?" he shouted.

"Get away," she demanded, swiping at him, but her voice was thick and her hand clumsy.

"Do you remember what happened?" he asked in the same overloud tone.

"I told you." It was Constance speaking. Joan's stomach roiled. "She fainted and hit her head on the paving stone."

"Yes, but she vomited," Genuold said. "Lady, did you vomit before or after you hit your head?"

"Stop shouting at me." She closed her eyes. "Before," she said. "Before."

"Lord be thanked," he sighed. "There are scratches and a bruise on your forehead. But a head injury that causes vomiting is reason for concern. Have you been ill? Have you reason to think you may be with child?"

Joan groaned. "Leave me alone."

"We sent to the Cuba for William," Constance said.

Charisse put in, "We were so frightened, lady. We could not think but to send for Genuold when you did not awaken. But the king—"

"I won't see him."

"He will be concerned." Constance's steady voice grated against her nerves. How did she dare?

"Tell him he need not be."

"He will want to speak with you," Constance insisted. "To see for himself."

"You tell him. I'm sure he will believe whatever you say."

"Lady—" Genuold began.

"Go away. My head hurts. I want to be alone."

JOAN STAYED A WEEK AT THE ZISA. FOR MUCH OF THE TIME, Constance sat with her, watching with a guarded expression, waiting for her to speak. William must be waiting also.

Her injuries were minor; there was no excuse to remain. Yet if she returned to court, what would she do?

On the seventh day, Charisse announced a visitor she could not turn away—the archbishop of Palermo. He came boldly to the privacy of her anteroom.

"My lady queen," he said, bowing from the shoulders rather than the waist. He was so short and round he'd probably topple over and roll across the room if he bowed properly.

"Would you care for something to eat or drink after your journey?" Her voice sounded as far away and false as an echo.

"No, thank you, lady. It was hardly far to come."

"It is kind of you to visit. Though I assure you I am well."

"I am pleased to hear it. But it is not your mishap that brings me." He lowered his gaze to the floor. "Or only in part—your mishap. It is being said there might soon be an heir?"

Her forbearance dissipated. "If it is so, it is too soon to speak of it."

"I beg your pardon, my lady."

Joan returned to her seat, gesturing to one of the yellow-cushioned benches opposite. He sat, gracelessly crushing the pillows. Embroidered pink-and-silver flowers wrinkled and disappeared beneath his dark robe.

"I've come because I know you have some influence over the king, and I hope to convince you that I am not—as he seems to think—his enemy."

"My influence is minimal. You might convince him yourself by behaving as a friend."

He smiled. "To my mind, I have never done otherwise."

"But you can understand how he might be confused."

The archbishop chuckled. How refreshing to hear someone laugh at irony. But then, Archbishop Walter was an Englishman by birth.

"Lady, the princess must be married before she is too old to tempt any suitor at all." He certainly did not dance around delicate topics. "You are probably not aware that the emperor's ambassadors have returned."

"What do you mean? How could they?"

"They made it no farther than Messina. I think they expected the king to send a messenger after them and were surprised he did not. They have doubled the promised subsidy to aid Alexius Comnenus, provided that the king accepts the proposed alliance."

"Constance cannot marry Prince Henry unless Sicily's succession is secure."

The archbishop ran his pudgy hands up and down his thighs. "If there is no heir, there will be war in Sicily, no matter whom the princess marries. The best hope is for the war to be short and decisive."

"I'm sure Barbarossa will promise that."

"The kingdom would not fall to Barbarossa, but to Prince Henry. Who will have enough trouble keeping his vassals from dismantling the empire at his back—Henry is not a strong man."

William had said the same.

"He wouldn't be able to spend much time in Sicily," he went on. "But he might send Princess Constance back to be regent."

"Sicily would still be annexed by the empire."

The archbishop shrugged. "Three generations ago, there was no Sicilian kingdom. The world changes, my lady. I think Sicily will not find a distant overlord too great a burden. Worse would be internal strife, division of the kingdom. Endless warfare."

As in her father's realm. She had heard that after Henry's death, Richard, as next eldest, became heir to England. But in return, her father commanded him to relinquish Aquitaine to John. Naturally Richard refused. Furious, her father gave John control of his armies, along with permission to invade Aquitaine. Her family was at war again.

"Why do you bring this to me?"

"You haven't the Sicilian temperament. You can weigh the options without irrational fear of the Holy Roman Empire. Talk to your husband. I suspect he is not so averse to the match as some of his advisers. He may only need stiffer support than mine."

She arched her brows at him. "Perhaps if you were to feign opposition to the match?"

"That," he answered, laughing heartily, "would serve the *familiares* right."

Joan could not help smiling. How simple it would be to rid Sicily of Constance. And William's kingdom could go to the devil for all she cared.

## FOURTEEN

A FTER ANNOUNCING THE BETROTHAL OF PRINCESS
Constance to Prince Henry, heir to the Holy Roman
Empire, King William began readying Sicily for war.

To her disgust, Joan discovered her husband's idea of war
preparations differed greatly from her father's. William had no
intention of taking part himself, but he would visit the shipyards
in Messina, where fifty new galleys were being built at his
command. Joan decided to go also—an opportunity to escape
Palermo seemed God-sent. She knew William would acquiesce.
He now acceded to whatever she asked, allowing her to take part
in councils despite the objections of his advisers, promising
Constance to Prince Henry, and banishing her to the convent
San Salvatore until Barbarossa sent for her. The fool must be
afraid. As if anyone would believe what Joan had seen.

The sight of Messina jolted her from her gloom. The city
sprouted at the foot of tall mountains to the west and overlooked
the strait. It had a mercantile heart; she could hear the clamor of
its vendors ringing in her ears. Peeking though the curtains of her
litter, she watched citizens along the narrow streets drop to their
knees as the cortege passed. William rode amidst a cadre of guards,
his scarlet mantle around his shoulders, a thick crown of gold
encircling his hair; he did not deign to turn his head. It was the
Sicilian way—the people shouting praises did not expect acknowledgment. Still, Joan thought he looked pompous.

She sat back, away from the curtains, before the urge to throw them open and wave to her subjects became strong enough to act upon. The smell of the marketplace—fish and fowl, unwashed bodies, smoke and cheap incense—permeated the litter, all underlain by the scent of the sea. They bounced slowly onward, then inclined as though going up a hill. The noise outside dimmed, and they came to a stop.

Messina's palace was built of limestone. It was sturdier than Palermo's, and not as pretty, with a haphazard design, as if constructed in stages by different men for different purposes. The elderly castellan hurrying to the porch had a Greek complexion, and his wife was as wrinkled and brown as a peeled apple left out in the air. William greeted them both in Greek, and they chattered away for several moments before he bothered to introduce her.

"Queen Joanna," he said, lifting her hand.

"An honor and a great pleasure," the castellan said, bowing. "My wife, Helena."

Helena smiled warmly. "You must be tired. There is no more torturous method of traveling than riding in a litter." Her French was as round and melodious as the Greek had been fluent and clipped. "Come. I'll show you your rooms and you can bathe before supper."

For two weeks, Joan and William acted as husband and wife, eating meals together, conversing politely for the sake of their hosts. He encouraged her to speak Greek, sometimes praising her efforts, sometimes gently laughing at her mistakes. One morning he even accompanied her on a tour of Messina's churches. She could almost join him in pretending nothing was wrong.

Until he appeared in her bedchamber, looking both contrite and determined. "Joanna," he pleaded, "it is our duty."

Perhaps she had been expecting it. Or else she felt too heart-sick and weary to fight. With resignation, she lay down on the bed and lifted her skirt.

"Joanna," he said gruffly. She didn't answer. "Is this how it will be?"

She turned her head and closed her eyes.

Every few nights, he lay with her, seeming as resigned as she was. Her courses came twice, marking the passage of time, marking her failure; she began to wonder if he considered it not duty but penance. What was he thinking? How could it be she still did not know him at all?

One breezy, cloudy September morning, a commotion interrupted their breakfast. A messenger entered to announce a shipwreck had occurred the previous night during a storm. The ship had lodged on a rock just before dawn and was slowly sinking.

"How many does it carry?" William asked, his eyes wide with concern.

"A few hundred, sire, including women and children. They launched a longboat this morning. It brought some of the better passengers to shore, but the boat broke up in the landing. The rowers have been begging use of other craft."

"Why is there no rescue?"

"It's a Saracen vessel, sire."

Joan pushed aside her trencher, appetite gone. What a horrible way to die.

William rose from his chair, his color up. "Do you mean to tell me those on shore are merely watching?"

"The wind and waters are still high. Only smaller boats might reach the ship without running aground, and even that is dangerous."

William turned to the castellan. "Saddle my horse."

"I'm coming too," Joan said, pushing on the table to rise unsteadily. She felt morbidly curious, but more, she wanted to see what he would do.

She rode a palfrey at his side, the discomfort of the saddle a pleasant change from that of the litter. No one tried to stop her. She realized that Marguerite's death and the discovery of William's shameful secret had freed her to be herself again—a Norman lady, not a Sicilian one—a Norman queen like Eleanor. At least she could be thankful for that.

Within an hour, they were at the quay. A handful of fishing boats had ventured out to offer transport to any merchants able to meet their extortionate demands. The rescued—there were pitifully few—milled about weeping. Joan began to wish she'd stayed at the palace. She glanced at William, gazing out at the rocks where the doomed ship was barely visible.

He turned abruptly to the castellan's man beside him. "Tell the fishermen to go back out."

"But, sire, they'll claim it isn't worth Christian lives and livelihood to save Saracens."

"They saved these."

The man smirked. "They weighed the risks and demanded fair price."

"I will pay what they ask," William said simply.

"Sire! There are hundreds. It will cost—"

"Go. Tell them I won't pay for drowned bodies."

The man shot off. Soon, Joan saw the first few boats

bobbing out into the waves. She turned to William, whose eyes were fixed again on the shoals. The knot of tension in her gut loosened. Several more small craft followed the first. She was glad of the rescue, even if they were infidels. Yet wouldn't others consider this evidence that the Sicilian king loved Saracens? He should have considered that.

Probably he had—and counted it no more important than the fortune he'd promised to the fishermen. What a strange man he was, self-assured only in kindness.

The musing brought her up cold. Kindness was a weakness. Heaven hated sinners and Saracens. And Eleanor's daughter hated weakness even more than sin.

ON JUNE 11, 1185, THE SICILIAN HOSTS SET SAIL FROM MESSINA. Before the month's end, Durazzo, the Greek empire's third largest city, was in Sicily's hands. The army, eighty thousand strong and led by the count of Acerra, marched onward to Thessalonica while Admiral Tancred of Lecce brought the fleet around by sea to blockade the port. They reached Thessalonica on August 6. That siege lasted just eighteen days.

Acerra's messenger did not downplay the butchery that followed. Looting soldiers desecrated Greek churches, scraping mosaics from the walls and urinating on the altars. The Greeks at Messina's court listened quietly, if dourly, but William was incensed.

"How did the count allow it? They behaved as barbarians, not men of Sicily!"

Joan said snidely, "How do you expect men to follow your example if you are not there?"

A messenger arriving a few weeks later told of a plague that struck the city. Three thousand of the foot soldiers died.

"God's retribution," William sighed.

Joan snorted. Her husband knew nothing of war.

In possession of both Durazzo and Thessalonica, the reduced army began its march on Constantinople. For several weeks, there was no word. During this time of quiet, Barbarrossa sent for Constance. Protocol required that William escort his aunt to Taranto to meet Prince Henry's representatives, but Joan returned to Palermo. If her absence gave them opportunity to compound their sin, she didn't care.

William came back and still it was silent, until November when Tancred returned. His fleet had been in sight of Constantinople, but the count of Acerra's army never appeared. It had progressed overland as far as Mosynopolis, a mere two hundred miles from Constantinople, when the Greeks rose up against Andronicus and murdered him themselves.

A man named Isaac Angelus was elected emperor; he immediately appointed a general to stop the Sicilian advance. The Greek army caught the Sicilians unawares and routed them. When the count of Acerra learned of Andronicus's death, he offered to negotiate. After all, their goal had been to depose the tyrant. But the Greeks had attacked while pretending to consider a truce. They slaughtered Sicilians by the thousands, and thousands more drowned in the Strymon River trying to escape. William's ally Alexius would never have a chance to be emperor—he was captured and blinded.

Stragglers managed to crawl back to join the garrison at Thessalonica, but now that the foreigners were the weaker party, the Thessalonicans took vicious revenge. Tancred's ships were able to rescue fewer than a thousand men.

William was stricken. Joan couldn't help but feel cheated. Her husband was pathetic. Her *father* had never lost a war.

WILLIAM HANDLED DEFEAT AS HE DID ANY OTHER UNPLEASANT-ness—by ignoring it.

Throughout the winter months, Sicily's fleet lay idle, divided between Messina and Palermo. Tancred had resigned command in favor of one of his captains. An energetic man, Margaritus of Brindisi had close-cropped hair, a scar beneath his left eye, and a barrel chest that provided the bellows for the loudest voice Joan had ever heard. She supposed he learned to talk on board a ship, for his father had also been a sea captain. Margaritus wanted nothing more than to return to the fight and avenge Sicily's honor. He had his chance soon enough.

As Eugenius explained, another of the Comneni had wormed from Constantinople's dust and proclaimed himself emperor. The pseudo-emperor, also named Isaac, had seized the island of Cyprus, claiming it as the new seat of the Eastern Empire. However, several of its ports relied on close ties to Constantinople for their livelihood, so it was doubtful that he could hold Cyprus without a navy.

The fact that Isaac Comnenus was every bit as much a despot as his cousin Andronicus had been was not at issue. Isaac Angelus had used dishonorable means to humiliate Sicily; therefore, his rival deserved Sicily's support. William sent Margaritus to Cyprus to put Sicily's fleet at Isaac Comnenus's disposal. Joan expected lackluster results.

The treacherous Greeks were not the only men busily stirring up wars. Joan heard news from England. Her father had previously unleashed her brothers upon one another in an effort to convince Richard to yield Aquitaine to John. According to Archbishop Walter, they had been devastating each other's inheritances. When her father finally realized his error, he made a new plan.

He ordered her brothers to stop fighting, then summoned Queen Eleanor from prison and asked Richard to yield Aquitaine to her. Perhaps he expected Richard to refuse and weaken his position in the eyes of his vassals. If so, Richard outfoxed him by yielding willingly. Eleanor might have bestowed Aquitaine on John, but she did not. Nevertheless, King Henry left things as they were, imposing a fragile peace among his sons. Geoffrey had been made seneschal of France, an honor that should have gone to Richard. If Richard had not yet complained, it was because he was currently occupied raising troops to threaten Count Raymond of Toulouse. Count Raymond had sided with the young king during the rebellion. With Richard fighting too many enemies at once, the count's son had found opportunity to seize Quercy. Joan thought it a courageous and ambitious move, one she might approve if it weren't so foolishly provocative. Richard would not stop at retaking Quercy if Mama wanted Toulouse.

After talking with the archbishop, Joan sat a long while in the garden court, her eyes fixed on the spiky yellow-green flowers of a carob tree. Mama had taught her to examine the significance of events from every angle, but every approach led to the same conclusion, as every needlelike petal led to the stalk. Her brothers would fight again, with or against one another, with or against Papa. Only now Lord Raymond would also sink in her family's mire.

*　　*　　*

JUST BEFORE HER TWENTY-SECOND BIRTHDAY, JOAN LEARNED of Geoffrey's death in a tournament in France, trampled by his own horse after a fall. They said King Philip cradled the broken body in his arms and wept. Guiltily, she recognized her own first reaction as relief. Geoffrey was dead, not Richard, and Richard had not killed him. Also, with unseemly thankfulness, she noted Lord Raymond had been nowhere near.

She hoped to find some blessing in the end to her elder brothers' rivalry, but Geoffrey's death settled nothing. Now Richard would simply fight with John, and that competition promised to be even more bitter. Geoffrey had been count of Brittany, a French fief. Although the French king aggressively asserted his rights, no one disputed that those lands would go to Geoffrey's son, Arthur. But as eldest surviving son, Richard claimed the rights to all of his brother Henry's lands—Normandy, Anjou, Maine, England—without relinquishing either of his own, Poitou and Aquitaine. It was as if he believed John should ever be John Lackland.

For a while, impending war between England and France became the favorite topic at court. Joan was forced to listen to stories of the French king outmaneuvering Papa and Richard by claiming custody of Geoffrey's two young daughters. As overlord of Brittany, it was King Philip's right. In the resulting tempest, instead of sensibly trying to appease the King of England, he added another demand—that Alice be married immediately or returned, along with the Norman Vexin and the county of Berry. He threatened to invade Normandy if King Henry did not comply.

Joan could imagine her father's fury. Especially since Philip flatly refused to negotiate while Richard was harassing one of his vassals. She suspected Richard was equally furious when Papa ordered him to leave Toulouse alone.

Philip agreed to a truce until the following summer, but no one expected it to hold. It was rumored that a vassal of Richard's had killed two of Count Raymond's messengers and Richard refused to surrender the man for judgment.

If only King Philip would invade Normandy quickly, it might bring Papa and Richard together. An unwieldy peace would only drive them apart. Yet winter gave way slowly to spring, and then to summer. Sicily lost interest in rumors of wars in faraway England, France, and Cyprus. These wars were always imminent and yet would not start.

It seemed to Joan it must always be summer in Sicily. Many of the courtiers left Palermo for the cool breezes of the countryside, and Bishop Palmer took a party to the Favara for the month of July. William spent half his days at the Cuba. She wished he would spend the whole summer there. One evening, she felt him watching her too intently during supper. When she excused herself before the entertainments, he did as well.

"It has been a month, Joanna," he murmured, drawing close behind.

She sighed. "Has it? Well, come then."

Ignoring his grimace, she mounted the stairs. She would just as soon get it over with. He hesitated a moment, then she heard his feet on the steps.

The maids in the day chamber jumped out of their chairs, blushing and bowing. High in color himself, William ducked into the bedroom. Joan followed wearily, shutting the door as she went in. She stood beside the bed while he methodically untied her laces, then she stripped off her gown and lay down. To avoid seeing him undress, she shut her eyes, and kept them closed as she felt the weight of him beside her.

Sometimes it helped to think of other things. It had been a while since they'd had any reports of Admiral Margaritus. She'd misjudged him. So far, he'd kept Angelus away from Cyprus's shores.

William grunted, shifting his weight. Joan turned her head.

Cyprus's shores—she guessed Margaritus would rather be Isaac Comnenus's opponent than ally. Maybe the disaffected Cypriots would be willing to rise up against him, the way the Greeks had risen against Andronicus. But then, they might not be any more willing to accept Sicily's rule.

"Do you think he would be able to take Cyprus?" Joan said aloud.

"What?" William stared at her. "Who?"

"Margaritus."

William grumbled something she could barely make out.

"What did you say?"

"Nothing," he answered, frowning, his lips tight.

"I heard you," she insisted, nearly taunting.

"Then I don't have to repeat myself."

It didn't matter. She'd heard enough. "I wasn't thinking about Margaritus, but about Cyprus. Don't you think—"

"Joanna! Are you even in this bed when I am here?"

She gazed at him coldly. "I try not to be."

His head jerked back. He looked beaten, like Papa when he told her Richard had been knighted by King Louis. Fighting pity, she climbed from the bed.

"I'm going to bathe now, William." She drew a robe around her shoulders and left the chamber, knowing he would be gone by the time she returned.

THAT SUMMER, ALL TALK OF ENGLAND AND FRANCE WAS disregarded in favor of a new rumor, one too frightening to believe, too terrible to ignore. Saladin had broken his truce with the Franks in Outremer—the Holy Land. Saracens defeated the combined Frankish forces and the Templars at a place called the Horns of Hattin. Even the name conjured the devil's image.

Ship after ship put into harbor carrying the same tale, magnified in horror. Saladin was now in possession of the True Cross. The Christians had been massacred. At the end of the battle, Saladin had all the captive Templars put to the sword. The king of Jerusalem, Guy de Lusignan, had survived but was in Saladin's custody, leaving no one to defend Jerusalem but Queen Sybilla and a handful of knights.

In October, Archbishop Josias of Tyre brought irrefutable word. The last bastion of defense was now in Tyre, fewer than two hundred soldiers under the command of Count Conrad of Montferrat. The unthinkable had happened. Jerusalem itself had fallen into the hands of infidels.

Yet it happened peacefully. In contrast to the slaughter at Hattin, Saladin accepted the Holy City's capitulation magnanimously, allowing the Christians within to buy their freedom with gold. He pardoned Queen Sybilla and her court without ransom. As a reward for his loyal service, Saladin's brother, el-Adil, asked for one thousand slaves from among the captives too poor to ransom themselves. Then he set them free.

But Saladin and his brother could afford to be generous after Hattin. They feared no one. There was no one left in Outremer to fear.

Listening to the archbishop, William fell into a fit of weeping. He left the throne room to seclude himself in his apartments. For a week, Joan presided over a court in an uproar. The archbishop of Tyre urged a new crusade. Bishop Palmer and Archbishop Walter found themselves, for once, in agreement: The Holy Land must be reclaimed.

But the king had yet to show his face. Finally, Joan went to his apartments and rattled the door until a page opened it. Seeing William wearing sackcloth, she felt a surge of exasperation. When he rose to greet her, his legs bowed and he put a hand to the wall.

Startled, she asked, "What is wrong?"

"Nothing." He shook his head slowly. "I have been fasting."

"Humph. Monks fast. Kings eat. Have you given thought to how to answer Josias?"

"I've prayed—"

"He must go to Rome as quickly as possible. Give him a fast ship and a strong escort."

"Yes," he answered sluggishly, as if waking from a dream. "Yes, of course."

"There will be a crusade. After Hattin, and now this, Jerusalem—"

William winced. His anguish surprised her.

"Will *you* take the cross?" When he did not answer, she cleared her throat. "It will be months before the pope can launch a crusade. Help is needed now. Saladin has been to Tyre once already, but abandoned the siege for easier victories. Josias fears he will return."

He squinted at her, finally listening.

Joan spoke more forcefully. "Christendom cannot afford to lose Tyre. When the crusaders are ready, they will need a toehold on the coast. Sicily already has a fleet halfway to the Holy Land."

"Margaritus?" The wrinkles on his forehead smoothed away. "Yes, of course. The fleet."

Appalled by his relief, Joan added cowardice to the long list of her husband's faults. He would answer God's call by sending others to martyrdom. *That* was how the king of Sicily prepared for war.

## FIFTEEN

R ICHARD WAS THE FIRST TO TAKE THE CROSS—RICHARD, who was everything her husband was not.

The duke was in Tours when word of the disaster reached him. He didn't wait to beg leave of his overlord or of his father but knelt before the bishop of Tours and swore the crusader's oath. Richard was his own man before God.

Joan sat in the library, an opened codex before her: a commentary on the Gospel of Mark. Ashamed of her previous complacency, she'd abandoned study of anything but God's word. But thoughts of the Holy War, or lack of one, distracted her. Where was the righteous fury of Christian kings?

King Philip had insisted Richard honor his long-delayed betrothal and marry Princess Alice or he would break the truce and attack Normandy. To avert war, the two kings held another conference at the beginning of the new year, a conference Richard refused to attend. According to Archbishop Walter, negotiations were failing until Tyre's archbishop arrived. The eloquent Josias turned the focus to Jerusalem, and at the conclusion, though nothing else had been settled, the English and French kings took the cross.

That was in January, however. It was now December, and the promised crusade was not yet under way.

In the spring, one after another, Richard's vassals in Aquitaine had rebelled, and one after another, he defeated them. Then had come more trouble with Count Raymond. Richard invaded Quercy, regaining castles in Cahors and Moissac among others, before advancing on the very city of Toulouse. But his attack on Toulouse provided King Philip an excuse to move against Berry again. With his northern border threatened, Richard could not continue besieging Count Raymond. He hurried to Normandy to join Papa. Together, they battled Philip's men throughout the summer and into the fall.

All of which meant Saladin had been in Jerusalem a year, and the only king who had done anything for the Holy Land was one who had not taken the cross. William sent several more galleys to Margaritus; while France and England fought each other, Sicily's fleet saved Tripoli, Tyre, and Antioch.

But Margaritus's success held a mixed blessing, for as soon as he left Cyprus the tyrant Isaac Comnenus made a truce with Saladin and banned crusaders from the island's ports. In response, William sent word to all the principals who had taken the crusading oath, urging them to use Sicily as their Mediterranean base instead of Cyprus. Joan convinced herself William intended to join the crusaders coming through Sicily. He could not, with honor, do anything else.

Of course, all speculation assumed the crusaders managed to put aside their differences to fight the common enemy. Master Eugenius said on that day Allah himself would tremble, but until then, Saladin had no cause to fear.

The library door creaked open, but Joan didn't bother to look up until she heard the soft voice of one of her eunuchs.

"My lady, it is time. The king is on his way to the council chamber."

Joan shut the codex and rose. William had asked the *familiares* and Archbishop Walter to meet him before supper. Usually, she had at least an inkling beforehand what they would discuss, but not this time.

The eunuch walked a few steps behind her down the wide hallways leading to the council chamber. Unlike the throne room, this chamber had unadorned walls and dull tiled floors, but it possessed a magnificent gilded oak table large enough to seat twenty. The three *familiares* and the archbishop sat far apart from each other. When she took a chair close to Bishop Palmer, they eyed her as if trying to guess what she knew.

The king entered the room. Everyone stood until he waved for them to sit. William was looking tired these days, older, though at thirty-five he was hardly an old man. His voice had lost some of its gruffness, sounding more nasal, and his nose-bleeds must have increased in frequency, because he often seemed to have crusted blood about his nostrils.

"The lord pope has asked Sicily's commitment," he announced, "and I have promised sixty galleys and thirty thousand men."

A smile bloomed on Joan's face. He *would* go.

"The count of Molise says he will go to the Holy Land if I give him command."

"The count of Molise!" Matthew of Ajello was first to object, but the others appeared equally appalled. "He would as soon dethrone you as Saladin."

William frowned. "I'll not have slander—"

"It is prudence, not slander, to question the motives of Molise." Bishop Palmer, ever diplomatic, leaned forward in his earnestness. "Sire, I think you should reconsider."

"Someone must lead Sicily's crusaders if the king will not," Joan jeered. Even if they considered her a harridan, as bad as her mother, she didn't care. Their king was a coward. It needed to be said.

William ignored her. "There is another option. Emperor Barbarossa has taken the cross. He might well be the first to reach the Holy Land." He faltered a moment, then declared, "Princess Constance wants Sicily's soldiers to fight for the Holy Roman Empire."

"No!" Joan's protest was lost in the loud disapprobation of the others.

Richard Palmer made himself heard. "Combining our forces with Barbarossa's would be conceding"—he paused only a moment before forging ahead—"conceding that we expect Sicily to become part of the empire." He managed to avoid looking at Joan.

"It means nothing of the sort," Archbishop Walter answered. "We have a truce. We'll fight as allies."

"Not allies if we subordinate our troops to Barbarossa's command." Now Palmer did look at Joan. "Lady, I know you and the princess were friends, but I beg you, think this through, for Sicily's sake."

Open-mouthed, she stared a moment, unable to reply. Did he think she was behind this absurd plot? She glanced at William; his face had paled to gray. She drew a steadying breath. "No friendship would come before duty to my lord's kingdom. *I* would not have Barbarossa command Sicily's army."

"But not the count of Molise!" whined Caid Richard.

"No." She had an idea to put Constance in her place. "Why not add Sicily's strength to that of the duke of Aquitaine?"

"Duke Richard?" Palmer repeated, his voice soft, considering.

The archbishop frowned. "But to refuse Barbarossa?"

"Surely, the emperor cannot take offense if the king refuses in favor of his wife's brother, the first man to take the oath." Joan looked to William, lifting her eyebrows.

He said, "The queen's suggestion has merit."

The murmuring of the others died away. Even the archbishop seemed disinclined to argue further, but then he blurted out, "Will it offend the king of England if we offer aid to his son rather than to him?" He cast an apologetic glance at Joan.

"My father will not begrudge Richard an alliance with his brother-in-law if the enemy is Saladin." Richard had fewer resources to draw from. Papa would approve, she hoped.

"I have one reservation," William said. "What if he and King Philip cannot come to terms? How will your brother honor his vow?"

"He'll find a way. Richard is a man of his word."

William nodded, seeming satisfied. "We must send word to Duke Richard, offering Sicily's support. And regrets to Emperor Barbarossa."

Joan felt oddly ill at ease after her exercise of power. What if it was a mistake? Richard once prided himself on being a man who did not equivocate—Richard Yea-or-Nay, men had called him. Was he still the same man? Or would her brother make a liar of her?

IT WOULD BE A DISMAL CHRISTMAS COURT. JOAN WALKED THE outer courtyard for air and stooped to pluck the brown leaf tips from a cluster of rosebushes. Had there been a change in gardeners or had they forgotten how to prune?

An atmosphere of wilt pervaded the Royal Palace, all of

Palermo—perhaps all of Christendom. Even William's beauty had faded. His temples and cheeks were hollow, his skin sallow. He wore an air of permanent fatigue. His visits to her bed waned to once a month, and he had ceased frequenting the Cuba. The last time he had bedded her his weight upon her was feather-light, and there were excoriations on the patches of skin she accidentally glimpsed. He must be fasting and wearing sackcloth again. As if that would gain a coward favor with the Lord.

Close by her cheek, Charisse's skirts rustled. "Lady, please stand up. Someone's coming."

She whirled about, rising from her crouch to see Bishop Palmer, Archbishop Walter, and Master Eugenius—an unlikely party. When they saw her, they slowed, almost visibly pushing Eugenius to the fore. Joan's throat closed. What was wrong?

"Lady," he said with a bow, "I beg your pardon for this intrusion. The king sent us to speak with you."

"Richard is dead?" she asked, her voice so tight she doubted she'd be heard.

"No," Eugenius said gently, though he was not a gentle man.

"Please, just say it outright."

"He is at war with your father."

"How? Eugenius, how? They cannot fight the French if they are fighting among themselves!"

The tutor winced and turned to Bishop Palmer.

"Would you like to go inside?" Palmer asked, solicitously taking her arm.

"No!" Joan wrenched away. "What are you afraid to tell me?"

"The duke has allied with the French king," the archbishop said.

No. She shut her eyes and tried to pray, but her thoughts were too scattered. How could God allow it? Did He want Saladin to win?

Bishop Palmer explained, "Last October, King Philip offered to return Chateauroux and Berry to King Henry if the Duke surrendered Quercy back to Count Raymond of Toulouse."

"He meant to drive a wedge between my father and brother." She could see it so clearly. How had Papa and Richard not? "Did my father agree?"

"He might have been inclined, but in the end, he was so offended by the French king's demands he broke off negotiations."

Good for Papa. "And then?"

"Duke Richard went to King Philip without your father's knowledge. At least, that is what the best sources report. He wanted to put an end to the strife so the crusade could begin."

Her own words came back to haunt her. Richard was a man of his word; he would find a way.

The archbishop took up the tale. "He insisted he would keep what he'd won in the Toulousain, but would recognize King Philip as his overlord for Toulouse as well as Aquitaine."

"But that is little concession," she protested weakly. "King Philip *is* overlord of those domains."

Bishop Palmer said, "Lady, he was offering to change allegiance."

She knew that, but could not accept it.

"A few weeks ago, Philip invited your father to Bonsmoulins for another attempt to negotiate. Your father arrived to find the duke already in the French king's company. King Philip offered to return Berry and allow Richard to keep his gains in Toulouse, with two conditions. Duke Richard must wed Princess Alice—"

Joan sniffed.

"—and King Henry must recognize Duke Richard as heir to the kingdom of England. King Henry refused."

"Refused! But surely he meant to make Richard his heir!" And surely her father was not so fond of Alice. Rather should Richard refuse.

"He said he would not agree to name Richard under compulsion."

"It was pride ruling him, not sense." She felt furious with them for falling into Philip's trap. "Richard must have thought Papa intended to name John heir." Richard, too, could be blinded by pride. But why would he be so foolish as to ally with Philip? It made it seem as though he thought the king of France had a right to choose England's monarch.

"Yes, lady. Duke Richard said he was now forced to believe what he previously refused to see. In front of your father, he knelt before the French king and paid homage for not only Aquitaine, Poitou, and his conquests in Toulouse but also for all your father's French lands—Normandy, Anjou, Maine, Berry."

A declaration of war. It was as if Richard had sworn to take what his father refused to give. And he swore it publicly, to Papa's face.

"God help them," she said. But God would not. God had abandoned them as they had abandoned His Holy City.

"There is still hope, my lady," Eugenius said. "They will not make war through Christmas. And they agreed to another conference in January."

Another conference would settle nothing. Joan could not bear the pity on their faces. Trembling, she reached for Charisse's arm. "Thank you. I will go inside now."

*   *   *

THE KING OF ENGLAND FELL ILL AND COULD NOT ATTEND THE peace conference in January. The truce expired. Word of scattered fighting reached Sicily. Sometimes England had the upper hand; other victories went to Duke Richard and the king of France.

Late in winter, Constance asked again for Sicily's support, and again, William refused. Joan was surprised—this time he scarcely seemed to consider the request.

"I promised our support to your brother," he said, sitting at the edge of her bed. "I won't go back on my word."

She certainly wouldn't argue, though he had a ready excuse at hand if he wanted to oblige Constance. Richard was making war against his own father, and not for the first time. Should such a man lead a crusade?

"Well, then, thank you," she said, grudgingly acknowledging his sacrifice. She slid sideways to make room for him to recline.

He did but sat up abruptly, coughing, one hand covering his mouth. His face reddened with the effort. Afterward, while he leaned close to the edge of the bed to catch his breath, she noticed him wiping his hand against his tunic, which was draped across the closest chair. A smear of blood appeared on the hem.

"William!"

He turned to her, looking aged and miserable.

"William, what is wrong?"

"Nothing," he said. "Nothing that can be helped. Genuold gives me possets."

"Do they work?"

"Sometimes. They used to." He sighed and scratched at a roughened spot of skin on his thigh. It wasn't fasting and hair shirts. Her husband was ill.

"The nosebleeds, do you still have those?"

"Sometimes."

"And you cough blood. What else?"

"I'd rather not talk about it, Joanna."

She clamped her mouth shut. Of course not. He had never invited her into his private world. For good reason. But would he recover? Was he dying? He couldn't die without an heir. "Can you . . . are you able to lie with me?"

"Sometimes," he said, turning his head away, his eyes so dull it hurt her. "I thought tonight . . . I felt stronger."

So, he came to her chamber on days he felt strong enough. And those days had grown farther and farther apart. Stupidly, she had been grateful for the reprieve.

"Oh, William," she sighed, tears of helplessness burning her eyes. "What are we to do?"

Emperor Barbarossa would have Sicily. Constance would return to find her old rival a childless widow.

"We do what we can, Joanna. And put our faith in God's plan."

God's plan. "Is this why you would not take the cross?"

He blinked at her. "I would have been a poor crusader. But yes, I might otherwise have taken the vow, though to the sure detriment of my soldiers and the other Christian kings. So, perhaps my illness is the Lord's blessing."

"God's feet, William, that sounds almost blasphemous. Most men I know would only speak like that in jest."

He swung his feet to the floor. "I cannot afford to blaspheme. And I am not one of most men you know."

"Are you angry with me?" she asked, startled.

"No." He shook his head and stood, using both hands to

push himself up. "I am tired. And angry with myself. I had hoped to keep this from you as long as possible. You have worries enough."

She scrambled to her knees on the bed. "Surely you know me better than that. You mustn't keep things from me. William, what does Genuold say?"

A small smile came to his face, accompanied by a faint light in his eyes. "You do that when you are eager," he said, gesturing to her posture. "I used to wonder . . ."

"Wonder what?"

"What it would be like if you were to welcome me some evening, perched like that, like a bird poised for flight." He shook his head, his sallow cheeks turning a pale pink. "You only do it when you want me to tell you something."

Feeling the heat of her own blush, Joan wished she could change position, but any movement would call too much attention to itself. Why on earth would he say such a thing now?

"My mother taught me to be curious," she murmured, knowing it wasn't an adequate response.

He nodded and said very quietly, "And mine taught me to be wary of saying too much. Good night, Joanna."

THEY HELD ANOTHER CONFERENCE AT WHITSUNTIDE. KING Philip raised his conditions of peace to three: Alice must wed Richard, Richard must be heir to England, and Prince John must take the cross. King Henry stormed from the meeting swearing to avenge himself on his son. But it was not to be.

Richard won La Ferté-Bernard, Montfort, Maletable, and Beaumont. He would have captured his father in Le Mans but for King Henry's quick flight and strong rearguard in Sir William Marshal. Marshal had once been Richard's fencing master, and the tale echoing throughout Christendom was that the two met face to face. Richard was not wearing armor and cried out that it would be dishonorable of Marshal to kill him. Marshal cursed him to the devil and killed his horse instead.

Joan didn't know which was worse, war or sickness. Now that she knew of William's disease, it seemed impossible she had not seen it before. At the same time, she wondered how many at court were aware.

He hid it well. In his heavy long tunics, no one could observe his wasting or the marks on his skin where incessant itching led him to scratch until he bled. If he no longer went to the Cuba, it was because events in the Holy Land drove him to repentance. If he stared distractedly at the walls during supper and entertainments—well, distraction had always been his way. Over Joan's solitary heart hung a doomed sense of waiting: waiting for him to die, waiting for her father and brothers to kill each other.

Early in August, amidst the bloom-filled beauty of her garden, Joan spent a morning scattering bread crumbs to the multicolored fish in her fountain. She liked to watch them bob to the surface and pop open their mouths.

From the balcony, Charisse called out, "Lady, the king is here. He wishes to see you."

"I'm near the fountain. Will he come down?" Joan called back. He had never visited her in the garden before, but it didn't surprise her. More often now, he sought her company during the daytime.

"I will," William answered. A minute later, he stood by her

side, wide-eyed, gray-faced. "Joanna, something terrible . . . I thought I should be the one to tell you." His voice cracked. "Your father is dead."

"Papa?" She swallowed rapidly, her legs turned to water, and she sat down. "How?"

"He lost the war. Several weeks ago, Duke Richard took the castle of Tours."

"Tours," she echoed.

"Your father met with King Philip and Duke Richard the next day and agreed to all of their terms. He was ill, very ill, or he never would have done so. His men carried him back to Chinon in a litter. He died two days later."

"Who was with him at the end? John?"

"No. William Marshal. Robert of Chenowith. A few others."

"Not even John." And she had not kissed him before leaving England. "My poor father."

She felt too desolate to cry. Hadn't she known it would come to this?

William sat beside her. "The duke's first decree was to have your mother freed from prison." He said it as a question, as if knowing it would please her, hoping it would be enough.

"Yes." She tried to smile, though her heart felt no less heavy. "Will there be any trouble with the succession, do you think?"

"It seems not—his coronation is set for next month at Westminster Abbey. The Normans and Angevins have already sworn oaths of fealty, even those most loyal to your father. Richard was lenient with them. He also sought absolution from the archbishops of Rouen and Canterbury for the unnatural war."

"He is thorough, isn't he?" she murmured, her voice catching.

Richard must be wild with despair. He had loved Papa, but they had been too much alike.

"They say he wants to begin his crusade."

Joan could not respond; there was nothing more to say. Suddenly she felt glad she and William did not love each other. Distance set a limit to the pain they could cause one another. If only Mama had warned her not to love her brothers, either, or her father.

A sob wrenched her chest, like a great hiccup, and she could not hold back her tears. William's arms settled around her shoulders. Back and forth, he rocked her while she wept.

IN AUTUMN, CHRISTENDOM LEARNED THAT SALADIN HAD released King Guy of Jerusalem. In defiance of the oath he'd sworn to his captor, Guy made fast for Tyre to join and—he must have assumed—take command of the Holy Land's remaining Christian knights. But Conrad of Montferrat, who held Tyre, refused to submit to him. Joan could not bring herself to fault Conrad. King Guy had shown such poor sense before the battle of Hattin.

But perhaps he had been shamed into better behavior. When thwarted in Tyre, he assembled an army from the few small contingents of crusaders who had made their way to the Holy Land in advance of the great kings, and laid siege to Acre.

William threw himself into a flurry of activity. Sicily's ships must be made ready; the army must be raised. Joan thought he seemed stronger. He bedded her twice in the month of October and even mentioned the possibility of another trip to Messina.

But the flush in his cheeks was fever, not health. His frenzy was a desperate one.

One morning he suffered paroxysms of coughing during morning prayers and had to be helped from the chapel by Genuold and two pages. When the service ended, Joan went to his apartments to find him asleep. Behind the door of his bedchamber she noted a chamber pot a quarter full of rust-red urine. Genuold must have seen her alarm, because he pulled her away from the door and bed toward a window.

"Was that his water?" she asked, feeling nauseated.

Genuold nodded. "I'm afraid, my lady, he hasn't much time."

She sat by his bedside for three days, leaving only when Charisse or Sati dragged her away to rest. Then Bishop Palmer cornered her on her way back and asked what was wrong.

"He is dying," she answered tiredly. There was no reason to hide it. They would all know soon enough.

To her surprise, the bishop merely sighed. "He has been ill a long while, hasn't he?"

She nodded.

"May I see him?"

It felt odd to have him ask her permission. When had she gained the authority to stand between Richard Palmer and the king?

"Of course. But don't wake him if he is sleeping. He sleeps so fitfully now."

The bishop sighed again, turning his head to blink at tears. Joan put a hand on his arm.

"He will be pleased to see you," she said, knowing it to be true. She had never paid attention to the fact that they were friends. There was so much about William she'd never bothered to know.

Another week passed, and Joan realized, counting the days,

that she had not had her flux in almost eight weeks. It had been late before—she'd learned not to hope—but never this late. She said nothing to anyone, not even a whisper in William's ear while he was sleeping, but she counted each sick twinge in her belly, each time fatigue threatened to overwhelm her, as more evidence in her favor. God was merciful. She would have a son after all. She would not be the barren queen who brought about Sicily's ruin.

She and Richard Palmer took turns keeping the bedside vigil. When William was awake, he seemed peaceful. But in sleep he was tortured, coughing, gasping for breath, calling out feverish words Joan never understood.

On the eighteenth of November, he woke suddenly and said, "Joanna!" She startled awake and reached for his hand. It felt cold and without the strength to grip hers in response.

"Forgive me." He coughed, weakly, and made a gasping sound. Then his eyes bulged, and blood dribbled from his mouth.

"Genuold!" she shouted, getting to her feet. "Genuold!"

The physician flew into the room, his tunic askew. "What is it?"

Joan dropped her husband's hand, which fell limply beside the bed. Genuold reached down and closed William's eyes, then lifted the hand to fold over his chest.

"Hand me a towel," he commanded.

Joan found one on the bedside table and gave it to him without a word. Genuold wiped the blood from William's lips and chin.

"Tell the bishop—he'll know what to do."

Tell the bishop. Joan plodded from the room, dazed. She didn't want to look for Bishop Palmer. She wanted to sleep. She hadn't slept well for a week. Her last bath had been . . . she couldn't remember.

With one hand on the railing, she descended the stairs. It was very early in the morning; only the kitchen servants must be awake. She'd have to wake Sati to find the bishop. Glancing down at her skirts, she saw a small splotch of blood. The first thing she must do was change her clothes. How could he have spat blood all the way onto her skirt when his cough had been so weak?

Then the whole world spun round. Joan collapsed onto the steps and sobbed. William was dead. And the blood was her own.

PART THREE

COUNTESS JEANNE

## SIXTEEN

*Palermo, Sicily, September 1190*

THE QUEEN OF ENGLAND WAS IMPRISONED BECAUSE OF HER sons; the queen of Sicily, for want of one. Who would fight to set a barren queen free?

Tancred of Lecce had usurped Sicily's throne before William was cold and immediately arrested Joan, confining her to her apartment in the Royal Palace. She'd been his prisoner now for nigh on a year.

Tancred knew he would have to defend himself against Constance and her husband, Barbarossa's son. To that end, he had kept for himself the fortune William had bequeathed to the English king in gold and provisions for the crusade: a large silk tent, fifty armed galleys, and four months' stores of grain and wine. Not that Tancred's perfidy would mean much to the crusaders. At last word, Richard and King Philip had met at Eastertide to discuss their plans, only to receive news of the death of France's queen in childbed. Once again, their departure had to be postponed.

Joan wondered how the Christians in the Holy Land could possibly hold out. King Guy de Lusignan's siege of Acre had lasted throughout the previous winter, despite harsh weather, sickness, and famine. Queen Sybilla died, and Conrad of Montferrat married her sister, staking his own claim to the throne of Jerusalem.

Sicily sent no more aid. In fact, Tancred had even recalled Margaritus, claiming he needed the fleet at home.

A knock on the door interrupted Joan's musings. A eunuch guard announced, "It is the tutor." Charisse hurried to the door and opened it. There stood Eugenius, a stunned expression on his face.

"Whatever is it, Eugenius?" Joan asked.

"The crusade is underway at last. King Richard is come." His voice sounded strained.

She stared. "My brother? Here?" He had come to deliver her. Warmth stole through her and she felt so overcome she nearly wept.

"He wants the ships King William promised."

Bewildered, she asked, "He thinks Tancred will give him aid?" It made no sense. Surely, Richard knew William was dead.

Eugenius snorted. "I doubt he cares for Tancred's intent. He's in Messina, along with the king of France, demanding your release and dowry."

Joan sat down, almost missing her chair. "Richard!" she said under her breath, as if swearing an oath. So he was not here for her sake alone. "Will . . . will Tancred release me?"

"He must. He can't afford to alienate any enemy of Emperor Barbarossa. And if he dares defy your brother, there will be bloodshed."

Biting her lip, Joan looked away. She was responsible for Sicily's impossible predicament. And now Richard must bargain or fight with Tancred, when he should be saving his money and men for the crusade.

"Lady?" Eugenius's voice was uncharacteristically gentle.

"Tancred will make peace with King Richard. You will be free of this prison."

What would happen to her now? Another marriage? The dowry William had promised her, Monte Sant'Angelo, had worth, but not enough to overcome the liability of her person: barren yet too young to conveniently die. An old man with sons might take her. Or there was always the convent. She'd exchange one prison for another.

Why had Richard bothered to come?

THERE STANDS A KING, JOAN THOUGHT.

In the frescoed dining hall in Messina's palace, surrounded by a dozen thick-limbed Norman knights with ragged beards and swords at their sides, Richard waited. He stared a moment before breaking into a wide smile and opening his arms. Joan flung herself against his chest. After a crushing embrace, he pushed her away to study her.

"Sister mine, you look like hell. Did Tancred do this to you or William?"

Flushing, Joan glanced reluctantly at the stained gown she had been wearing since leaving Palermo. Her belongings were supposed to follow on the next ship, but she suspected Tancred would keep everything of value.

"I get seasick."

"God's legs! Seasick doesn't account for your hair."

She touched her head. The coils Charisse and Sati had painstakingly wrapped were all in place. Scowling, she said, "It's the Sicilian fashion, Richard."

"There," he bellowed, laughing. "I know that face."

He had not changed in the least. But what did she expect him to do? Weep for joy at the sight of her? This was Richard, not Henry or John.

"Ah, sister mine. There's someone you must see. Philip is very anxious to meet you. You're the only one who has eluded his spell."

"Spell?"

"You will think he is simply flattering you, until you wake one day distrusting your own heart. I'd keep you from him, but you always did have more sense than the rest of us."

At the end, his voice gentled. His eyes, pale blue and sad, met hers. Pride would never allow Richard to admit his regrets, but he had loved their brothers and Papa, too. Joan touched his arm. When he smiled, she felt unburdened. She forgave him and he knew it, as if their souls could speak without sound.

"Must I meet him now?" She gestured to her dress.

"He won't even notice. You're cleaner than he is, and not half so ugly. We'll go to him. He's expecting me to send a messenger requesting the honor of his company or some such foolishness. Tell me if you don't think he's a maggot."

"But Richard—"

"Come." He pulled her arm eagerly, and together they traversed the halls of the palace to a small chamber at the back. Joan thought it had once been a storeroom. Richard pounded on the door. "Philip! I've got her. Come see!"

The door opened. A page dressed crisply in scarlet blinked up at Richard, then bowed.

"Please come in, my lord, lady."

He backed out of the way. Richard winked and ushered her inside. Philip glided forward out of the shadows. Joan had to bite the inside of her lip to keep from giggling. His greasy tunic stank of sweat. He was shorter than she was, puny beside Richard. His dark hair was already receding, and he was obviously blind in one watery, drifting eye.

"Richard," he said curtly without looking at his rival, "and Lady Joan." When she gave him her hand, he bent and kissed it. "Please accept my condolences. It is a great tragedy for Christendom, but I am sure an even greater loss to you."

His good eye fixed on her face. She opened her mouth then shut it. She hadn't expected sympathy. Even more surprising was his evident sincerity. But then, he had just lost his wife.

Meeting his unsmiling gaze, she replied, "You've suffered an equal loss. I—"

"Not quite equal," Richard interjected. "Philip got a son for his pains."

"Richard," she scolded weakly, feeling as though he had kicked her, seeing Philip's face also go gray. Richard must be the most insensitive man alive.

Philip turned aside. "Your brothers have always sung your praises, madame. I now see why. I hope you will grace us often with your company while we're in Messina."

He sounded less sincere, as if a veil of courtesy had dropped between them.

Richard laughed. "If we don't invite her, we'll find her hiding under the table. Let's go, Joan. There must be a woman somewhere in Messina who knows how to plait hair. If I have to look at that hive on your head any longer, I'll take my knife to it."

Joan rolled her eyes, knowing Richard too well to take offense. She curtsied to the French monarch and turned to follow her brother. In leaving, however, she caught Philip's expression. Not pitying but compassionate. Apparently, the French king knew Richard as well as she did.

JOAN HAD BEEN IN MESSINA LESS THAN A WEEK WHEN DISAS-trous word came from the East: On the tenth of June, Barbarossa had drowned in a river crossing. His second son, Duke Frederick of Swabia, managed to keep only a small army together to push on to Acre.

Although she believed this meant Richard and Philip were more urgently needed, they saw it otherwise. There was no risk the Holy Land would be saved without them; so, rather than subject themselves to a winter sea journey, they would set out again in the spring.

But Richard could not abide idleness any more than their father; it didn't take long for the novelty of Messina to wear thin. Daily clashes occurred between the merchants of the city and Richard's soldiers, and he did nothing to discipline his men. When the violence came to a head, Joan was certain he welcomed it.

Early in October, a fight over the price of a loaf of bread escalated into a riot. Instead of reining in the instigating soldiers and asking the magistrate to quell the disturbance, Richard donned his armor and roused his knights with a call to war against the "Grifons," as he called the Greeks of Messina. At the end of the day, England's banner flew over William's city.

While Richard and his knights celebrated loudly through-out the halls of the palace, Philip, whose men had taken no part in the skirmish, came to her apartments. He was followed by the same young page she'd met before, who carried a flask of wine and two goblets.

She'd not turn away a king, though it was poor judgment for him to pay a call with no more of an escort. She did not offer him a chair. As if oblivious to the thinness of her welcome, he plucked a goblet from the page's grasp and poured it full of wine.

"Divided loyalties?" he asked, putting the drink in her hand.

"Pardon?" She closed her fingers tightly around the stem so her hand could not tremble. Although she didn't want wine, she brought the goblet to her lips. The warm, sweet bouquet of French wine filled her nose, bringing Poitiers closer. She sipped.

He answered while pouring his own drink. "Daughters are reared to be loyal to their fathers. Then those same fathers, or brothers, marry them off to the enemy."

"William was not my father's enemy."

"No. But you were Sicily's queen for twelve years." His mouth quirked into an awkward smile. "It shouldn't bother you to see Richard's standard flying over one of Sicily's proudest cities, but it does."

She sniffed and looked toward the windows, but didn't refute him.

"I thought I should tell you, I plan to see him this evening and insist France's banner be raised also. We agreed before setting out that any of the spoils of the crusade would be evenly divided."

"Sicily is *not* a spoil!"

His smile reappeared. "Divided loyalties." He took a drink. "I have no intention of conquering Sicily, and neither does Richard. He wants to frighten Tancred into keeping your husband's promises."

Joan squeezed her goblet tighter. What was Philip doing? "Do you wish to frighten some concession from Tancred also?"

"No. Nor am I interested in stealing half of your dowry." He looked at his hands. The insinuation was clear—he thought Richard would take what was rightfully hers. "But I do want to remind Richard that we are partners in this war. I believe Tancred will try to play us off each other. I have little patience for such games when our goal is Jerusalem."

"How noble of you."

He laughed. "You have Richard's tongue for sarcasm."

"Why are you telling me this?"

"Perhaps because I anticipate what your brother will say about me after we argue tonight."

"Do you expect me to defend you?"

"No. I'd rather he not know I talked to you at all."

"I won't lie to him."

"You may tell him whatever you like." Philip glanced around the room, then drained his goblet before looking back at her. "Would you like more wine?"

"No, thank you, though I enjoyed it." She handed back her goblet, the wine unfinished.

He smiled thinly. "Do you mind so much that I spoke with you?"

"Not at all."

"Perhaps I'll come again?"

"You are welcome."

"Come," he said to the page, and to Joan, "Good evening, madame."

IN THE MORNING, RICHARD BURST INTO HER ANTECHAMBER. His boots scuffed loudly on the marble floor until he stood directly in front of her couch, his beard flecked with food and his pores redolent of last night's wine.

"Did you hear what that coward . . . that shirker . . . it is like him to claim credit when he did none of the work!"

"Mmm-hmmm," Joan said, wetting floss between her lips to thread her needle. "What work is that? Using knights to mow down burghers?"

Richard stood still. The muscles of his jaw twitched with his anger.

She cast her eyes down and said, "I was their queen, Richard."

He stared at her before saying evenly, "Had they been Londoners, I would still have put down a riot."

"Had you been in London, you wouldn't have let your knights steal from merchants and force the women."

He held silent a moment. "Maybe not," he granted, then with a snort of laughter said, "What do you think Tancred will give us to go away?"

Joan shook her head. "You've nowhere to go until spring."

"By then, he'll be desperate for us to leave."

"Unless Emperor Henry is on the march. In which case, he'll hope one of you stays."

"One of us?"

She laid down her sewing. "Tancred needs an ally, Richard. And everyone knows you and Philip are uneasy friends. If he gets any word of dissension, he'll be quick to take sides."

"You're suggesting I need fear either Tancred or Philip?" He sounded irritated.

"Not individually."

"So you think I should remain cozy with Philip?"

"Unless you plan to ally with Tancred yourself."

Richard retreated to the windows and gazed toward the mountains.

"Your voice is so like our mother's." When he turned to face her, his eyes were hard. "Perhaps that is why Philip's words sound so much more convincing from your mouth. When was he here?"

Swallowing her nervousness as he advanced again, she answered, shrugging. "It was yesterday evening, while you were carousing."

Richard grabbed her wrist. "How often do you meet?"

"Don't be absurd." She tried to shake off his pincer grip.

"Are you aware"—his voice was low and sly—"that people are saying there will be a wedding at Christmastide? A widower already blessed with an heir and a barren widow—"

"Holy Mary! Who would start such a rumor?"

"I did." He laughed in her face. "It embarrasses him to hear it whispered about. He's afraid I'll guess how much he wants it."

"He doesn't," she said, wishing her voice were stronger.

He released her arm. "Even a man half blind can see your charms, pretty sister. But I'd never give you to him."

She let out her breath.

"Unless your honor is at stake. They say a young widow is easy prey, and if I were to understand Philip has been calling on you in secret—"

"You wouldn't!"

"I'm your brother and protector. It would be my duty."

Had this been his plan all along, to marry her to Philip? To the enemy? She bit back angry words. It would be a mistake to challenge Richard.

As if misunderstanding her silence for submission, he smiled falsely and said, "Don't fret. If his company pleases you so very much, you can enjoy it as often as you like, in my presence."

"But then I must suffer *your* company."

The forced smile disappeared, and his voice grew husky. "Jeanne, I know him. I warned you. Don't let him do this."

He left her with the protest still on her lips.

IN MARCH, RICHARD AND PHILIP TRAVELED TO CATANIA TO meet with Tancred. In lieu of his predecessor's promises, Tancred offered Richard twenty thousand ounces of gold. Richard accepted and, in return, gave him Excalibur, King Arthur's sword. Richard also accepted twenty thousand ounces of gold in his sister's name, relinquishing her dowry rights to Monte Sant'Angelo.

When Richard and Philip returned from the parley, Philip refused to disembark, saying his fleet would sail for Acre at first light. Joan joined her brother in the dining hall, sitting quietly while he paced back and forth between trestle tables, boasting of his success, mocking Philip's pique. In Catania, Tancred had accused Philip of authoring a letter warning him Richard meant to conquer Sicily and offering an alliance against the English. When Philip denied it, Tancred produced the letter, which Philip promptly declared a forgery.

"Did you write it?" Joan asked sullenly as Richard related the tale with ill-concealed glee.

"Me? Of course not. It bore Philip's seal." Now standing beside her, he nudged her elbow. His forearms were dirty and grainy with salt. As she turned up her nose, she heard him add under his breath, "Though I'll admit it was conveniently timed. Now Philip can't hold me to marrying Alice."

Richard had rejected Alice? Joan managed not to smile.

"Here now, sourpuss. You'll forgive me for Monte Sant'Angelo when I tell you who is in Naples, who should be here in a few days." He set one hip against the table, and hitched his foot onto the edge of her chair. "My bride-to-be."

"Bride! Who? How could—" Marriage negotiations were not concluded overnight. He had never had any intention of marrying Alice.

"The princess of Navarre. Berengaria. And guess who is bringing her."

What would Philip do when he heard? Bad enough Richard had spurned the French king's sister. But Navarre was a Spanish kingdom that was traditionally at odds with or alternatively trying to ally with Toulouse. Was Richard still harassing Philip's vassal?

"I can't guess, Richard. Tell me."

"Our mother, of course. Do you forgive me now?"

Gaping and breathless, she insisted, "I never faulted you for taking my dowry money. I simply wish you'd allowed me to offer it first." Her head spun. "Mama is truly coming? Do you know this princess? How old is she?"

"Almost your age." He scratched his nose. "Twenty-two?"

"I'm twenty-five."

"No." He looked alarmed. "She isn't that old."

Richard was thirty-three, yet he had just pronounced her to be ancient. Irked, Joan balled her hands into fists on the table and pressed, "Have you met her?"

"I know her brother, Prince Sancho. I met her once, I think, at a tournament. Sancho said I carried her kerchief."

"You don't remember?" Joan wagered the girl did.

"It was a long time ago. But, Jeanne," he continued, ducking his head as if imploring a favor, "we cannot marry during Lent, and if Philip really means to leave for Acre, I can't stay here through Easter. Berengaria will have to follow me." He let the words hang a moment. "She'll need a chaperone, and I need Mother at home keeping watch over John." His eyebrows rose; he grinned, in obvious delighted anticipation of her response. "You will come, won't you?"

She stared. Go with him? Joy washed through her as she understood his intent. How could she have imagined he meant to lock her away in a convent or marry her off to some old ogre whose favor he needed? Richard was taking her on crusade.

AT SEVENTY YEARS OF AGE, ELEANOR OF AQUITAINE HAD grown thinner but not frail; grayer, yet she did not appear old. Disembarking at Messina, she greeted her daughter with smiles and embraced her as matter-of-factly as if their separation had been one of weeks, not fifteen years.

Sparing no notice for the many ships lined up along the quay or the bustle of the men on shore, she asked, "Will you survive your mourning?"

"Of course." Hadn't she heeded Mama's warnings against love?

Her mother patted her arm and turned sideways to introduce the woman trailing behind. "This is Berry, Richard's fiancée. Be good to her."

Berengaria stepped forward timidly and curtsied. "Lady Queen—"

"I am queen no longer," Joan said. "To my sister, I am Joan."

The brown-haired Spanish princess was not particularly

pretty—her mouth and nose were too small, her dark eyes set too close. It made her appear almost elfin, an impression her whispery voice did nothing to dispel. "It is an honor to meet you."

"And a joy to meet you," Joan replied, feeling ridiculous under her mother's amused gaze. "Richard tells me we are to accompany him to Jerusalem."

"Yes," Berry murmured, pulling her cloak tighter about her shoulders.

Joan guessed she was frightened and pitied her.

The queen said, "We had hoped to be here sooner, but Tancred wouldn't let us put into harbor until Richard talked sense into him." Eleanor shot a look at Joan. "Philip is gone now?"

"Yes." Joan wasn't sure how else to respond. Richard had said nothing about Tancred preventing their arrival.

"I daresay Richard could have been more tactful. But I suppose the gold appeased Philip." Although her mother spoke offhandedly—and cryptically—Joan realized the words were directed at her.

"What gold?"

"Tancred's. Richard and Philip agreed to divide everything equally."

"Richard gave him half of Tancred's gold?"

"No." She studied her daughter. "Philip would only take a third."

Though she guessed his reason, Joan asked anyway. "Why?"

"He said he promised you he would not touch your dowry." Mama's voice was high and clear. "Richard did not tell you?"

"No, Mother. He must not have thought it important."

"I simply wanted to be sure you were aware of Philip's motives. I heard rumors—"

"Richard started that rumor himself. And I would not have Philip for all of France."

"Hmmm. France would be a fair prize. As I said, Richard might have been more tactful. But," she laughed softly, "that ship has sailed."

They quieted, seeing Richard approach, swaggering and smiling. At her shoulder, Joan felt Berengaria grow rigid.

"Mother, the horses are ready, finally. The stable tried to send a litter." He shook his head, incredulous. "Joan, what is wrong with these Grifons? Please tell me you haven't been going about veiled like a—"

"Richard," Mama interrupted sharply, "will you greet Berry or not?"

His mouth snapped shut, and he turned to Berengaria. "Forgive me, Princess. In my delight at seeing my mother and sister reunited, I nearly forgot."

Joan rolled her eyes. His excuse was as insulting as the offense. But Berengaria seemed not to notice. Her face glowed, and she trembled as she curtsied.

"My lord king, I . . . I . . . ." Then she blushed and curtsied again.

"Berry, is it? It suits you. I do apologize for the delay. I had hoped we'd be wed here in Sicily. But Joan is so excited to be going on crusade"—he clapped Joan's shoulder—"I'd almost think she finagled her own imprisonment."

"William did not enjoy traveling," Joan said. "Have you traveled much, Berry?"

Joan nearly had to hold her breath to hear her answer, "Not until now. But your mother says I did well." She looked up at Eleanor with a puppyish expression.

"She didn't lose a meal," Eleanor said. "Which puts Richard to shame."

"God didn't mean for men to walk on water," Richard said laughing. "You should have seen what sea travel did to Joan's hair."

"Richard!" Joan started to protest. How could he have made fun of her when he suffered from the same malady?

He turned his back on her and swept a hand toward Eleanor. "Mother, is it true you are leaving before the week is out?"

"At first favorable tides. You must be off, and the longer I stay, the longer you will."

"Well, then, let's leave this stinking harbor for the palace. You should see the city. Most of it is foul, but there are some quite remarkable churches." He took his mother's arm and began to lead her away.

Joan turned to the princess, whose eyes were soft with disappointment. She remembered her own sorrow when her husband-to-be had ignored her. And she'd been a child then, with nothing to tempt a man's interest, while Berry was closer to her in age than Richard realized. She'd probably been in love with Richard since he carried her kerchief to joust.

"He won, didn't he?"

"Excuse me?" Berry whispered.

"When he wore your token, Richard won?"

Berry nodded.

"He said he didn't remember winning, but I'll wager he was just being modest." She offered her arm, and Berry took it, beaming shyly. The poor girl didn't know Richard at all.

RICHARD SHOWED HIS MOTHER ABOUT THE CONQUERED CITY AS if he, not Joan, had been its ruler all these years. While he courted

Eleanor, Joan entertained his betrothed. She was glad to find Berry decent company. She could not play merels but excelled at chess. Years ago, she had been introduced to Ermengarde of St. Gilles and found her charming. Ermengarde had given birth to twin girls, or so she'd heard. And once, she had met young Raymond of Toulouse and thought he was not so bad as his father. Joan quickly changed the subject. Richard would not appreciate their good opinions of that lord.

On the third day, the master of Eleanor's ship announced they could sail the next morning. That night, she sent Berry for a walk with Charisse.

"What do you think of her?" Mama asked, sitting straight-backed as always.

Joan corrected her own posture. "A little colorless for Richard."

"That's why I chose her. Richard is colorful enough."

"He'll ignore her. He does already."

"Then you must be doubly kind. He's thoughtless, not cruel. Make sure they marry as soon as possible. He has to get an heir on her before he gets himself killed."

The thought of Richard dying knocked the wind from her. "God won't let Richard fall to Saladin," she said, half in prayer.

"God keeps His own counsel. But I do know John is not suited for kingship. His spine is made of water. And Geoffrey's son is smart enough, but he lacks nerve. We must be practical, Joan. You, of all people, should understand that."

Joan hung her head. For her, it would always come back to this: She had failed as a wife and as queen. "You know I'll do whatever you ask."

"You must do whatever *Richard* asks. Support him. Even when you know he is wrong."

Their eyes met. She felt the tug of her mother's will, her mother's love for Richard.

"Whatever he needs," she vowed. *But not whatever he asks.*

## SEVENTEEN

IT WAS A RELIEF TO WATCH MESSINA RECEDE INTO THE distance. Joan didn't feel she was leaving anything behind. Not even Sati, she thought wryly. She'd granted the maid her freedom, believing it unfair to compel a Saracen, even a baptized one, to journey with crusaders. But Sati chose to stay with her mistress. Joan felt guilty for ever doubting her loyalty.

The first two days passed pleasantly with sunshine, calm waters, and a stiff breeze to fill the sails. The third day, Good Friday, dawned bloodred before the skies darkened to gray. Joan's stomach roiled with the waves. The day's drizzle turned to heavy rain at eventide.

The shipmaster, whose white hair and deep voice inspired confidence, said, "Don't worry, my lady. The king won't lose a vessel."

Joan nodded, seeing a faint light glowing on the masthead of Richard's ship. She retreated to the shelter the women shared beneath the forecastle, an airless dark closet of a room with one small mattress to serve as a bed.

No one slept that night. The ship shuddered and bounced as though tossed into the air. The wind, heard through the wooden hull, sounded like a beast's death throes. They prayed for hours on end, alternating with bouts of seasickness. To Joan's shame, she could not always reach the chamber pot, but then it no longer mattered when the pot overturned.

Finally they were too exhausted for anything save to cling to each other and wait for morning or for death.

It was near noon before the waters stilled enough for Joan to venture from the cabin. She wandered the deck, climbing over debris. The sailors, bleary-eyed and drenched, paid no heed to her. In the distance, she could discern dark, fluttering shapes that assured her they were still with the fleet, though she could not see Richard's light.

At last she located the master. "Thank you for preserving us," she said, her voice raw.

"The Lord be thanked, not me."

"I don't see the king's ship."

He ground his teeth. "No, my lady. We lost sight of it during the night. We've caught the signals of six other ships, but they seem to be adrift also."

"Adrift?" Her stomach dipped. "Then we don't know how the others fared?"

"No, but we haven't come across any wreckage. The sun is out. Tonight we'll have stars. We'll find our course. There's no need to worry, my lady. It was not so bitter a storm."

If that had been a gentle storm, she'd not survive a harsh one. "Thank you. Please keep us informed."

One day of sunshine was followed by more than a week of wind and rain. They traveled in a fleet of seven now instead of two hundred. Two of the ships had signaled they were taking on water. In addition to seeking King Richard, their flotilla now began searching for land.

Then another storm arose out of nowhere, black clouds chasing white ones, erasing the pale hint of blue from the sky. One of the shipmaster's mates sent them to their cabin with the warning, "Bolt the door and keep to your bed."

Heart pounding, Joan made for shelter, pulling Berry with her. Sati blew out the swaying lamp—the smell of oil smoke thickened the damp air. In utter darkness, Joan found the bed and clenched the nearest hand.

They lay in a jumble of arms and legs tangled in skirts and bed linens, their moans blending with the wind. After a jolt, Joan heard a thud, then Berry's whimpering. A bony elbow caught her cheek.

"Jesus' knees," she swore, as Richard would.

"Don't blaspheme!" Charisse commanded, her voice tight with panic.

Then they heard a crack. Like a tree falling. Like the world breaking in two.

"The mast," Sati said.

Above the storm, the shouts of sailors on deck were audible for a moment. The walls sweated with moisture. Joan did not dare stretch a hand or foot to check the floor. Were they sinking?

A vision of William on Messina's dock came to her. *Send the fishing boats back out. I'll pay what they ask.* Her heart cried out, *William! Save us.*

Instantly, she wrenched her hand from Berry's to cross herself. William was no saint to intercede for anyone.

*Oh, merciful Father—*

Tossed against Sati, she heard deep-voiced Arabic murmuring. She understood enough to know they were praying to two different gods.

"Joan!" Berengaria gasped. "I will be ill."

Joan grabbed for her in the dark and pulled her head toward the edge of the bed, holding her hair as she vomited. Thunder boomed as loud as the cracking of the mast. She stroked Berry's hair, feeling her tremble.

For a long while, they rocked and jounced, until gradually, Joan began to imagine she was riding in a wain. Had she been sleeping? Berry's sour breath warmed her ear. They were alive. Heaven would not stink like this cabin, and Berengaria would never be in hell.

The wind had died. Joan untangled herself from the other women, waking them into groans and complaints. "I'm going out."

Sati said, "I will accompany you, lady."

They helped each other from the bed and stretched their arms and legs. Water coated the floor. They stepped out the door onto the slick deck.

The shipmaster greeted them.

"Lady, I was just coming to—"

"Land," Sati said. "Look there. Land."

"Yes," he said. "We think it must be Limassol harbor."

"Cyprus!" Joan gasped. They were in danger. "Isaac Comnenus has a truce with Saladin."

"But we must—"

"Are we sinking?"

"Sinking? No, the ship is sound." He rubbed the back of his hand against his jaw. "But lady, we can't go anywhere without repairing the mast."

"Then we stay here. If Richard lives, he will find us."

The master turned from her, grumbling. "We'll sit until the gulls pick our bones clean."

OF THE FOUR BOATS ANCHORED OFF LIMASSOL HARBOR, ONE sank, necessitating the division of its seamen and soldiers among the remaining ships. Because a good deal of the stores had been ruined in the storms, the master ordered the rationing of food and drink.

The smallest galley set out again to search for the fleet. Its master offered to take the princess's party, but Berengaria wept and refused to leave sight of land.

"We'll await the king," Joan said, both irritated with Berry and relieved for an excuse to stay close to shore.

After a week, several longboats approached, flying rags with the king of England's colors. The knights came aboard to report to the master. Three ships had beached during the storm, losing half their crews to the sea. Those who reached land were slaughtered or taken captive, but these prisoners had managed to escape.

The next day Isaac Comnenus sent an invitation to Joan and her escort to disembark, promising succor in memory of her late husband's support. She declined, asking instead for fresh water and food. The Cypriot king refused. Being right about the tyrant was small consolation.

But she was right about her brother also. Four days later, a scout cried, "A ship!" Joan stood on deck, peering back toward the west. Within an hour, the harbor was filled with English and Sicilian galleys, and Richard held her in his arms.

"Thank God, Richard. Thank God, you're here."

"I've had ships and messengers all over creation looking for you." He shook her shoulders. "What is this I've been hearing about the usurper? He tried to lure you to shore?"

"Heaven knows what he planned. But he still holds some of your knights."

"We'll remedy that." He turned to one of his men. "Send a message to Comnenus. He has one day to surrender my people and apologize for the insult to my sister and the princess. And I'll expect restitution for my lost ships."

"Sire, the beach is well fortified and shallow. You can't mean for us to take them by storm from longboats."

"I can't?" He smiled grimly. "By God, we will."


THE NEXT MORNING, JOAN WATCHED THE LONGBOATS STRAIN toward shore under a hail of arrows and stones. Buffeted by waves, a few were swamped; but Joan kept her eyes on Richard, stalwart and foolish, standing tall in the center of his boat.

They disembarked in a horde; Joan made out only that the men gained the beach. All day long she stood at the rail, while Berry hung on her arm with a thousand whispery questions she couldn't answer.

Toward sunset, the king sent word to his loved ones—they would spend the night on solid ground. Taking note of Berry's glistening eyes and nervous smile, Joan said, "You'll sleep with me, Berry."

She needn't have worried; her brother was not in the fort. Isaac had made camp only five miles away, so Richard ordered the travel-weakened horses brought on shore to set out after him. In the morning he returned, loaded down with plunder—strong Cypriot horses, food, gold, and arms, but not Isaac, who had managed to flee.

Buoyed by success, Richard grew boastful and expansive, handing out gifts all too generously, playing tricks, matching wits with Joan. But when she saw him draw his bride-to-be under his mantle to kiss her and Berry emerging flustered and pink, she decided she must act.

"Richard," she announced over supper, "I hear there is a lovely chapel here in Limassol, and the bishop of Evreux is in your company."

He glanced up from his plate. "Eh? What are you up to?"

"A wedding. It won't take but a few days to plan."

Richard grunted, then looked to Berengaria. "Are you still willing?"

Berry blushed a deeper shade of red than Joan thought possible.

"I'll talk to the bishop," Joan said. "May twelfth. That gives us four days."

Richard took a large swallow from his cup and set it down with a thud. "May twelfth? There is nothing inauspicious about the day." He reached across the table and pinched Joan's wrist. He said in Occitan, "I wasn't going to forget."

"I'm simply Mama's agent," Joan replied, also in Occitan, hoping Berry would not be offended.

"Ha! As am I, sister mine, as am I."


ON MAY II, GUY DE LUSIGNAN, THE ERSTWHILE KING OF Jerusalem, and his brother Geoffrey arrived in Limassol to beg Richard hurry to Acre. Not to aid in the siege, Joan noted cynically, but because King Philip had taken the part of Conrad of Montferrat, who had conferred upon himself the title "king-elect." Irritated by their inopportune timing, she almost pointed out that Saladin was, in fact, king of Jerusalem, but better sense ruled her tongue.

At the same time, a scout reported Isaac Comnenus had fled with his army to Famagusta, on the east coast of the island.

Throughout the afternoon, while the men held conference, Joan attended Berry. The princess shuffled through her wedding preparations nervously, as if afraid to be joyful. Richard had been handed two perfect excuses to postpone the ceremony.

When Joan could no longer bear the uncertainty, she left Berry with Charisse and Sati and went to Richard's quarters. Barging inside, she demanded, "What are you plotting?"

Richard flinched. The barber trimming his beard recoiled.

"God's toes, Joan! Would you have my throat cut?"

"Maybe. Berry has tried on every gown in her trousseau twice. What are you doing?"

Richard pushed away the barber's shaking hand. "What does it look like? You may report back to Mother that I did my duty bathed, barbered, and confessed of my sins."

She noticed several steaming buckets of water against the wall. Her brother didn't appear very martial in his undershirt and braies, a piece of linen draped across his chest. Hesitantly, she pressed, "What about Guy?"

"I invited him to the wedding. He's very pretty, don't you think? A widower . . ." He drew out the word, his voice warbling.

Joan ignored the taunt. "And Comnenus?"

"He's withdrawn as far as he can go. I told Guy if he aided me in Cyprus I would support him against Conrad. You know everything. Are you satisfied?" He pointed to the door. "I'm going to be washed."

"I'll leave. I'm sorry, Richard. I just . . ." What? Why hadn't she trusted him?

He shut his eyes, and the hard line of his jaw relaxed.

"Mother needn't have put the goad in your hand. I do want to marry Berry."

"You do?"

"I am king. I have to be married to someone."

An old wound reopened. "Don't ever say that to her."

ON HIS WEDDING DAY RICHARD WORE A ROSE-RED SAMITE tunic and cap, a matching mantle richly embroidered with golden threads, and a girdle of the finest Sicilian silk. Gold and silver encrusted the scabbard for his sword. Beside him, poor Berry possessed no more substance than a ghost.

Richard had asked that his own chaplain, a beefy Norman Englishman named Nicholas, say the wedding mass in the small Greek chapel of Saint George. Afterward, the bishop of Evreux placed a crown on Berry's dark hair.

Even at the celebratory feast, Richard seemed to behave himself, yet Joan would not breathe easy until morning. As the shadows grew longer, Berry's eyes grew wider and her complexion more pale.

"Come," Joan said at last, "we'll make you ready." She rose from her chair, beckoning to Charisse and Sati.

Richard smiled up at them, then reached after his bride and let his fingers trail down her arm. Joan thought Berengaria might faint. She took her elbow and led her from the dining hall to Richard's apartments.

The bedchamber was a shambles, the bed linens dirty and half torn from the bed. It stank of men's sweat and boots. Berry's face fell.

"Soldiers' quarters," Joan said brusquely. She should have thought to inspect the room.

Sati began straightening the linens; Charisse opened the shutters for air.

"Let me help you," Joan said, awkwardly gesturing to Berry's robe.

The frightened girl blinked and held up her arms. With Charisse's aid, Joan managed to strip Berry to her chemise before Richard pounded on the door.

"How long does it take to undress?" he shouted, laughing. He sounded drunk. Joan cursed under her breath. She should have made sure he watered his wine.

"Give us a minute, Richard."

Sati put a hand on the wild-eyed queen's shoulder to steer her to the bed.

"Sit," she said, and began unplaiting her hair.

Richard banged on the door again. Berry's lips moved without sound. After their near death at sea, her fear would have seemed comical, except Joan knew exactly how she felt. She could think of nothing soothing to say.

Sati spread her fingers through Berry's hair and said, "You are ready."

The door shook.

"All right, Richard! Enough." Joan pulled back the latch and opened the door.

Richard leaned against the wall, smiling maliciously. "You've done your duty, sister mine. It's my turn."

She wanted to slap him. When Charisse and Sati slipped into the hallway, Joan followed, feeling as if she'd thrown a child to a lion.

*He is thoughtless, not cruel. You must be doubly kind.*

Her duty had just begun.

THE KING OF ENGLAND CONQUERED CYPRUS IN LESS THAN three weeks. Kindness was weakness, and Richard was nothing if not strong.

Immediately after the wedding, they had sailed for Famagusta, only to find Isaac Comnenus had already decamped. Instead of Greeks, an envoy from Philip and Conrad awaited Richard. His allies were growing impatient. Furious, Richard accused them of encouraging the tyrant to avoid battle, knowing the crusaders would soon have no choice but to move on.

He chased his enemy into the island's interior and on to the mountain fortresses of the north, though he could ill afford a protracted search of Cyprus's mountaintops. Then Guy and Geoffrey captured Kyrenia, a small town on the northern coast where Isaac's daughter had taken refuge. As soon as he heard of Kyrenia's capitulation, Isaac surrendered, begging only that he not be put in irons.

The court gathered in the great hall of the local Greek palace for Guy's triumphant return. As Joan took her place next to Richard, he grumbled regrets that he had no time to pry the mosaics from the walls. She didn't bother replying. Enough of Cyprus's prodigious treasure was portable. It was not simply his greed she found offensive, but his lack of discernment. The mosaics were pretty but hardly fine.

A herald announced King Guy, who marched in and nodded to Richard, proudly, as if they were on equal footing. His floral perfume permeated the four corners of the room. He was a handsome man, as everyone said, yet Joan considered his looks too sculpted, too delicate. William had been far more beautiful and not half as vain.

"Lord King," Guy said, "I give you the Cypriot 'emperor.'"

The gilded door opened once more; two guards half led, half dragged the captive across the carpets. A gasp rose from the assembly, followed by laughter. Isaac Comnenus was fettered with immense silver chains. Richard's sense of humor—he had not put Isaac in irons. The joke must have cost a fortune, but everyone would sing of it.

Richard asked, "And where is the girl?"

"Bring Lady Theodora," Guy commanded.

The daughter who entered the next moment, head held high, was no child. Although her face was youthful, she had a woman's body—rounded hips, a small waist, and a bosom so large it seemed unnatural. No one had bound her hair, which fell to the small of her back, shining like a crown of black glass.

"The tyrant is yours," Richard told Guy, his voice coming from deep in his throat, "but the girl I remand to my sister's keeping."

Joan winced. He should have sent the girl to a nunnery. His intention was clear enough.

Mama was right about men. The devil take them all.

## EIGHTEEN

O N THE EIGHTH OF JUNE, 1191, KING RICHARD OF ENGLAND arrived at Acre. It seemed the whole Christian world had come: French, Danes, Flemish, Champagnois, Germans, and now the Normans under England's ruler. United, the Christian horde would be insuperable.

The king of France had been there since the twentieth of April. In seven weeks, he had assembled a catapult and a large siege tower, which he attempted, several times, to put to the walls. He ordered men called sappers to dig tunnels beneath the Accursed Tower, one of the Saracens' primary defensive towers. But King Philip had not taken Acre.

King Richard was welcomed with daylong festivities. Trumpets and cymbals sounded loudly enough to alert the Saracens that their position had become even more tenuous.

Richard asked Joan to sup with him that evening, but he did not include Berry. He claimed it was because Philip would be there—Joan thought it a weak excuse. Philip could not truly have expected Richard to marry Alice after what Papa did.

Her brother's pavilion was centrally located in the English camp. His tent was multichambered and made of silk, the workmanship obviously Sicilian. She entered through an actual wooden door, hung by leather hinges from a sturdy frame. The entrance hall served also as dining room. The table before her held a fortune in silver plate, and the smell of meat roasting had reached her all the way outside. How must that sit with men who had gone hungry for two years?

Richard stood beside the table, gnawing a knuckle of pork. Obviously, it had not occurred to him to wait for his guests.

"Hunh," he greeted her, chewing. "Philip will surely be glad to see you."

"It's not as if Philip doesn't know about Berry," Joan said, continuing the argument she'd been having with her brother in her head. Besides, did Richard think she was blind to the amount of time he had been spending with Theodora? "How long do you intend to ignore your wife?"

He tossed the knuckle to a hound sitting quietly in a shadowed corner. The dog pounced, and she heard the bone crack between its jaws.

"Shut your mouth. I want you to sit quietly and try to look pretty." He wiped his hand on the tablecloth then circled his finger beside his head and teased, "Why didn't you do that Sicilian thing with your hair?"

She sat without answering and awaited Philip's arrival. The French king gave her a thin smile and took the seat opposite, then obliged her by ignoring her throughout the first course. By the second, an argument was in full force. Richard wanted to reorganize the entire siege strategy. Philip insisted he was making good progress and could take Acre in another month, with or without Richard's help.

Richard scoffed. "You've set your sappers at the Accursed Tower."

"The wall is weakening."

"And if it falls, no one will be able to get through the rubble.

Your infantry will have to scale a mountain of debris. You've chosen the worst possible spot."

Philip stood. They glowered at one another. Joan refilled Philip's goblet before Richard's unobtrusive cupbearer thought to do so.

"Sit, please, my lord. If you leave, I'll be alone with Richard in this temper."

Philip sat, grudgingly, and Joan suspected she'd diffused their anger only by taking it upon herself.

Richard raised his jeweled cup and swirled it. "Do as you like. I'll lay my own siege."

"I didn't expect cooperation."

"Meaning?"

Philip sneered, deferring to Joan. "What do you think of the valiant Guy de Lusignan?"

She kept silent.

"He captured Isaac Comnenus," Richard said.

"He captured a girl," Philip scoffed, pulling on the edge of his mustache. "Everyone here supports Count Conrad of Montferrat for king of Jerusalem over Guy. I only confirmed their choice."

"You hadn't the courage to make an unpopular decision?" Richard mocked.

"I don't make *stupid* decisions simply to prove I can enforce them."

Joan felt the knot in her stomach tighten.

Philip was the first to look away. He sighed, then stabbed a piece of boar with his knife and put it into his mouth. Joan couldn't watch him chew. His blind eye dipped and bowed.

"You'd do well to make peace with Conrad," he said, without looking at Richard.

"If Guy hadn't kept Saladin occupied here for two years, Tyre would be in infidel hands. Conrad would do well to make peace with Guy."

Joan said, "I thought they'd reached an understanding until you two stirred the pot."

"Their 'understanding' was to make war against each other as soon as Saladin is beaten." Richard chopped at his food so hard the table rumbled.

"At least they are willing to wait until then."

Richard's knife stilled. After a pause, he looked at Philip and shrugged. "My mother's tongue."

Philip smiled grimly. "You shouldn't encourage her."

"God's feet," Joan muttered. Richard had invited her to be the shield that blunted their blows.

The French king rose once again. "I've overstayed my welcome. Madame"—he made a curt bow—"I'll leave you to your supper."

Richard waved his knife at him and continued to eat; Joan scrambled to her feet to curtsy.

With Philip gone, she sat and stared at the table. Richard got up and opened the door. After peering outside, he flapped it open and shut several times. "The man stinks."

"You both do. You know, Sicilians have a fascinating custom. They call it 'bathing.'"

He returned, grimacing, and sat. "Eat something. You're thinner than I found you at Messina."

She put a morsel in her mouth. Then another, so she would not have to speak.

Toying with his food, Richard said, "Guy is an idiot. His brother Geoffrey is worth three of him."

She'd heard it said that Geoffrey de Lusignan was a remarkable warrior. Older than Guy by several years, he was inoffensively plain, with a large nose and small chin. She choked down her meat.

"Is it true Philip shouldn't have placed his sappers before the Accursed Tower?"

"He saw it himself. He was ready to move them, but won't now I've pointed it out." He sounded pleased, and Joan couldn't follow his reasoning. "The Saracens will concentrate their defense there. It will give me opportunity to mine the south wall of the city with my own sappers."

So Philip's men would suffer the worst of it, and Richard would claim the victory.

"That is low, Richard."

"If sense ruled him, he'd move them anyway. I can't be blamed for Philip's pride."

"No," she said, rubbing her temples. But he could be faulted for his own.

JOAN DREAMED OF THE ZISA'S GARDEN. SHE WOKE DISGRUNTLED. How simple life was when one was imprisoned.

For three weeks, she had tried to support Richard while he neglected Berry, trysted with his Cypriot captive, and squabbled with Philip as if they were both spoiled children rather than kings. When Philip executed another assault against Acre, Richard refused to take part, claiming they'd do better to wait until his men finished assembling the catapults he'd brought from Sicily. That wretched day the garrison beat drums to signal they were under attack, and Saladin responded with an assault against the crusaders' camp. Joan had never been so terrified.

Soon after, Joan learned that Philip had been taken sick. It seemed a quarter of the army was ill with arnaldia, a wasting disease with fevers that had their physicians mystified. They said Philip hadn't risen from his bed for two days and some of his fingernails had fallen out.

Joan looked at her own filthy hands. No wonder everyone was sick. Tonight she would bathe, in seawater if necessary.

"Lady," Charisse whispered, stirring, "you're awake? I'll set out your dress."

"Where is Sati?"

Charisse shrugged. "She rose early."

Joan wouldn't voice her fears. She had suspected—from Sati's guarded sighs, the way her eyes searched the horizon, her increasingly secretive prayers—that the maid was looking for a way to escape to the Saracens.

Joan donned a faded red dress, choosing to ignore the fraying hem and discolored bodice. She regularly wore only two of her gowns; the rest she kept packed away. After having been queen of one of the world's wealthiest kingdoms, Joan had only a few trunks left to her name.

She stood to have her hair fixed. After two strokes, Charisse dropped the comb with a gasp. "Lice."

Joan shut her eyes and held her breath until the urge to shudder passed. "It's unavoidable. If that is the worst we suffer—"

"Lady." Sati's muffled voice came from the other side of the curtain that screened their beds. "The lord king has sent a page."

"Oh?" Thank God she was still with them. The devil only

knew what might happen if a beautiful Saracen woman were caught wandering alone in a crusaders' camp. "I'll be right there."

Gingerly, Charisse wrapped a broad flat ribbon around Joan's hair and tied it to the back of her dress.

"Yes?" Joan pulled back the curtain and greeted the boy. He was round-faced and wide-eyed, somebody's nephew, too young to be here.

"The king requests you to come at once. He . . . he has the arnaldia."

No wonder the boy looked so scared.

Joan took the shortest route, past the compound of the wounded, a cluster of tents she generally avoided. The groans of the suffering, the stench of gangrene and clotted blood appalled her. With aching lungs and burning thighs, she climbed the hill that gave Richard's pavilion its vantage point.

As she yanked open the door, Geoffrey de Lusignan came forward, perspiration beaded on his lip.

"The physician just left. Now Chaplain Nicholas is with him."

"Oh!" She felt a stab of fear as she drew her next breath. "Let me see him." She brushed past into Richard's sleeping chamber.

He lay on a wood-framed bed with a thick mattress. He had pushed off his sheet, and the room smelled of his fever sweats. The chaplain sat on a stool at the foot of the bed. He nodded in greeting but didn't rise, appearing too exhausted to do so.

"Ah, sister mine. Come nurse me." Richard looked pale and defenseless.

When Geoffrey delivered a chair to the bedside, she sat, tears stinging her eyes, and combed her brother's matted hair with her fingertips.

"You are not so bad off," she said, making her voice as crisp as Mama's. "I have lice."

Richard's laugh was little more than a whimper. "Then you must also take sick. The physician said my hair will fall out."

"Oh, Richard. Then how will we tell you and Philip apart?"

"King Philip is the one *behind* his troops," Geoffrey said. "Our king is the man in front."

Joan gazed up at Geoffrey gratefully. No doubt Richard preferred admiration to her banter.

"Let him sleep as much as he can," Nicholas said, getting to his feet. "I can't stay. Everyone wants to say confession today. Who would think sin would be so rampant in a crusaders' camp?"

Joan nodded without thought for an answer, too worried about her brother's body to be concerned for anyone else's soul.

"I must be off, too, lady," Geoffrey said. "The king has set me a few tasks."

"Yes. Wait, I'll see you out." She escorted them from Richard's bedroom to the area that served as entrance and dining hall. Armor, clothing, parchments, and maps lay scattered about.

She touched Geoffrey's arm as he reached for the door. "What did the physician say?"

Geoffrey hesitated. "He said the king shouldn't have taxed himself in yesterday's heat. He should stay abed until he's recovered."

"Recovered," Joan echoed. "What else?"

"He should expect to lose his nails and hair. His mouth will bleed. He might lose teeth."

"God in heaven. What else?" Joan waited until he continued in a husky whisper.

"Some men in camp are dying. But God won't permit the king to die."

"God keeps His own counsel."

"That's what he said." Geoffrey sounded awed. "He said, 'God keeps His own counsel. Fetch my sister. Joan will not let me die.'"

SHE EMPTIED RICHARD'S CHAMBER POT, CHANGED HIS SWEAT-drenched clothing, mopped his brow, and spoon-fed him luke-warm sops of bread and broth. Meanwhile, his officers interrupted his rest at all hours, and he refused to let her banish them.

Upon hearing Philip was well enough to supervise the French troops, he decided he must check on his own. When Joan insisted he stay in bed, he commanded his men to carry the bed outdoors. After each unwise exertion, he relapsed into fevered moaning and lethargy, then slept, only to wake and overtax him-self again.

Then one night, Geoffrey de Lusignan appeared at the king's tent. When he saw her, he seemed reluctant to speak, but Richard had heard his voice and called him to the bedside.

"What word?"

Refusing to look at Joan, Geoffrey said, "He said he'd send el-Adil."

"Perfect. Bring him."

"What are you talking about?" she demanded. Wasn't el-Adil Saladin's brother?

"I've been trying to meet with Saladin." Richard finished with a rattling voice. He coughed, winced, and rubbed his chest.

Meeting in secret with Saracens? How foolhardy! What if they took him hostage or killed him? Or Richard's allies might strike Geoffrey down just as readily for negotiating with the enemy.

Geoffrey frowned. "El-Adil is as anxious to observe our camp as you were for me to scout theirs. Are you sure he should see you this ill?"

Joan wondered who else would be brave enough to tell Richard he appeared weak.

"I am not dying. That much, he will see."

"Then you may expect him the day after tomorrow." Geoffrey avoided Joan's stare. "This will not remain secret, sire."

"No matter. England's king needs answer to no one."

JOAN EXPECTED SALADIN'S BROTHER TO BE OLDER, FOR THE sultan was an old man. But el-Adil looked to be William's age. Beside Geoffrey he seemed tall, but when he passed the curtain she'd hidden behind, she guessed he was closer to her own height. In the center of his forehead, a few locks of gray-streaked black hair escaped from under a richly woven turban. He would have been handsome if not for a sunken scar extending from his right nostril to his ear.

Geoffrey led him into the king's bedchamber. She crept close to the silk wall to listen—Geoffrey's Arabic, though rough, put hers to shame. She repeated silently the words she needed to remember, the speech she had practiced for two days.

Richard praised the bravery of Saladin's garrison but assured el-Adil that Acre would fall. The Saracen disagreed, saying reinforcements had come from Sinjar and Egypt, and an even greater force was on its way from Mosul.

"That simply means more of your people will die," Richard said.

El-Adil asked what he proposed, but Richard answered vaguely. Joan suspected he wanted to hear Saladin's offer first. After a few careful exchanges, he said he would send his envoy to Saladin again on July 1, in one week, with gifts to show his goodwill.

Hearing movement, she scrambled away from the wall. As soon as el-Adil emerged, she stepped into his path and curtsied.

"Sir, I am the king's sister. I—"

"Joan!" Richard roared from the next room. "What are you doing?"

She tried to continue quickly, but el-Adil's panicked response made her forget the words. His body grew rigid, his cheeks ruddy, and he averted his eyes to the side of the tent.

"Oh," she gasped, swallowing an oath. She wasn't veiled—what must he think?

Richard threw aside the curtained flap of his bedchamber; his clothes were wrinkled and sweat-stained, his colorless face betraying the strain of rising. El-Adil rolled his eyes toward the ceiling, and he seemed to be holding his breath. There was nothing to do but finish.

"I want him to find a place for Sati. I've been watching her, Richard. She's looking for a way to leave."

El-Adil tilted his head toward Geoffrey and asked, "Is this the Sicilian queen?"

Joan answered him. "I was."

Without looking at her, he said, "Your husband was greatly admired. A just and generous man."

"Yes." Joan added haltingly, "As are you." When Jerusalem fell, he'd set a thousand Christian prisoners free.

He stole a glance then raised his eyes twice as quickly,

blushing harder. To Joan's surprise, Richard remained silent. She struggled to remember her speech.

"In Sicily, when I was a child, I was given a maid. She wants to live among people of her faith. But—"

"Send her to my brother. She will have a place in his household."

Joan bowed. "Thank you."

"Geoffrey," Richard said, "please take the lord el-Adil back to his escort."

As Geoffrey led el-Adil away, Joan braced herself for her brother's fury, but he wore a curiously benign expression. He slung an arm over her shoulder.

"Help me back to bed. You nearly killed me."

"I'm sorry. I—"

"I'm not angry. Will he take Sati? She can be one of my gifts to Saladin." Joan jumped when he barked a laugh. "Did you see his face? By God, sister mine, you damn near killed *him*!"

AFTER A FEW MORE WEEKS OF FIGHTING, THE SARACEN GARRISON capitulated—against Saladin's orders. In addition to the city, they surrendered the Egyptian galleys in the harbor and promised the return of fifteen hundred Christian prisoners, the True Cross taken at Hattin, and a payment of two hundred thousand dinars. In return, they were granted their lives.

Joan, Berry, and Charisse watched from a hilltop as the garrison opened the gate and marched out across the plain into captivity, their wives and children following. For the first time, Joan felt glad Sati was gone.

Geoffrey de Lusignan brought them horses so they could join Richard's party, massing before the gate. The nearer they drew, the worse the stench. The ground was still saturated with old blood and tissue, intermingled with the scent of vinegar, the only liquid capable of extinguishing Greek fire. Berry's skin looked sallow, and Joan wagered her own face was green.

Richard waved and called, "At my right side, sister mine, for Mother's sake. And Berry beside you."

The cortege began moving. The English and French would enter through different gates simultaneously. Germans, Franks, Danes, Pisans, Genoese, Austrians, and any of the other small contingents might march behind, if they so chose. Joan suspected they might choose not to. Weary of being disregarded by Richard and Philip, many of those crusaders were selling their arms to raise passage home.

"When we leave," Richard said, leaning toward her, "you'll stay here with the bishop of Evreux. I'll leave a light garrison and the pilgrims."

"Who will Philip leave to guard his half?"

Richard turned his head and spat. "Philip? That dog. I asked him to take oath with me we'd give the Holy Land three years or die."

"Three years!" Her heart sank.

"He refused. He says he's sick with dysentery. The maggot is going to crawl home to France. Wait and see. He'll whisper in Johnny-boy's ear, God damn them both."

"Richard!" Hot dusty air flooded her lungs. "Mama is with John."

Richard grunted. Then he drew rein and shouted, "What! How . . . the cur!"

Joan followed the direction of his gaze to the citadel. Three banners fluttered above the portcullis: Richard's, Philip's, and that of Duke Leopold of Austria, a vassal of the Holy Roman emperor. The spoils were supposed to be split two ways, not three.

"Pull it down!" Like Papa in a temper, Richard was so red-faced, Joan feared he would fall from his horse in a fit. "Two bezants to whoever brings me Austria's flag!"

The first three knights to reach the portcullis climbed over each other's shoulders until one tore the banner down and ran it back to the hands of the king. The shouts and curses of Leopold's men inflamed Richard further. He dashed the banner to the ground and trampled it beneath the hooves of his horse.

Joan breathed easier as his color returned to normal. The tantrum seemed to sate him. But at what cost? The Austrian duke was no threat here, but Richard had already jeopardized relations with Emperor Henry by making a treaty with Tancred.

She wondered if Philip would be entertaining Leopold that evening. Richard said himself it would take a united Christian army to take and hold Jerusalem. Yet if he wasn't careful, he'd be crusading alone.

## NINETEEN

K ING PHILIP DEPARTED ACRE ON THE LAST DAY OF JULY.
Richard did not leave until August 25. By then, he and Joan
were no longer speaking. Princess Constance had once called
Richard barbaric and Joan had defended him. *Barbaric* now
seemed too gentle a word.

Saladin had been given less than three weeks to come up
with the ransom the garrison had promised. Never mind that he
had not agreed to the terms or that no Christian king at war for
so long could have produced two hundred thousand dinars in
such a short period of time. Richard accused the Saracens of
stalling to keep him in Acre until the campaigning season was
over. He said he could not drag the captives along, nor afford
the soldiers necessary to guard them. Perhaps these things were
true. But had he forgotten how generously Saladin treated the
Christians in Jerusalem? What of Richard's word to the garrison, who had surrendered on the condition that their lives and
families would be spared?

On the twentieth of August, after three weeks of listening
to her brother grumbling over Saladin's duplicity, Joan woke to
trumpet blasts. She sped to the castle gate to see Richard armed
and mounted, with a troop of knights.

"What is happening, Father?" she demanded of Nicholas,
Richard's chaplain, the first man she recognized in the crowd.

"The king is executing the captives."

Feeling dizzy, Joan clutched the chaplain's arm. "What . . . what do you mean? Not the women and children?"

"He said all."

She ran blindly to her brother's side, forcing her way through the knights, choking on the dust stirred by their horses. "Spare the innocents, Richard. You—"

He struck her with the back of his gauntleted hand, knocking her to the ground. If he made any answer, she never heard it. She didn't know who picked her up, who brought her inside.

They beheaded twenty-seven hundred Saracens in one day. Then the army was gone.

She listened to dispatches of the crusaders' progress. Richard chose the coastal route to travel south to Jaffa. The fleet followed to keep the men provisioned. The sea protected the right flank, and the shields and armor of the infantry protected the left. Plagued by summer's heat and the constant harassment of Turkish arrows, the men marched on, bent to Richard's will.

When Saladin saw the usual tactics would not stop the crusaders' relentless advance, he forced a pitched battle near Arsuf. How the heralds sang of it. The Saracens outnumbered the Christians three to one. Had Richard's troops not possessed complete confidence in his generalship, they would have broken ranks and been cut down. But Richard claimed victory that day. The Saracens were so disheartened that they abandoned Jaffa, burning it before retreating east toward Jerusalem.

How proud Papa would have been.

By mid-September the crusaders had settled in Jaffa, where Richard set his men to rebuilding the fortifications. However, because he had forbidden any women save laundresses to accompany the march, soldiers now took unauthorized leave to return to Acre.

Richard returned to roust the reprobates. Arriving at the palace, he accepted the court's welcome, suffered Berry's fluttering embrace, then set her aside to regard Joan.

She knelt at his feet. *Mama would have cared nothing for Saracen prisoners.* "Forgive me for questioning your judgment, my lord."

He clamped a hand on her shoulder and raised her, muttering, "I had not known you loved infidels so well."

They remained in Acre while Richard received messengers and sent dispatches. As if regretting their quarrel, he made an effort to be pleasant, even managing a small celebration for her birthday, killing a stag for supper and finding among the pilgrims an Occitan troubadour.

With Richard holding court, the dining hall served as a gathering place throughout the day and into the evening. At first, Joan had felt uncomfortable mingling with knights taking their ease, watching Theodora saunter about in silks that fluttered like a Saracen slave dancer's costume. But then Geoffrey de Lusignan asked Joan to play merels. For two weeks, they'd been engaged in a tournament. A native of Poitou, he spoke fondly of their shared homeland, though as a middle son of a younger son he would not likely return. Especially since Richard had promised him lordship of Jaffa and Ascalon.

"Your move, my lady," Geoffrey urged.

She bit the inside of her cheek and laughed. "You know very well you've won this round."

He chuckled. "Yes, well. It took a while to break your streak. I was beginning to worry I'd need a new adversary."

Behind them, Richard snorted. He'd been in a sour mood all evening, and she hadn't realized he was following their game. He leaned between them to stir the pegs with his fingers.

"I had thought better of you, Geoffrey. If you can't beat your opponent, you should consider changing the game. Joan is not very good at chess."

Geoffrey smiled. "But neither am I, sire."

Richard straightened, staring ahead. Abruptly, he walked out of the room.

Joan and Geoffrey gaped after him. Rudeness was not out of character for Richard, but they had done nothing that would provoke him.

"Excuse me," she said, nodded to Geoffrey, and followed her brother. The worst he could do was order her away.

He walked stiffly and didn't acknowledge her presence behind him, but when he reached his antechamber he held the door open until she entered also. The room was dim and empty but for two chairs, a dusty table, and a bowl of flowers Berry had placed there for welcome. The bowl was long dry, the flowers wilted.

Richard slouched into one of the chairs and said, "Sit, since you are here."

She sat opposite him and leaned her elbows on the table. "What's wrong?"

"Saladin's power is at an ebb. His allies are reluctant to campaign in winter."

"But so are yours." Men who knew the region had warned Richard not to attempt an advance on Jerusalem until spring. Mud would make the mountains impassable. Still, she knew he would not be inclined to delay.

"Yes. And already the duke of Burgundy is threatening to go home." He mimicked the duke's whining. "'*I am King Philip's representative. You are to treat me as your equal in command.*' Ha. I'll treat him as Philip's equal, not mine."

He fell silent, and Joan dared not interrupt his brooding.

When he spoke again, his voice sounded weary. "Jeanne, if I march now, I could take Jerusalem, but unless I appoint myself king over it, there's little point. Guy can't hold Jerusalem without me." He clenched his fists then slowly unclenched them. "Conrad might have been able."

Joan caught her breath at the admission that he'd backed the wrong man. "You might reconcile."

He shook his head, more with frustration than to refute her. "Conrad has been meeting with Saladin. He offered to lay siege to Acre as soon as I leave for Jaffa."

"The traitor!" No wonder he was brooding.

"Yes, treachery. Which brings us to Johnny-boy."

*John.* She had been dreading this since leaving Messina. She buried her head in her hands.

"He was supposed to stay out of England. Or at least refrain from meddling in the kingdom's affairs. But he has been turning men from posts I assigned, installing his own lackeys. He has been collecting the new tax I levied to support this crusade, but he has not forwarded a penny of it for three months. And—"

"He met with Philip." Patterns in the table's dust seemed to take on ominous forms.

"John believes I stole his throne. But if our father meant to name him heir, he had ample opportunity to do so." Lowering his head, he said, "Our father had too many sons." No one could have missed the pain in the words. But then his voice grew sardonic.

"Yet Saladin has even more. Worse for him, many of his emirs would prefer to see his brother succeed him. When he dies, his empire will crumble."

"Is he ill?" She'd heard that rumor also.

"Not ill enough."

"And what of el-Adil?"

Richard's heavy eyebrows flickered. "What of him?"

"You've been negotiating, Richard. That's no secret. What does he want?"

"Unfortunately, *he* is utterly loyal to his brother." He stared at her a little too long. "Jeanne, if I cannot defeat this adversary, I must change my game. What I need is a workable peace. Saladin is old and ill. I hear he is losing the support of his emirs. The stumbling block is el-Adil. His spies are as efficient as mine. He knows my position and has not been willing to make any concessions." He scraped back his chair and stood. "I do have a plan, but I'll have to placate Guy somehow. Under such circumstances, *everyone* must accept what needs be done."

His emphasis made her skin crawl. "What is your plan, Richard?"

The way he studied her face, she thought for a moment he might confide in her. "If it succeeds, you'll know soon enough."

JAFFA WAS A PORT CITY. ITS COLORLESS STONE HOUSES WERE piled one on top of the other, and the dirty streets thronged with men who looked as if they couldn't remember their last decent meal. Inside the walled palace, a fountain graced the garden court, but though Richard pointed it out cheerfully, saying, "Just like Sicily," Joan was not heartened. The gritty white stone walls had been stripped bare. The very air tasted of sand and salt. She was sick of the godforsaken Holy Land.

Although he reopened negotiations with el-Adil immediately, Richard didn't wait for an answer before marching inland to claim two nearly demolished Templar castles and setting troops to rebuilding them. Joan imagined he had a twofold purpose—pressuring Saladin to accept his terms and preparing the way to Jerusalem if Saladin did not.

The second week in November he returned to Jaffa in order to receive el-Adil. Saladin's brother brought a small retinue; Joan watched their approach from a window in the castle tower. Toward dusk, from the same window, she anxiously watched them depart. There were many, especially the French, who grumbled about Richard's dealings with the enemy. What terms had he made? How acceptable would they be to his allies?

A page found her. "Lady, the king would like to speak with you."

"Of course," she said, a sinking feeling in her belly. Their mother's words haunted her. *Support Richard. Even when you know he is wrong.*

Richard was in the bleak council room, surrounded by the residue of men's celebrations: crumbs on the floor, spilled wine. The courtiers had all gone save for Geoffrey, bleary-eyed in the corner.

"Sister mine!" Richard called. "Come. Sit by me."

She approached warily and chose a chair near but not beside him. Geoffrey roused to draw closer, though he didn't sit. He appeared uncharacteristically nervous.

Richard beamed. "I knew el-Adil desired this. He'd have to,

to put such a scheme before Saladin. In my heart, I thought the most we'd accomplish would be to drive a wedge between them, but Jeanne"—he leaned forward—"Saladin said yes."

Geoffrey growled, "Tell her the terms. Don't lead her by the nose."

Richard shot him a dangerous look.

"You haven't permission to speak." He returned to Joan. "You'll be queen of Jerusalem."

*Queen?* The word struck like a blow, leaving her gasping. She wouldn't marry Guy. She wouldn't live in exile for the rest of her life.

"No, Richard." The scratchy sounds she made were hardly words. "Please, not Guy."

"Tell her," Geoffrey said.

Richard didn't take his eyes from her. "Not Guy. El-Adil will be king."

She thought she'd misheard. A Saracen king? And herself queen? Marriage to an infidel?

"No."

"Jeanne, I've given my word."

"No!" Trembling, she stood. She could hear her own voice rising, echoing off the bare wall. "Would you sell your sister to the very devil? I'll curse you. I'll curse your sons—"

He sprang from his chair, face ablaze, but Geoffrey was quicker, stepping forward to block the king chest-to-chest.

"After you flaunted yourself before him!" Richard shouted.

"Sire, don't!" Geoffrey begged.

Richard's eyes darkened. His voice shook. "Say yes, you useless, barren witch. Or we lose everything."

What good was a truce after the departure of the crusaders?

If el-Adil were king, Saladin would still hold Jerusalem. How dare Richard do this to her?

She drew herself up tall and threw the word back at him. "No."

"Get her out of my sight!" he roared. "She is no sister of mine."

THE WOMEN RETURNED TO ACRE. BANISHMENT FROM Richard's grace was far worse than any prison; time passed more slowly than ever it had in Palermo. There was little to sew or spin, little for women to do but pray. Joan's only comfort was that Richard had sent Theodora with them. Not that they enjoyed her smug company, but it meant Richard was no longer enjoying her either.

Richard sent no messengers. Rumors abounded, but only hearing of his exploits in bits and fragments, nothing made sense.

The week after Easter, an English abbot arrived in Acre with an urgent message. Richard's chancellor had been overthrown and exiled by Prince John. Discovering that the king was not in Acre but Ascalon, the abbot hurried along, leaving Joan and Berry in despair.

"What will Richard do? What can he do?" Even after Berry ceased hounding her, the refrain echoed inside Joan's head.

The abbot was two months gone when the answer came. Returning to her chambers after morning prayers, Joan was startled by a sharp hiss. Down the shadowed hallway, she caught a glimpse of a plain knight with a large nose and weak chin.

"Geoffrey!" She flew down the hallway.

"Lady," he said, but spoke quietly and stepped close to the wall as if seeking the shadows.

"Richard didn't send you?"

He shook his head.

She sighed raggedly. "You shouldn't have come. I won't have you out of favor on my account." His grimace said he had not come to be scolded. "But I'm glad you're here," she admitted. "I've been so desolate. My brothers are—" She caught her tongue. It was unfair to speak ill of men he must serve.

"How much do you know?"

"Nothing. We've heard nothing since the abbot left us."

Geoffrey clenched his jaw, trying to decide where to start. "When King Richard heard about his chancellor, he called a council to elect a king for Jerusalem. Conrad was chosen."

"But of course, they would. What was he think—" Joan stopped again. Clever Richard. "I suppose he gave Cyprus to Guy as consolation?"

"No. He *sold* it to Guy."

With a wry laugh she said, "Typical."

She wondered what Theodora would make of that. No one would attempt to wrest the island from Richard, but from Guy? Any knight with more ambition than discernment might be willing to champion her cause for such a prize.

"Then he sent Count Henry of Champagne to Tyre to tell Conrad of his good fortune. And three days later, two Turks cornered Conrad on a street and struck him dead." Joan gasped, but Geoffrey said hurriedly, "The murderers confessed to being followers of al-Din Sinan."

"The Old Man of the Mountain?" Joan felt a frisson of awe. The Old Man was a Saracen mystic, an enemy of Saladin and Christians alike. It was said he put his followers into trances, and they would kill at his will. Joan had thought it a myth, though

Richard claimed he was real enough to terrify Saladin. "Why would he kill Conrad?"

"Conrad ambushed one of his caravans. But the French accuse your brother of bribing him."

"That's absurd!" Richard needed Conrad. "Why kill him after finding a way to reconcile?"

"The French feel no compulsion to back their slander with reason. They say your brother has also paid al-Din Sinan to have King Philip murdered."

"Pshh," she said, shaking her head. "Who would listen to such lies?"

"Everyone who wants to believe ill of your brother, lady. But that's not the whole of it. When Count Henry brought word to the widow—"

"Humph. You can't tell me she was too upset by his death."

"No, indeed." He smirked. "She married the count."

"No!" It grew more incredible with each word. She closed her eyes to think. "Richard would prefer Henry to Conrad. The French will make much of that."

"Count Henry has reunited the French, Conrad's men, and Guy's, and is marching south to join King Richard. If we win Jerusalem, no one will care who murdered Conrad."

"And if we fail?"

Geoffrey's voice dropped low. "If we fail, Conrad's death will be counted the least of your brother's sins."

## TWENTY

A MERE TWELVE MILES FROM JERUSALEM, THE CRUSADING army degenerated into factions. They abandoned the goal, though it lay within sight; Richard had no choice but to make a truce. Under its terms, though the crusaders might keep the coastal cities they had taken, Saladin retained Jerusalem. The Holy Crusade had failed.

Eleanor had told her daughter to support Richard. Joan had not. His failure was her own.

The women's ship left Acre late in September. Richard insisted his queen set sail before winter's approach turned the seas treacherous. They were to sail to the east coast of mainland Sicily and then travel overland across the peninsula to Rome, where they should await him.

After three weeks of uneventful sea passage, they landed on the coast of the Sicilian mainland in the city of Bari. There they learned how quickly fortunes could change. King Philip had already petitioned the pope to condemn the king of England for sins committed in the Holy Land: bribing assassins to kill Conrad, despoiling the Christian island of Cyprus, and colluding with Saladin to reach an ignoble peace. Joan prayed the presence of Queen Berengaria would remind the pope of Richard's faithful service. If the Church turned against him, his fate would be sealed.

The lord of Bari welcomed them grandly. He called Joan "my lady queen" and told her they still grieved over King

William. He provided them with strong horses and knowledge-able escorts, and Joan discovered the expedience of well-maintained Roman roads. They covered over two hundred miles to Rome in a week.

Hospitably received by a Navarrese bishop, a cousin of Berry's, Joan luxuriated in simple comforts: warm baths, soft beds, palatable food. She found the very antiquity of her surroundings gratifying. Man might damn himself by bringing soldiers against the city, or mock its purity by setting up false popes, but the Holy See would endure. Mass was not simply mass, but a pilgrimage. Surely, from these exalted altars, God would hear her prayers.

*Bring Richard home safely. Let us reconcile.*

But God mocked her. In November, a Pisan sailor sought audience with Queen Berengaria. With grave foreboding, Joan watched him drag his feet across the marble floor of the bishop's hall. In his outstretched hands, he held out a torn mantle of red samite, faded but unmistakably Richard's.

Releasing a strangled cry, Berry sprang forward, tearing it from him to clasp against her cheek. "Where did you get this?"

With a moan, he answered, "A ship foundered on the Istrian coast. Debris washed ashore."

Berry sank to her knees.

"Were there survivors?" Joan asked, her voice sounding hollow, the words dropping into a void. Richard was not dead. The mantle could have been lost a thousand ways.

"None have been found, lady."

"The dead?"

"None have been found."

Later, after Berry had been put to bed with a posset, Joan paced in the villa's receiving hall, unable to escape her thoughts. Before undertaking the crusade, Richard had named their nephew Arthur, Geoffrey's son, as his heir, specifically excluding John. But Arthur was a child. And John had already proven he would not be content with the inheritance Papa had left him. Who would Philip back now that Richard was gone? Who would Mama support?

She'd told Berry the mantle meant nothing. She'd told Charisse she wouldn't cry because Richard was not lost. But now, alone, she wept. Death had prevented her reconciliation with too many estranged loved ones. Surely, it was God's punishment for her willfulness. If He would only bring Richard back, she would not cross him again. She'd never quarrel with anyone she loved again—if only Richard lived.

IN ROME, THEY WERE SURROUNDED BY RICHARD'S ENEMIES. For a week, they had turned away all visitors, so deep was their grief and their fear. Yet some had come twice, even three times— sincere mourners or wolves circling? Joan doubted she had the wits to discern. She knew only that she had a duty to Berry, and no desire of her own save to go home. But to return to Aquitaine, they had to cross Italy, Provence, and Toulouse, all held by enemies of England.

They were waiting to be summoned to supper—a supper no one would eat except the Cypriot captive, Theodora. Listless, silent, Joan turned her sewing over in her hands, unable even to stitch. Berry held a prayer book closed on her lap.

A dull rap sounded on the door.

Charisse opened it enough for them to hear a servant announce, "Ladies, another visitor requests audience. Sir Aimery of St. Gilles."

"St. Gilles." Joan's heart leapt to her throat. Might this be the answer to her prayers? "Aimery is lord of St. Gilles in Provence. If he can help—"

"Count Raymond is lord of St. Gilles," Charisse said. "Aimery is merely the castellan's son."

Joan insisted, "He's Ermengarde's brother." For that reason alone, she would hear him, even if it was foolish to imagine he could help. She cast a pleading look at Berry, who clutched the prayer book tighter.

"Bring him to us," she said, her voice trembling.

The servant led Aimery into the hall. Shrouded in a pale blue mantle, he appeared a beacon of calm amid the room's harsh red-and-gold decor. He swept a low bow.

"My sympathies, ladies, and those of my sister and my lord count."

"How does your dear sister?" Joan asked, refusing to acknowledge condolences. Richard was *missing*. She would not admit his death until she saw his sea-bloated corpse.

"Well of late," he said, straightening. "Though widowed, if you've not heard."

"Widowed? Oh, poor Ermengarde."

"No. You needn't pity her. Lord Raymond's wife invited her to be an attendant at court. She's grown quite content."

Joan started at the news. Ermengarde in Toulouse? She should feel glad for her friend, but . . . had Lord Raymond suggested it to his lady? It was not a question she could ask.

Berry said. "Please, tell us what brings you."

"My lord Count Raymond invites you to Toulouse for Christmas court. A somber one under the circumstances, but one he hopes might bring you comfort. Afterward, an escort will see you to Aquitaine."

Joan bit her tongue. Instinctively, she trusted Aimery, yet who could trust Count Raymond of Toulouse, enemy of her father's house and vassal of Philip of France?

"Tell him he is very kind to think of us," Berry said, her whispery voice unexpectedly strong. "But my husband bade me wait for him here."

Aimery turned to Joan with a flustered, quizzical look, as if the queen had just proved herself mad. Yet Joan knew Berry was simply emulating her own stubborn denial. Swallowing disappointment, she said, "Take my love to Ermengarde."

His eyes still on her face, Aimery's voice grew quieter. "That's not the only message I was asked to carry. Lord Raymond asked me to remind you that you're always welcome in Toulouse."

"Pardon?" The words fanned a flicker of memory into a blaze. The vision of a young knight pulling a doll from a satchel rose before her eyes. She remembered the strength of his hands scattering her tormentors and preventing her fall.

"He said you mustn't fear his father. If need be, he will escort you to Aquitaine himself."

Her heart beat so hard she thought it must be audible. "I . . . I can't answer now. The queen—"

Charisse moved toward Aimery. "I'll show you out, sir. The queen will send for you when she's reached a decision."

Aimery bent his knee, then followed her from the room. Joan felt Berry's stare, yet she could not face her. Rattled, she wished for just a moment to think.

"Do you trust Lord Raymond?" Berry asked, rising and coming to stand closer.

What if she led Richard's wife into a trap? Hardening her heart, she forced herself to answer sensibly. "I have no reason to.

He knows we'd never go to Toulouse on his father's invitation. How better to lure us there?"

"Yet you want to trust him," she said. Joan turned away, wondering why it should be true.

"I want to go home." Her voice caught.

Leaning over her, Berry wrapped both arms around her shoulders. "Then we'll go."

THE POPE ASSIGNED A CARDINAL TO ESCORT THEM AS FAR AS St. Gilles. Lord Aimery returned from Toulouse to meet them there with ten knights, four palfreys, and a thickly cushioned wain spacious enough to carry them as well as their baggage. For Berry, raised with a Spaniard's love of horses, the choice was simple. Theodora also proved a surprisingly competent horsewoman. Joan rode for the sheer pleasure of being outdoors, while Charisse, offered the company of Theodora or the baggage, chose the wain.

Though it was December, Joan needed only a light cloak. Leaves crunched beneath the horse's hooves, and the scent of wood smoke brought back memories of traveling with her father. *Know the scents belonging to the locale,* he'd taught her. Cows and sheep. Drying hay. Each night they ate fresh game and drank new wine.

Aimery, Joan soon learned, was as loquacious as Ermengarde when talking about nothing.

On the sixth day he told them they would reach their goal by nightfall. That afternoon the walls of the great city loomed in front of them. The stones had a pink cast, so that Toulouse seemed to exude warmth. The blue-green Garonne coursed alongside, with numerous barges, mills, and fishing boats clinging to its banks.

As they drew closer, a troop of men spilled forth through the east gate. At the head, two heralds carried scarlet banners embellished with the twelve-pointed cross of Toulouse. The count rode between them. Five knights followed, riding abreast. One was Lord Raymond.

"Ladies," the count called, holding up his hand to halt the dust-raising approach of his party.

Joan noticed Lord Raymond's hair was still a shade too long but now thinning in front. He must be near thirty-six, William's age when he died. He still looked fit, though it was hard to tell when a man was on horseback. He swiveled his head, as though searching for something. Then he saw her and smiled.

His father's horse pranced daintily up to the women. "Lady Joan. I'd know you anywhere. You have your father's eyes."

It sounded like an accusation, but Joan bowed her head and said, "Thank you for your kindness, Lord Count."

"And you are Queen Berengaria," he said, turning to Berry. "Welcome to Toulouse."

"Your generosity redounds to your good name."

"I am not so hard a man I cannot be moved by the plight of grieving ladies." He shifted his gaze. "Princess Theodora? Welcome."

Joan tensed. Theodora was the captive daughter of a deposed usurper. What did he mean, calling her princess?

"Please, ladies, come along."

Surrounded by the knights, enemies of her family, Joan's small party entered Toulouse. Her stomach bubbled with fear, and each step of her horse jarred her spine. Had they made a mistake in coming?

The streets were wide and lined with square wood-and-stone

houses, stoops swept and shutters in good repair. She smelled leather and wool, but not butchery, tanning, or sheep. The count was showing them a prosperous quarter.

The burghers on the street bowed to the passing cortege, but almost perfunctorily, as if they had more important business to attend to. She heard Lord Raymond's laughter and saw someone had tossed a bouquet into the street. A girl waved from a high window, and he waved back.

When they reached their destination, Joan had to blink away unexplainable tears. More graceful and compact than the Norman fortresses of her youth, less fantastical than the pleasure palaces of Sicily, Toulouse's rather ordinary castle seemed comfortably welcoming. The hooves of their horses clattered against the paving as they entered the gates. Grooms swarmed about. Her escort had already dismounted and held a hand to her. Joan grimaced and slid from the horse, hoping she didn't look too awkward.

Several ladies wended closer, led by a tall, gray-haired woman whose smile appeared carved in stone. Seeing Ermengarde among them, Joan let out a breath of relief.

"Ladies." The gray-haired dowager caught hold of Berry's hand and Theodora's. "You'll want to refresh yourselves after your journey."

Joan shot a glance at Ermengarde, who mouthed something she could not interpret. Not until they crowded into a narrow hallway did she worm close enough to catch Ermengarde's hand and squeeze it. "Who is that?"

"The count's mistress, Lady Ponsa."

A mistress pretending to be a countess. "Where is your lady? Lord Raymond's wife?"

"Shh, later," she whispered.

Lady Ponsa led them along a narrow corridor to an antechamber subtly scented with herbs. The room contained a few cushioned chairs and two small tables arranged on a thick green carpet; two narrow couches sat against the far wall. At either end of the room were doors. Ponsa opened one to display a tall bed swathed with opaque curtains.

"For the queen and princess," she said with a slight curtsy. "Your women may share the anteroom."

Berry turned red. "Lady Joan will share my bed. Theodora can have a couch."

"Oh! Of course, you may choose who shares your bed, lady, but we won't put the princess with the maid." Lady Ponsa had the courtesy to look flustered, but the insult was clearly intentional.

Joan could understand why they would demean her; she was her mother's daughter. Eleanor of Aquitaine had pressed her own claim on Toulouse too vigorously for one of her offspring to find a true welcome there. But were they deliberately favoring Theodora?

"Princess Theodora may have this chamber," Ponsa said. She crossed the room to open the second door. Inside, linens were stacked as though it were a storage room, but it also held a bed, half hidden by the piles. "It needs but an airing. Lady, is this to your liking?"

"Certainly," Theodora said.

"Your trunks should be here shortly." She smiled her granite smile at Theodora before turning it on Berry and Joan. "We'll see you at supper."

Ermengarde cast an apologetic glance toward them, then followed her lady. When the door closed, Theodora whirled around.

"The king is dead, my father avenged." She sneered. "I expect I will go home before you do, Joan."

*     *     *

"LADY JEANNE," LORD RAYMOND MURMURED. HE CAUGHT hold of her hand and brought her fingertips to his lips. "You've come."

They stood in a narrow corridor before the massive oak doors of the castle's great hall. As if her desire had conjured his presence, Lord Raymond had slipped through the crowd of courtiers and caught her unawares, though she'd been looking for him.

This was not the youth she remembered. His skin was coarser, with fine laugh lines around his mouth. The gray eyes she'd once thought coldly metallic now radiated heat like molten lead. Lankiness had given way to broad shoulders and muscular limbs, and the hand holding her own was pleasantly callused. William's hands had ever been soft.

She merely nodded, tongue-tied, as he released her. She hoped the heat rising to her neck would not be visible in her face. How absurd to come undone in his presence simply because he'd been kind to her when she was a child.

He turned to Berry. "Lady, you do us honor."

She held out her fingers to be kissed. Joan noticed *she* didn't blush.

"And where is Lady Theodora?" he asked.

"Having her hair combed," Berry answered flatly and turned away.

Joan didn't elaborate. Lady Ponsa had sent a half score of maids to unpack their trunks and help them dress for dinner. Berry possessed a fairly simple trousseau—her gowns were well-made but modest. It was not Joan's intention to outshine her. She had meant to wear her plainest robe until she saw Theodora's choice: a samite gown of imperial purple, the molded bodice decorated in bold Greek style. Joan switched to a rich blue silk with silver beading.

The doors opened to reveal the count and his lady.

"Raymond," he said, a scowl on his face, "what are you doing?"

"Dining, sir. Had you something else in mind?"

"Come here."

Raymond left Joan and entered the hall beside his father. Scarlet cloths lined the walls to muffle noise. The room had only tiny windows close to the ceiling, so torches provided illumination. With the flickering light and faintly smoky air, Joan felt she was walking into fire.

Lady Ponsa showed them to their places. Joan was to sit at the far end of the high table with Berry to her right. The seat to her left remained empty—for Theodora, she surmised. Several courtiers were interposed between them and the count, then Ponsa and, beside her, Lord Raymond. The chair next to Raymond remained unclaimed. Did it wait for his wife?

Joan swept her eyes across the hall. Chairs surrounded the head table; the others were flanked by benches that were rapidly filling.

"They will honor Theodora," Berry said, her voice even quieter than usual.

Theodora chose that moment to make her entrance. All eyes turned. Even, a quick glance confirmed, Raymond's. Lady Ponsa beckoned to her, and Theodora glided across the room to claim the empty place beside Raymond. Yet at the same moment, assuaging Joan's outrage, Ermengarde appeared at her side.

Joan jumped from her chair to embrace her old friend.

Ermengarde flushed with pleasure, then curtsied low before Berengaria as Joan seated herself again.

"Where is Lord Raymond's wife?" Joan asked, tipping her head toward the offending parties.

"He doesn't have one," Ermengarde answered, voice low, gaze wandering, as if making sure they could not be heard by anyone who might understand their French. She slid into her chair. "She entered a . . . a religious house."

"A nunnery? But why?"

"No, not a nunnery. She held Cathar views." Defensively, she added, "Many gentlewomen of Carcassonne do."

"A heretic!" The hair on the back of Joan's neck prickled. She had heard of this strange religious sect. They called themselves true Christians, but they had been condemned by the pope. And Raymond had married one? "No wonder he put her aside."

"It wasn't like that." Ermengarde shook her head with vigor. "He thought she would recognize her error. But she was so unhappy. She *wanted* to be a Cathar goodwoman."

Uneasily, Joan realized it meant Ermengarde and Raymond were now both free. Yet the heir to Toulouse could not marry a woman with no dowry or property. Would Ermengarde settle for less than a marriage? Joan prayed she'd hear no more confessions.

To Joan's relief, uncomfortable silences could not last in Ermengarde's company. She seemed to feel the awkward topic had been disposed of, and now she might chatter every thought that entered her head. Joan laughed to listen, glad for an informer who never needed prompting.

The food was faultless: roast pheasant, bread and cheese, baked honeyed apples, Provençal wine. While she ate, Joan learned that Count Raymond had been ill—not deathly, but feeling his age. Lord Raymond had taken over many of the day-to-day duties of the court, and the courtiers adored him.

As much as Joan enjoyed Ermengarde's company, she could not help but keep one eye on Lord Raymond's end of the table, where Theodora appeared to be entertaining the count and his son.

After supper, a talented troubadour sang several Occitan songs. The last, humorously bawdy, he sang in French. Rocking with mirth, Theodora bumped her shoulder against Raymond's chest. It pained Joan to see the light in his eyes as he laughed along.

Afterward, they retired. Joan could not complain of their quarters. Airy and clean, the chamber was lit by candles on the wall as well as a lamp that sat on a small table. After helping the ladies undress, Charisse sank to the couch.

"Pardon me. I cannot stand any longer."

"Nor I," Joan admitted, watching Theodora strut to her chamber. She looked as though she could easily dance.

Berry stumbled toward the bed the widowed queens were to share. Joan followed and lay beside her, exhausted by the long days of travel, the anticipation and fear. Her prayers swirled senselessly. Then she realized Berry was weeping.

"Oh, darling." There was no point asking what was wrong. The list was endless.

"I hate her." Berry's sobs shook the bed.

"Theodora? You mustn't let—"

"You don't know. She's afraid of you, but when you aren't here she . . . she tells me the things she and Richard did together."

Joan gasped. "You mustn't listen to such . . . She was less than dirt to him."

"More to him than I was."

"No. He loved you. He told me so." God forgive her untruths.

The sobs subsided into whimpers. "What will we do with her?"

Joan had no answer. For all she might wish to abandon the Cypriot to her fate, she could not—Richard had made her responsible for his prisoner. Berry had good excuse to hate Theodora; she had no such cause.

IT RAINED THEIR ENTIRE FIRST WEEK IN THE CITY: MISTS, drizzling, and, at last, a deluge with lightning and thunder enough to make the dogs howl. Cold and damp seeped into the castle. Lord Raymond apologized as if he were at fault.

"I want to show you Toulouse," he said wistfully, including Berry yet directing his words mainly to Joan. Or so it seemed. His eyes on her face melted her bones. "There's the church of St. Sernin, perhaps not so impressive as Sicily's cathedrals, yet beautiful after our fashion. And I'd hoped to take you across the bridge to St. Cyprien. The street markets are as lively as a fair."

Joan sat in the great hall with her small entourage apart from the general congregation—the ladies spinning, the lords throwing knives at improvised targets.

He heaved a sigh, loud enough to be playful. "Now I'm boring you with repetitious complaints. But wait till the sun shines, my ladies. You won't find us so dull."

She smiled, knowing it was what he wanted. "Dull, my lord? Wearying, perhaps, but never wearisome."

The days were filled with entertainments he'd devised: word games, jugglers, and a hunt for painted wooden coins complete with prizes. Joan took part in the more subdued games, often at Berry's urging, though Berry would do no more than watch.

It was a youthful and lighthearted court he presided over, yet Raymond never seemed frivolous. His smiles were always measured, his tone reserved. He attended daily morning worship service without fail, and Joan learned from Ermengarde that the prayers for King Richard were included at his insistence.

"Raymond, there you are."

Lady Ponsa came toward them. Joan's heart sank as he rose without a hint of irritation at the interruption. She enjoyed his company more than she wanted to admit. Was it simply wishful thinking to imagine he enjoyed hers?

"Princess Theodora has asked to see the rose bower. Will you be so kind?"

"Of course. If she doesn't mind muddying her feet on the garden paths."

Berry said, "Theodora doesn't mind mud." Her sweet, soft voice made the jab sound complimentary. Ponsa turned to her with a puzzled smile and furrowed brow, and Joan stifled a laugh.

"Will you come?" Raymond asked, addressing Berry. "The bower is remarkably constructed. The bushes intertwine to form a"—he made a tent with his fingers—"a little house. Of course, it's prettier when the flowers are in bloom."

"No, thank you," Berry answered. "I want to spend time in the chapel before supper."

Berry would not stomach Theodora's company if ever she could avoid it. Joan refused to meet Lord Raymond's gaze. If he asked, she would accompany him; otherwise, she would do her duty and pray with Berry.

He cleared his throat. Lady Ponsa said, "The princess is waiting."

Joan saw his bow from the corner of her eye.

"Good afternoon, ladies."

When he walked away, Berry stood, sighing a little. "She'll make a conquest of him."

Charisse rose and set down her spindle. "Or he'll seduce her. He's like the king your father," she said to Joan. "Half the women at court worship him, but that isn't enough. He must bed one and all."

Had they been alone, Joan would have rebuked her for her impertinence. She glanced at Ermengarde. Eyes cast down and cheeks pink, she seemed to hope no one would notice her. Joan's anger leaked away. How terrible it would be to love such a man.

THE TOULOUSAIN COULD NOT BE EXPECTED TO RESPECT THE grief of its guests at Christmastide but rather gave itself over to merriment. Joan was relieved when Christmas finally passed into the new year and the festive atmosphere waned. Several of the visiting courtiers left, but a new troubadour named Folq came to court. Those who were so inclined gathered in the great hall to listen to his songs. Raymond left his seat near the front of the hall to join the circle seated near Joan. He sat behind Berry, close enough for Joan to see the gray of his eyes.

*"Sai, a la dolor de la den, vir la leng', a leis cui mi ren,"* Folq sang.

As the tongue is drawn to the toothache, so I am drawn to the one who scorns me. A labored analogy. Ladies giggled and men groaned. Joan inclined her head toward Berry to translate and caught Lord Raymond's eye. He tucked his tongue into his cheek as if his tooth hurt. Joan rolled her eyes and turned away. He was shameless.

The door to the great hall suddenly swung open, admitting a herald who called, "A messenger!"

Folq stopped mid-verse. Lord Raymond stood.

The man entered, dripping wet, tracking mud. "The king of England lives!"

"How so?" Raymond demanded over the gasps and shouts of the court.

"His ship foundered, but he and some fellows made shore. The king was attempting to cross the lands of Duke Leopold of Austria when he was recognized and captured."

Duke Leopold. Whom Richard had so gravely insulted in Acre. The Holy Roman emperor's man.

Berry slid from her chair in a dead faint. Raymond joined Joan at her side, patting her hands and fanning her face until her lids fluttered open.

Raymond waved two knights nearer. "Take the queen to her apartments."

"Charisse," Joan said, clutching the maid's arm, "go with them."

She should go also, but she would not leave until she heard all the messenger had to report. One of the men hoisted Berry and carried her from the room.

"Where is the king now?" Raymond asked.

"In custody of the duke, to be handed over to Emperor Henry."

"Has the emperor said what he plans?"

"In a letter to the king of France, he stated only that King

Richard was in his power. The letter should have reached France by now. They rejoice, my lord. The world rejoices."

In the babble around her, Joan heard an echo of France's joyous gloating. Raymond glanced quickly toward Joan.

"He lives," he said, as if that were the reason for their joy.

She couldn't find voice to defend Richard, to accuse Philip and the emperor. She needed to weep. For joy. For fear. Raymond put a hand on her arm, but she shook him off and stamped from the hall, painfully aware of the court's attention.

She must go to Berry. It was her duty. Yet instead she mounted the stairs to the second floor. Near the chapel's entrance, a door exited onto a balcony. It connected with an open walkway that led around the perimeter of the castle, but the balcony itself, partially overhung with a roof and protected by a low guard wall, allowed a measure of privacy. She slipped outside.

How beautiful Toulouse was in the moonlight. She could see past the gleaming white cathedral to the shimmering waters of the Garonne. Pressing her hands on the top of the wall, Joan leaned over and pulled in great lung-drenching breaths.

Richard lived.

He lived, but in the Holy Roman emperor's custody. Constance's prisoner. What would Philip do? Richard dead at sea was a martyr. Richard alive and imprisoned could be prosecuted for his sins. And John, almost a king, must be trembling. Would he fight for his brother's freedom? Or pray Richard languished in the emperor's jail?

Joan heard footsteps behind her and knew it was Raymond.

"I'm glad I found you."

How had he known where to look? She turned to gaze silently into his concerned face.

"Jeanne, what are you feeling? Please, talk to me."

"Why?" Why was she so tempted to unburden her heart?

With low, rumbling earnestness, he said, "I want to know you."

He bent his face closer to hers. She didn't turn away.

His kiss was so tender. She felt curiously unsurprised it should happen, that she allowed it to happen. Had she expected him to follow her here?

The pressure of his lips increased, and for a moment, she yielded. So this was how it felt. His hands moved from her elbows to her waist. His lips parted and she felt his breath hot on her cheek. He wanted her. It was a heady sensation. He kissed her again, pulling her closer, enfolding her as she melted against him. *This is how it feels.* She wanted him.

"No," she said in a sudden panic, turning her head, shoving away his hands. Shame engulfed her.

Flushing deeply, he retreated a step. "I beg your pardon."

"How dare you!"

"I hadn't intended that. I'm sorry."

"Would you take advantage of my . . . my confusion?"

His eyes caught hers and held them, searching. Pride kept her from revealing what he sought. He blinked, and his warmth was snuffed like a candle.

"My lady, I've offended you, and for that, I apologize. I won't intrude again."

IT SEEMED THE PEOPLE OF TOULOUSE HATED NO ONE MORE than King Richard. Now that the mighty warrior had been brought low, nothing could stem the celebratory tide. Joan and Berry were loath to leave their apartments even for meals, even for prayers. But not Theodora. Some nights, lost in celebration, she even failed to return to her chamber.

After five days had passed, the count summoned them. Joan had a strong suspicion as to why. Another messenger had come to court, this one from France. The count had probably been taking orders from Philip all along. If Richard was a prisoner, they would be also.

She ascended the stairs and passed the door to the balcony, averting her eyes. Ahead she saw Lord Raymond, blocking the council room door.

"Lady Queen," he said, bowing his head to Berry, then to Joan, "my lady. I must have a moment. A messenger has come from King Philip. I was not privy to his missive, but I'll repeat, I've given my word you will go home."

"We also have the word of your father," Joan said. "Forgive me for being skeptical of the word of Toulouse."

"My father's allegiance belongs to his overlord," Raymond answered, an edge to his voice.

"His lord? Yet I was in Limoges when your father pledged homage to mine."

"I was there, too. Perhaps you'll recall, even then, I chose to serve you."

The assurance was bittersweet, warm words delivered coldly. Joan was glad Berry interrupted to say, "You've been very kind. Certainly, we will hold you to your promise. It was on your word, not your father's, that we came."

He nodded once again, then rapped on the door.

Joan expected the count to disapprove when he saw his son

enter in company with the enemy, but he only smiled. He sat at the head of a long walnut table in a chair as plush as a throne. Toulouse's elderly bishop stood beside him. Lady Ponsa was present, standing off to the side, and with her, Theodora. The two looked smug, confirming Joan's fears.

"Ladies," Count Raymond said, "we have much to discuss." He didn't offer them chairs, so they stood before the table like petitioners. "If you are ready to leave us, I will arrange an escort to Aquitaine."

Joan stared. Warm relief coursed through her veins. She looked to Berry, whose mouth hung open.

"I am also to tell you the king of France sends his regards."

Joan felt an odd urge to laugh. She wagered the count was as confused as she was. Yet, somehow, it was in character for Philip.

"Thank you," Berry said. "You've been a generous host. I'll remember you to my husband."

The count's smile broadened—maliciously, Joan thought.

"Unfortunately, I fear I owe your husband some restitution. My son has been indiscreet, an incorrigible habit of his."

Joan felt dizzy. She didn't dare look at Raymond. Had someone seen them?

"He'll marry her, of course. And I'll compensate the king for the loss of his ward when his own unfortunate imprisonment is ended."

*Theodora.* Joan's eyes were drawn against her will to the hated captive. Theodora hadn't even the decency to blush. Her eyes blazed with triumph.

"You have no right!" Berry said shrilly.

"I have the obligation." He sighed as if pained. "Unless,

Raymond, you deny that the princess has cause to expect you to wed her?"

Joan had to look at him, to see his face for herself. He was pale, jaw clenched. Had he gone straight from her arms to Theodora's? *Deny it*, she begged.

"Raymond?" the count pressed.

"No, sir. The princess has cause."

TWENTY-ONE

Eleanor would not abide her son's imprisonment. Scarcely wasting a moment's time to welcome her daughter and daughter-in-law home, she explained what had transpired and what they must all do next. The king of England would be released from captivity if he renounced his alliance with Tancred of Sicily and paid a fine of one hundred thousand marks to the Holy Roman emperor. It was up to Richard's subjects to raise a king's ransom.

In Aquitaine, no one could stir the people more effectively than their Duchess Eleanor. However, she was not so loved in England, and there, Berry was unknown. So Joan sailed across the Channel to sing her brother's praises and vilify the emperor and French king. She badgered tax collectors and flattered abbots. Slowly, Richard's ransom coffers filled.

Joan also met with John. It took only a glance to know she pitied him still. She told him what their mother commanded: Don't cause any more trouble. Stop communicating with Philip. Mama would effect his reconciliation with Richard.

"Will she?" John asked, his eyes sad. "And what will she do for you? Fontevrault? Is this what we were born for? To serve Richard's ambition or be shut away?"

"We serve our family, John. We must stand together."

"When has Richard ever served anyone but himself? No. I've

done nothing I'm ashamed of. I'll continue to fight for what is rightfully mine."

John would not win. Who could stand against Richard, right or wrong? Only King Philip might prove Richard's match, and they could not allow that to happen.

In the spring, the French king moved his army into Normandy, seizing Gisors and several other border castles. He stirred the ever-rebellious lord of Angoulême to raid Richard's lands in Poitou.

Yet Richard had been busy also, forging an alliance with his captor. Having received the bulk of the ransom, Emperor Henry announced he would release the king at the beginning of the new year. The news made Philip wary enough to arrange a truce with Richard's men in Normandy. If allowed to keep his gains, he would attempt no further advance.

As always, the French king spoke from both sides of his mouth. At the same time, he recognized John as Normandy's duke, and John, more desperate than ever, formally ceded the entire duchy to France.

At January's end, the emperor invited Queen Eleanor and two of Richard's advisers to Mainz to pay the last installment of the ransom. On February 4, after nearly fourteen months in captivity, Richard was free. Free to seek revenge.

"HE WON'T SEE YOU." AS HER MOTHER SWEPT INTO THE women's chamber, Joan dropped her sewing and stood. How could a woman of her age travel so fast? She was a week early, at least, in returning from Mainz.

"Mama, what do you mean?"

Finger by finger, her mother pulled off her dark woolen riding gloves. With narrowed eyes she scanned the four corners of the poorly lit room as if assuring herself of Joan's solitude. "He said it is still his wish that you enter the nunnery, but he no longer expects you to gratify his wishes. He understands how hard you've worked for his release, but said he never would have been imprisoned had you obeyed him."

"That is unfair." Though in despair she'd often thought the same, she knew it to be untrue when Richard accused her.

"You needn't go to Fontevrault."

Joan sank back onto the chair. "I don't care. I would have gone. Better to serve God—"

"Richard did consent to see you to give his blessing if you decide to take the veil."

So, there it was. He would forgive her only if she bowed to his will, yet he dared pretend he was giving her a choice.

"That," Eleanor said, slapping the gloves lightly against her palm, "is why I said he won't see you. It's nonsense. What good could you do him there?"

"I could pray for his soul," she muttered. Mama wouldn't even pretend choice existed.

"You can do that here. Besides, I don't know what Berry would do without you. I can't blame Richard for finding her unappealing but—"

"She worships him. She's docile and sweet. What more could he want?"

Eleanor shrugged. "I told Richard I'd bring her to Barfleur next month. Before he begins his spring campaign, he's going to lie with her if I've got to stand over the bed and supervise."

Joan almost laughed. If that threat didn't frighten Richard, nothing would. "Will I be permitted to accompany you to Barfleur?"

"One thing at a time. He's got to reconcile with John first. I can only push him so far."

BY MAY, IT WAS CLEAR PHILIP HAD NO INTENTION OF HONORING any truce. He laid siege to Verneuil, a castle Joan well remembered. As Richard marched to the aid of his garrison, he was met by his younger brother, who fell at his feet begging forgiveness. In typical fashion, Richard tinged generosity with scorn.

"Don't be afraid, Johnny-boy. You fell into bad company. We'll punish those who've led you astray."

However John felt about the matter, he now fought on Richard's side. King Philip abandoned the siege of Verneuil.

Throughout the summer, Richard put Philip on the defensive, punishing France's allies in Touraine, in Aquitaine, and in Angoulême. Philip moved his army back to Normandy. At the end of July, the two exhausted monarchs agreed upon a fourteen-month truce.

Although there were no major battles the rest of the season, it was hardly a truce. Richard concentrated on making his presence felt in Normandy, strengthening his fortifications, raiding the countryside up to the very walls of Philip's castles.

"Richard says Philip has learned from Saladin how to wage war," Eleanor said, reading one of his reports aloud. "He's destroying some of his own castles rather than see them fall."

Berry smiled weakly. "Then my lord will certainly defeat him also."

Joan scowled at the inane comment. "He didn't defeat Saladin."

The great sultan had died while Richard was in prison. Joan refrained from pointing out that if Richard had stayed in the Holy Land rather than stupidly sailing for home so late in autumn, he could have taken advantage of the resulting turmoil among the Turks instead of landing in the emperor's jail.

"You won't win any favor with your brother with that attitude," her mother chastised her. "And he's coming to Poitiers for Christmas court, so you might practice your meek smile."

"Is he?" she and Berry demanded almost simultaneously.

"And John, also." Eleanor rose from her chair, pressing a hand to her chest. "God be merciful and grant us a month's peace and quiet."


THREE DAYS AFTER HIS RETURN TO POITIERS, RICHARD received Joan into his presence. With its damp gray walls and deep-set windows, the council chamber was as cheerless as a dungeon.

Surrounded by family and a few knights currently in favor, she knelt and kissed the hem of his tunic. "Will you forgive me, sire?"

He stood silent until their mother cleared her throat. Then he said haughtily, "When I've ascertained that you are truly contrite."

With a burning in the pit of her stomach, she stood and backed several steps to the wall, keeping her head low. She would suffer him humbly, as John did, for their mother's sake.

"I understand you've made my pretty little captive a countess."

"Pardon?" Joan asked, head jerking up. Richard's smile was so cold, she almost shivered.

"You haven't heard? The count of Toulouse is dead."

For a moment, she could not think to answer. Then she said, "Good. The devil likes company."

"Count Raymond VI will pay homage to Philip in January. If he takes one step in the direction of Quercy, I'll go south, truce or no truce." He paused, staring hard at her. "Will he press Theodora's claim to Cyprus?"

"The old count might have wanted Cyprus, but I cannot say what tempted Lord Raymond."

Richard laughed. "No? I can."

"Richard!" The queen's razor voice sliced the air.

He glanced lazily at Berry, whose face had turned bright red. Then he returned to Joan. "I told you to await me in Rome."

"Yes, my lord. But we believed you were dead."

"You were quick to believe it."

"Richard, I was heartbroken."

For just a moment, the coldness left his eyes. It returned so abruptly, she decided she'd imagined any thaw.

He said, "That's no excuse. From now on, you do as I tell you."

Joan hung her head. "Yes, my lord."


THROUGHOUT THE FOLLOWING SPRING AND SUMMER, UNDER the guise of the truce, the French and English kings talked of peace while making war.

In Poitiers, Joan listened for news of Toulouse as carefully as for word of her brother's progress. Although Richard expected— even welcomed—trouble from that quarter, the new count seemed to have little interest in the squabbles of the kings. He had troubles of his own—a border dispute with Foix; a treaty with his father's old enemy, the king of Aragon; and the disputed election of a new bishop of Toulouse. Joan refused to give credence to a discussion she overheard between two clerics that the count needed a sympathetic bishop because he wanted his marriage annulled. John, bearing messages for their mother, confirmed it.

"By God's ears," he said, "the man takes his marriage vows lightly. Isn't this the third wife he's cast off? You might think he shouldn't put her aside for barrenness after only two years, but his courtiers say two years is more than enough. Whenever he takes a new mistress, he swells her belly in three months."

It served her right for chasing after rumors.

Whatever Raymond's distractions, Richard had foes enough and should simply be glad the Toulousain was quiet. After celebrating Christmas with his troops, Richard finally returned to Poitiers in February. His mood was edgy, and Joan avoided him as assiduously as he ignored her. Nevertheless, she was present in the great hall one evening when a knight arrived from Quercy.

"What word?" Richard said, jumping to his feet. The table jiggled, upsetting several of the chess pieces on the board in spite of his adversary's attempt to catch them. "Has Count Raymond dared—"

"No, sire. He's a careful one. I've come to tell you he no longer has a quarrel with the viscount of Carcassonne. The old man died. The new viscount is just a boy."

"And the boy is Raymond's nephew," Eleanor put in. She was seated ten feet away, nose buried in correspondence, but she had not missed a word. Neither had Joan, beside her.

Richard pulled on his beard. "Damn him. He's either exceedingly clever or completely oblivious. Has he a rival left in the south?"

The messenger shook his head. "Only you, sire. He's pacified all his borders, made friends with all his father's enemies. But have you heard about his wife? The annulment for barrenness?"

"Huh. What about it?"

"Apparently in Toulouse *barren* means 'caught in bed with the chamberlain.'"

"Is that so?" Richard threw back his head and laughed.

Joan felt a sick mixture of satisfaction and embarrassment. It was no more than Raymond deserved, and yet . . .

"So," Richard said. "The girl goes to a nunnery? I can't think of anyone less suited to the life. And the chamberlain?"

"They say the count was loath to punish him. It would only prove the rumors, of course, but more, he was fond of the man."

Eleanor made a disgusted noise with her tongue. Richard laughed again.

"He sounds weak," Eleanor said. "Richard, you should forget about waiting for him to attack Quercy. Take your men to Toulouse."

"Perhaps I should. Philip may have given him time to set his house in order, but he's still vassal to France. He'll be more than ready to join the campaign in the spring."

"Not only vassal, but also Philip's cousin. He's plotting something, you can be sure."

THE KING CAMPAIGNED NEXT IN BRITTANY, RETURNING TO Poitiers after Easter, but spent only two days at court before vanishing for three days of hunting. Joan sat with Berry in the chamber they shared, trying to convince her that Richard was not avoiding her.

At the door, three raps sounded, then a pause, then three more. "Lady?"

· 333 ·

"Come in."

Charisse looked disheveled, as if she'd been running. Her cheeks were flushed and her eyes wide. "Men at the gate," she said, panting. "From Toulouse."

"An attack?" Berry gasped.

"Don't be silly, Berry. An army would never have made it so far north without warning."

"An envoy," Charisse continued, slowly catching her breath. "Queen Eleanor had to receive them, but they wouldn't state their purpose to anyone but the king."

Joan cursed the location of the women's apartments—high in the west tower of the castle. It was impossible to see the entrance gates from their window. They were always the last to know when anything happened.

"Your mother lodged them in the knights' tower. I'm to ask if you have any idea why they're here."

"Me? Why would I know?" Joan chewed her lip. "I haven't even a guess. But if Richard isn't back, I'll try to speak with them in the morning."

Charisse nodded and left. Joan and Berry stared at each other.

"Do you think," Berry asked, "he wants to make peace with Richard?"

"It would be a terribly strange way to wage war. What on earth . . . ?"

Berry rose to wash her face. At least her mind was no longer on her own troubles. "You know, I don't really blame him for Theodora," she murmured, drying her face with a towel. "It was his father's fault."

Joan scowled. "His father didn't lift her skirts. That was his choice."

"Was it?" Berry asked, her voice strange. "It seemed a conspiracy to me. I pitied him."

Joan didn't have to try to arrange a conversation with the emissaries. Her summons came at daybreak. Although Richard must have returned late the night before, his formal blue mantle and jeweled tunic made it obvious that he'd already met with the Toulousain envoy.

In the chill council chamber, Richard, leaning lazily against a small desk, couldn't have appeared more intimidating if he'd sat on a throne. He gestured for Joan to take a stool before him, then folded his arms. Their mother sat on a bench of dark wood to his right, her back flat against the wall.

Joan waited for Richard to speak.

He shook his head. "Well, sister mine. You never cease to surprise me."

"Enlighten me, my lord. What have I done?"

"The question is what will you do?"

"Richard, amusing as this is for you, we'd all be better served by forthrightness." Eleanor sounded tired.

"Fine." Richard straightened. "The count of Toulouse wishes to marry you."

Joan gripped the sides of her stool, afraid of falling as the floor spun away.

"Imagine that." His smile was dark with contempt, and he spat his next words at her. "Do you know what dowry he suggests? That I reinstate Quercy. You should be insulted, Joan. Surely you're worth more than a few battered castles."

Did he suppose she had anything to do with this? Colluding with the enemy? God help her, what next? "Richard—"

"Be quiet. Listen while I tell you why you should wed him."

*Wed him?* She cast a pleading glance at her mother, but Eleanor's eyes were fixed on her son.

"Because it will deprive Philip of an ally." He took two steps forward so he towered over her. "Because he needs an heir, which you cannot provide. Because when he tires of you—and he will—he'll learn that it is not so easy to cast aside the sister of the king of England."

She'd known her brother had not truly forgiven her, but she had not thought even Richard capable of this—wielding her own inadequacies against her as a weapon. And Mama allowed it. Tears wet her cheeks. How could Raymond make such an error?

Crowing with laughter, Richard continued, "Guy was a sage compared to this suitor. El-Adil had not so many wives. You might imagine how well I relish this moment." He brought his face to within an inch of hers. Malice shone in his eyes as he crooned, "Will you marry Count Raymond, sister mine?"

THEY GATHERED IN ROUEN FOR THE CEREMONY. HER MOTHER insisted she wear a gown of good English wool. Just as well—the wool was warmer than silk, and the gown, dyed as blue as her eyes, suited her better than the ornate dresses she'd worn in younger days.

Peering at herself in Queen Eleanor's mirror, Joan could not escape the conclusion that she'd grown old.

How long until Raymond lost interest?

Time came to pack into a wain bound for Rouen's cathedral. During the subdued journey, Berry held her hand limply. With the other hand, she rhythmically wiped away tears. Poor girl. She was fading away before Joan's eyes; soon Richard would cease to see her altogether.

The wain clunked to a halt. Groomsmen helped the women climb out. Joan smoothed her dress and gulped in the cold air of a Normandy October. The sky was overcast, and dampness permeated everything. At least Toulouse would be warm.

She mounted the steps of the cathedral at her mother's heels. At the tall entrance doors they stopped. Her mother turned.

"Jeanne." She pushed back a few tendrils that had slipped from Joan's braids then laid the back of her hand against Joan's cheek. "You look beautiful."

"Thank you," she said, surprised.

"He'll be pleased. Use it while you can. Remember Richard needs Toulouse's soldiers."

Joan swallowed the sharp lump in her throat, jerking her head angrily away. She waited in silence for the summons. To get through this she need only say the words, hold Raymond's hand, eat the food, drink the wine, lie beneath him. The queen's daughter knew what was expected of her.

Music started, and her mother pushed her forward. Joan stepped inside the inner doors and met Raymond. She'd known he'd be in scarlet. She knew they'd look fine walking down the aisle. Thank God he was taller than she, if only by an inch.

She nearly stumbled over a wrinkle in the carpet, but Raymond's hand went automatically to her elbow and he turned his head toward her with an easy smile. A few more steps, and they stood before the altar.

The bishop's voice had a monotonous, withered quality. His words landed on her ears but didn't penetrate. She found it unusually difficult to breathe, requiring conscious effort. Giving her responses by rote, she wondered if Raymond ever tired of repeating the same vows so many times.

She must draw a breath again, yet her chest was so tight air moved in and out of her nose but never reached her lungs.

The bishop's voice stopped, and Raymond kissed her lightly on the forehead. They walked back down the aisle, but now his grip was firm on her upper arm.

"Hold fast," he said into her ear. "It's almost done."

The church seemed to darken as they sped along the nave, a narrow gorge lined by cliffs of blank faces. She could see only a few flickering candles near the door. Her feet felt like boulders. Raymond caught her around the waist and dragged her outside.

The air cooled her cheeks. She sucked it in greedily. Gradually, she grew aware she was leaning heavily against Raymond's chest, one of her feet atop one of his.

"Pardon," she murmured, shuffling her foot.

"Take your time," he said. "You're all right." His hands still gripped her arms.

"Yes," she said, embarrassment flooding her as she realized how many courtiers had gathered.

Raymond wrapped his arms around her shoulders and kissed her hair. "I'm not sure what happens if a bride faints in the middle of the ceremony, but I was terrified I was going to find out."

"I . . . I don't know what came over me."

"Shh. Here are the horses. Ride with me."

She would have begged to go in the wain. Certainly, she didn't trust herself to sit a horse. But Raymond lifted her into his saddle as though she were a rag doll, then mounted behind her. She saw Richard, who called out, laughing, "There's a palfrey for the bride."

Raymond laughed, too.

"I prefer this." He spurred his horse forward to the front of the party as others found their horses or piled back into the wains. "Shall I spirit you away, lady? I'd fain avoid the feasting and speeches and be alone."

"You've married the king's sister." She tried to match his lighthearted tone, but the last thing she wanted was to be alone with him. "Feasting and speeches are part of the dowry."

"I didn't marry you for your dowry."

She flushed. "I'm sure Richard would be glad to take it back."

Because he held her so close, his laughter jostled her. "It would be impolite to refuse his generosity."

When their escorts caught up, they lapsed into silence. With Raymond's arms about her, wrapped in his mantle, Joan felt unaccountably secure.

The reprieve was short-lived; the castle was close to the cathedral. The wedding party descended upon the great hall, which was decked out for the feast. Though the tables were already laden with food, servants carried trays holding more. The wine goblets were full to the brim, and cupbearers stood at both ends of each table ready to pour. Raymond had the seat of honor beside the king. Richard drained his cup even before the chaplain said grace.

Joan and Raymond shared a trencher—he had impeccable manners. Joan hoped her mother took note. She noticed, too, that after every few sips of wine, he added water to the drink before anyone topped off his goblet. After the first few toasts, she copied his trick and blushed when he caught her and smiled. He ate a little of everything, but didn't gorge himself, and paused frequently from various conversations to talk quietly to her.

"Jeanne, I've been watching you. You haven't eaten enough to sustain a rabbit. It's no wonder you nearly fainted."

"I can't eat when I'm nervous," she admitted.

"But the hard part is over," he said, pushing a slice of pear toward her side of the trencher. "Here. This is very sweet and mild."

The hard part was over?

"I almost fainted on my wedding day. Would you also like to see me ill?"

He snatched back the pear. "I'm sorry. I'll be less annoying when I know you better." He slid his hand under the table and squeezed her thigh. With effort, she kept herself from brushing it off. He pulled back and looked at her questioningly. Had he felt her recoil?

"Behave," she managed to whisper.

He laughed very low.

"You seem well entertained," Richard said, intruding.

"I am," Raymond answered. "But the matter is private and no great credit to me, I'm afraid."

Richard's laughter resounded across the hall. If Joan didn't know better, she'd believe Raymond was winning her brother over. Or perhaps Richard hoped to charm Raymond.

If only the feast could last. But already servants were clearing the tables, and a harpist set his chair before the head table. The cupbearers refilled goblets as he tuned the instrument. Raymond was one of the few men who did not immediately lift his drink.

Sweet notes filled the air. The harpist sang an Occitan love song. Listening to the joyous melody, Joan gazed around the table. Richard's face had lost some of its hardness. Mama's lips curled contentedly. When Raymond reached for her hand, a dream came upon her, a dream that she was young again and this, her first wedding. She might have found happiness. Instead . . .

The last strains faded. Joan's eyes were wet, but she was not alone. Even some who didn't understand the words were moved by the music. Raymond stood and tossed a purse to the singer.

"There is more," Richard said.

Raymond smiled. "I'm glad of it. With such splendid entertainment, our presence will not be missed."

He laid his hand on Joan's shoulder, and she rose, though her legs felt like pudding. Appreciative tittering spread among the celebrants. A new round of toasts was raised, but Raymond was already leading Joan toward the door.

They walked down one corridor and turned at the next. The moment they were out of view, Raymond took hold of her shoulders and pressed her against the craggy wall. His mouth was hard against hers, as if he would devour her. When he stopped to breathe, she turned her head before he saw her fear.

"You'll have to lead, Jeanne. I don't know the way to the bridal chamber."

Without answering, she slid past him and walked down a long hallway then up a flight of torch-lit stairs. When they reached the landing, he pulled her close and kissed her, more gently.

"Too far," he complained.

"Please, stop. Someone will see us."

With a laugh, he peered down the deserted stairs.

"We're almost there," Joan said, breaking away.

A girl had been set at the door; but she'd fallen asleep, a bouquet of dried roses across her lap.

"Marie," Joan urged in a loud whisper, "we're here."

The girl startled awake. "But where . . . ?" She'd obviously expected more of an entourage.

"Go back to sleep, child," Raymond said, handing her a coin. "We won't need anything."

He pushed open the door.

The small room was beautifully arrayed with fall blossoms. An oil lamp burned low on a table near the door, surrounded by slender tapers they might light if desired, and a flask of wine with two chalices. Three mattresses were heaped on the bed, covered by a bright yellow blanket. Underneath would be crisp linen sheets that had been soaked in rosewater before drying.

"Would you like wine?" she murmured, gesturing to the table. Anything to stall what was to come. He shook his head.

"You hardly touched your drink at dinner, my lord. Is it not to your liking?"

"It's very good." He smiled down at her. "But I've reached a stage in my life where I no longer try to indulge competing pleasures."

She didn't know whether the comment required a response of laughter or flattery. While she debated, the moment passed.

Raymond shut the door, lit one of the tapers, and taking her elbow, moved toward the dressing table and chair along the far wall. The table held a hairbrush, a bowl of scented water, and an empty bowl to spit in. Draped over her chair was a pretty, light-weight gown. Didn't Raymond know he was supposed to allow her time alone with her maids to prepare?

He set the candle down and stared at her. When he spoke, his voice was low and heavy with desire. "Since leaving the church, I've been imagining undressing you."

Joan blanched. He chuckled softly.

"Here. Sit down." He guided her into her chair. Standing behind, he began plucking the wooden pins from her hair—not as deftly as Charisse but less clumsily than some maids she'd known. The plaits gave him more difficulty, but he persevered until her hair was completely unbound.

"Hairbrush?" he said.

She handed it to him, and he began brushing her hair with smooth gentle strokes. Her nerves grew calmer. With the last tangle gone, he pushed his fingertips against her crown and massaged her scalp. Her skin tingled all down her spine.

He swept her hair aside and kissed the nape of her neck.

"Stand up." He pulled her to her feet and began untying the laces of her dress. Just as she wondered if he was having second thoughts over the numerous knots, the cloth loosened. He pushed the gown from her shoulders, down over her hips, to fall in a pile at her feet.

He turned her around and lifted her chin to kiss her, soft and slow. She didn't know if she was floating or drowning, but after a few minutes, she dared attempt to kiss him in return.

"Now you undress me," Raymond whispered.

Her blood chilled. "I . . . I don't know how."

He pulled back to see her face. "That's all right. I won't mind a few mistakes."

He was teasing her. The chill left. Her embarrassment was hot. "You do it, please. I can't."

Perhaps he responded to her piteousness, because he backed away and untied his girdle, letting it drop where he stood. Then he stripped to his undershirt and braies. She averted her eyes, wishing she could faint again. Memories of all the shame and pain she'd endured with William flooded back to her. And they'd do this for naught. There would be no heir.

The chair legs scraped against the floor. Raymond sat.

"Come here."

She stepped forward and he drew her onto his lap. With kisses and caresses, he pulled her closer until she resisted.

"What is wrong?" he asked, ceasing abruptly.

"Wrong?"

"The more I kiss you, the more you tie yourself into a knot. You must talk to me. I can't guess your thoughts. Is it . . . are you so unhappy to be with me? Is your heart still with your husband?"

"My . . . ? William? No, of course not."

"Of course not?" He seemed bewildered.

Mortification made her irritated. "I'm nervous. God's legs, is that so hard to understand?"

"No." He shifted her weight on his lap. "Well, yes. It's not going to hurt."

"That's something men say." Words ran out of her mouth, though she regretted them even as she spoke. "It will hurt *me*, and you won't care."

"Jeanne!" His face grew pinched. He cupped her chin with his hand. "Are you nervous or frightened?"

Jerking her head away, she said, "I'm not frightened. I wish you'd just get it over with instead of—"

"Get it over with?" He sounded aghast. "What did he do to you?"

She didn't answer.

Raymond stood, setting her on her feet. He returned to the wine table and poured a chalice full. She was about to protest she didn't want a drink, but he brought the cup to his own lips and gulped. "Go lie down."

Joan stomped to the bed and climbed into it. He followed, nudging her over to make room.

"You needn't scowl at me like that. I'm not going to 'get it over with.'"

"But—"

"Not tonight and not until you're ready. Nothing will hurt."

She lay flat on her back, arms crossed over her chest. Her face burned with humiliation when he snuggled beside her and ran his fingertips down her arm. She'd prefer quick pain to this prolonged embarrassment.

"If you don't like anything that I'm doing, tell me and I'll stop." His hand rested lightly on her belly. He started kissing her shoulder, then up along her neck to her ear. He must have felt her tense again, because he moved away and whispered, "Won't you trust me, Jeanne? Grant it to me as a gift, just this once."

His earnestness pulled at her heart. What would it be like to trust someone?

He wrapped a lock of her hair around his wrist and kissed it. "I won't fail you. I swear."

JOAN COULDN'T REMEMBER EVER SLEEPING SO SOUNDLY. SHE woke feeling languorous but rested, then blushed to feel her husband's warmth and the hair of his chest tickling her back. Although she was naked, Raymond, true to his word, had not removed his braies.

Shame fought with desire as disconnected images of the night flitted through her memory. The things he'd done—and she'd let him, her body betraying her with its response.

She rolled over very slowly so he wouldn't awaken and studied him. That was her idea of a perfect face. His jaw was strong, but tapered enough not to be square. When he laughed, he had not dimples but crevasses. And she was glad he wouldn't change the cut of his hair. It was silken against her fingers, and he had liked her to touch it.

His eyes opened and slowly focused. He flung his arm around her and pulled her close for a kiss. "How are you feeling this morning?"

She said, "Ravenously hungry."

"Me too." It sounded like a growl. He nuzzled her neck and stroked her hip and flank.

"Oh!" She pushed his hand away. "Raymond, that tickles."

"It didn't tickle last night."

"Yes, it did. I just didn't mind."

Lord help her, she could fall in love with that smile.

"Do we rise and greet the day or linger?" he asked.

"You're giving me the choice?"

"If you choose lingering."

His hands grew busy again, and she buried her fingers into his hair, lifting her face for his kisses, then becoming bold and kissing him, his chin, his neck, his collarbone. He hugged her tight.

"You tell me when, Jeanne."

"Now."


THEY STAYED IN ROUEN FOR SIX DAYS, THE PLEASANTEST SIX days of Joan's life. They hunted and rode, played games and listened to troubadours, feasted and prayed, with everyone as polite and happy as angels in God's own court.

But the morning of their departure, Joan was summoned into her mother's chamber—alone.

How well she remembered the room from her youth. A large tapestry covered one wall, depicting dancing maidens and a unicorn. The unicorn wore the most mournful expression; it had always bothered her. Now it seemed fitting that her mother could make even a unicorn mourn.

"Joan." Eleanor stood tall and straight, a brittle smile on her face.

Joan bent her knee. "Mother. I'm sorry to have to go so soon. But the weather is turning—"

"Raymond needs to get back." Her lips pursed. "I must say, he's been very kind to John. It's done the boy good."

It was true. Raymond had made a point of seeking John out. He treated him like a prince and peer instead of merely Richard's ill-favored younger brother, all this without annoying Richard. Joan wanted to point out Raymond's presence had been good for everyone—Richard was even flirting with Berry—but something in her mother's stance kept the words in her mouth.

"You've done very well, Joan. To all appearances, the man is smitten. Richard is encouraged." She sighed, her face as gray as Sarum's winter clouds. "I shouldn't worry. You've always been sensible. But it's what mothers do."

"Why are you worried, Mother?"

"When you reach Toulouse, be sure to keep an eye on that . . . the count's natural son, Bertrand. I've heard it said Raymond dotes on the boy." She frowned a moment then added, "A man should not let his by-blows rise so far. Perhaps he married you *because* you are barren."

That dagger sliced Joan to the bone.

"He's fickle, the count. You know that. I hope you aren't so very fond as you're pretending. Don't love him, Joan. He doesn't love you. Remember, he chose Theodora first. If she hadn't betrayed him, he'd be married to her still."

"Yes, Mother."

"He's kind, Joan, and your heart has always responded to kindness. The same way you took pity on John when you were children. Some men are simply weak, and you can't make them strong, no matter how much you pity or love them. Sweetling, you mustn't love Raymond."

"Because he's kind?" She meant to sound sarcastic, but she was so hurt, she didn't succeed.

Her mother answered sternly, "He's kind because he needs to be. He appeases his enemies because he isn't strong enough to fight them. If you love that kind of man, you deserve what you get. Now, go to Toulouse and do your duty. Richard is depending on you."

## TWENTY-TWO

"Y OU CAN'T TURN A CORNER WITHOUT TRIPPING OVER ONE of the count's brats," Joan grumbled.

Charisse didn't answer, except with a sigh that said *What did you expect?* She continued unpacking their trunks.

Upon arriving in Toulouse, they had been met by a swarm of young courtiers, Ermengarde at the forefront. Ermengarde had shown Joan to her apartments, along the way introducing many maidens of the court. Six of the girls—six!—were Raymond's natural daughters. And there was one more who'd already been married away.

But it wasn't the daughters who concerned Joan. On the journey to Toulouse, they had been met by Raymond's son, Bertrand, who was no longer a boy but a fine young man. They rode alongside one another during the long days and sat together at supper. Raymond even made a point of saying good night to him before retiring, even if he had to seek him first, a habit that became more irksome each night. The other knights deferred to Bertrand, not excepting men who were older. Worse, he was perfectly well-bred, deferential without being obsequious, and polite even when Joan was not.

Her mother had said to keep an eye on him and, try as she might, Joan could not banish the ominous words. Her brothers had risen up and destroyed their father over inheritances they were assured of but impatient to claim. How far should one trust a man with no birthright? A man whose only fortune would be what he could win by guile or by force? She would not see Raymond's heart broken as her father's had been.

The last two days of the journey, Raymond had been grumpily preoccupied by reports messengers had brought from Toulouse—reports he did not share with her, but did with Bertrand. Bertrand—his only son. God help her, she could not look at the young man without seeing her own failing. How long until Raymond realized he must put her aside?

Ermengarde's animated tour failed to lift Joan's spirits. The first time she had seen Toulouse's castle, she'd been struck by how comfortably welcoming it seemed. Yet now she rattled about in its vastness feeling like an interloper. Then, she had known who she was—Richard's sister—and what was expected of her. Now, she was Raymond's wife and didn't know how to behave.

When they arrived in the city, she thought he would show off his home—their home—even though she'd seen much of it before. She hadn't anticipated this—being shunted off to the countess's apartments.

She'd grown accustomed to their conversations before sleeping, to being awakened each morning with kisses. Now what? Would he send a messenger for her whenever the mood struck him? Or come to her door like William?

With Ermengarde chattering in her ear, Joan tried to appreciate her surroundings despite the moldering disappointment that had gripped her. Her apartments occupied the third story of a turret. The bedchamber was spacious, with a window overlooking the cathedral and city. The walls were warmed and softened by remarkably well-made tapestries decorated with familiar

Arthurian scenes. Jutting out from one wall was a large hammered-metal basin. Ermengarde presented it, bursting with pleasure as if it were gold.

"Raymond asked what you'd like in your room, and I told him how you missed Sicilian baths."

Joan had found it difficult to respond with enthusiasm. Did she have to refer to him so familiarly? Had they really discussed the way she preferred to wash?

After her tour of chamber, toilet closet, and antechamber, Joan had asked Ermengarde to grant her a few hours alone. "I'm exhausted. If I seem peevish, I apologize. Let me sleep awhile and begin again."

Ermengarde's relief proved she'd noticed Joan's distance. She shooed the other maids from the room, leaving Joan alone with Charisse to finish unpacking. Charisse wasn't fooled. She didn't offer to loosen Joan's gown or turn down the bed. She simply carried out her tasks, letting her mistress pace about.

"Lady Ponsa must have had some strong attachment to Camelot," Joan mused, running her fingertips over a tapestry.

"Lady Ponsa or one of the previous ladies," Charisse said absently.

"The nunneries of southern France are peopled with former ladies of Toulouse."

Charisse set down the linen sheet she was folding. "You seem unhappy."

"No, just out of sorts."

She missed her husband. It was ridiculous. She doubted it had been two hours since he fobbed her off on the women. And yet . . .

Richard had said Raymond would soon tire of her. And

Mama had warned her not to love a man who didn't love her. Charisse was right—Joan was unhappy.

TOULOUSE WAS A BUSY PLACE, AND JOAN DISCOVERED NEW duties daily. The kitchen steward required her to order the menus; the head chambermaid reported to her. She was expected to minimize discord among the courtiers and distribute patronage evenly among an extravagant number of troubadours. Visitors and messengers came and went, and they all had to be flattered, entertained, and fed.

The court attended prayers each morning in the chapel and every Sunday went to mass in St. Stephen's Cathedral. Even if she didn't cross her husband's path all day, she knew she would see him at prayers, at supper, and at night.

Initially, she had been wary, not knowing what he expected of her. But each evening as supper drew to a close, he took hold of her hand. When he retired to his chamber, she went along because he was still holding on. She thought at first it was because he wanted to make love to her, until one night when he didn't. He merely helped her disrobe while asking about her day. He smiled at her successes and offered suggestions for her difficulties. Then he undressed and climbed into bed, complaining about a suit he'd heard between two merchants whose shops shared a wall that had fallen into disrepair. She giggled as he mimicked them and yawned after he yawned. He put his arm around her, kissed her, and went to sleep. It occurred to her then that perhaps he craved her presence as much as she did his. The thought filled her with a terrifying joy.

They went on in such a way for three weeks before Joan made a bold decision. Summoning several women and menservants, she packed her trunks and her washtub, even the tapestries, and had them carted from her chambers to Raymond's. That evening, when they returned hand in hand, he turned slowly, taking it in. Joan held her breath, afraid of his reaction, afraid she'd revealed too much of herself.

"Jeanne," he murmured at last, and a pop of laughter came from his mouth. He scooped her up and carried her to bed.

"What possessed you?" he murmured afterward.

Inexplicably shy, Joan covered by saying archly, "My mother said the best way to keep other women out of a husband's bed is to be there." But seeing his puzzlement, she yielded to her heart and whispered, "Besides, I like the way you feel next to me."

His arms enfolded her. "I never want to be anywhere else."

STILL MIXING UP NAMES OF THE TOULOUSAIN LADIES AFTER A month, Joan couldn't understand how Ermengarde knew everyone. Not only the ladies at court but women in Foix, Quercy, Carcassonne, and Provence. She knew every broken engagement, every second cousin, every rumored harsh word. It astounded Joan that a girl who talked incessantly could still have heard so much. Ermengarde's timely cautions had prevented Joan from making several mistakes in seating arrangements and scheduling entertainments.

Yet no matter what else she reported, Ermengarde never divulged the names of Raymond's previous lovers. There were jealousies enough without the countess adding to them.

It all gave Joan a headache. There were several women who attended her—pretty, charming, amusing women—whom she could not befriend. She would not be deceived as she'd been by Constance.

She couldn't help watching to see whom he spoke to, who received his smiles. She hated the fact that, most often, it was Ermengarde.

In December the weather turned rainy and chill. They kept a fire burning in the hearth in the great hall, and smoke hung in the air and saturated their clothes. Joan bathed more frequently, but it didn't help. Never before had the smell of wood smoke so offended her. Even the blankets stank of it. Raymond said she was mad, he couldn't smell anything, but she insisted the chambermaids launder the bedding twice a week.

In three weeks, it would be Christmas. Her first Christmas court as countess. One day her mind soared with plans: a winter hunt, a tournament, a Court of Love like her mother enjoyed. The next day she would feel so tired and sodden-headed she wanted to take to her bed until January.

One morning she found Raymond had risen and left the chamber without waking her. Struggling from bed, she padded across the floor to peer out the window. The sky was a dismal gray, but light enough to show she'd slept far longer than she should have. She opened the door to the antechamber.

"Charisse?"

The maid looked up from her sewing. "Lady? Are you well? The count said to let you sleep. You were complaining last night that you felt ill."

"Whatever wood they used in the cookstove, everything at supper tasted burnt. But I'm not ill. Help me dress."

Charisse laced her into a clean gown. Joan sniffed it suspiciously.

"Where is the count?"

"It's Tuesday. He's hearing petitioners."

"Already?"

"It's almost noon, lady. Shall I send for a tray from the kitchen?"

"No, I'm not hungry." The thought of food brought the burnt taste back to her mouth. "If it's almost noon, I should find Ermengarde in the music room."

They were supposed to listen to a harpist recommended by the count of Comminges to grace their Christmas court. Unfortunately, two other harpists also expected the honor—fine musicians, but nasty, spiteful men. She'd told Raymond she'd like to give them swords and let them decide for themselves.

She hurried to the music room, leaving Charisse to her mending. The door was ajar. As she stepped into the doorway, her heart stopped.

Ermengarde was with Raymond, in his arms. Quickly, Joan backed out of the room and whirled flat against the corridor wall. Her breath came in short, sharp gasps. She heard her mother's voice calling her coward. She couldn't faint, not this time.

Drawing herself up tall, she stalked back to the door and threw it open so that it slammed against the inside wall. Startled, they both looked toward her. Joan's rival was pallid, her face streaked with tears. Raymond hadn't even the decency to let go of her elbows.

"Send her away," Joan said, her voice throbbing with anger. "I won't be made a fool of."

"My God!" He finally let go. A vein bulged purple against his temple. "Be quiet before *you* make a fool of yourself!"

"Send her away, or I'll go!"

Tears still poured down Ermengarde's ashen face. She turned slowly to Raymond, her mouth open in mute appeal.

"I'll talk to her," he said, so gently, so kindly, it broke Joan's heart.

"Not for my sake," Ermengarde rasped, the voice of a woman who'd been sobbing a long while. She walked toward the door with a slow dignity, as if she'd aged. When she reached Joan, she said, "You needn't have me banished. I'm going to St. Gilles."

Joan watched her go, feeling small in her triumph. Why bother fighting for Raymond? He wasn't much of a prize. She faced him again, head tilted back to look down her nose, but something was wrong. He was staring at her with something akin to revulsion.

"What in God's name is wrong with you?" he demanded.

"Wrong with me? Me? You're a pig! She was my friend!"

"You don't know the meaning of the word." He hurled this at her, fists clenched as if he'd rather strike her. "*Aimery* was a friend. My friend."

Her stomach heaved with fear. "Was?" Pray God she had misheard.

He turned his head from her, blinking. She whispered desperately, "Was?"

"He's dead. Fallen from his horse."

"Oh!" She couldn't breathe. What had she done? "Oh, Raymond. I—"

"God damn it."

"Raymond, I—"

"Be still." Clutching his hands to his head, he muttered again, "I'm taking Ermengarde and her daughters to St. Gilles for the funeral. I'll be there as long as it takes."

AT WHAT AGE SHOULD A WOMAN'S COURSES CEASE? CERTAINLY, she was too young, but perhaps it happened earlier for barren women. After all, her body had never functioned properly. Her flows had always been erratic, sometimes earlier than expected but more often a week or two late, especially when she was ill or not eating. *And when William died, and she'd thought—*

But she had not bled since two weeks before her wedding, and she'd been married ten weeks. Ten weeks, and she'd already managed to earn her husband's contempt.

Raymond had set out for St. Gilles the very day of their argument. While she understood his obligation to take Aimery's body home as quickly as possible, still, it made her feel as if he could not bear to remain in Toulouse. The responsibility of being overlord of St. Gilles weighed heavily upon him, and she knew how concerned he must be about Ermengarde. She grieved for the ache in his own heart. Yet how busily he avoided her in the hours before his departure! When she tried to speak to him before he joined his guard, he only shook his head and put a hand on her arm. His face as haggard as an old man's, he said, "We'll talk when I return."

And Ermengarde was worse. With her weeping daughters bundled beside her, surrounded by ladies offering condolences, most of whom were crying also, it was impossible to find a moment alone with her.

Joan could say nothing but "Ermengarde, I am sorry."

And Ermengarde, drawn and so pale she appeared bloodless, looked away and said without emotion, "I know."

Joan did not feel forgiven.

Raymond returned a week after Christmas, and she greeted him at the castle gate. With everyone watching, he was kind enough to kiss her. But he had other things to do. She went to their chamber and waited. She expected to wait a long time, but within an hour, he came to her.

"How is Ermengarde faring?" Joan asked, determined to air their difficulties.

"She bears it. I'm more worried about her mother."

"Oh." What else could she say? "What . . . what of Aimery's wife?"

"She died two years ago," he said, a little impatiently. "In childbed. Ermengarde didn't tell you?"

Joan shook her head, embarrassed that she'd never asked Ermengarde about her own family. "Who will be castellan?"

"Aimery had a son. A good boy, poor thing. He's seven years old." Raymond sighed. "Aimery's father is still healthy, for now. If he dies before the boy reaches maturity, Ermengarde will hold the castle as his guardian. In a year or so, I'll try to arrange a marriage for her. She shouldn't be alone."

It sounded strange to hear him talk of finding a suitor for her. But that was a count's duty, after all.

"Do you . . . do you think she'll ever forgive me?"

"Of course she will if you ask. She has a very generous heart." He sounded sad, but no longer angry. He shook his head. "But, my God, Joan, it was so hurtful of you."

"I can't bear to think of it. I know I hurt her—"

"You hurt *me*."

"I'm sorry." Her eyes prickled hotly with tears. "But you did love her once."

"Everyone loves Ermengarde."

"You know what I mean."

"No, Jeanne, I don't." He rubbed his cheeks hard, a sign of his exhaustion.

"When you kissed her," she insisted. He had to understand

before he forgave her. "In the garden. Before she married Anfusus."

His eyes widened, and he dropped his hands to his sides. "She *told* you?"

"Yes."

"Why would she tell you such a thing?"

"Not . . . oh, Raymond, not recently. She told me years ago. In Sicily."

"Oh, for all the . . ." He exhaled loudly. "Well, there's payment for my conceit."

"What do you mean?"

"She was a child. She wasn't in love with me; she only thought she was. I was her brother's dashing friend, heir to the county." He waved a hand in the air. "She had some notion in her head and chased me into the garden to tell me about it. What was I supposed to do? Laugh at her?"

"But you kissed her!"

"In three days her father was sending her off to England. I thought it unlikely I'd ever see her again. I believed she'd learn to love her husband. She'd grow up and forget about me. But in the meantime, there she was, with her heart in her hands and her eyes big as moons. Of course I kissed her."

Joan sat heavily on the bench by her dressing table. "I'm a witch."

"Is that a confession?"

"Oh, don't tease me, Raymond. You don't know. I have so few friends. My God, I have *no* friends." She was as isolated here as she'd been in Palermo. Except there, it had been Marguerite's suspicions that kept her secluded and lonely; here, it was her own. Joan decided to send a messenger to Ermengarde at once. She would go to St. Gilles as soon as Raymond allowed it.

He crept up beside her. "You have me." His voice turned gentle, warm.

"How could you have married me?"

"I'm sorry, Jeanne. You've used up your self-pity ration."

"I'm serious, Raymond, and you must be also. Aimery was young and hale, and look! If he hadn't a son, Ermengarde could marry someone, and you could make him castellan. But—"

"But what if I fall off my horse?"

She nodded, unable to look at him. The very thought of him dying made her feel lost.

"My brother Bauduoin is my heir."

"Everyone in Toulouse hates him."

Raymond's jaw set. "Be that as it may—"

"And you know how the younger lords love Bertrand."

"Bertrand?" His brows knit. "Darling, you don't understand him at all. He won't—"

"And you have my brother and Philip waiting to swoop in and carve up everything between them." She had to tread lightly. She should have realized he wouldn't hear a word against his son.

"For the love of God, Jeanne. Is this what you lie awake at night and think about?"

"Someone has to. I saw what happened to Sicily. When William died, there were riots in the streets. Tancred and the emperor are still warring." Her throat tightened. "Do you know how it makes me feel, to think this will happen to Toulouse?"

"Let me sit down." He lifted her high enough to slide under her, then rested his chin on her shoulder. "I'm not a fool, Jeanne. At least not an utter one." He laced his fingers through hers.

"Did you never wonder why, when William died, Sicily had to look to his uncle's natural son for a usurper?"

What was he talking about? "Because there was no heir!"

"But why was there no little William from the wrong side of the sheets? By all reports, the man was no saint."

"What are you saying?" she scoffed. "William was barren?"

"Not barren exactly, but . . . well, he died young. How long was he ill?"

"Only the last year." But, no—it had been longer. She remembered the first time she'd witnessed his nosebleed; she'd been but a child. How long had he suffered and kept it from her?

"Well, whatever the cause. God didn't bless you and William with children. That doesn't mean he won't bless us."

"Oh, don't. Don't build dreams on false hopes." She had to tell him. It wouldn't be right to hide it even if she could. Blushing hot with shame, she whispered, "There's something wrong with me. I . . . I don't even have my courses anymore."

He stared. "Since when?"

"Before we were married."

"How long? A few months? A year?"

"Two weeks."

"Two weeks before we were married?"

She nodded, waiting for his repugnance, his pity. What if he didn't want her anymore? *Men prefer young wives.*

But he was grinning like an idiot. "They'll come again. In seven or eight months." Then he started laughing. "'Oh, the food tastes funny. Oh, everything stinks of smoke. Let me sleep, I'm so tired.'" His laughter turned to hoots.

He thought she was with child? "You mustn't think it, Raymond. Don't." She had known too many false hopes.

"Tomorrow I'll have the midwife come. But I'm right, Jeanne." He chattered as rapidly as Ermengarde. "I've seen it before—and don't give me that scowl. You'll be glad one of us knows what he's doing. I can't believe you—" He stopped and puffed out his chest. "You know what they'll say about me, don't you? I can get a babe on a barren woman."

"Shush." She blushed all over again as she recounted his arguments and thought, prayed, maybe he was right. She was as stupid as a cow. But if he was right, she was willing to be stupid.

"Jeanne." He poked a finger into the flesh of her waist. "I'll bet it happened that very first time!"

WHETHER RICHARD BROKE THE LATEST TRUCE OR PHILIP, IT didn't matter; the two continued to ravage each other's lands. Richard had invaded Flanders, where he was enjoying success more typical than the misfortunes he'd suffered the past summer. Joan listened when Raymond repeated news he'd heard, but it sounded far away and unimportant. Her home was Toulouse, and Toulouse was not at war.

The weather was dry in the new year, drier than usual; but even though Raymond commented on it often, Joan didn't give it much thought. She couldn't think of much but the midwife's cautious optimism and Raymond's certainty. Her fatigue and illness dissipated, to be replaced by a mix of restless energy and contentment. At the end of February, with a pouch of a belly beginning to appear, she felt the baby quicken. She interrupted Raymond in conference with the bishop to insist he come to their chamber. Of course, when he put his hand on her middle there was nothing, but she maintained she had felt movement. He said, "I'm sure you did. I told you she was in there."

"She!" Joan crossed herself. "It won't be a girl."

"Jeanne," his voice sank to a low caress, "we'll love the child no matter. If this one's not Toulouse's heir, we can always make more."

The whole month of March passed without rain. Joan knew that would be a worry for the farmers, but she was surprised by Raymond's concern. His meetings with the town councilmen lasted longer and longer. After going over reports with his chancellor, he seemed disturbed. Yet by suppertime, he always found a smile for her.

One evening, as he brushed out her hair, a task he insisted on performing each night, he sighed and said, "Thank God you're in bud, Jeanne."

"What do you mean?" she asked coyly, expecting to hear how much he loved her—how glad and thankful he was that she would be the mother of his son.

"We're going to see a drought this summer. Already the shepherds are complaining they can't find good pastures. It will mean thin fleeces and stringy mutton. If the grain yields are poor, farmers can't pay their rents, lords can't pay their taxes, tithes fall, the churches complain, and everyone blames each other. Old rivalries will flare, and some hothead young lord will attack his neighbor."

"Huh." He paid more attention to the weather than to her. She wanted him to share her joy, not haunt the palace, glumfaced. "Surely it's too soon to predict all of that."

He set down the hairbrush. "Perhaps. I'm praying there won't be famine, but it will be a lean year. Fortunately, sometime in the middle of summer when everyone is moaning, we'll have an excuse for celebration."

"For heaven's sake, Raymond. Is that all this baby means to you? Distracting farmers from their misery and providing the court with a summer celebration? This is our son, not some convenience for Toulouse's—"

"My love, whether son or daughter, our child's birth, life, and death are all dedicated in service to Toulouse . . . well . . . to God and Toulouse," he amended.

He sounded self-righteous, so she scoffed, "Is that how you lived your life?"

"I served my father. Oftentimes against my will, but I obeyed my lord." His answer was stiff, almost cold, but abruptly, he sighed. "I spent a lot of years imagining how I would do things better. Now it is my turn, and I miss his guidance."

"You can't mean it! He was a liar and—"

"Jeanne." He put his finger on her lips. "He was my father."

She drew a breath and let it out slowly. "I assumed you hated him."

"Hated him? My father?"

How could he sound so aghast? Why shouldn't he hate him? The man was hateful.

Raymond walked away from her, to the wall, where he pressed a hand against one of the tapestries. "I disagreed with him on many things. I hated the way he treated my mother. The way he treated Bertrand's mother. I suppose there were times I didn't like him. But he was my father. I loved him very much."

Joan swallowed painfully. "I loved my father also."

So had Richard. So had Henry and Geoffrey. Family bonds were strange, confounding things. She remembered her father talking about their family, his love for his children. But it wasn't her father's voice she was hearing now. It was her mother's, reminding her not of love but of duty. She'd have to be a mother to this babe in her womb. She felt a twinge, like regret.

"Jeanne?" When she glanced up, she saw he had turned and was regarding her intently. "I loved my father and admired his strengths, but love did not blind me to his faults. I hope to be a better man."

"You are," she said. Of course he was. But then she understood he was not seeking reassurance. His gaze did not falter. Was he waiting for her to say something more? She tried to smile. "You are not your father."

He nodded as if satisfied. He wasn't smiling when he said, "And you are not your mother. Thank God."


IN THE SMALL HOURS OF A STIFLING MID-JULY MORNING, JOAN woke with a shuddering pain in her womb. She rolled against her husband for comfort, but it was so unpleasantly hot, he rolled away without waking. She couldn't be angry; he wasn't supposed to be there at all.

She'd been lying in for three weeks, confined to her room—to her bed, if anyone asked. At least she was permitted visitors during the day. To her joy, her most frequent companion was Ermengarde. In the spring, Raymond had taken Joan to St. Gilles. She had prepared a few versions of an apology. None quite explained how she could have imagined Ermengarde capable of such deceit, but all begged for forgiveness. Her old friend would not even listen, but instead insisted on pretending the shameful event had never even occurred. Now Ermengarde spent hours telling Joan everything she needed to know . . . and more . . . about childbirth.

At night, Raymond pretended to sleep in the antechamber,

relegating Charisse to a storage room across the hall, but each night he slipped into bed beside her.

Joan had almost drifted back to sleep when another pain gripped her. This time, weeping with fear, she woke Raymond. "Get the midwife. Hurry."

"When your women come, they'll make me leave. Wait a little longer."

For the next few hours, he rubbed her back, sang troubadours' songs, sponged her skin, combed her hair. He even helped her from bed to the narrow window where they watched dawn break over the city.

"It won't be so bad. You're strong. Like your mother."

When her water broke and the pains came faster, he sent Charisse for the midwife. She arrived with four other women and banished Raymond, who swore he'd go no farther than the anteroom. Joan called out to him twice. In response, the door opened, but the women barred entrance. The second time the midwife slapped her hand and told her to stop.

"Do you want the count to see you like this?"

So she hung on his words. She *was* strong. Concentrating on the midwife's instructions, on Charisse's hand gripping hers, she pushed the baby into life.

"A boy," the midwife said, as proud and smug as if she'd made the child herself.

Joan reached for her son.

"Just a moment," Charisse said, lifting him. "We'll dry him."

"Raymond. Tell Raymond."

The door was already opening. He came straight to her side and fell to his knees.

"Jeanne," he murmured, laying his cheek against the back of

· 366 ·

her hand limp on the bed. His face was gray, his eyes sunken. His bravado had been for her sake. She loved him so terribly she thought her heart would split open.

"Our son," she said, her voice raspy from hours of groaning. "Did you hear?"

He raised his head. Tears glistened on his cheeks. "My love, yes." Then he said the strangest thing, "Thank you." And kissed her hand.

Charisse placed a swaddled bundle in her arms, and one of the women dragged a chair to the bedside for the count. After a few moments, he said, "Jeanne, let me see him."

Reluctantly, triumphantly, she handed over the prize and watched her husband adore the heir she'd given him. Yet, by the joy shining in Raymond's face, she could see he had not fallen under the spell of the future count of Toulouse. He loved *the babe*. In due course, their son would be count because it would be his right and his obligation. What a fool she'd been to worry about Bertrand just because he was Raymond's son. No matter her husband's faults, he had always known his duty to Toulouse. He'd tried to explain to her: His beloved Bertrand understood duty too.

"We should give the babe suck," the midwife said. "The wet nurse is waiting."

Raymond growled, "He won't starve in the next few minutes. We'll summon you when you're needed."

With a huff of indignation, the midwife left, followed by the other attendants. Raymond laid the babe back in Joan's arms. He took hold of her hand and with his other hand, he brushed back a stray lock of her hair. Then he gestured with his chin to their son.

"I remember the first time I saw you, cradling your poppet just like that. The weight of the kingdom was on your tiny shoulders. How I despised our parents for the position you were in."

"That was the start of the war," she remembered. Raymond had been so young himself, and no friend of her family. He had come to her aid out of simple kindness. Mama said that was his weakness, but Joan saw now that kindness had ever been Raymond's strength.

"You were often in my thoughts over those years. I was pleased to see you again at St. Gilles. To see how well you had weathered the storm. You were but a child, yet it was easy to see what a beautiful woman you would be. Jeanne, it's strange how you haunted me."

"I thought of you, too."

"Did you?" He squeezed her hand, smiling a little as though he didn't believe her.

"You were the champion of my youth. I could imagine you to be whoever I needed you to be."

He laughed softly. "The reality is doomed to disappoint."

"No. You offered us succor when we were stranded in Rome, believing Richard dead."

"Ah," he said, nodding. "I wanted to help. I didn't expect . . . my heart was lost from the moment you appeared in Toulouse. But none of my usual tricks seemed to work."

"They did. Only not on me."

His jaw hardened. "Of the many mistakes I've made in my life, I most regret Theodora. You mustn't judge her too harshly. All she wanted was to go home, to avenge her father. She imagined if she married me, I'd march an army back to Cyprus and set her up as empress."

"I cannot think you promised her those things."

"No. Though I'd wager my father encouraged that plan. I paid very little attention to her beyond taking what she offered. My mind was on you, Jeanne, but you gave every indication of despising me. I accepted Theodora's favors out of bitterness. Perhaps I was hoping to make you jealous. I can't say what petty lovers' games I thought I was playing. When I realized what I had done, I felt I owed her marriage. But I was not what she wanted. And she . . . she was not you. Terrifying as it was to try again, I had to set things to rights."

"Have you?"

"You tell me. I confess I still don't understand your heart as well as I'd like. My profoundest desire is your happiness. Have I succeeded?"

Eleanor possessed such lofty ambitions for her children, but happiness had never been one of them. Likely Mama thought only fools believed in happiness. Yet how, with the warm weight of her babe against her chest, could Joan feel anything but joy?

"You've given me a son."

"God gave us our son. Are you happy with me, as my countess, my wife?"

As Sicily's queen, she had tried to live by her mother's precepts, only to discover too late that William's kingdom was nothing like England and William's faults differed from her father's. She had not been happy in Sicily. Could she be happy in Toulouse?

Raymond pressed her hand again, awaiting her answer. "I love you, Jeanne. You know that, don't you?"

Looking past him, she murmured, "My mother says there is no greater fool than a woman who loves her husband, unless it is a woman who believes a husband who says he loves her."

She heard his sharp intake of breath and saw his expression, stunned, turning to hurt. She hadn't meant for him to take her words at their value; she was merely thinking how she had come to be the person she was. A good girl listened to her mother. Even if . . . especially if . . . her mother was Eleanor of Aquitaine.

But she was more than just Eleanor's daughter. She was Countess Jeanne. She was *Joan*. Quickly, she turned her palm over and laced her fingers through his.

"A thousand times over," she assured him, "I am happily a fool."

## AUTHOR'S NOTE

IN HISTORY BOOKS, JOAN IS KNOWN BY THE COMPANY SHE KEPT: Eleanor of Aquitaine and King Henry II, Richard the Lionheart and Prince John, King William the Good, the last great Norman king of Sicily, and Count Raymond VI of Toulouse. However, unlike these well-documented historical figures, Joan left no record, with the exception of a will. And yet, imagine the life she must have led in the presence of such company! Imagine being Eleanor of Aquitaine's daughter. This is why I love historical fiction.

If this novel inspires you to read more about this time period, or if you are already familiar with twelfth-century England, you may notice this book has omitted facts and embellished stories. For example, I've neglected to mention Joan's older sisters, who would have been married away by the time the book opens, as well as King William's older brother, who died in childhood. I've omitted much of the chronology of the crusade but embroidered Joan's role. Joan and Berengaria did accompany Richard to the Holy Land, but we know nothing about how they spent their time there. It is reported that Richard tried to arrange a marriage between Joan and el-Adil; however, some historians doubt that this happened or that the offer was ever sincerely made.

Raymond's wives are another puzzle. While his marriage to Joan is well documented, lesser-known ladies did not fare as well. The name of Isaac Comnenus's daughter was never recorded, and historians have debated whether Raymond married her before or after marrying Joan. His first marriage, to the heiress of Melgueil, took place in either 1172 or 1173, when Raymond was only sixteen years old. For the sake of Joan and Raymond's story, I've used the marriage sequence that best suited the tale and pushed back the year of Raymond's first wedding.

I've tried to adhere to the facts about Joan's life where they are known, but verifiable details leave only the sketchiest outline. So I've filled in the story with anecdotes as they have appeared in historical texts, even when the accuracy might be debatable. For example, the scene of Joan asking her father to give the imprisoned Eleanor an allowance for clothes is in the historical record but not in primary sources. Even with anecdotes, there is little historical documentation to give us true insight into Joan. And therefore this is primarily a work of fiction. Much of the book is plausible (to my mind) but purely made up. I admit there is absolutely no historical basis for the notion of a love affair between King William and Princess Constance.

Also, this story suggests Joan was unhappy with William but found love and joy with Raymond. Historians have variously speculated that her marriages were happy or unhappy, drawing opposite conclusions based on the same meager evidence. Raymond and Joan had a daughter together the year after their son was born. Joan had another son the following year who did not survive. Unfortunately, neither did Joan. Raymond was in another part of his domain at the time, at war with one of his vassals. Some Toulousain lords rose up in revolt and Joan, although pregnant, took an army to lay siege to their stronghold. When a group of her own knights turned against her, Joan fled, ending up at Fontevrault. She died in childbirth, in her mother's company, not her husband's. She was only thirty-four years old.

I encourage you to discover for yourselves the rich historical record surrounding the company Joan kept, consider the sometimes contradictory assertions in history books, and come to your own conclusions about Joan's fascinating family.

Imagining Joan's life is one thing. Putting it to paper and getting it out to a reading audience is entirely different. I could not have done this without a great deal of help. I need to thank my husband, most of all, for being my first reader and moral support. Next in line are my young "beta" readers, Anna Burke, Lila, and Lucas. Also crucially important is my writers' group, all the talented people at Novelpro, especially Jamie Lankford, who founded the group and keeps it functioning. I also want to thank my marvelous agent, Irene Kraas, for taking me on and having faith in this book. Finally, it was a pleasure to work with my editor, Noa Wheeler, and I appreciate her dedication, her insight, and her tact.